Reena Was Shivering Almost Uncontrollably . . .

as she tried to unclasp the frogs that held her soaked cloak together.

Suddenly long brown fingers were at her throat working the clasp to her cloak free. Startled, she looked up into the concerned face of the man she had silently and so violently cursed this past hour.

"What are you doing?"

"I'm taking these wet things off you."

"No!" she cried out, slapping at his hands.

"Madam, now is not the time for girlish modesty. Lest you wish to come down with the fever, I'd advise you to comply."

"Ou-out of the question," she stammered, trying to sound authoritative. He was dangerously close. Reena shivered as his eyes met and held her own. For an endless moment out of time, he held her inches from him, and caressed her lovely features with his fathomless gaze.

She would later realize she could have, should have stopped him then.

Dear Reader,

We, the editors of Tapestry Romances, are committed to bringing you two outstanding original romantic historical novels each and every month.

From Kentucky in the 1850s to the court of Louis XIII, from the deck of a pirate ship within sight of Gibraltar to a mining camp high in the Sierra Nevadas, our heroines experience life and love, romance and adventure.

Our aim is to give you the kind of historical romances that you want to read. We would enjoy hearing your thoughts about this book and all future Tapestry Romances. Please write to us at the address below.

The Editors
Tapestry Romances
POCKET BOOKS
1230 Avenue of the Americas
Box TAP
New York, N.Y. 10020

Sweet Revenge

Patricia Pellicane

A TAPESTRY BOOK
PUBLISHED BY POCKET BOOKS NEW YORK

Books by Patricia Pellicane

Charity's Pride
Sweet Revenge
Whispers in the Wind

Published by TAPESTRY BOOKS

An *Original* publication of TAPESTRY BOOKS

A Tapestry Book published by
POCKET BOOKS, a division of Simon & Schuster, Inc.
1230 Avenue of the Americas, New York, N.Y. 10020

ISBN: 0-671-61761-3

First Tapestry Books printing April, 1986

10 9 8 7 6 5 4 3 2 1

To my sister
Mary Dietz Elberfeld
who lent me her courage
when I couldn't find my own.

Prologue

In the predawn stillness of a gray day, the bedroom's antechamber was cast in eerie shadows. His bare feet were nearly numb with cold as he stood upon the uncarpeted floor. It wasn't the first time he had stood in the darkness and listened to her tortured cries. For as long as he could remember, her soft whimpers in the dark of night had awakened him, leaving him shaking upon his bed, his covers pulled protectively over his head while the cold terror only a small boy could know clutched at his heart.

With a trembling hand he reached for the doorknob. He couldn't stand to hear her anymore. What happened to her at night that she should cry so? Did she, too, have nightmares? Did she see the same slight movement in the shadowed corners of her room? Did she lie in bed and tremble while waiting for the terrifying beast to pounce? If so, she gave nary a sign of it upon the morn. In truth her cheery disposition often gave him cause to wonder if he had imagined it.

The pounding in his small chest nearly obliterated all sound from the bedroom as he turned the knob and pulled the heavy oak door from its jamb. Her cries had become muffled, as if she covered her face, while the accompanying low, male laughter grew in strength as he stepped inside.

Due to the overhanging canopy and drapery, the forms on the bed were shadowed darker than the rest of the room, and it took some time before his innocent mind could grasp the horror that played out before his wide-eyed stare.

Her face was pressed to the mattress, while the man held her on her knees, her naked body tight to his. Equally naked, he drove into her softness with vicious thrusts, unmindful of her obvious suffering.

He had seen dogs perform this act. It was unthinkable that she should be subjected to this horror.

"Nooo!" he screamed, never realizing the utterance as he charged into the room and threw himself upon his mother's attacker. Small fists flew and contacted with amazing force to the master's chest and face.

An instant later he was flung, as if weightless, from the bed. His head struck the leg of the armoire with a terrifying thud, leaving him completely helpless against the coming attack.

His mother screamed as the man leaped from the bed amid a stream of vile curses and gave his dazed form a powerful kick.

From somewhere far away he heard her shriek, "No! Please, no!" as there came another vicious blow to his midsection. Pulling at his arms, she tried to drag him away, only to be flung to the floor, her cries for help unnoticed.

The man loomed above him momentarily, as his menacing glare glittered with terrifying fury in the pale light of near dawn. Then, he continued his vicious attack upon the little boy produced from his own loins.

A heavy chair was suddenly lifted from a dark corner and

2

flung at the man with a strength born of fierce protectiveness. A look of astonishment, a muffled groan, and the man crumbled heavily to the carpet.

"I'm sorry, darling," his mother whispered. "I'm so very sorry," she continued, as she lifted his head to her bare legs.

This was not the first time he had taken his fury out on the boy, but it would be the last, she vowed silently as she allowed her gaze to rest upon the hated form lying unconscious near her son's feet.

Returning her gaze to the boy, she once again began to soothe with tender words.

He was left dazed from the powerful blows and couldn't bring forth the assurance she needed.

She was gone from his side and he again began to feel frightened. Moments later she returned fully dressed. Pulling off his nightdress with shaking fingers, she somehow managed to get his aching body into his clothes. Soon after, taking no more than a change of clothes and a few saved coins, she held his thin young form to her as they hobbled into the dark damp streets of New Orleans.

Her heart ached with guilt that her child should have suffered for so long simply because she was too cowardly to leave the security of the man she had once been indentured to.

Dominic said nothing as he allowed his mother to lead him from the hated house, her soft urgings unheard as his heart suffused with a rage that would grow and fester. Waiting, always waiting for the day he could obtain his revenge.

Chapter One

MARY GIGGLED AS REENA'S DARK BLUE EYES GREW HUGE and expressive and her soft, throaty laughter mingled with the younger girl's delighted merriment.

"God's truth, Mary, he was watching me so closely, he walked right into a tree. Indeed it was most hard not to burst out laughing. I'm sure the blow that dastardly tree struck brought the poor man untold discomfort."

"Did he come calling again?"

Reena sighed wearily as she remembered his all too often appearance. "Indeed. For a time Mr. Sinclair was a most determined suitor. It took much to dissuade him." Reena grinned mischievously, waiting for her cousin to ask how she managed to relieve Mr. Sinclair of his amorous tendencies.

Finally the young girl prompted, "Well? Are you going to tell me before I expire from curiosity?"

Reena smiled at her young cousin's exuberance and gave a slight shrug. "'Twas not so difficult to persuade him to look elsewhere. I merely related the sorry fact that senility had attacked our dear Aunt Agatha. Of course, I tried to impress upon him the condition was not to be feared. Even though the dreaded affliction did strike the poor old lady down in her youth, still the doctors doubted the defect to be inherited." She shrugged and continued with a straight face, "I was forced to confess, however, that more than one distant relative had been rumored to walk the moors in the dark of night." Reena shook her head vehemently. "I, of course, denied as total nonsense the reports that the dark nights would often echo with the repeated sounds of animal growls."

Mary clutched her midsection as tears of laughter streamed down her softly rounded cheeks. Her voice kept breaking as she groaned out between gasping breaths. "Indeed, Reena, you are a wretch. How could you? We don't even have an Aunt Agatha."

Reena's eyes grew wide with feigned surprise. "Do we not? Oh dear," she continued softly, apparently overcome with remorse, but for the slight twitching at the corners of her lush mouth, "I must have been thinking of someone else's Aunt Agatha. Now who do you suppose it could have been?"

After a long pause, during which Reena managed to suppress her merriment, she finally remarked with no little sarcasm, "Still, 'tis amazing how well the heart can heal. Why barely one week's time past and he had ingratiated himself with one of the young ladies—a lady known to have an enormous yearly income. 'Twas a thankful sight to be sure, to see them exchange loving glances and endearments."

Mary shook her head. "I doubt the man sought your wealth alone. You possess startling beauty."

Reena waved aside her cousin's compliment with a delicate wave of a slender white hand. "Oh pooh, Mary, a

5

comely wench perhaps for a schoolmistress, but a startling beauty? Not likely. In truth I'm getting on in years."

Mary laughed. "Indeed. In a year or so you'll be positively ancient. I've often wondered how a woman of a score and six manages without her walking stick."

Mary grinned and shook her head at Reena's attempt to insist she spoke the truth. She knew full well that neither the deliberate, somber cut of her clothes, nor the forced severity of her thick golden hair could take away from her cousin's extraordinary loveliness.

Reena had spent the last few years teaching French at Mrs. Bark's school for cultured young ladies. Still, no matter her efforts, she could not succeed in making herself look the drab old maid she often professed to be. Her eyes, forever twinkling with deviltry, were so dark as to appear purple. And, although Reena thought to disguise them with a pair of ugly bifocals that Mary knew to be nothing more than glass, the spectacles merely emphasized the pertness of her slender nose and, if anything, brought more notice than ever to her full, enticing lips. Lips, Mary knew, when relaxed from her rigid control or softened as now in laughter, caught many a gentleman's eye.

Unpracticed and natural, Reena carried her slender, delicate form with a captivatingly provocative manner, which caused more than one gentleman to suck in his breath at the sight of her. Unaware of the sensual essence she exuded, Reena was often surprised and annoyed at the bold responses she incurred. Being a lady, born and bred, she was quick to snub, in a most cool and disdaining fashion, anyone who might misinterpret her spirited manner as perhaps a promise of some future reward.

"Were there no others that caught your eye? Surely many prospective suitors visited the school."

"Aye, in truth there were many," she agreed, "but none that cast a glance to a dowdy schoolmistress among so many of firmer flesh.

"Mrs. Bark gave many an afternoon tea and an occasional ball." Reena sighed wearily. "These social engagements often reminded one of buyers at an auction. I could well imagine Mrs. Bark calling out, 'Gentlemen, if you please, what would you offer for this one? Examine her closely, if you be inclined. Notice her teeth, an obvious sign of good stock, the health of her skin, the thickness of her hair. The width of her hips, perhaps, excellent for breeding, I'm sure.' "

"Oh Reena!" Mary gasped, her face coloring with shock. "She wouldn't!"

Reena laughed softly, while glancing out the carriage window. "Nay, she would not. In truth, she'd be horrified to hear tell of my wicked thoughts. Still, I often felt that to be the case, and often thanked the Good Lord I was not one of the anxious young ladies bent on making a favorable match."

For a time the coach moved over the rutted dirt road, bouncing its occupants about the leather upholstery quite ruthlessly.

"Oh dear," Mary exclaimed, as her bonnet slipped forward and momentarily covered her eyes. "I'm afraid I shall be quite bruised before we reach Philadelphia."

"Aye," Reena offered absentmindedly, as she continued to gaze out the window. "The roads in this godforsaken country are in a sorry state." But her mind was not on the conditions of the road. Knowing the uselessness of her constant nagging, she nevertheless ventured once again. "Mary, have you given the matter further thought? You are so young. As yet not a score of years has past since your birth. You need not accept your first offer. You have the means to do anything you desire."

"Reena, Monsieur Coujon is a man of impressive reputation. His wealth matches my own, therefore I know he has not sought this match for monetary gains alone. I realize he is many years my senior, but I find nothing in his person to

7

disgust me. Upon his visit to England, he singled me out above all others. He was very much the gentleman in my presence. What more could I want?"

"Mary, for God's sake, must you be so amicable?" Reena snapped. Ignoring her cousin's gasp at her flagrant use of profanity, she went on, "Good God, the man is an American! That in itself is reason enough to reject his offer. I doubt there be one among the lot worthy of you."

Reena took a deep breath and forced herself to control the disgust she felt, for she had long believed Americans to be no more than gun-slinging barbarians fighting off wild-eyed red men. Her voice was softer when she spoke again. "Mary, you've met the man but one time. How know you his true worth? Does it not strike you odd that a man of two score and eight has not married before? One wonders if there is not some serious fault that has kept the ladies at bay."

"Reena, you are being overly suspicious. I appreciate your caution, but believe me there is no need. I'm sure I could not have made a better choice if I had searched many years over."

Reena groaned in frustration. Granted, Monsieur Coujon was exceedingly handsome, but looks did not necessarily make the man. Indeed, in her experience, frequently the more handsome the man, the less he could boast of admirable qualities. For she knew of few who did not preen before mirrors admiring their own attractions and expect their lady to do the same.

She sighed wearily. For Mary's sake, she hoped there was more to the man than his looks. Perhaps Mary was right. Mayhap she was being overly suspicious.

Still, try as she might, she could not get rid of the feeling of foreboding that came over her at the mere mention of the man's name. Surely his manner upon their meeting had been exemplary. As Mary said, he was polished, cultured, and acted very much the gentleman. What was it then that bothered her about him? Why couldn't she shake this uneasiness about Mary's marriage to the man?

"Very well," Reena finally sighed. "Perhaps you are right. If you've set your mind on the matter, I'll no longer try to dissuade you." She smiled gently as she continued. "Mayhap you have already lost your heart to the handsome M. Coujon."

Reena had bearly spoken these last words when there was a sudden loud, grinding sound, and the carriage dipped most terrifyingly. Mary screamed, her tiny form flung across the interior of the coach, and landed with a sickening thud against the far wall.

Reena felt a bit dazed. She realized the carriage had turned on its side. With a heart-stopping chill of fear, she also realized that Mary was unusually quiet. Reena's shoulder ached miserably as she reached out to comfort the girl who lay so limply at her side.

"Mary! Mary, can you hear me? Are you hurt?"

Reena found herself breathing a long sigh of relief as she watched Mary's long-lashed eyelids flutter and heard a low moan escape her delicate mouth.

"Have we overturned?"

From outside the carriage came the deep sound of the guards' voices as they scrambled over the side of the coach. One of them cursed just before the carriage door was flung open and sunlight flooded into the darkened interior.

"Are you injured, madam?" Seth Grimes asked, as he stuck his bearded face into the carriage.

"Nay, Seth," Reena responded. Her hands shook as she patted down her hair and retrieved her bonnet. She straightened the bifocals that had become dislodged and set them once again across the tip of her nose as she continued, "I fare well, but I'm not sure of my cousin's wellbeing. She seems a bit dazed."

"Jamie," Seth growled, "help me get Mistress Braxton out. I'll get in and lift her." And then addressing Reena, he

9

added, "I'd have more room, madam, if I could get you out first."

"Of course," Reena agreed, as she came to her feet, standing on one door while Seth pulled her out of the other. She was lowered over the side into Jamie's waiting arms, and stood leaning against the carriage as Seth immediately jumped inside. The two men brought Mary's dazed form out into the sun and lifted her gently to the ground.

Reena smiled to see her cousin exclaim her mortification at being so handled, but she knew this tiny woman caused many a brash heart to grow tender, and the burliest of men to act the simpering fool in her presence.

"Please, Mr. Grimes," Mary cried, as Seth continued to fuss over her, "you need not worry so." She colored prettily as she added, "I promise you I am quite recovered."

"You've taken a nasty bruise to your forehead, miss. Are you sure?"

"Quite sure," Mary returned, as she came to her feet, adjusted her bonnet, and smoothed her skirt.

"We cannot be far from a posting house, Seth," Reena remarked to the old family servant. "Perhaps we might find help there."

"No doubt, madam," Seth returned.

It was decided the two ladies would ride Seth's horse the few miles to the inn, while Seth and Jamie took the carriage horses.

"You should feel better once you've rested, Mary," Reena remarked, as she held out a cup of tea for her cousin and poured herself a liberal amount of the steaming brew. "I don't want you to stir from that bed until dinner. I'm afraid it will take at least that long to repair the coach, in any case. We may as well stay the night. I've no wish to travel these beastly roads in the pitch of night."

Mary murmured her agreement as she sank back against the recently fluffed pillows. Her head throbbed, and the

10

cool cloth she held there brought little relief. "I think you are right, Reena. I've no doubt a few hours of rest will see the end to this headache."

"Do you suffer greatly?" Reena asked.

"Nay," Mary smiled weakly, "but an hour or so of sleep can bring no harm."

Reena watched her cousin's eyes close and soon left her to sleep the afternoon away. Entering the tap room, Reena ordered a light lunch of clear soup and another cup of tea, as the owner graciously led her to a table and seated her quite ceremoniously. Reena grinned, wondering if she'd have attained such gallant ministrations had she not earlier deposited a hearty sum of coins into the man's meaty palm.

While she was waiting for her meal, Reena's gaze swept the small, darkly beamed room. All present seemed to be travelers like herself, who had stopped for a short respite or a hearty tankard of ale to cleanse the parched throat free of dust. She was well aware of the raised eyebrows among the dining room's occupants and put it to the fact that she sat alone. She realized a lady never ate unescorted. She could only imagine what their thoughts were regarding her temerity.

Reena gave a small shrug. She'd not worry of appearances. If eating alone caused her to be the object of such attention, so be it. She'd not stay cooped up in her room simply because of what others might think.

Directly across the room sat a gentleman whose dark, admiring gaze openly followed the swaying skirt of the comely serving girl who was just now bringing Reena a piping hot pot of tea. His hair curled black and thick around a disturbingly familiar and handsome face. Dark brows lifted with pleasure, and his mouth curved into a sensuous smile as he studied the serving girl's posterior, while no doubt allowing his imagination full rein.

Reena's eyes narrowed in thought. Had she met this man before? For the life of her she could not recollect such a meeting. Why, then, did she feel she knew him?

Suddenly, she realized his gaze, which had followed the serving girl to her table, had lingered on, and he had been watching her for some time. Reena's cheeks pinkened, and she wished Seth had not insisted both he and Jamie should return to the disabled carriage.

Lifting her head, she returned his bold stare with cool disdain. She gave him her sternest look, the exact same that had made many a giggling young lady quake in her shoes. Reena grew irritated when her icy glare merely brought about an answering, taunting smile. Her surprise was obvious. How dare he display such audacity? He actually seemed to be enjoying her growing anger. She almost groaned. The oaf was surely a simpleton not to realize a setdown when he saw it.

Unwilling to prolong eye contact, she looked upon her cup of tea and took several deep breaths to settle her agitation. Her skin prickled uncomfortably. She could almost feel those dark eyes move over her.

Reena forbid it, and yet time and again she found her gaze helplessly drawn to him. She mouthed a curse and then flushed pink as the bloody cur's smile broadened as if he had read her lips. Why couldn't she ignore him? Why did her gaze constantly stray? Once he had the gall to lift his tankard toward her, as if in a toast, before he brought it to his grinning lips.

"Damn," she groaned, only barely beneath her breath. "One would think I was spotted with the pox the way the beggar continues to stare." She flitted nervously, unconsciously adjusting her spectacles, while barely tasting the rest of her meal.

Reena was not unused to the attention she received from the opposite sex. Still, this man's scrutiny irked her beyond anything she had ever known. Unable to enjoy her meal, her full lips thinned to a menacing snarl as she finally pushed her half-finished broth from her and came to her feet. She took her long cloak from the chair at her side and slid it over her shoulders.

Reena walked the length of the room and paused for a moment at the man's table. Uncaring that her cheeks burned, she forced herself to return his bold stare. "I do not appreciate your attentions, sir. Should I again have the misfortune to come across your person, I sincerely hope I am accompanied by one of my guards. 'Twould do you justice, I think, to have that arrogant smirk wiped off."

Expecting his stuttering apology at her sharp setting down, Reena was stunned into silence as she heard his low husky chuckle. "Do you now?"

It took a great deal of effort to restrain the gasp that threatened. His voice was devastating to her senses. She felt as if her chest had suddenly shattered and realized, with no little surprise, that she had to force air into her starved lungs in order to breathe.

His heated gaze openly caressed her lips in frank appreciation. His voice was low, silky, almost hypnotic as it washed over her, leaving her suddenly weak and trembling, her mind a muddle. "If the lady were to do the wiping, I confess I'd not object overmuch."

It took a long moment before his comment penetrated the mush that had suddenly replaced her quick mind and registered as the barely veiled lechery intended. She straightened her shoulders as her hands clenched into fists at her sides. She dismissed the mesmerizing effect of his softly spoken words as pure imagination on her own part and answered his teasing with an angry sneer. "How dare you?" And then, gaining some control over the desire to inflict physical abuse, she shrugged and fixed him with a haughty glare as she adjusted her perfectly adjusted cloak. "In truth one cannot hope for more than impertinence from you American barbarians."

Dominic chuckled softly, not at all disturbed by her insult to his nationality. He leaned arrogantly against the wall. "I gather Englishmen do not look at beautiful women?"

"Sir, they may look, but they do not display such boorish scrutiny."

" 'Twould seem, madam, you displayed your share, lest you'd have no knowledge of my interest."

Reena groaned at the truth of his statement and closed her eyes against the delighted humor she read in his. Her face burned with mortification. She gave a sound of disgust and lifted her skirt away from his foot as if he were something vile. Having no need to further this most unwelcome conversation, she spun on her heel and left him to watch her straight back while the sound of his soft laughter vibrated through every pore of her body.

Chapter Two

DOMINIC RIVERIA ENTERED THE LOW-CEILINGED DINING room of the inn with a grateful sigh. His stomach rumbled with hunger and his body ached with bone-weary exhaustion. Having personally seen his second mate on a long, arduous journey home after a particularly harrowing voyage had not left him in the most jovial of moods. God, he couldn't imagine a chore he more despised.

Still, Anna Peterson had been so filled with relief and happiness to have her man home she couldn't have cared less if he never walked again. Luckily, Dominic had been able to assure her Peterson needed only time and exercise for a full recovery.

The memory of the lady's happy tears brought a tender smile to the corners of his firm lips and transformed his ruggedly tanned features into a handsomeness that sent the serving girls scurrying to see that the dashing captain had all he desired.

Hanging his heavy, blue coat on a peg near the door, he made his way to one of the empty tables and sat with a weary sigh, thankful to be able to rest his aching back against something solid at long last.

After leaving Peterson in the care of his wife, Dominic had made a quick stop at his bank before returning to his ship. The fruits of his last voyage had brought a pretty penny at auction. Even after sharing the profits with his crew, Dominic found himself a rich man.

For the first time he allowed a broad smile to soften his hard features. Excitement tightened his chest as he realized his plans would soon come to fruition. Coujon was slowly boxing himself into a corner—a corner from which he'd never escape.

In the past two years Coujon had lost three ships to the English frigates that often accompanied a merchant ship. Another dozen or more had suffered serious damage. Dominic grinned with satisfaction. Luck was finally turning from the man. His fleet's repair had seriously drained his reserve. His empire was on the brink of financial disaster.

Dominic knew everything Coujon owned was mortgaged to the hilt. He had made it his business to know everything the bastard was about. When another loan was applied for, Dominic immediately extended Coujon's line of credit.

Nathaniel Pennwick, the bank's president and a friend of long standing, had tried to dissuade his friend from backing an obviously failing business. When it became apparent Dominic would do it regardless, he merely shrugged his shoulders and professed it none of his concern if he wished the loan's origin to remain confidential.

Dominic almost laughed out loud. It wouldn't be long now. He couldn't wait to extend another loan or two. Soon he'd be able to watch his unsuspecting victim squirm as he called in all the notes. It would mean his downfall at last—at long last.

Scanning the occupants of the inn's dining room, Dominic wondered if she had yet arrived. He knew he wouldn't be here today were it not for Josiah Pennwick, and he silently thanked his luck at being in the right place at the right time.

The doddering old man had long ago relinquished the running of his bank to his capable son and had been puttering about in a small outer office. Since the old man's retirement, his son had taken pity on the endless idle hours his father was forced to endure and had offered the man a few hours' work a week.

Dominic had been passing the small office on his way to see Nathaniel when he heard a small thump and an accompanying groaned oath. Glancing inside, Dominic had smiled as the elderly gentleman got up off the floor while retrieving a fallen piece of paper. His hand was pressed against his head where it had contacted with the desk and he grinned sheepishly.

"Monsieur Coujon!" the elderly Pennwick exclaimed, as he came full to his feet.

Dominic smiled and was about to correct the banker once again—for this was not the first time he had confused the two men, when he was brought up short by his next words.

"Let me be the first to congratulate you. I hear your future bride is a beauty. I confess I've listened to all the gossips. She's reported to be lovely, very lovely indeed."

Dominic never heard the rest of the old man's chatter as he digested this startling information. So Coujon had finally found someone to take to wife. She must be something special, he reasoned, for he had known the lecherous bastard to favor many a lady with his nocturnal expertise, but never before had it been hinted that he lost his heart to one of them.

Knowing better than that, Dominic reasoned, the lady in question must assuredly possess a fortune. Surely Coujon could not be in greater need. How much simpler to marry money and solve his problems. Still, she was reported to be

17

a beauty. Could not a young heiress, and a beautiful one at that, find better than that monster?

By the time Dominic quit the offices of Pennwick and Pennwick, he had gained the lady's name, the ship that was bringing her to the states, the time of her expected arrival and the route she was taking to meet with her dear betrothed. Without conscious thought he had, hours later, found himself astride his horse as it thundered south. Why, he could not say. He seemed unable to resist the macabre need to know the woman who would wed herself to this unconscionable bastard.

According to Pennwick, Mary Braxton was to have boarded a French ship after stopping briefly in the West Indies and proceeding then to Charleston. Since it was a fact that the Union Jack was not a welcome sight along these coastal waters, she might then attain some degree of safety in the last leg of her journey.

Dominic reasoned she would eventually stop at the Pirate's Cove for a night's rest before continuing her journey to Baltimore. He need only wait.

Dominic leaned back against the wall again and closed his eyes for a long moment. Was there a living soul he hated more than Coujon? Just thinking of the man twisted his mouth into a menacing snarl. He was anxious to feast his eyes on the chosen one and wondered how long he'd be forced to cool his heels.

Forcing aside his disagreeable thoughts, Dominic allowed his mind to return to his ship. The clipper *America*, berthed at Baltimore, sat nearly crippled while awaiting repairs. Since receiving a "letter of marque and reprisal" from President Madison, Dominic had easily and most happily combined his trading with the West Indies with the more dramatic and exciting plunder of English merchant ships he might encounter en route.

The goddamned ship had looked ripe for the plucking. "Jesus," he groaned, only barely beneath his breath. What a shock it had been to find the damn crew armed to the teeth and opening fire just as the boarding pikes had been thrown.

A partially hidden cannon had nearly been the end of them. Luckily, his men had been quick to react. Carrying their muskets and cutlasses to the ready, they had worked feverishly to save not only his ship, but their necks as well. In the end he and his men had taken a wealth of lace and crystal bound for the West Indies.

With a small shrug, he turned his thoughts to the buxom brunette who approached and amicably set his plate of hot roast beef and boiled potatoes before him.

His smile turned into a grin, and he felt a tightening in his loins as she leaned forward to needlessly wipe the already gleaming table. Her blouse gaped away from her smooth creamy skin, leaving rose-tipped, unencumbered breasts displayed for his pleasure.

Her answering smile, as her eyes met his, spoke clearly of her hopes for the coming night. Dominic reasoned a night spent in the warm arms of such a willing female might make this trip worthwhile. Aye, it had been a long time since he had pleasured himself between the warm thighs of some hungry wench—far too long.

His almost frenzied trading between the United States and the West Indies left him little time in port but to see to the unloading of tobacco and cotton and to fill the ship's hold for their return voyage with rum, sugar, and spices. Those who dared speak, found a deaf ear as they warned the captain of working himself into an early grave. In truth, he was not a man to idle his time away. He smiled again, for it wasn't merely the work he so enjoyed, but the money he was slowly accumulating. Money, he had learned long ago and from bitter firsthand experience, was the only way to secure his place in the world and, most importantly, the only way he might obtain his revenge. He grunted and nodded slightly; the hatred that had eaten at his gut for nigh on twenty-five years would take much to appease.

Dominic finished his meal and leaned back, enjoying another tankard while watching the saucy sway of the serving girl's skirt as she brought a cup of tea to a woman at another table. For a long minute he watched as her slender white fingers poured cream into the cup and then lifted it to the most beautiful, pink-lipped mouth he had ever seen.

Dominic felt the previous warming in his belly spread to tongues of fire through his abdomen and into his chest, leaving him breathless at the sight before him. He cursed himself as he felt his face flush with the extreme emotion that suddenly wracked his body.

My God, he groaned silently. He had been too long without a woman if one affected him so drastically.

Gaining some control over himself, he forced aside his instant throbbing desire, while berating himself for his schoolboy emotions. He had to think of a way to meet the lady. For a lady she most obviously was—not a serving wench one could accost in a public eating establishment.

No doubt she had guards or a traveling companion close by. Puzzled, he wondered why she was dining alone.

She had removed her bonnet. Her thick, honey-golden hair was pulled back severely, leaving her exquisitely beautiful features to his view. His fingers ached to release her hair from the large knot at the back of her head as a few tendrils of errant curls fell lusciously around her creamy, pink cheek.

Spectacles were perched upon her adorable, slender nose and looked ridiculously out of place on a face that could only be described as angelic in its beauty.

Dominic caught the impish glimmer that flashed behind her glasses as her eyes swept the room. Suddenly she seemed to remember something and brought the impulse to an abrupt end.

Soft, dark lashes fanned her cheeks below fine feminine brows as she brought her gaze to her cup. Perhaps feeling his notice, she raised her eyes to meet his.

Dominic's lips parted and he almost gasped aloud at the

20

shock of it. For a long moment he was incapable of breathing at the sight of the blue fire that reached across the room and seared at his being.

My God, he had never seen a woman to compare! He knew he was staring, thereby acting in a most ungentlemanly manner. Still, he seemed unable to stop. He felt as if the wind had been knocked out of him and he found himself gasping to fill his lungs again.

Her cheeks grew pinker and her full lips parted as if she too had some difficulty with her breathing. Belligerently, her gaze continued to hold his, while changing subtly to annoyance and then to anger.

For an instant she reminded him of a schoolmistress. He sighed with a wistful smile. He should only have been so lucky as to have had a teacher such as she.

He knew she was trying to stare him down, but it wasn't working. Nay, he could look at this lovely creature for eternity and still not have his fill.

Finally giving up, her brow lifted in disdain, and those dark blue, almost violet eyes shifted from his person to scan the doorway, leaving him suddenly empty and aching for her notice. Apparently not finding the one she looked for, she made a slight scowl.

Dominic smiled. God, how easy it was to read her every expression. Forcing his gaze from her, he allowed his eyes to seek out the others in the room. Aye, he nodded slightly, 'twas not he alone who noticed the lady's loveliness. More than one set of eager eyes were examining her delectable person. For one wild moment he felt unreasonable rage that others should dare to look upon her and then almost laughed out loud at his unbelievable possessiveness. Good God, what had come over him? Could it be that one look from this beauty had left him besotted and nearly wild with desire?

She was looking at him again, no longer bothering to hide her anger. Dominic couldn't control the smile of delight that formed. Christ, he had better take a room and bed the willing wench that simpered so sweetly while coyly allowing her breast to brush against his arm as she cleaned away his finished meal. If he didn't act soon he feared he'd do something he'd later be sorry for.

Still, he reasoned, another moment spent feasting his eyes could surely bring no harm. He watched as she slid her chair back and placed her bonnet upon her head. Her slender fingers fumbled for a moment before the ribbon was retied under her delicate chin.

She stood. Her high-waisted dress of blue nearly disguised the voluptuous curves he spied beneath the heavy material. She was so tiny, he doubted her head would reach the middle of his chest, yet she carried herself with an elegant poise that would rival the most fashionable of ladies, while her stark sensuality left him nearly breathless.

Dominic almost choked on a last sip of ale as she made straight for him, rather than either of the two exits from the room.

She stopped at his table and leaned down ever so slightly. When she spoke her voice was low and so sensuous he nearly stood and pulled her into his arms. Later, he realized he should have risen, but at the moment, the scent of gardenias filled his mind, and he forgot what should have come most naturally.

Her blue eyes blazed as she glared at him, and when she finally moved past and left the dining room, all thoughts of bedding another left his mind. He knew this woman would be his.

Unable to stop himself, Dominic moved from his chair to the window facing the courtyard. Spying the lively, brisk walk of the young lady, he grinned and muttered low, "No demure miss here." Nay, this one had fire, and he suddenly ached to see how hot she could burn.

Chapter Three

REENA STRODE IN A HUFF PAST THE BARNS, STABLES, AND out buildings. A quick glance told her Seth had yet to return with the carriage, and she was loathe to cool her heels, waiting in the yard, lest the beast inside be so bold as to follow her. She sighed with disgust. It was impossible to return to the inn after her disgraceful display of temper. What she needed was something to occupy her thoughts, so she might clear her mind of the grinning oaf. Turning on her heel, she walked toward a clump of trees that might afford her a bit of privacy from the probing eyes she could suddenly feel on her back.

What an absolute boorish creature, she raged silently. She should have known better than to think she could set that sort down. Why the man was simply too ignorant to realize when a lady was issuing him an insult.

She groaned as she remembered his words of retaliation. Her face flamed again. What had ever possessed her to address him in the first place? Surely others had done as much and she had easily ignored their ogling.

"Damnation," she groaned quietly. Of course she had made it all the worse. It galled her to know she had admitted her discomfort to him. Why hadn't she simply ignored him? What was it about the man that made her hand itch to slap his face?

Reena reached the edge of the inn's courtyard. A narrow path led between the heavy growth of trees and underbrush. As yet, she was too jittery to return to her room. The path tempted her to follow, and she gave only a moment's hesitation before acceding to its silent invitation.

The damp scent of rotted and decaying underbrush assailed her senses no more than ten feet into the dark forest. Still, the scent was not repulsive to her. It smelled of earth—dark, warm, and full of life. She breathed the tangy moistness with great lusty gulps deep into her lungs. A bird flittered overhead singing his high-pitched song as he landed on a thick branch and then, seemingly changing his mind, flew off to another.

Reena smiled in appreciation of her surroundings and a calming peace began to fill her soul. The path widened now and the underbrush thinned so she felt less enclosed. Her eyes were on the trail as she carefully avoided thick roots and gopher holes that dotted her way. Reena started at a sudden movement near her and then laughed with relief as she spied a family of rabbits dashing quickly across her path. Overhead a squirrel and robin argued noisily over territory, and her heart grew light as she became absorbed in the lively beauty of her surroundings.

A moment later she came to a fork. Having no fear of losing her way, she veered to the right. A dozen yards or so later, she stepped out of the wooded area and into the sweeping majesty of Virginia's rolling blue hills.

It was a breath-taking sight, and she knew not if even her beloved England, always green and fertile, could compare to this lush and wild beauty.

Hesitantly, almost as if she loathed to infringe upon God's perfection, she moved away from the trees and up the gentle slope of grass-covered hills. She walked slowly, stopping to pick a handful of yellow daffodils on her way, knowing their bright color would cheer her cousin.

Coming to stand atop the hill, she gaped at the beauty that stretched as far as the eye could see. Absorbed in the lushness of Virginia's countryside, she stood for some time, never noticing the menacing clouds that were gathering overhead. Quite suddenly, powerful gusts of wind tore at her cloak, nearly pushing her off the flat ridge of the hill.

Reena looked about, somewhat startled to see the sky behind her black and fierce. Turning, she ran back from whence she had come. It took some time before she found an entrance to the woods again. And only a moment longer to realize it was not the same path she had previously used. By this time fat drops of icy water slapped at her face, while the wind pushed and pulled at her slender form, leaving her breathless with its intensity. She lowered her head from the force of the wind as she scurried back to the inn.

Soon her hurried steps faltered and slowed to a standstill as she realized she was quite lost. Cold water ran in rivulets down her back. The hem of her dress was thick and heavy with mud, her soft kid slippers ruined. She was soaked to the skin, and shivered as the cold water kept up its relentless assault. She slipped in the now-slick earth and fell to her knees, her hands covered with the heavy wet mud.

On her feet again, she raced wildly through the trees. Head down, she had unknowingly veered off the path, and came unexpectedly upon a small clearing. In the center of the open area was a dark, rain-soaked, delapidated cabin. One corner of an overhanging porch roof had slumped with age, and rain from the roof ran off like a tiny waterfall.

For an instant Reena wondered if indeed she would be better off inside, since the building actually seemed to sway in the mighty gusts of wind. But as the wind rushed against the worn-down shack, so did it pummel her. For a time she was knocked about so cruelly, she found she was forced to hold on to a tree or be swept away and perhaps slammed into one of the many rain-darkened trunks.

She could hardly breathe and was forced to keep her face down or take in water. She waited for what seemed an eternity before the wind slacked enough to allow her to stand unassisted. By then she was stiff from the cold, her hands and feet long grown numb.

Finally, she lunged toward the cabin. From the side of her eye she caught movement, but she was too cold, wet, and intent on reaching shelter to care who or what it might be.

After a moment Reena could see that it was a horse and rider. Obviously the rider, too, meant to take cover in the cabin. She felt no need to detour from her chosen path, assuming the pair would steer clear of her. But the rider had not seen her as the wind also whipped rain into his face, and her dark wet dress and cloak blended perfectly into the trees and shrubbery.

Not ten feet from the cabin, she came clearly into view. Strong brown hands jerked at the reins, but it was too late.

Trying to avoid a large puddle, Reena moved quickly to her right and grunted as she came to a sudden stop. Amazed, she realized she had smashed into the side of the chestnut mount. Her soft gasp was lost in the wind as she was thrown completely off balance. With helpless fascination she watched as her feet slid out from beneath her, and her slender form went flying backward, landing on her backside in the exact puddle she had hoped to avoid.

Astonished to find herself sitting in the midst of a freezing puddle, Reena did no more than blink. Cold water seeped through her clothes, biting at her warm flesh. Her bonnet had been whipped away to be forever lost in the underbrush. Her spectacles tipped to a ridiculous angle while torrents of water ran down her face.

A hearty burst of laughter sounded from above.

Mindless of the howling wind and choking rain, she looked up to see the same arrogant beast she had left at the inn sitting atop his horse.

For a long moment she simply stared. Why she should have been surprised, she had no idea. Indeed, if anyone could cause a lady to fall into a puddle of mud and then laugh as though that surely was the funniest sight imaginable, it would be him.

Her words were almost lost in the howling wind as she snarled, "What are you doing here?"

Dominic grinned as he watched her straighten her askew spectacles with muddied fingers. "I noticed the clouds forming, and since you had not returned, I thought you might be in need of some assistance. As it turns out I was right."

"Of course," she agreed snidely. "I had been wondering who might assist me into this puddle." Between gritted teeth she added, "How lucky for me that you should have come along."

Reena's lips thinned at his further laughter, while a silent sneer stole across her lovely features. An instant later she regained control of herself. She'd not give this man more to laugh at.

She tried to rise, only to find it impossible to stop sliding. The weight of her waterlogged clothing felt as if a heavy hand were tugging her down.

Finally he was at her side offering his hand. At first she thought to refuse it but knew that would have been a stubborn and useless gesture indeed. A moment later his hand caught hers and she was pulled free.

Shooting him a withering glance, she blotted out his happy laughter with a disdainful lifting of her chin. Leaving him in the rain, she entered the cabin.

"Goodness," she groaned, as she staggered into the

27

cabin, holding the wall for support. Her knees almost buckled under the weight of her clothes. She could hardly stand—never mind walk. With disgust she looked down at herself. Her clothing must have absorbed half the afternoon's rainfall, coupled with mud; it was completely ruined.

She was shivering almost uncontrollably as she tried to unclasp the frogs that held her cloak ..ogether. A brow lifted and she eyed the door warily. There was no lock and therefore no hope of keeping the evil lout from invading her privacy. Indeed, no sooner had the thought entered her mind did he come crashing inside the tiny cabin.

Reena refused to move aside, even though his huge form seemed to fill the cabin and left her strangely trembling and nervous. Lifting her chin, she glared fearlessly. No arrogant beast would cause her to back away. Nay, this bloody beggar had another thing coming if he supposed she might cower in fear at his close attendance.

Dismissing his presence from her mind, she turned and allowed her gaze to sweep the ramshackled cabin. The frame of a bed stood in one corner, its roped springs hanging to the floor in rotted threads. A stone fireplace covered one wall. A few dry logs lay near the hearth.

Dust and cobwebs covered everything, and she shivered all the more at the thought of spiders. Still, it was a refuge. Dirty, nowhere to sit but the bare wooden floor, but at least it was dry.

She was shivering violently now, and her jaw ached with the effort it took to clamp her teeth together.

Long brown fingers were at her throat working the clasp to her cloak free. Startled, she looked up into the concerned face of the man she had silently and so violently cursed this past hour.

"What are you doing?"

"Your lips are blue. I'm taking these wet things off you."

"No!" she cried out, slapping at his hands and his unwanted assistance.

"Madam, now is not the time for girlish modesty. Lest you wish to come down with the fever, I'd advise you to comply."

Reena stared at him in disbelief. "Do you believe I'd be warmer unclothed?"

Dominic shrugged away her sarcasm. "I will build a fire, and you may wear my shirt while your clothing dries."

Reena found it extremely difficult to talk, as her trembling jaw refused to cooperate and caused her to stutter like a mindless idiot, while her body trembled with violent chills.

"Ou . . . out of the question," she stammered, trying to sound authoritative, but gave a silent groan as the words came out shaky and without conviction.

Her cloak was over his arm and he was reaching for the tiny buttons that secured the front of her dress. When she realized his intent would not be thwarted, she slapped at his hands and backed away. "I will do it! Start the fire."

Dominic grinned at her easy order. He gave a slight shrug and turned from her. Obviously, she was a lady who was not unused to wielding authority.

A few moments later a small fire blazed in the hearth. For some reason, as the warming air caressed her damp, icy form, Reena only shivered all the more.

Dominic turned to find her standing behind him, still fully clothed—the few open buttons of her bodice her only concession to his demands.

"What are you waiting for?"

"Sir, since the choice presents itself that I must freeze or expose myself to your lecherous gaze, I choose the former."

Dominic eyed her speculatively. A stubborn wench to be sure. And he had no doubt he would most certainly eye her quite lecherously, given half the chance, but for now it was imperative she put aside her modesty and listen to him. "You labor under a misconception, madam, if you believe I have never before seen the female form."

"Sir, it interests me not in the least what you have or have not seen. I am perfectly content to stay as I am."

Unused to having his orders ignored, he almost shouted, "Take them off!"

Reena jumped, startled at his menacing tone, but her chin lifted stubbornly and, although she trembled with a mixture of cold and trepidation, she faced him bravely. "I will not! The room warms. There is no need."

"Damn it, woman!" he raged as he unbuttoned his jacket and slipped it from his broad shoulders. "Your trembling increases with each moment. Your lips are nearly purple. You will take them off, or I will!"

Reena gasped with outrage. "Nay, you would not dare."

But she knew from the determined look in his narrowing gaze he would indeed dare that and much more. Unwilling to give him the opportunity to touch her, she stepped back and began to pull the sodden dress from her shoulders.

"Be quick about it!" he growled needlessly, for she glared at him and moved as fast as she pleased.

Her traveling dress soon fell heavily to her feet, and Dominic's belly tightened to a hard knot of desire as he attempted to ignore the swell of firm creamy breasts that were clearly visible beneath her thin, clinging chemise.

"Your shirt, sir?"

Dominic opened his shirt and slid the white muslin from his shoulders.

Reena's eyes widened. She never realized her gasp of surprise. Involuntarily, she took a step back. She had never seen a man in this state of undress. Helplessly drawn, her gaze moved in slow fascination over his broad shoulders and wide chest that was heavily matted with black hair.

Dominic grinned at her obvious reaction to him. She didn't seem to realize she was staring, or that he was watching her. He could almost feel the heat of her gaze as her eyes wandered over his chest and stomach. His muscles hardened and contracted as she followed with no little amazement or admiration the line of black hair that disappeared into his trousers.

Reena's lips parted as she forced air into her starved lungs. Had she been holding her breath? The pink tip of her tongue moistened her suddenly parched lips. What was happening to her? Why couldn't she take her eyes from him?

She disliked the brute intensely, and yet her heart threatened to burst as it slammed against her breast, simply because his chest was bare. What was the matter with her? She took another step back.

My God, she almost groaned aloud, he was so big! She had never felt so tiny as when she fully realized his size. His skin glistened in the firelight like polished bronze, smooth and beckoning. How had he become so tanned? She felt her body grow warm as she wondered if he were dark all over.

She felt an almost uncontrollable desire to lift her fingers, her whole being suddenly ached to touch him. God in heaven, she could smell him! A wave of dizziness assaulted her at this new sensation. His scent filled her being, causing her to sway and almost stumble against him.

Reena wasn't alone in her appreciation. Had she lifted her eyes to Dominic's dark, smouldering gaze, she would have read a hunger that would have enflamed her warming flesh. The chemise offered less than nothing in the way of protection from his devouring gaze, and Dominic gladly took the opportunity offered to drink in the lovely sight before him. Her breasts lifted with every breath she took, the pink tips rose hard and pointed from her chill and pressed enticingly against the damp, gauzy material.

Dominic felt his body tighten, caught up in a desire he could barely control. His breathing came with gasping effort as he fought the urge to take her. He wanted her more than he could remember ever having wanted another, yet he held back. Instinctively he knew her innocence to be no act.

This was a lady unused to the ways of love. When he took this one, and he surely would, he wanted it with all the fire he suspected her capable of. Aye, he would have her, to be sure, but he wanted her complete and total surrender. God, he wanted her to burn for him.

It was only when she managed to tear her gaze from his body and lift her eyes to his that she realized he had been watching her stare. Angrier than ever to be caught in the act, she snatched the shirt from his outstretched hand. Eyes snapping, she slid it over herself.

Dominic grinned at her anger and remarked casually, "The petticoat too, if you don't mind."

She bristled at his nerve. "Whom do you think you're talking to? I most certainly do mind!"

"Take it off!" he warned ominously.

"Or what?" she snapped, as she lifted blazing eyes to his, her anger pushing her past the point of reason.

Dominic grinned at her show of defiance. Obviously his size did not instill fear. She faced him like a tigress. Finally he shrugged and remarked, "I could take it from you faster than you could blink." His voice grew softer, his eyes more tender. "I don't think you'd appreciate that overmuch. Take it off."

Reena ignored his short chuckle at her unconscious remark that left him in no doubt as to her belief of his parentage. Clearly the brute would do it himself if she failed to comply. Good God, she almost groaned aloud, how did she ever get herself into this predicament?

Dominic dragged the bed closer to the fire. He spread her discarded clothing over the frame to aid its drying, while Reena sighed and untied the strings that held her petticoat at her waist.

Her chemise was short, barely brushing her knees, a mere confection of muslin and lace, which offered no protection whatsoever from his penetrating gaze. His shirt swallowed her in great folds. Buttoned securely over her half-naked state, she breathed in the warm, manly scent it carried and willed away the mortifying thought of any further discovery of its owner's essence.

Her flesh-colored silk stockings were mud splattered and damp, but she left them in place, knowing the thin material would soon dry. She knew he was watching her, but refused to lift her eyes to his. Instead she worked the cuffs of his shirt into short neat folds until her hands and wrists were exposed.

Unable to stand the strained silence between them, she belligerently raised her eyes to his burning black gaze. Her face suffused with color and she had not a clue as to why her voice should tremble so as she spoke. "Must you stare at me in that distasteful fashion? In truth I prefer my clothes returned regardless of their state."

Ignoring her remarks he ordered, "Sit before the fire," and surprised himself as he found his voice gruff and oddly unsteady. Even though she tucked her feet beneath his shirt, the picture of her perfectly formed slender legs refused to leave his mind. His hands burned to reach beneath the cover of his shirt and touch what his eyes had so clearly seen. He cursed himself soundly. How was it that this woman should affect him so drastically? How was it that with every breath he took, her scent flooded his being and caused him to want her more?

Reena reached shaking hands toward the comforting warmth of the flames. They were still caked with mud, and she rubbed them together so the drying dirt might fall away.

Dominic chuckled. Taking a sodden handkerchief from his jacket, he knelt beside her, removed her spectacles and silently began to wipe away the splatters of mud that dotted her face.

Alarmed that he should be so close, she pulled back while reaching for the cloth. "I'll do it."

"Nay," he returned, "I've nearly finished." His finger lifted her chin as he worked to clear away the dirt around her mouth. Gently the damp cloth brushed at her sensitized skin. Her lips parted as he moved his fingers near her mouth, and chills spread unexplainably down her back. Her eyes lifted to his. His dark gaze on her mouth, he concentrated on removing the dirt.

He was dangerously close. Reena shivered as his eyes met and held her own. The fire reflected a deep glow in their black depths. For one wild moment she thought he was going to kiss her, but the moment passed, and Reena felt somehow disappointed.

My God, she groaned silently, what could she have been thinking? Had she actually wanted this stranger to touch his lips to her own? What in heaven's name had come over her? Had the chill she experienced left her feverish that she should fantasize such nonsense?

"Your hair is soaked. It will never dry unless you unbind it."

Reena reached up to pull at her pins, but noticed the mud still caked on her fingers and hesitated.

"Never mind, I will do it."

"No! Oh please, do not!" she cried, shocked that this man should dare to touch her so intimately and then mortified that the thought of his touch should fill her with such choking emotion. Her voice broke as she continued, "'Tis most unseemly."

"Nonsense, it will take but a moment."

An instant later her wet hair fell heavily to her waist. Dominic gave a choking sound. He couldn't resist. All thoughts of restraint fled as the luscious tresses fell over his hands. His blood began to pound and the air grew heavy with the need to touch her. It was without conscious thought that he threaded his fingers through the mass of damp waves, luxuriating in the silken strands. God, he'd known it would feel like this. His hands were slowly pulling her face toward his descending mouth as pure, unadulterated flames of desire licked through his being, threatening to consume him with need. His free arm closed around her slender shoulders and brought her helplessly toward him.

For an endless moment out of time, he held her inches

from him. His ebony eyes compelled her, and his clean breath teased the flesh of her mouth as he caressed her lovely features with his fathomless gaze.

She would later realize she could have, should have, stopped him then. She had no excuse for her wanton response to him. It baffled and confused her as it would for some time to come.

Reena could feel the heat of his body warming her though they barely touched. Her breathing grew uneven and gasping as his clean scent filled her senses, and her heart pounded wildly against her breast. She wondered what it would be like to have his mouth against hers. Would he taste as he smelled, clean and woodsy, with just a trace of the ale that still lingered?

An instant later she was to know, as his mouth covered her lips. Her breath caught in her throat, and she felt herself gasp at the sudden surge of emotion that blazed like living fire within her breast. She had been kissed before, but never with such intensity and manly strength. Never had powerful arms held her in a breathless embrace against a warm, hard, muscled chest.

She had no idea a kiss could be so wonderful, nor that a man's touch could fill her with such sweet sensations, such mindless longing for more. The rushing of pounding blood in her ears all but obliterated the ragged sound of their breathing. She never realized the soft moan of pleasure that escaped the back of her throat, nor did she hear his deep, hungry answering growl.

It never occurred to her to stop him. Her mind could only register her delight, while her body yearned for more. His lips moved over hers. His tongue teasing her full lips, coaxing them to part. His teeth tugged and his head twisted, intent on tasting the sweet essence that lay just beyond this luscious softness.

"Open your mouth for me," he murmured against her throat. "I want to taste you."

His words made her dizzy, and she gave a choking sob. It

was madness, insanity, and yet she had not the power to stop it. His warm, moist breath left her no room to reason. He pushed aside his shirt, his mouth searing the slender curve of her shoulder, sending chills down her back and causing her to tremble all the more.

Her mind swam in a daze at his hungry assault, and she moaned again, helpless to do more than savor each delicious touch of his mouth.

His eyes were level to hers, his breathing harsh and irregular. His stare grew blacker than coal, waiting, questioning, longing for her response. From the first moment his gaze had touched upon her, he had thought of nothing but this. How soft he knew she would be, how sweet she would taste, how her lush body would feel crushed beneath his.

His lips touched hers again, feather light, whisper soft. "Open for me, pretty lady," he groaned, his voice aching with need.

He was weaving a hypnotic web around her, leaving her without the will to protest. Her lips softened, parting slightly with a silent sigh, as she leaned mindlessly into his warm embrace.

His mouth sucked at hers, his tongue running along the sensitive flesh inside her lips. Enticingly slow he passed the barrier of smooth white teeth and groaned as he finally gained access to the sweetness he knew awaited him.

Rough and smooth, firm yet gentle, his tongue plunged deep, eager to explore every crevice within. Drinking in her honeyed taste, he took her breath with his every hungry gasp and returned it to fill her with his dizzying scent.

A burning heat was spreading through her veins. Slowly it crept, spreading from her stomach until not an inch of her escaped the fire. A warning voice echoed in the deep recesses of her consciousness. Stop him! You must stop him now! Yet she only willed away the annoying thoughts as he tore his mouth from hers and spread a delicious path of liquid fire along her throat.

His hands had brushed his shirt from her shoulders and

she could only whimper soft sounds of delight as his brown fingers slid inside her thin chemise to cup a heavy, firm breast. Running his thumb over her nipple brought a curious ache to her midsection. She felt herself softening even more. Every movement of his hands, every whispered caress made her feel even closer to bursting into flame.

The straps of her chemise slid down her arms and then his hungry gaze was on her breasts. Amazingly she felt not a moment of shyness as his dark gaze caressed her. She felt him tremble with emotion, and a wave of pure power spread over her when she realized that she was the cause. With eyes half-closed, the pink tip of her tongue moistened her parted lips and she straightened her back, lifting her breasts for his longed-for touch.

"Oh God," he said, his voice no more than a broken whisper as he looked upon her unconsciously wanton pose. Then his mouth covered hers, slanting over her softness with excruciating need.

She was floating in mindless ecstasy by the time his lips moved over the soft sweet mounds of offered pleasure.

His shirt slid from her unnoticed, and Dominic spread it on the floor behind her. Gently, he eased her back to lay upon it.

Gusts of rain and wind beat against the cabin. Thunder exploded in a wild crescendo, and the small structure fairly shook with the viciousness of the storm, yet Reena never heard it. Nor did she realize the change in her position as his mouth took hers with an urgency he could no longer hold in check.

Gasping, he left her aching lips and moved over the softness of her. Hot and wet, his mouth left a blazing trail of fire. Tracing the delicate shadow of blue vein along creamy white flesh with long tasting kisses, the warmth of his mouth reached the pink tips of her breasts at long last and a strangled groan escaped her lips as he hungrily filled his mouth with her.

She held his head to her burning flesh. As her fingers

37

threaded through his thick black curls, she groaned for more of this new pleasure.

Her chemise moved easily down and over her full hips. The pink tights followed.

Dominic's breath caught in his throat at the beauty of her. He groaned softly as his brown fingers reached out to touch the satin smoothness of white, flawless skin. Her hips were full and lush, her legs long and shaped to perfection.

His hand against her stomach strengthened the ache she felt within her. Her eyes closed with desire. She couldn't think. Her body controlled her mind and her body needed more of this delectation.

His mouth left her aching breasts and eased lower, as he revelled in the taste of her warm flesh. He buried his face in the softness of her stomach while his hands slid down the length of her, moving over her hips and down the slender curve of her smooth legs.

Slowly his hands reversed their course and slid up to the more sensitive flesh of her inner thigh. He parted her legs, his hands discovering her every secret and bringing with them an aching need she could not deny. She moaned, delirious with sensation, and gasped as his mouth descended to meet his hand.

Her body stiffened, her mind fighting to emerge from behind clouds of desire. She murmured a weak, "No."

"Oh yes, beauty, yes," Dominic groaned. He lifted her hips to his searching mouth, his warm, moist breath brushing against the damp flesh his tongue longed to taste. He growled hungrily as his lips moved against her.

"Oh God," Reena choked out, not able to believe such ecstasy could exist.

His mouth, drinking in her musky scent, pressed hungrily to her. He groaned as his tongue, burning hot, sought to discover the sweet essence of her beauty with achingly slow seduction.

Reena's body answered his demands of its own accord.

She never knew the disjointed, broken words she uttered as she strained her body to meet his hungry mouth.

His hands moved over her hips. His fingers, probing the soft, pliant flesh of her buttocks, held her still.

She was wild for him. Her fingers moved through his hair, holding his face against her warmth. Her stomach ached as the tension increased to almost blinding pain. She couldn't stand any more. He had to do something! He had to bring her suffering to an end. "Please," she cried out. "Please, I can't bear it!"

Dominic ignored her pleas, intent on bringing to her all the pleasure he knew.

With a strangled cry her back arched and her trembling body stiffened as waves of ecstasy convulsed her entire being. Lights sparkled behind her closed eyelids as every glorious tremor was felt, leaving her bathed in a delicious, warming glow of contentment.

Reena never felt him leave her. She never heard the sounds of his disrobing. Slowly her consciousness recognized the feel of his nakedness against her. She opened her eyes and looked at him with some puzzlement.

Dominic smiled into the loveliness of her blue eyes. "Did you think it finished, beauty?"

Reena had no chance to ask his meaning as his lips were covering hers again and all thought seemed to vanish into the sweetness of his mouth. She could taste herself as his tongue moved against hers, and she groaned with the further delight this new sensation brought.

Her legs parted again at the slight prodding of his knee, and he lifted her hips so that she could more readily accept his swollen, throbbing desire. She felt the heat of him as he sought to enter. His lips clung to hers, stealing her breath, leaving her dizzy and pliant beneath him.

He moved slowly, feeling the slight obstruction. He pushed his body past it and held her to him as she stiffened and cried out in sudden pain. Dominic cursed softly against her hair. His long, brown fingers threaded through the tumbled strands as he breathed soothing words of comfort to ease her sudden tenseness.

For a long moment he remained still, waiting for her body to accept him. His mouth moved against the slackened lips beneath him, and he comforted softly, "I know. I promise you'll never feel such pain again."

After a moment her mouth began to answer his as he drew her once again into his spell of enchanted pleasure. Slowly he began to move against her, easing far into the depth of her and then pulling back with a steady, effortless motion, until only the tip of his body was held in her warmth. With aching tenderness he pressed forth again and smiled as he heard a low moan of building excitement tear itself from her parted lips.

God, she was luscious. It took every ounce of strength not to ram his body into hers and devour her sweetness. Again he repeated the movement and then again until she felt her stomach begin to tighten. Vaguely she wondered if it was to happen again, but soon forgot her thoughts and unvoiced questions as he guided her hips into answering movements.

She murmured low sounds of aching pleasure as he moved over her. Whispering words of delight, he subjected her body to masterful, silken caresses, bringing sensations she could not have dreamed possible.

His pace quickened, and she groaned again as he plunged deeper. She met each gentle thrust until the tenderness between them was a forgotten thing, and ravenous need melted their every thought. His hands reached beneath her shoulders and lifted her against him as he rose to his knees.

"Wrap your legs around me," he groaned into her neck, while holding her in a breathless embrace, suspended above the floor.

She couldn't believe it! It *was* happening again, only this time the sensations threatened to drive her insane. Her equilibrium gone, she clung to his neck as if he alone were the center of a swirling universe. She was beyond speaking. The soft whimpering that escaped her throat went unnoticed as deep gasping sounds of strenuous breathing filled the room. She knew nothing but this moment of taste and touch as she strained closer. She thought of nothing but to answer the demanding thrusts of his body and tongue.

Her nails bit deep into his back as she urged him on, desperate to find a release from the painful ache that had swelled within her.

"Oh God, yes, yes," she cried breathlessly as tears of relief slipped from her closed eyes and it finally began. She threw her head back and gave a frenzied cry of pure animal satisfaction as her body arched viciously into his. He felt her throbbing spasms of release and groaned into her neck as the last of his control vanished and his body joined hers in mind-exploding ecstasy.

Dominic cradled her limp form close to him as he fought to bring his breathing under control. God, she was magnificent! More than he could have imagined. She had held nothing back. He smiled into the dampness of her neck as the scent of her warm flesh filled his senses. Unbelievably, he felt a quickening, an instant rekindling of desire, and knew this one taking would not be enough. He had thought to find relief and found in its stead more to crave. He couldn't remember when a woman had filled him with such wonder and delight.

Slowly he lowered her to the floor. Propped on his arms, he held himself above her. His eyes lingered over her softened features. Gently his fingers caressed the softness of her slightly swollen lips. "Are you all right?" he whispered.

Slowly her mind returned from the ecstasy she had suffered, and her eyes grew wide with the horror of her actions. *What had she done? What had she allowed him to do?* Good God, they didn't even know each other's names!

Gasping sharply, she managed to clear her head of the remnants of his masterful lovemaking. Gathering his shirt

41

about her in quick, sharp movements, she groaned with disgust as tears of remorse filled her eyes.

Dominic smiled tenderly, his fingers tracing the delicate line of her jaw, as he murmured gently, "You need not feel regret. It was lovely, almost as lovely as the lady herself."

Reena couldn't bring herself to look at him, never mind answer his softly spoken words. What could she say? What excuse could she offer for her lapse of sanity? She couldn't explain it to herself. How was she to make him understand?

He shrugged as he watched her profile in the flickering firelight. "Perhaps we've rushed things a mite. It occurs to me we've yet to be introduced."

Reena's face flamed with mortification. She trembled with shame. Suddenly she felt an hysterical urge to giggle. No need for introductions at this point. She already knew him more intimately than she'd ever known another human being. A low moan escaped her as she closed her eyes and wished herself miles from this place.

It was easy to see that the lady suffered pangs of embarrassment, but to Dominic's mind the suffering was needless. They had both enjoyed these past moments and would, with luck, enjoy many more before this day was done.

He lowered himself to her side as a tender smile played across his lips. Gently he cajoled, "I realize it's a bit late, but my name is Dominic Riveria. Won't you tell me who you are?"

God in heaven, why did he feel this disgusting need to talk? Couldn't he simply go away? She could feel his dark gaze upon her face. What more did he want? How was she to get out of this, she cried in silent agony. What did one do after such an act? What did one say? She could find no words. Perhaps she should simply get up, dress herself, and leave with the last of her dignity intact. He had gotten what he wanted, hadn't he? Surely he'd make no effort to stop her.

But on that count she was in obvious error, for as she

tried to rise, his arm slid around her shoulder and pulled her into his embrace. Like steel bands his arms held her against him. She had not a prayer of breaking his hold.

"Do you believe you can run from me without a word spoken?" he asked softly. "Nay, pretty lady, I will know your name before this day is out."

"Why?" she asked, her voice no more than a muffled groan as she pressed her flaming face to his chest. "Why? 'Tis finished, done. What more do you want of me?"

Dominic chuckled tenderly, breathing in the clean scent of her hair as he nestled her beneath his chin. His hand had unconsciously found its way beneath his shirt and gently grazed the silkiness of her side and hip with absentminded strokings. Indeed, there had been others he would have let, nay encouraged, to leave. But she was not like any other he had known. Already he needed to feel again the lushness of her body beneath him. He needed to experience, at least one more time, her wild response to his kisses, to his touch.

It was a long moment before he realized he had not answered her questions. Finally, he responded. "Parting thus would only enhance your mystery. Perhaps I would then find myself searching you out."

He felt her stiffen and heard her softly uttered groan of horror.

"I doubt I'm mistaken in the belief that you would prefer no further encounters."

She nodded almost imperceptibly, still unable to raise her face to him.

"Then lie with me, love, tell me your name, and after today we'll be done with it."

Even as he said the words, he wondered as to the truth of them. Would one day be enough?

Chapter Four

REENA COULDN'T BELIEVE THE WORDS AS THEY CAME tumbling forth. It was as if another spoke in her place. "Mary. My name is Mary Braxton." Silently she gasped in pure shock as she wondered what had possessed her to say that. She almost groaned with disgust. My God, how could she? Was there a more evil deed than defaming another to hide her own misconduct? A wave of self-loathing washed over her. First she had lain with a man she did not know, nor did she care to know, and then she compounded her misdeed by lying. Good God, if she had to tell him a name other than her own, why had she chosen Mary?

What in hell had come over her? This was a new Reena, one she couldn't honestly say she cared for, one she had never seen till today, one she prayed she might never see again.

Since meeting this man, a lifetime of morals and honor

44

had simply vanished, as if it had never existed. Why? What was it about him that caused this heretofore unknown evil to surface?

Reena sighed softly and prayed for forgiveness. There was no help for it now. If she suddenly told him the truth, he'd only doubt her more. She had done her worst. Now she had to continue the lie and convince him a future encounter would be impossible.

Her voice broke as she forced out the words. "I'm on my way to Baltimore to be married."

Dominic nearly gasped out his astonishment. He hadn't immediately recognized the name, so caught up was he in the touch of her soft skin as he pressed against her. He felt his body stiffen with shock, yet he somehow managed to act naturally as his mind screamed, *No!* He had come to search out Mary Braxton to see for himself the kind of woman who would marry a man like Coujon. What he found was a woman of incredible beauty and spirit. She was too good for the bastard.

Dominic felt an irresistible urge to laugh. She wasn't too good for him. She was perfect. A whore like all the rest. She beds one man while on the way to wed another. God, he couldn't have dared to hope for a better mate.

Suddenly, it was anger that filled the core of his being to overflowing. The intensity of the emotion was so powerful as to astound and confuse him. Why should he feel such rage? What was she to him, after all? Nothing but a wench to bed, and there were dozens of them about, nay hundreds! So why should he feel this sudden, senseless fury? Why should his chest constrict at the thought of Coujon bedding her, kissing those sweetly tender lips, touching this silken flesh?

A long moment of uncomfortable silence ensued and Dominic was no less shocked than Reena as he heard himself ask, "Do you love him?"

Reena, lost in thoughts of self-disgust, only vaguely heard him, but when she didn't reply a flame of hope sprung to life and began to warm his chilled body. He pressed on, hardly daring to breathe as he waited for the words he suddenly and desperately longed to hear. "Do you?"

Reena lifted puzzled eyes to his and answered without thinking. "Who?" And when no answer was forthcoming, she realized his meaning, "Oh, my betrothed? Of course," she added absentmindedly. "Monsieur Coujon is a fine man. I've no doubt I'll be extremely happy."

Reena, so lost in lies, never noticed the sudden tensing of the man who lay at her side. He knew her answer before he asked, still he was unable to resist lest there be one shred of hope. "Could it be Monsieur Coujon from New Orleans and Baltimore, of which you speak?"

Reena gasped in surprise, her face flaming again, thinking she was about to be caught in her lie. She tried to escape his hold as she lifted fear-filled eyes to his freezing glare. "Do . . . do you know him?"

Dominic nodded as an icy disgust filled his heart. His mouth thinned as he snapped, "We've met." For a moment it was all he could do not to swing his fists into her beautiful face. God, how he hated her! How could she marry that swine? How could a woman of such loveliness give herself to that villainous coward? He almost laughed as he realized she, like all the others, saw only his pockets swelling with coin. A humorless grin touched the corners of his mouth. What a surprise she had in store. The man was a step from being penniless.

Perhaps she didn't know him as he did, a small voice reasoned. Perhaps she believed him to be as she had said. Nay, he returned. They were all the same. He'd not search for an excuse. Would he not be double the fool to do so? Did she not succumb to his every advance while on the way to greet her love? Did his Amanda not turn to Coujon the moment the doors to that godforsaken prison had shut behind him?

He almost laughed out loud. Aye, she had gone to plead

46

for help and had done just that, but she had not returned to him. Nay, she had stayed to be Coujon's slut, only to die in the birth of yet another bastard child.

He shrugged almost perceptibly. In the end it mattered not. This one would not go to Coujon. That man had stolen from him for the last time. Now Dominic would return the favor. He almost smiled at the delicious thought. His revenge would be sweet as he relished the charms of the luscious lady. Sweeter still as he brought her betrothed down to the gutter where the slime belonged.

His hand slid up and cupped a soft breast. His thumb brushed lightly over the nipple and brought the tip to a hard bud. He felt her body respond before she realized his intent. His mouth hard, his black eyes glittered with his first tasting of revenge. This would be a purposeful seduction. He grinned menacingly. The bastard would know, he'd see to that. He wanted Coujon's guts to cry out with the same impotent torture he had once felt. Only then would his own raging hatred begin to ebb.

His mouth lowered, his lips nearly touching hers. Realizing his intent, she twisted her face away and sought to dislodge his hand. "No! Please, I cannot." She made to sit up, but his hand again at her shoulder kept her securely in place.

His smile softened; his eyes teased beguilingly. "Can you not?" He nuzzled her neck with warm kisses. His tongue flicking out, tasting again the heady sweetness of her flesh.

"Mr. Riveria, stop. Please stop!" she groaned, as chills spread in delicious waves down her back. "I cannot begin to relate my remorse. I've no answer as to why this should have happened. I know only it cannot happen again."

He laughed softly, feeling her body grow languid and pliant despite her words of protest. His voice was low and husky. "There be only one reason why it happened, Mary, my love. We wanted each other, plain and simple."

She tensed, her voice breaking as she fought the unwanted sensations his mouth caused. "No! I don't want this!"

His mouth moved across her cheek, hovered a hairsbreadth from her own. His eyes warmed with rekindled desire as he murmured, "The first time you barely realized what you were about. This time I'm going to show you just how much you want me."

Chapter Five

REENA BIT HER LIPS AND LOWERED HER GUILTY EYES FROM
Mary's concerned gaze. Her face colored as she remembered again how easily she had defamed her cousin. How
could she bear to see Mary's sweetly innocent face and not
groan with the knowledge of her own lie? She couldn't even
bring herself to look at the younger girl.

"Mary, I promise you I fare well. Indeed I am sorry for
causing you needless suffering, but as you can see I am
unharmed."

Mary watched her cousin with a puzzled expression as
Reena pulled away the last of her wrinkled, muddied
clothing before she hastily stepped into the waiting bath.
Was it her imagination, or was Reena behaving oddly?

Reena shuddered, and for the first time in her life felt
embarrassed to bathe before her cousin. Why? She almost

laughed a humorless sound. Surely this afternoon's events had not changed even that?

Reena knew Mary was watching her. Could she detect a difference? Had his touch left a telltale sign? Did her body show what she had done these last hours?

She gave a silent groan and slid lower into the tub. She had not felt a moment's qualm at his warm, sensual glances, nay, she had welcomed them. Reena's eyes lingered on her breasts, swollen and tender, and seemed to feel once again his hungry assault as the water swirled gently around them.

Her flush grew deeper as she remembered this afternoon's happenings. How badly she had craved his touch, and how readily he had acceded to those cravings. She had not known she possessed such qualities—be they qualities, in fact. She had not dreamed such things could happen between a man and a woman.

"You've yet to say where you were."

Rubbing the soap against the cloth with a good deal more concentration than needed, she responded, "While waiting for Seth to return, I thought I might stretch my legs and get a breath of air. I became confused in my direction when the rain came. I found a deserted cabin and waited out the storm."

Mary watched her closely, suddenly sure she was holding something back. "And?" she prompted.

Reena sighed with disgust as she realized she was forced to lie yet again. Carefully examining the soapy cloth, she forced a nonchalant shrug, "That's the whole of it. There is nothing more to tell. When the storm ended, I found my way back to the inn."

Leaning back in the water, she breathed a deep sigh at its warming comfort and gave yet another silent prayer for forgiveness. Eyes closed, she swore that lie to be the last. She couldn't live like this. She couldn't stand the strain.

Reena cursed herself soundly. Were she not such a coward, she would tell her cousin of the awful deed. But to

50

what avail, she reasoned. Surely no good could come of confessing. Indeed, it would only bring the girl needless suffering and mortification.

Take hold of yourself, Reena, and think before you do further damage. It is extremely unlikely that you will ever meet the man again. Surely he would not try to contact a married lady. And if by some chance he should again meet Coujon, he will, of course, realize Mary is his wife. You will by then be long gone and the matter finished. Her spirits lifted at the thought. Indeed the more she thought on it, the less disastrous the whole matter seemed.

Mary's soft voice invaded Reena's thoughts. "Seth promised the carriage will be fit for travel on the morn."

"Good," Reena sighed thankfully. She had a great need to leave this establishment posthaste. No doubt the wretched man would be spending the night. With a bit of luck she might never see him again.

Reena eased herself slowly out of the bed. After hours of restless tossing, she had finally given up any hope of sleeping. Soon she'd have Mary awake and, above all, she wanted to be alone.

Silently she began to pace the floor. What in the world had come over her this night? Never before had she harbored such wildly provocative thoughts as those that ceaselessly bombarded her now. Each time she closed her eyes, the happenings of this afternoon replayed in her mind's eye. Over and over again, she remembered until she thought she'd go mad. A slight smile quirked her full lips. Perhaps she was mad. Had she been able to give an excuse or reason for her strange behavior? Nay! There was no answer for it. Never in her life had she acted in so thoughtless or foolish a manner.

Her face flamed as she remembered his every touch, his tenderly murmured words of endearment. She bit her lip, trying to keep the thoughts at bay. She didn't want to think of it. She didn't want to remember!

Perhaps if he hadn't shown her just how wanton she could be she could have forgiven herself. But he had shown her. He had teased and taunted her flesh until she had cried out for him to take her. Thankfully he had fallen asleep at last and she had been able to slip away.

Still, if it was relief she felt at escaping him, why then was she pacing the floor in the midst of night, yearning for . . . for what?

Sighing with disgust that she should feel this unsettling confusion, she walked to the room's large window and pulled the drapery aside. God, how she wished she were back in England. What a fool she had been to agree to accompany Mary on this awful journey. It had proved beyond a doubt just how vulgar these colonists were. Why could she not convince her young cousin of this fact? In truth she doubted a gentleman existed among them, Coujon included.

Reena gave a weary sigh. Life had been so simple at home. She had chosen to teach rather than marry. She supposed many would consider her an old maid, but she cared not. She was content and satisfied with her life.

Upon reaching her twenty-fifth year, she had come into substantial wealth. Lately she found herself toying with the possibility of taking her long-empty family estates and turning them into her own exclusive school.

Understandably, her one problem was public opinion. It was a bit unorthodox for a lady of tender years to be trusted to care for others only a few years her junior. Therefore she constantly strove to maintain a somber attitude.

Unfortunately, she was not always successful in forcing aside her readiness for laughter or the gleam of deviltry that often entered her eyes.

Still, if she wished to open her own school, she had to develop an air of composure and studied elegance. A touch of dowdiness could surely bring no harm. The glasses were a good ruse. They made her appear older and more serious. Her hair too, although its natural curliness gave her a bit of trouble keeping it secure, added years to her face with the severity of her chosen style.

Still, her somber dress and manner mattered little. Not when it came to a certain rogue. Reena groaned again and for the hundredth time wished herself home. At least in England she could squash her restlessness with hard work. But not here, not tonight. "Nay," she groaned as she pressed her face to the windowpane. Tonight she burned, shamelessly, desperately, and now she knew it for what it was.

Even though she wore the thinnest of chemises, she could find no relief from this suffocating heat. A heat that burned within and without.

She opened the window as wide as it would go. Confident no one was wandering about at this late hour, she sat her hip on the window sill and raised her leg for balance, baring her leg to the thigh in a most unladylike manner. What did it matter, she reasoned, no one could see her in this black, moonless night.

She almost sighed out loud as the desperately needed breeze began to bathe her heated flesh with its cooling caress. Thank God she'd be gone from here in the morning. She wished they could have left tonight, but the roads were dark and dangerous. Seth had assured her a small delay would bring no harm. She almost laughed at the thought. No harm indeed. No harm if she kept herself hidden in this tiny room.

Dominic walked aimlessly through the stretch of wooded land that bordered the inn's courtyard. He smiled wryly, for the night was as black as pitch and, he reasoned silently, a good companion to his mood. Earlier he had sent word to his ship and expected his men to join him within a few hours. In a day or two at the most, he and his guest would be on his ship and the lady in his arms, his first step toward revenge complete.

Angrily he pushed aside a fleeting pang of guilt. No

matter her morals or lack thereof, he knew she didn't deserve this. Silently he cursed his own weakness. What cared he if she didn't deserve it. The bitch was no better than the bastard she was to marry. In truth they deserved each other. Too bad, he mused sardonically, there would be a slight delay in the arrangements.

For an instant Amanda's laughing face came startlingly clear to his mind. Her wide, brown eyes were filled with joy for the love of him. Suddenly her laughter turned to reproach. He cursed again as his mind wandered back in time and he wondered if he'd ever be free of the pain.

His friend, or so he had thought at the time, had left him a package for safe keeping. How could he have known it was all Coujon's evil plan to see the last of his bastard son?

Granted, the man had reason to be angry. Dominic, his prices lower, had managed to convince two of Coujon's buyers they'd be better off working with him. Still, was that reason enough to have him flung into prison? He gave a vicious curse as he remembered the conditions he had been forced to endure and shook his head trying to free his mind of the horror.

When the authorities came, Amanda had begged to go to Coujon. No matter Dominic's insistence she'd not. She swore she would convince him to drop the charges. Dominic chuckled humorlessly. Well, she had done that. She not only got him to drop the charges, but had had his child to boot. Damn her and her evil lot to hell.

He had let a woman close to him once. It would not happen a second time. This Mary could parade her sweetness before him, she could declare her innocence, she could smile and taunt and tease, but not another would hurt him. He would take her to be sure, and like all the others she would succumb to him. He would use her until he'd had his fill, and then perhaps he'd drag her back to Coujon.

He shrugged. The time was at hand to see the revenge he had so longed for, and if he had to use Mary to bring it about, so be it.

His thoughts fled back to this afternoon. Suddenly he couldn't wait to see the fruition of his plan. Somehow he'd known before he'd touched her of her passion. Aye, she'd been a lusty piece, he grinned. If today had been any example, they had many hours of enjoyment ahead.

He could feel a stirring in his loins at the thought of her creamy skin. His eyes lifted to the windows of the inn, wondering in which room she slept.

Suddenly he almost choked as he saw her. She was sitting on the window sill. Her chin was resting on her propped-up knees, the thin garment she wore riding nearly to her hips. God, she was a beauty. Even if she wasn't betrothed to that animal, he'd have her again. He felt his body grow hard with desire. His eyes strained as her gown fluttered in the slight breeze.

For a long moment, he took in her beauty, his imagination filling in what he could not clearly see.

He leaned back against the tree, his arms crossed over his chest, as he waited in breathless anticipation, silently willing her to leave the room and join him.

From the shadows came a flicker of light as someone struck a match and lit a pipe. Oh God, she almost groaned out loud as the light illuminated his face. Was she forever doomed to see him at every turn? He'd ravaged her thoughts, and now here he stood. She dared not move. She couldn't even breathe. Good God, what if she made a sound and he looked up to see her so boldly displayed?

His pipe was in his mouth, his head slightly raised. Could it be her imagination? Was he looking up at her? He couldn't possibly see her, could he?

It seemed hours before he finally finished his smoke. Knocking the ash against the tree trunk, he put out the tiny flame with the heel of his boot. At last she dared to relax, confident he'd walk inside and never know she'd been watching him.

His voice was barely above a husky whisper when he

spoke, but Reena was positive the whole inn would awaken from the din. "Would you care to join me for a walk, Mary?"

Reena gave a startled, strangled shriek as she jumped and fell. Luckily she fell inside, which caused only a painful rump and bruised pride.

"What . . . what is it?" Mary murmured sleepily.

"'Tis nothing, Mary," Reena whispered, "I've opened the window, is all." And then she silently cursed as she heard a clear, deep chuckle from below her window.

Chapter Six

REENA'S ATTEMPTS TO DOZE, AS THE ROCKING CARRIAGE jolted her about, were useless. What little sleep she had managed the previous night had been filled with wildly sensual dreams that had left her exhausted and vaguely jittery upon awakening.

She sat across from her cousin, feigning sleep as she questioned herself. Why can you not shake the evil lout from your mind? Pull yourself together, she berated herself silently. What happened yesterday is done, finished! Are you such a fool as to allow the man control of your thoughts? Forget the shameful occurrence. Forget *him!* Surely your paths will never cross again.

Thank God, he had not shown himself at the morning meal. She knew not how she could have borne his presence and managed to eat at the same time.

Reena sighed softly and allowed a slight smile to curve her full lips. She was looking forward to the round of parties she knew awaited their arrival in Baltimore. Yes, that was just what she needed to take her mind off this unbelievable experience.

Spying the trace of a smile on Reena's lips, Mary ventured softly, "Are you awake?"

Reena opened her eyes and smiled at the lovely sight of her cousin. "Aye. The bouncing of this carriage offers a person nary a chance to sleep."

Mary gave her typically sweet smile, and Reena was once again plagued with remorse and guilt. Had she searched this country twice over, she doubted she'd find another friend as nearly perfect as this woman. What right had she to despoil her name?

"Enough!" Reena grunted sharply.

"Enough?" Mary questioned. "Were you speaking to me, Reena?"

"Nay, Mary, 'twas a fleeting thought 'tis all. Are you faring well? We should be approaching the outskirts of the city before long."

"Aye," Mary smiled. "The journey was not as arduous as I feared. Still, I am anxious to soak away the bruises from this jolting carriage."

Reena smiled and leaned out the window. "Seth, how much longer do you think?"

Before the guard could answer, two shots were fired, and the carriage came to a sudden stop, throwing Reena to the floor. At first she didn't realize what was happening and gave a series of unladylike oaths at being so cruelly tossed about. She could hear the muffled sound of horses' hoofs as they pranced upon the dirt road, but it wasn't until she heard Mary's name called out that she realized someone had stopped the coach.

Perhaps M. Coujon was so anxious to see his future bride again that he had ridden out to meet them, Reena reasoned, but was quickly dissuaded of the notion as the carriage door was flung open and a masked man peered inside.

"Mary Braxton?" the rough voice questioned.

By this time Reena had lifted herself from the floor and was once again seated. But at the sudden appearance of the stranger, the two women simply gasped and remained silent.

"Which of you ladies be Mary Braxton?" the man inquired in a gravelly voice.

Mary turned white as a sheet. Reena knew she was about to faint. Obviously they were being robbed, but how did this highwayman know Mary's name? Someone at the inn, no doubt. Surely it would not have been difficult to watch their carriage leave and then hurry on ahead to stop them at some deserted, lonely point.

Reena knew Mary could not bear the terror of a robbery and, therefore, answered him.

"I am Mary Braxton."

But Mary was not the delicate flower Reena had supposed. She'd not allow her cousin to be put in danger on her account. "Nay," she countered with a trembling voice, "'tis not true. I am Mary Braxton."

The highwayman chuckled as he stepped away from the carriage. "They both claim to be Mary Braxton, Captain."

A low, muffled curse rang out before the voice continued, "I've no wish to delay this overlong. Pull them out to the light. It's Mary I mean to take."

Take! Reena's mind screamed. Take? Take where? What was he talking about? She thought they meant to rob them, but Mary was being kidnapped! Good God, she could not permit this to happen!

The man's burly hand reached in to grab at Mary's arm as Reena pulled a long pin from her hat. Holding it as if it were a dagger, she jabbed it repeatedly into his thick arm.

Howling with pain and clutching his arm, the man jumped back. The attention of everyone was centered on the highwayman, who shouted obscenities at the carriage door, when shots rang out and Reena heard Seth groan. Obviously, he had reached for his gun during the ruckus and had been shot for his trouble.

A low curse rent the suddenly silent air. Reena gasped as another masked man filled the carriage door. His gun pointed at one and then the other woman. "Which of you did that?"

Reena quaked. How could she have been so foolish to incur the wrath of these villains? She was so terrified she could not get out the words. Slowly she raised her hand. In its palm sat the offending hat pin.

The man grunted and knocked the pin from her. Admiration sparkled in his eyes.

The man pulled at her hand and dragged her carelessly from the carriage. Her skirts scraped along the dirt road, her spectacles fell to the ground, her bonnet flew from her head, and her severely coiffured hair came tumbling down her back in a wild disarray of golden curls. He pulled her back and shoved her hard against him.

"Have ye another weapon, mistress?" the low, laughing voice inquired silkily and then, with the most outrageous audacity, he proceeded to run his hand over the front of her body, cupping the softness of her form as he leisurely searched her.

Reena stiffened at his touch and pushed herself free of his hold. In an instant she spun around and slapped him hard across his masked face.

After a moment of shock at her temerity, his eyes crinkled with humor and he laughed out loud. "Spunky wench aren't you, Mary? Have you not the sense to fear your captor?"

Again he reached for her, only to be interrupted by a loud cry from the coach. "Nay, you've got the wrong one. I am Mary! Leave her be!"

The masked man's deep voice sounded again above her. "Bring the second wench out here."

Reena's attention was averted from the man who held her as Mary was forced from the carriage, kicking and screaming. The man that held her cursed as she ran her fingernails down the side of his face, leaving bloody welts in their wake.

"Keep her quiet!" the man who held Reena ordered sharply. And Reena gasped as the other man's fist smashed into the side of Mary's face and the young girl collapsed in a crumbled heap on the dirt road.

"Sweet Jesus!" Reena's captor grunted, as he shoved her from him and lunged at the man responsible. His dark eyes burned with anger. A vein pounded at his temple as he swung his fist into the man's face. The man crumbled instantly at his feet. His voice was low and measured with icy rage as he spoke, "I told you not to hurt her!"

The man's face turned white, and his eyes bulged with fear. His hand came to nurse his recent injury as he stammered, "Capt'n, she was screamin' and a clawin' my face. There weren't no other way I could stop her."

"Pick her up," he returned, his voice low and vicious. And then added with ridicule, "I trust you can manage her now."

The man muttered as he picked up Mary's unconscious figure and mounted his horse with her in his arms.

"Which of you be Mary?" he asked Reena, as he pulled her again toward him, his hands held tight to her shoulders.

Silently, she lifted her chin. Her eyes narrowed and her lip lifted in obvious contempt. This lout would get no information from her.

The masked man shrugged, "There's no help for it. We'll take both of them. Johnny, bring that one to Mr. Steele, and I'll meet you on the island. I've no wish to have two females on the same ship," and then, muttering almost to himself, he added, "No doubt one will bring trouble enough."

Chapter Seven

REENA'S MIND SWIRLED AS ONE PLAN OF ESCAPE AFTER another came and was simultaneously rejected. She couldn't fling herself from the running horse without the threat of serious injury. She couldn't fight and hope to win against her captor's superior strength. She couldn't wait until they stopped for the night. For one thing, she was sure she'd be constantly guarded, and she had no guarantee they would be stopping at all.

As it happened, it was the simple call of nature that provided her the means.

It was nearly dark when the group pulled their horses to a stop. Reena's captor whispered with a decidedly evil snicker, "Should you feel the need for privacy, madam, I'd advise you to be quick about it. These woodlands abound with wild and ferocious beasts, both two-legged and four. I'd not see you come to harm."

Reena grunted as he slid her from his horse. She leaned against the animal as her legs wobbled from the exhausting hours of riding, as she snapped nastily, "Nay, sir, if there's harm to be done, no doubt it would be yourself wanting the privilege."

From atop the horse came a muffled laugh and a quick low warning, "You'd do well to remember what I said."

Reena spun away from the bloody beast only barely concealing a fervent wish to see the monster in hell, where he no doubt belonged. She parted the thick greenery with an angry slash of her hand and cast an eye about for a likely place.

A moment later she was rearranging her clothing when the anger came suddenly bursting forth. "Damn his maggoty soul to hell! Does he think me so dimwitted to believe his threats of boogeymen and gaping jaws?" She laughed at his attempt to instill fear. After today, she doubted much more harm could befall her. Surely if she made good her attempt to escape, help could be found.

It took not a moment for her to realize this was the opportunity longed for. She knew the men were stationed somewhere close by, but if luck were with her, she just might be able to slip between them. If she didn't move immediately, it would be too late.

An instant later she was flying through the woods away from the low male voices behind her. Her feet moved so fast she barely felt the ground beneath her soft kid slippers. Branches slapped at her face and pulled painfully at her hair. A heavy thorn caught the shoulder of her cloak and dress, penetrating the thick fabric and tearing as Reena, nearly strangling herself, broke free. She ignored the thorn-caused pain and refused to look at the wound as blood began to seep down her arm. Desperately she fought against a forest that seemed of no mind to allow her entrance.

It was some time before Reena paused long enough to lean into a tree. Every breath brought knifelike pain as she fought to bring the much needed air to her starved lungs.

Another pain sliced into her side and she bent over, breathing deeply as she tried to sooth its sharpness with the pressure of her hand.

It was pitch dark when she stopped again. The twinkling of a few stars in the inky black sky was only now and then visible through the thickness of overhanging trees. It would be folly to continue in this blackness, she reasoned. More than likely she'd only wandered about in circles and would perhaps end up within her abductors' grasp again.

Her face stung from the endless branches that had barred her way, leaving deep scratches against flawless skin. Tentatively she reached a hand to her head and to her surprise found most of her hair intact. She'd have sworn more than half was missing, for every branch and thorn had seemed intent on seeing her relieved of the heavy mass.

Sliding to the ground, Reena used the trunk of a tree to support her back. For warmth against the damp night, she hugged her legs close to her with aching arms. Her shoulder was stiff and throbbed miserably, but Reena clenched her teeth and willed away the discomfort. To be free of those monsters, she'd take that pain and much more, she vowed.

Weakly she laid her head upon her knees and wondered how long it would be before she came upon some form of civilization. A smile of triumph curved her full lips as she thought of the frustration her kidnappers must surely be experiencing. No doubt, thinking her weak and defenseless, an easy prey to their horror stories, they were more than a little surprised to find her gone. Idly she wondered how long they had searched for her before giving up.

Silently she prayed Mary had used a similar opportunity for escape. She laughed softly, imagining their happiness if they were to suddenly come upon each other.

The picture of Seth holding a bloodied arm came to her, and her chest constricted with pain at the knowledge that he had suffered on her account. "Please God," she whispered softly, "let him be all right. Let all of us be all right."

A squirrel stood on its hind legs and chattered out an angry tirade at the gall of his unwelcomed guest. Reena opened her eyes as a shaft of sunlight fell across her face. Her head rested still upon her raised and now achingly stiff knees and she couldn't resist a grin as her gaze took in the little creature's obvious censor. Apparently she was invading his territory, and he didn't like it a bit.

A smile tugged at her lips; she lifted her head. Still the squirrel dared to issue his insults.

Laughing with delight, she remarked, "If you ever visit my home, I promise you a more polite welcome." She laughed again as the furry animal bolted with obvious terror into the underbrush.

Breathing a deep sigh, Reena managed by sheer willpower to unlock her stiff legs and stretch them out before her. With a soft groan of pain she crawled to her knees and managed to pull herself into a standing position while using the tree for support.

Her stomach rumbled with hunger. "I'm famished," she groaned aloud, while realizing for the first time that she'd eaten nothing since yesterday morning. Tentatively she released the tree and breathed a sigh of relief that she was able to stand unassisted. A few moments later she was walking toward the rising sun, keeping an eye out for something to eat, knowing she would sooner or later come upon someone who could bring her to safety.

In her eagerness, red juice slid over the fullness of her lips onto her chin. Hastily, she wiped it away with the edge of her petticoat just before she once again stuffed a handful of strawberries into her mouth. She sighed with relief as the sweet fruit began to take the edge off the worst of her hunger and continued to eat until she was full.

It took well over an hour before she managed to pick

enough for still another meal. Having no means to carry them and feeling a need to be on her way, she finally removed her petticoat and used it as a sack.

So it was with a great deal of cockiness that Reena brushed away a swarm of gnats and continued on her journey. Her heart was light, her step quick and agile. She knew now she could take care of herself and felt no fear of what this forest might bring.

Flies and mosquitoes might be bothersome, but she had found nothing as yet to strike fear in her heart. Even the occasional growl of a distant animal did little to mar her confidence.

Suddenly a loud rustling instantly relieved her of this arrogance. The underbrush moved. Something was charging through. She jumped, nearly shrieking, her hand jammed to her mouth to stifle her scream.

An instant later she laughed with relief as a bear cub came bounding through the thick underbrush and stopped to inspect this newest addition to his playland.

"Hello there," she laughed, with untold alleviation. "My goodness," she said, and shuddered involuntarily, "do you know the fright you gave me?"

Unconcerned, the cub lifted his front paws and leaned playfully against her, snorting as he sniffed out her scent. Reena laughed as she stroked the thick fur of his back and felt him increase his pressure against her.

"You wouldn't have any food on you, would you?" she asked wistfully, feeling a sudden urge for a hot cup of tea.

She gave a startled cry as the weight of the cub caused her to step back. She stumbled over a heavy tree root and landed abruptly on her knees.

A few moments later Reena was laughing, rolling on the ground as the cub tried to lick her face, when a deep growl rent the air and brought their playful antics to a sudden stop.

With a sense of unreality, Reena watched as the thick foliage parted and the most enormous bear she could have ever imagined came into view. Standing on her hind legs, the teeth of the cub's mother glittered in the sun's rays. Saliva dripped down her gaping jaws as she let out a growl of horrendous rage.

"Oh my God," Reena gasped as she scrambled to her feet. Her strawberry-filled petticoat forgotten, her long skirts proving no obstacle, she bolted with a high-pitched scream of pure terror.

Again branches struck her face and went unnoticed. Glancing back, she saw the huge bear take off after her. Reena was in a panic. She could barely think. She needed help, and she needed it fast. If that beast caught up with her, she was doomed.

She was running with blind terror, willing her body to outdistance the huge animal. She dared a quick glance behind her and then cursed herself soundly at her stupidity as she smashed into the solid trunk of a tree. Knocked on her derrière, she sat for a moment staring in a daze at what had so abruptly brought her flight to an end.

A thickly branched tree loomed before her, stretching its heavy limbs in silent adoration toward the clear blue sky. The deep growl sounded again, bringing her instantly back to the problem at hand. She knew she hadn't a chance to outrun the bear. A moment later, with another glance over her shoulder, she realized she had to climb that tree or die in the attempt.

Jumping for one of the branches, she held on and walked up the trunk to where she could bring her legs up and over the sturdy limb. At first on her belly, the branch between her legs, she finally maneuvered herself to a sitting position.

Her long sigh of relief was caught in her throat as the bear came to a stop beneath her. Suddenly she screamed again as the bear stood on her hind legs once more. Her hungry jaws were level with Reena's lap.

Reena came to her feet so fast she almost lost her

balance. Her hands scraped across the rough bark, leaving them bloody and sore, yet she felt nothing as she scurried higher.

A moment later she was three branches up, clinging to the tree as the bear, enraged at her escape, shook the tree with what felt like earth-shattering force.

Reena clung on, as if her life depended on it, which indeed it did. Barely able to breathe, helpless to do more than pray for the animal to get tired and leave her alone, she closed her eyes and pressed her face against the bark, while growls of rage split the air. The sound of splintering wood brought still another scream, and she knew her struggle to survive was near its end.

The cub, till this moment, was enjoying the chase, thinking nothing could be more fun than romping through the forest on the heels of its protective mother. Now it grew bored watching his mother beat a tree to death and started to wander off in search of more interesting quarry.

It was a long time after the bear scrambled in pursuit of her young cub, before Reena realized the tree was no longer shaking, and she dared to open her eyes.

A huge sob tore itself from her trembling form, and tears came to blur her vision. She was shaking so hard, she feared to release the tree.

A vine hung close by, and she reached out for it so she might better balance herself and sit for a moment.

Another scream tore itself from her throat as the vine turned out to be not a vine at all, but a snake already beginning to coil around her wrist. Instantly and with a violent shudder, she flung it to the ground.

Gasping for air, she leaned back into the tree and shivered with disgust. How could she have ever thought this land beautiful? It was horrid, and the sooner she was gone from here, the better.

"I'm going to kill them," she promised in a tear-filled voice as she swore her revenge on her kidnappers for the suffering forced upon her.

Her immediate terror was fading, and Reena suddenly became conscious of a throbbing leg. Lifting her skirt to find the cause, she gasped at bloody claw marks. She had been so frightened she'd never felt the injury.

Waiting endless moments before she dared leave the haven of the tree, she tried to calm what she felt was dangerously close to hysteria. Nothing could be gained by losing control, indeed she chanced much. She had to remain calm. Without a doubt she would eventually find her way out of this mess. She simply needed to keep her wits about her and remain patient.

Her eyes smarted with unshed tears as she finally lowered herself to the ground and put pressure on her leg. For the first time she wondered if indeed she had made the right move in running from her abductors.

A low curse slipped from her lips as she realized she had lost her petticoat. Already she was feeling hungry.

"How much longer?" she wailed softly.

Hours later, her stomach rumbled loudly. Her leg ached miserably with each step taken. With a groan of disgust she swatted the ever-present mosquitoes from her face. She was swelteringly hot, but dared not remove her cape. At least it offered her some protection from the increasing number of insects.

Reena squirmed as perspiration trickled down her back and sides. Damp ringlets stuck to her face, and she pushed them back only to find them returning to her sweat-soaked cheeks and forehead.

She prayed for a breeze. She could hardly breathe without inhaling flies or mosquitoes. God, she longed to be free of this damp, sweltering horror.

The sky was darkening. A heavy mist enveloped the tree tops. Reena glanced up with surprise. Surely she could not have been walking that long.

A long roll of thunder sounded in the distance.

"Oh Lord," Reena groaned wearily, "just what I need."

Instinctively she began to hurry her pace, and then found herself smiling. Where was she hurrying to?

Reena whirled about in fright as a flash of lightning zigzagged across the sky, while another crash of thunder split the air around her.

The rains came in a sudden sheet of gray water. Reena pulled her cape over her head, but moments later the water had soaked through anyway.

The water was icy against the heat of her skin, and she shivered with the shock of it. Must everything be so extreme in this horrible country? One minute she was steaming from the suffocating heat, the next shivering from the cold.

It wasn't long before Reena was soaked to the skin. She could scarcely find the strength to put one foot in front of the other. Her slippers were sucked into the mud. She moved on, only vaguely aware that she was barefoot. Her knees nearly buckled against the weight of her wet clothes. When the cloak fell from her shoulders, she couldn't find the strength to retrieve it. The thought crossed her mind that she'd be sorry later, but for now she was too exhausted to worry over it.

Reena didn't see the cabin until she'd nearly walked right into it. Her head down, she moved along its perimeter, feeling her way more than seeing. Finally she found the doorway and fell inside. There was no door, only an opening in one wall, and no means, had she the strength, to prevent the rain from coming in with each gust of wind.

The cabin was totally bare. Not even a stick of wood had been left. A wave of sadness washed over her as she realized she couldn't stop shivering. A misty smile touched her lips. She never thought she'd meet her maker in a deserted cabin somewhere in Virginia.

She hadn't the strength to come to her feet again. Whipped and broken, she crawled to the farthest corner and curled herself into a tight ball.

Her leg was so sore she couldn't bear to touch it, and she

shook so badly from the cold she thought she might literally shake apart.

Now that the end was near, she was amazed to feel no fear. Only bone-weary exhaustion. All she wanted was to sleep. And even though she knew once she closed her eyes, it would be forever, she couldn't find it within herself to care.

Chapter Eight

SHE WAS SO HOT! SHE COULDN'T REMEMBER EVER BEING this hot before. The forest! Of course, she was still in the forest—the wretched, wretched forest. When would she find her way out? How would she find the strength? Where in God's name was help?

She knew she never should have come here. What a terrible place America was. Barbarians all. She longed to feel again the cool breezes of England. It seemed if she concentrated very hard, she could smell the sharp, salty scent of cool mornings. Morning, when she had walked along the cliffs at the rear of Mary's estates. The warm sun would gently touch her then as the cooling breezes teased the hem of her skirts.

Oh England and home, she wailed silently. How much more she loved it now that it was lost to her.

She moaned as something cold slid over her. It hurt. Everything hurt. Her hands reached out to stop the torture.

"Please," she groaned weakly.

"Rest easy, love," an unexplainably tender voice whispered from somewhere above her. "I know this is uncomfortable, but it has to be done."

Was it her imagination? Was she not alone? Was someone talking to her? Aiding her? Reena tried to open her eyes. She could see no more than a red haze. Everything, even her eyes burned. Had she died then? Was she in hell!? Is that why everything felt so hot? Is that why she hurt so bad?

"Please, no," she murmured. "Please."

Again the soothing voice whispered to her, and again she felt a cold ache. She was beginning to drift. Like a feather that escaped its pillow, she was floating. And like that feather she was so light, so small, she was nearly weightless. The pain was fading. She sighed with relief as it vanished completely and she was once again engulfed in a black void of deep, soothing sleep.

Dominic sat at her side, replacing the wet cloths as soon as the heat of her body warmed them. Her eyelids fluttered and she cried out with pain, but he did not hesitate in his ministrations.

A fever such as he had never known raged within her. He had never seen a body suffer so and live. But this one would live. Aye, if he had anything to say about it she would.

He could easily imagine what would have been had he not found her when he did. Another few hours in those wet clothes would surely have been the end of her.

He shrugged aside the thought as a fresh wave of guilt washed over him. How had he been so remiss regarding her welfare? His dark gaze grew black as he studied her white face. He should have known from the stubborn lifting of that beautiful chin and the icy glare in those eyes, those eyes that could spread blue fire, eyes that could read into a man's soul, eyes that could draw and compel away reason. He shook his head, forcing away the erotic ramblings.

73

He should have known she'd not cower before him. She was a feisty piece, this one. She had spirit. Perhaps too much for her own good—and his.

His shoulders slumped as he reached a hand to her fiery skin. Was this fever never to abate? He gave a low curse. Why in God's name hadn't he kept her close to his side? He smiled as he imagined her rage, should he have denied her privacy. Still, no matter her embarrassment, it would have ensured her safety and wellbeing as well as his own peace of mind.

The memory of her disappearance returned once again with haunting familiarity. When she had not returned after a few minutes, he had begun to feel a prickle of fear that she might have taken it into her head to do something foolish. Once he had realized her escape, he had momentarily panicked. Sweet Jesus! She was a lady. At home in a drawing room, not a forest! She couldn't fend for herself. Lost in these woodlands, her death was a foregone conclusion, and Dominic suddenly felt very much a murderer.

Jesus! What the hell was it about this twit that caused him constant guilt and self-recrimination? She seemed so delicate, so damned fragile that he was filled with a protectiveness, the strength of which he had never known. What was she? Lady or whore? He shrugged away the question, for it mattered not, and felt a smile touch his lips as his dark gaze moved with tender affection over her body.

She was beautiful beyond belief, a prize any man would do much to attain. Her golden hair lay fanned out over the white pillow in a wild confusion of luscious curls, and he felt no compunction to refrain from touching its beckoning silkiness. Her lashes formed dark half-moons above high cheek bones. A soft flush touched her golden coloring, and he felt his chest swell with possessiveness that he should have been the only man to have touched her.

Suddenly he wanted to see more of what lay behind those haughty glances of ice. He knew well her passion, but unbelievably it wasn't enough. He longed to witness her laughter. He wanted to argue, fight, be with her, but most of all he wanted to hold her protectively against him.

How, in such a short space of time, had this little piece of fluff become so important to him?

A knock at the door interrupted his thoughts, and he pulled a sheet over her partial nakedness. Dr. Barrett entered at Dominic's call. For four days he and the doctor had taken turns at her side administering to her needs as best they could.

"Any change?"

Dominic grunted as he stretched his stiff back and came to his feet. "She was beginning to fight me, but slipped back before she gained total consciousness."

Dr. Barrett nodded, " 'Tis the fever. There be little else we can do since you won't allow the leeches. The rest is up to her."

Dominic's lips tightened and his body shuddered at the very thought. He couldn't hear the word without remembering his mother and the slow, seemingly endless suffering she'd been forced to endure. The doctors had bled her, and Dominic swore each drop of blood taken had brought her closer to the end.

Dr. Barrett removed the bandage and lifted the hot-bread poultice that was slowly drawing the infection from the gaping wound. His long fingers gently probed the tender pink flesh around the draining injury and caused Reena to groan out in pain.

"Good," he nodded, as he leaned closer and sniffed at the damaged area. "There seems to be less swelling and inflammation. For a time it appeared she might lose it. I think we can safely say she's past that danger."

Dominic breathed a sigh of relief at the long-sought reassurance.

The doctor covered her leg with another hot poultice. Reena cried out and tried to reach the source of her discomfort, while Dominic's lips tightened with undisguised pity as he fought to hold her flailing arms.

"She's beginning to feel it."

"Aye," Dr. Barrett agreed, "she should be coming to her senses soon. She's a strong young lady. Between the chill she took and the infection, I gave her not a chance. If you are right about how she came by this wound, I'd venture to say she's lucky to have escaped with her life."

Dominic's chuckle belied the terror he had felt upon first sight of her leg. "Judging from our short acquaintance, 'tis likely 'twas the bear that got off easy."

Reena opened her eyes to soft candlelight. She felt confused, disoriented. She was in a high four-poster bed, but where was the bed? She didn't recognize this small, low-ceilinged room. Suddenly it was just too much of an effort to think about it. A sound of a door closing drifted toward her just as she allowed her eyelids to flutter and close again.

"No you don't," a deep voice grated annoyingly. "You've been sleeping for days on end. 'Tis past time for you to take a bit of nourishment."

It took Reena some effort to turn her head toward the low sound. A man stood just inside the room, bathed in shadows; he appeared to be holding something. Slowly he approached the side of the bed.

She closed her eyes. God, she was so ill! Had she ever felt so poorly? Her tongue felt like cotton. Her throat seemed coated with shards of glass, and her body and head ached as though she had been beaten.

Again his voice sounded from out of the darkness, forcing her from the comfort only sleep could bring. "I'm happy to see you've rejoined the world of the living at last."

Reena's eyes narrowed as the timbre of his voice struck a haunting note. Did she know him? She couldn't quite get her thoughts in order, but he did seem somehow familiar. Her mind was fuzzy, her sight none too clear, her throat unbearably sore. She forced herself to speak. As sick as she was, she had to know. "Who are you? Where am I?"

Dominic leaned closer so his face was visible in the soft light.

"You! How did you . . . ? How did I get here?" She tried to lift herself to her elbow but fell back with a weak groan.

"Later," Dominic chuckled gently. "You're going to have to gain some strength before you can fight with me."

Placing a bowl of beef broth on a table at the bed's side, he leaned toward her and lifted her into a sitting position. In silence he adjusted her pillows, slid her toward the head of the bed, and pressed her back.

The mattress dipped as he cautiously sat at her side. His eyes never left her pale face as he spooned small amounts of the warm broth to her parched lips.

Reena obediently opened her mouth and took the offered liquid, having not the strength to argue or question him further. She groaned with pain as she forced the soup past her fiery throat, but after a few mouthfuls the pain began to ease.

She hadn't taken a dozen spoonfuls before it became too much of an effort to keep her eyelids open. She drifted off to sleep.

Later, she dreamed a cool, hard body slid into the bed at her side and Reena, even in sleep, sighed with contentment as a strong arm wound itself around her waist and pulled her heated body into a close, comforting embrace.

When Reena awoke the next morning she felt somewhat better. Her fever still lingered, but the raging heat that had burned was gone. The time since she had fallen asleep in the empty shack was no more than a blur. She knew she had been very ill. Vaguely she remembered someone holding her close, speaking tenderly over her, wiping her fevered brow. Cold cloths had been pressed repeatedly to her feverish skin and someone had spoken soothing words, but it was all a fog, as if she dreamt it.

Her stomach rumbled from hunger. When had she eaten last? With a great deal of effort she finally managed to lift herself into a sitting position. Her arms shook like jelly. She felt as weak as a baby, and a headache pounded viciously behind her eyes. She needed something to drink, but most of all she needed to use the chamber pot.

Her gaze searched the room for the needed object. Gritting her teeth, she slowly swung her legs over the side of the bed. For the first time she noticed her half naked state. With nothing less than amazement she stared down at her bare legs. Her body was covered in a man's white shirt and nothing else. Lifting the shirt slightly, she realized she was in the midst of her monthly flow, and someone had matted a protective cloth between her legs.

She edged toward one of the bed's four thick posts and held on as she came to her feet. The pain that seared at her leg was not to be borne. The room swam, and she gave a soft cry as she crumbled to the floor.

Dominic chose just that moment to look in on her and growled out a vicious curse as he watched her slide to the floor. An instant later he was at her side. His mouth was tight with anger as he lifted her into his arms. "Sweet Jesus! Don't you have the sense to call for help?"

Reena's eyes were closed as she pressed her warm face into the comfort of his cool, crisp shirt. Feeling safe and relaxed, she didn't realize to whom she spoke as she blurted out. "I've a need to use the . . . ." She opened her eyes and looked up into Dominic's tender expression. Her mouth gaped with shock and she choked on a silent gasp.

"The chamber pot?" he finished for her with an easy grin.

Even in her weakened condition, Reena felt fire flame her cheeks at his question. She lowered her eyes, unable to look at him. Oh God, it was so mortifying, she couldn't find the words. What the hell was he doing here? She thought she'd seen the last of him at the inn. Was she doomed to be forever haunted by this man? A small sound of suffering escaped her throat.

"May I presume you haven't yet?"

She didn't answer, but kept her eyes closed, wishing him gone from her presence.

"I'm sorry, but I'm afraid there's no help for it. Since there is no one else and you cannot do it yourself, I will assist you."

"I'll die first," she snapped fiercely, suddenly gaining untold strength. Her blue eyes were suddenly aglow with determination. Her headache grew worse than ever, and she grunted nastily, "Put me down this instant and get out."

"Perhaps we might work out a solution to this problem," Dominic reasoned, in a voice that was too close to laughter for her liking. Gently he placed her on the bed again. "I will bring the pot to you," he continued over his shoulder as he went to retrieve it. Holding it out to her, he grinned at her obvious abhorrence.

Clutching her head, she wailed, "Put the damn thing down and get out!"

Dominic grinned, but did as he was ordered. As he left, Reena eyed him with a dangerous glint and wished she had the strength to throw the blasted pot at his grinning face.

She was just pulling the sheet up over herself when the door opened again. Reena closed her eyes with a groan, for she couldn't imagine why Dominic should return but to cause her further suffering.

His hand was cool as he pressed it to her forehead. "You're still warm. How do you feel?"

Reena had to use the last of her strength not to scream out, I'm sick! How do you think I feel? Instead, she responded evenly, "Mr. Riveria, I cannot imagine why the condition of my health should concern you. Why, in God's name, are you here? Where am I?"

"Captain."

"Excuse me?"

"Captain Riveria."

"Oh," she breathed weakly. "Very well, Captain, if it wouldn't cause you too much trouble, would you explain to me just what is happening?"

"Later," he grunted, as he lifted her to rest upon freshly fluffed pillows. "First you need to eat and get cleaned up. Then we'll talk."

Dominic grinned at her questioning gaze. He had hoped to delay any discussions until she was completely well, but clearly the little spitfire wanted none of that. Her rage was sure to be magnificent. Her eyes would snap fire. He couldn't say why the thought should excite him, he only knew it did.

Indeed, he admitted easily, he longed to know every facet of her. He couldn't deny that she intrigued him, more so as each day passed. Suddenly he realized his need for revenge had become strangely less urgent as thoughts of her filled his mind.

Chapter Nine

DOMINIC CHOKED BACK A LAUGH AS REENA NEARLY bellowed "Good God Almighty! You cannot be serious!" Her dark eyes narrowed and snapped pure outrage, while moving from his to the bowl of water he held and back again to his twinkling eyes. Her pale cheeks pinkened delightfully as her anger came to full bloom at his obvious enjoyment of her suffering. Even in her weakened state, her voice rose strong and determined, "I care not if I be crawling with vermin. You, sir, will not bathe me."

Dominic grinned as he placed the bowl of soapy water on the bedside stand and relaxed his hold on the sheet, allowing Reena to pull it beneath her chin once again. Moving a chair closer to the bed, he sat and smiled down at her. "I believe I've mentioned before the female form holds me in little awe. Who do you suppose has administered to your needs throughout this illness? Do you believe that I, aware of the lady's tender sensibilities, kept my eyes averted during my tasks? Nay, sweet Mary, you have a lovely body, one a man might go to great lengths to obtain. More the fool I, had I not taken the opportunity offered.''

Dominic watched as her face flamed and her lips grew thin with rage. "How dare you?! Obtain? As if I were naught but a possession? You beast! You vile, bloody beast!''

Dominic laughed softly. "It matters little if the truth angers you, love. The deed is done. It cannot be reversed. And since I am already so well acquainted with the beauty of your form, I see not why you should object to my further ministrations.''

"Do you not?'' she snapped, her brow lifting with disdain, her lip curling in disgust. " 'Tis apparent, Captain, your perversion, coupled with your lack of intelligence, hinders you overmuch. Perhaps I should then endeavor to explain my meaning in simpler words. Words even you should be able to understand.'' She ignored his soft chuckle at her insult and continued on very slowly, pronouncing each word carefully and clearly as if she spoke to one of considerably less than normal intellect. "I care not the circumstances. You do not now, nor at any time in the future, have my permission to touch me, no matter the reason, need, or cause. Do I make myself clear?''

"Indeed, mistress,'' he grinned, obviously enjoying this verbal skirmish as much as she abhorred it. "Still, the question persists.'' Reena cast him a puzzled glance as he lifted his brows and gazed back in all innocence. "If you will not allow my help, who then will do it?''

"I will do it, damn it!'' she raged, as she lifted herself to her elbow and then fell back against the pillows with a soft moan of exhaustion. Her head was pounding. Her body ached miserably. She longed for him to be gone from her sight. In a decidedly weakened voice she finally continued, "I will do it, Captain. Please leave me to my privacy.''

Dominic shook his head, all humor gone as he replied,

"Forgive me, Mary, but 'tis necessary that I ignore your demands, for the present at least. You are in no condition to object overmuch and even less to do this chore yourself. Indeed, you have a need of much rest before you can fight me as I know you long to do.

"You are quite right. I am a beast to tease one so helpless. It seems you bring out traits I had not before been conscious of.

"From this moment on you must think of me as a doctor or nurse. Someone must see to your care. I will be finished momentarily, and you will be feeling much more the thing."

Reena watched with wary suspicion as he dipped the small cloth into the warm water and soaped it. Ringing out most of the water, he spread a thin film of soap over her face and neck. She searched his stony expression for a flicker of amusement, but found nothing amiss. He might have been washing a doll for all the notice he displayed.

Reena's sigh of relief caught in her throat as he tried to lower the sheet. Her sky blue eyes darkened to indigo fire and clung to his as her hands refused to relinquish hold of the sheet. "Nay."

"It will take but a moment," he returned, while ignoring her protests and easily disposing of the sheet. "You have not the strength to argue at this point. Later you may berate me till your heart's content."

Her lips tightened with undisguised hatred as she tried to prevent the unbuttoning of the shirt she wore and found her feeble attempts easily thwarted by strong, brown fingers. Her eyes glistened with tears of frustration and shame as she turned her face from him and helplessly allowed his ministrations.

Reena was positive her cheeks would be forever stained a vivid red, for she could imagine no greater distress than to have this particular man move his hands over her body in so intimate a fashion, no matter his apparent clinical attitude.

83

Still, a short time later, she was forced to admit she did feel a great deal better. While waiting for Dominic to strip the bed and replace the linen with crisp clean bedding, she had changed into a fresh shirt and sat comfortably wrapped in a lightweight coverlet.

Once the pillows were fluffed and the oversheet pulled down to await her, he turned and for the first time allowed a smile to enter his dark eyes at the exquisite picture she made. Only her face and hair were visible beneath the huge folds of a blue summer blanket. She looked no more than a waif. Her eyes, shining with fever, peered huge and dark from a pale drawn face. Obviously unsure of his next move, she looked as if she might bolt at his slightest movement.

Dominic briefly considered giving her ample reason to look at him thus as vivid pictures of grazing the soapy cloth over her softly curving flesh played again and again in his mind.

God, had he ever known such exquisite torture? It had taken nearly all his strength not to hold her in his arms and make love to her regardless of her weakened, feverish state or the monthly flux she was still experiencing. Indeed, he could not imagine a cause that might diminish this desire. It wasn't until he had lifted her from the bed and placed her in a chair across the room that he had been able to breathe with any degree of normalcy. He had almost thrown the shirt at her as he ordered her to change and had given a silent prayer hoping she had not heard the trembling in his voice.

For an instant he cursed himself for acting the fool. What the hell had gotten into him to put aside this tormenting hunger? He had not a doubt he could convince her to accept and return his amorous advances. From the depth of his soul a twinge of conscience made itself felt, and he gave a silent curse as he realized the only course open to him. She had been grievously ill, and even though he wanted her desperately, he wanted her as before, willing and eager in his arms.

It wasn't until he gathered her stiff form into his arms and placed her once again amid the soft mattress and pillows that Reena breathed a visible sigh of relief. He drew up the sheet and began to gather the soiled linen as Reena snuggled deep into the soft down. She was exhausted from fever and the emotional turmoil she had just experienced and was nearly asleep when she felt his cool lips brush gently upon her warm brow. Suddenly she felt as a child, at ease and safely protected in the comfort of his caring. This combined with her weakened, sleepy state caused her a deep, relaxing sigh, and it was with unconscious thought that her lips lifted and grazed the cool skin of his neck in return. She never realized, nor saw, the surprised expression in his eyes turn to tenderness as a gentle smile softened his firm lips. Again his mouth sought the warmth of her, though this time in less a brotherly fashion. It was a long moment before he found the strength to release her warm lips.

Filled with a tenderness he had not before known, Dominic ran his fingers over the silken softness of her cheeks and into the tangle of golden curls that fanned out like luxurious waves against the white pillow. An unexplained emotion twisted in his chest, and he felt no need to resist the impulse to pull her against him and hold her in a close, comforting embrace.

The mattress sagged against his weight and, Reena sighed, more asleep than not, as she snuggled closer and heard his low, whispered, "Rest easy, love."

Reena awoke the next morning soaked in sweat. The bedding and shirt stuck to her uncomfortably. Her hair was a tangle of damp knots. Her fever had broken at last, leaving her weaker than ever.

"How do you feel?"

Reena glanced to her right, surprised to find Dominic approaching the bed with a tray of steaming dishes. "Your fever broke during the night, so you are over the worst of it. You need only to rest and take some nourishment and you'll soon be your old self again."

While Reena leaned against the headboard and sipped at the cup of tea, Dominic rummaged through the bottom drawer of a huge armoire that nearly covered one whole wall. A moment later he returned to her side and handed her a lady's brush and mirror.

Reena smiled at the offered items. "Forgotten, no doubt, by the last lady you rescued? I assume it was you who found me."

Dominic nodded as he pulled a chair to the side of the bed and sat. With obvious fascination he watched as the brush was pushed through the heavy, damp waves, leaving the thick, silken lushness to tumble smoothly over her shoulder and reach nearly to her waist.

"But how?" she continued, her eyes a mirror of confusion. "How did you happen to come across that particular cabin? You couldn't have known I was there. What ever made you look inside?"

"Mary," he sighed, knowing the dreaded confrontation was at hand. He anticipated her anger and wished she were stronger before she found out the truth. For a moment he thought to make up a story, but shrugged away the notion. She would have to know sooner or later. He might as well be done with it. "A child could have followed the trail you left. Broken branches, strands of golden hair hung upon thorns, a torn piece of clothing, a petticoat filled with strawberries, and then finally your cloak."

"You were following me?" she asked with obvious amazement. "But . . ." The only people who knew where she was . . . the only people who could have followed her were the men who . . . "Oh my God," she groaned as realization hit. The brush fell from her hand as she clutched her throat in horror. Her eyes grew so huge it seemed they might swallow her pale face. "Why?" she rasped. "Why did you do it?"

Dominic shrugged, unsure as yet as to how much he was going to tell her.

Reena growled out in instant rage. "Sweet Jesus, I

cannot believe your unmitigated gall. You kidnap my cousin and myself, cause me untold suffering, nearly cost me my life, and all you can do is shrug? I demand an answer!"

Dominic grinned at her audacity. Here she was, his prisoner in every sense of the word, and yet she was ordering him about as if she were lady of the manor and he her serf. "I seriously doubt you are in a position to demand anything, Mistress Braxton."

"If you mean to see me cower in fear, Captain, think again. I will have an answer and I will have it now!"

Dominic shrugged again. "Perhaps in the future you will be more particular of the men you encounter in deserted cabins."

"Good God, you cannot be serious! You cannot mean you've abducted me simply to repeat that disgraceful act. Surely a man with your experience can find another more willing in her tendencies."

"I take exception to your description of a most lovely afternoon, but, no, I did not abduct you simply to repeat it."

"Then why?"

For a moment he seemed to have forgotten her existence. His smile turned hard and bitter. His lips thinned to a menacing snarl. His dark eyes burned with feverish hate and narrowed into bone-chilling slits. Reena was somewhat taken back by his sudden change in appearance, but refused to back down in her demands. Finally gaining some control over his emotions, he shrugged and his eyes cleared of the distant, haunting memories. "I see no reason why you should not know this much. You hold the key to a debt I claim."

"You mean to collect a debt from me, a woman you hardly know?"

"Nay, not from you. You are but a pawn in this scheme."

"Me?" she asked in disbelief. "How?"

"You need not know the whys and wheres. Know only

that a man must be destroyed, and I will use you and anyone else, if need be, to do it.''

"You're insane! There is no one you could destroy by dishonoring me.''

"Is there not? What of your betrothed?''

"But I have . . .'' Reena gasped as she remembered he thought her to be Mary, and Mary very definitely was betrothed.

"That's right, my love,'' Dominic snarled, "M. Coujon, the pillar of Baltimore's society. A lucky catch indeed for any young lady.''

Reena nearly groaned aloud. Because of her unseemly actions and untruths, she and Mary had been unwittingly caught in a trap. How could she have been so foolish as to believe the illicit afternoon would come to nothing?

An idea flashed. She could tell him the truth! She almost shouted out that she had lied, that she wasn't Mary, but instantly thought better of it. If he were to believe her, which she seriously doubted, she would only cause Mary further harm. She would not allow the dishonoring of her cousin to fall on her shoulders. Nay, he had to believe she was Mary until she found a way to free the both of them from his evil clutches.

"What are you going to do?'' Reena asked, while eyeing him with obvious trepidation.

Dominic grinned at the look she shot him. "Nothing so horrid as all that, my fancy English lady. Your betrothed already knows I have you. He knows too of the luscious afternoon spent in the cabin. 'Tis enough for now to know his guts ache with the knowledge.''

"When will you release me?''

"After I've done with you.''

"You bastard!'' she raged, her blood instantly boiling at the thought that this man sought to use her and then discard her once his appetite was appeased.

Dominic gave a bitter laugh as he stood and walked to the

door. Just before he closed it behind him, she heard his softly spoken, "If you say so, my love."

Reena choked at the fury that assailed her being and marveled at the untold strength that suddenly filled her. She grunted with satisfaction as the brush's handle snapped into splintered pieces as it contacted against the closed door. She wrenched the blanket away and came unsteadily to her feet as her mind searched for a word bad enough to call him. With a sweep of her arm, she instantly relieved the night stand of every dish and cup perched upon it. It was his face she wanted to smash, but being unable to do that, she settled for breaking anything she could reach.

When she was finished, the cabin was in shambles. Ink stained the Persian carpet and dotted the papers that had been hastily cleared off the desk and left to flutter in disarray upon the floor. The washstand was lying on its side, and water ran lazily amid the broken bowl and pitcher as if a storm had vented its rage upon the inanimate objects.

When there was nothing left to break, she collapsed to the floor and sat cross-legged among the debris and allowed tears of frustration and anger to spread their course down her softly rounded cheeks.

Desolate in her wretchedness and plagued by unbearable guilt, she knew she had no one to blame but herself. She couldn't stop the huge, soul-wrenching sobs that tore at her throat, taking with them the last of her strength, and she tumbled to her side into a tight ball of misery, her arms wrapped tightly around her raised knees.

Dominic found her thus only moments after the barrage of flying objects had ceased, and his chest constricted with pity at the suffering he had brought upon this tiny, courageous woman. It was at that moment he realized fully the beauty of her fierce spirit, and knew he had not the desire to see to its destruction. He would keep her with him till his end was accomplished, but he would not, no matter his original intent, force her to do more than that.

Reena sobbed into his chest as he turned her toward him, unmindful that she was seeking comfort from the very man who had brought about her suffering. His arms came around her and he lifted her into his warm embrace. Tenderly he soothed her tears away as he sat on the bed holding her, until she succumbed to the comfort of his arms and drifted into a deep sleep.

Chapter Ten

A GRIN TEASED THE CORNERS OF DOMINIC'S MOUTH AS HE nonchalantly stuck a pipe between his teeth, leaned back against the headboard, and stretched his long legs out comfortably before him.

"Mistress, do you believe me so sterling in character as to gallantly abandon the comfort of my bed for propriety's sake?"

Reena paced the small distance the room afforded as she eyed him and the bed with equal and undisguised aggravation. "Surely you cannot believe me so wanton as to desire your company? I understand your remaining at my side during my illness, particularly since you were the cause of it, but I am well now and wish for this cohabitation to cease. Good God, whatever can your men think of me?"

A pale blue cloud of aromatic smoke drifted over the bed.

Dominic casually shrugged as he lifted his arms and linked his fingers behind his head. "I care not what anyone thinks. In truth I see no harm in sharing this room. After all, we were once of a mind to indulge in more intimate pursuits. Why should we not continue in the same vein?"

Reena gratefully allowed her anger at his careless words to distract her from the sudden lurching of her heart as erotic pictures of twisting naked limbs came instantly to mind. "You boor! No gentleman would remind a lady of a past indiscretion."

Dominic gave a lazy grin as his dark eyes wandered appreciatively over her trim form. While waiting for the ship's repair he had sent a man to the nearest town for the things a lady needed most. Granted, she did not possess an extensive wardrobe, but she hadn't said so much as a thank-you for his generosity. He shrugged aside his thoughts. "Perhaps you might explain to me your change of heart. There was a time when you were eager enough."

"Indeed, sir, I've no wish to explain anything to you. What I did and why I did it is, of course, none of your business. In truth I can only claim temporary insanity for even speaking to you, a mere colonial barbarian."

Dominic chuckled softly as he came silently to his feet to search out a dish for his now cold pipe.

Reena watched as he disposed of his smoke and began to discard his boots. "Well? Are you going to allow me the privacy I asked for?"

"Demanded, wouldn't you say?"

Reena sighed, "Perhaps my words were a bit strong, sir, but I ask again with all due respect."

Dominic laughed at her feeble attempt to make amends. "No doubt."

"Well?" she asked again when no answer was forthcoming. Her hands rested belligerently on her hips while her booted toe tapped out her annoyance on the floor.

"I'm sorry, mistress, but I see no sense in your request. Shall I share a narrow bunk with my first mate while you luxuriate alone in this great expanse?" he asked. "Nay, I think not."

"Very well, Captain," she returned determinedly, "I may not be able to persuade you to abandon your bed, but I shall not share it with you."

Flinging the second boot aside, Dominic gave her a long hard look. "Mistress, you have little choice in the matter. You have been grievously ill, and any foolish gesture on your part may only cause you a relapse.

"Remember, you are on my ship, and my word is law. You, my fine and fancy English lady, will do exactly as you are told."

Reena's chin jutted out in defiance. "Will I indeed? And how, sir, do you propose to keep this word you call law? Will you tie me to the bed if I refuse your gallant offer?"

"If need be, mistress," he sighed, as he began to unbutton his shirt.

"Then set about the noble task and be done with it, brave sir."

Dominic flung his shirt to the corner of the room and walked to within inches of her. Tilting her stubborn chin up, he searched her angry face with an expression so tender as to take her breath away and leave her wondering as to why she was arguing in the first place. "Mary, I've no wish to bring suffering upon you. Surely as two rational adults we can come to an agreement."

Reena breathed deeply in order to steel herself against the debilitating weakness that slowly invaded her arms and legs and then cursed herself soundly as the dizzying scent of clean male suffused her senses. She closed her eyes against the sight of his bare chest, so wide, so muscular, so thickly covered with black hair, and so damn close she needed only to lean forward to touch the delicious warm flesh.

Nay, her mind screamed. You do not want to touch him! You will *not* touch him. Reena, come to your senses. For God's sake, the brute has kidnapped you. He is a villain of the lowest sort. Are you insane to imagine you feel something for him? But Reena knew it was not her imagination that brought about the warmth that filled her and caused her breathing to grow rapid and uneven. She wanted him. She wanted to experience again the hours of ecstasy she had known in his arms.

Think Reena, she berated herself silently. There would be long hours of pleasure should you give into this reckless impulse, but what then? He offers no future, he pleads no tenderness in his feelings, not that you wish it in any case, she reasoned righteously.

What the devil is wrong with you to desire a man such as he? Was she a wanton to feel such depraved emotion? Did other women suffer the same torment?

She pulled away from his intoxication, confused and shaken. Her skin tingled still where his fingers had caressed her jaw. You have but one chance, Reena. You must remain angry. Without your anger you will surely succumb to his magnetic pull. Remember, damn it, he means to use you for his satisfaction. He wants nothing more than that from you.

"I see but one adult in this room, sir," she finally responded, "rational or otherwise."

Dominic was fully aware of the effect his bare chest had upon her and realized, too, her stubborn refusal to give in to this burning desire in the set of her chin and the glare of her dark blue eyes. He smiled and purposely chose to misinterpret her words. "Mary, you need not be so hard on yourself. I know you are of tender years, still I would certainly consider you an adult."

Reena threw her hands up in disgust and breathed a long weary sigh. "'Tis useless to continue this ridiculous conversation. One cannot expect to argue with a baboon and win."

"Indeed," he returned, his laughter barely held in check, "and since you have conceded me the victory, I expect no further arguments."

"Expect again, colonial lout!" she countered angrily, as she shoved him aside and walked to the washstand.

"Should you be so dimwitted as to expect no further arguments from me, you are sadly mistaken indeed."

Reena stifled a groan of frustration as Dominic nonchalantly stripped off his pants and walked with an unashamedly naked swagger toward the bed. He threw back the coverlet and settled himself comfortably beneath the sheet, unmindful of her embarrassed glances and her ever-reddening cheeks. How could he be so casual about exposing his body, she wondered? Were all men so inclined?

Reena eyed his still form warily. It had been nearly a week since her fever broke, and as yet he had made no advances toward her. Still, just knowing he was lying naked at her side was enough to keep her awake long into each night.

Even though she made it a point to sleep as far from him as the bed allowed, every morning found her snuggled deep into his warm embrace, their legs wrapped indecently around each other, while her head rested against the comfort of his warm chest. And that was not the worst of it. She was terrified by her reaction to the touch of his body. It was growing more difficult daily to extricate herself from the warmth of his arms. Not that he refused to release her. Indeed, he gave her no argument as she nearly jumped, red-faced and stiff with shock, from the bed the moment she opened her eyes.

It was mortifying to admit, but just this morning she had found herself feigning sleep for a few minutes simply to enjoy the warmth of his naked body against hers.

It had to stop! She had no doubt as to the outcome should she allow further close contact. And it would not do. Nay, it would not do at all.

Dominic watched her from the shadows of the canopied bed. His eyes opened to mere slits as he feigned sleep. His body tightened with an endless hunger as his eyes moved boldly over the soft curves of her body. His heart pounded as she untied the strings that held her petticoat and watched

95

with longing as the soft material slid over her hips and legs. She rolled her stockings down well-remembered, shapely legs, and he reveled in the sight of her sleek, smooth limbs.

Reena folded her garments and hung them over a chair. Unconsciously, she did the same with Dominic's clothing. Dressed only in her short, frilly chemise, she took the broken brush from the washstand and pushed it through the heavy silken locks until the length of it shimmered like liquid gold.

Dominic smiled. He had seen others do much the same things countless times and yet, as he watched her go about this nightly ritual, these every-day actions seemed to grow in fascination. He wondered why he should suddenly find such interest in the shape and movement of her long, slender fingers, or the soft curve of a gleaming shoulder, or the provocative hint of a slim waist beneath her loose chemise. How had he lived so long and never noticed the lovely angle of a raised arm as a woman brushed her hair, and how the movement lifted her breast in the most innocent and yet seductive manner possible?

Reena turned suddenly toward the bed, her eyes narrowed with suspicion as if she could feel his eyes on her. With a weary sigh she gave the bed a look of longing. Having yet to regain her stamina, she was completely exhausted by the few hours spent on her feet and ached to curl up amid the soft feather pillows and mattress.

How could the brute be so cruel? Why could he not see her position? She sighed wearily. In truth he more than likely did, but simply cared for neither her sensibilities nor her comfort.

For the rest of her life she'd curse the evil forces that drew her to him on that fateful day and wondered how much longer she'd be forced to pay for that one mistake?

At present she had no alternative but to do as she was bid. Still, the thought of escape rarely, if ever, left her mind. She had to bide her time now that she was aboard his ship. It was unlikely she'd have an opportunity until they reached the islands. She resigned herself to waiting, and yet a moment didn't pass that she did not imagine her happiness once she was reunited with Mary. Somehow, some way, she would manage their escape.

After finishing her toilet, she searched the armoire for a heavy blanket and another bed linen. Silently she moved toward the bed and rolled the blanket into a thick pad and placed it between them. Lying atop the light coverlet, she pulled the extra linen over her and blew out the candle. Turning her back to Dominic, she tried to relax her stiff form so sleep might come.

Dominic grinned into the darkened room at her attempts to separate them and wondered how long it would be before she gave up the ridiculous notion.

He had no doubt the morning sun would find them locked in each other's arms. He almost laughed out loud at the imagined pleasure, for not only would the blanket be gone, but perhaps her chemise as well.

Chapter Eleven

REENA STOOD WITH HER BACK TO THE RAILING AND watched with awe the hub of activity on deck. Hammers rent the air with the sound of pounding while men called out crisp orders and huge lengths of heavy planking were heaved to and laid snugly into place. She could only imagine, not having her senses about her when brought aboard, the destruction that had been done this ship. If so, the work thus far accomplished had been nothing short of miraculous. The whole crew seemed to work as one. The gaping hole centered midship, that had once been in clear evidence, was a thing of memory, and upon the closest inspection could barely be detected.

The ship was nearly ready to set sail, and Reena anxiously looked forward to it since each mile covered would eventually lead her home again, and she could put this disagreeable time in her life to rest.

Preoccupied with her thoughts, Reena did not notice the approach of the ship's captain and never realized he stood at her side until he spoke.

"Good morning, Mary. I trust you slept well."

Dominic leaned his hip against the railing and turned his body to her. Standing closer than need be, his ever-present grin threatened once again to show itself.

Reena bristled beneath his good humor. What in God's name did the brute find so amusing? Suddenly her cheeks heated with embarrassment, for she knew the exact cause of his merriment. She turned her gaze from his and faced the water, for she definitely preferred the soothing calm of the blue sea to the glint of fire that sparkled in his black eyes.

In sleep they had again reached out for each other. This time the intimacy of their embrace left little doubt as to what awaited her should she continue to share his bed. Somehow the barrier of the rolled blanket had been flung to the floor and her chemise slid up! Worst of all, Dominic had used the softness of her breast to pillow his head.

Upon awakening she found herself clutched to his nakedness with her arms sleepily entangled around his neck. His leg had slid intimately between her own, his one arm around her, holding her close, his hand resting familiarly upon her derrière, while the other held her breast to his cheek.

Idly she wondered whether it had been him or herself who had reached out during the long night. Tonight, no matter his objection, she would make a pallet on the floor.

"Your fever has not returned, Mary?" he questioned, his laughter held barely in check, for he had not a doubt as to her thoughts. "Your cheeks seem pinker than usual."

Reena's gaze snapped up and met his taunting amusement with cold disdain. His handsome white grin was obviously meant to sway the coldest heart, she reasoned, but more would be needed than a teasing smile to rid her mind of her dislike. Bristling under his easy familiarity, even though the name he used was another's, she responded icily, "Captain, I realize the complexity of our relationship, still I have not given you leave to address me by my Christian name."

"True enough," he shrugged confidently, "but I'll take the liberty regardless."

"Like you take all else," she grumbled with undisguised disgust, as she turned from him.

"Are you inferring our afternoon spent in splendor was not enjoyed by both parties?" he taunted heartlessly.

"It appears your mind runs in but one direction, sir. In truth I was speaking of my abduction, nothing more."

"Mary, it hurts no one if we are civil to one another."

Reena turned to face him, her eyes flashing daggers of hatred. "Captain, you cannot be serious! You kidnap me to suit some evil whim and yet you expect me to be civil toward you? Why, I'd as soon run you through as look upon you."

Undaunted, Dominic chuckled at her fearless response. "Perhaps, Mary, but you will do it nonetheless. Should you dare to defy me, you tread dangerous ground indeed. I'd not have my crew witness your insolence."

Reena laughed harshly. "What more can you do, Captain, that I should fear you?"

Dominic regarded her for a long moment, his admiration for her bravery hidden behind his closed expression. Finally his lips twitched. "If you believe I've not the stomach to see my demands met, think again."

" 'Tis not your stomach I dread, Captain," she snapped, and then cursed her impulsive tongue. Despite her raging, Reena felt a smile threaten at his answering, hearty laughter. Turning her head, she again rested her gaze upon the smoothly rolling sea. "How can you expect me to act civilly with the constant threat of your lechery hanging over my head? No doubt the moment I relax my stance, you will cart me off to your bed and have your way with me."

"Your attitude has naught to do with that eventuality,

mistress. Should I feel the need to cart you off to my bed, your obvious hatred will not hamper me."

"You would take me against my will?" she asked softly.

Dominic shrugged aside her question as insignificant and grinned. "It would not be against your will."

Dominic watched as Reena's spine straightened and her lips thinned. "Rest easy, mistress, oddly enough I do not find you so desirable that I lose all control in your presence. Nor do I long for your body my every waking moment. I wish only for an amicable relationship, one devoid of hatred and snarling comments, lest my crew believe me incapable of controlling one rather small female."

Dominic knew his words were far from the truth. Indeed the woman occupied more time in his mind than he would have cared to admit. For the greater part of the last hour, he had watched the smooth trimness of her form, her skirts swaying with delicious ease as she walked the deck, or pressed enticingly to her every curve when the winds were so inclined to bring about this favor.

At night his body ached as he lay knowing she was but an arm's length from him. The need to touch her was every bit as strong now as when he had first caught sight of her.

Reena couldn't believe her ears! He claimed, at least, to be offering her a relationship devoid of debauchery. She looked at him in astonishment. "In truth?"

"What say you?"

With a wide smile she met his taunting grin. She extended her hand with an offer of agreeability and relented. "For the sake of your crew, Captain?"

"Aye," he grinned, as he took her offered hand in friendly response, "for my crew."

It wasn't until some time later that Reena sat in the cabin and thought over his taunting words with a mixture of relief and surprisingly enough, annoyance. Gazing into the small mirror above the washstand, her face flamed at his jeering words. "Not desirable . . . do not long for your body." Had he not found pleasure in their coupling? Was she somehow lacking?

Confused, she began to pace the small cubicle, unable to sort out her feelings. Why should his words cause her such annoyance? What cared she if he found her undesirable? In truth she couldn't imagine anything more perfect. Still, no matter her relief, his comments continued to rankle. 'Tis smarting pride, she finally allowed. She doubted a woman existed who didn't wish to be held up to the highest regard, and probably that brute of a captain held no one in that favorable light. Indeed, she ranted silently, his intent was obvious, to abuse anyone who crossed his evil path.

Chapter Twelve

REENA SMILED AND COVERED HER GLASS OF WINE WITH her hand as the cabin boy made to refill it. "Thank you, Jimmy, but I've had more than enough."

The young boy nodded and gave a short bow as he left her side and filled the glass of Mr. Graves, the ship's quartermaster, who sat to her right.

"Mr. Graves," Reena ventured, "I've been meaning to speak to you."

"Yes, ma'am," the young man answered awkwardly, and then turned beet red to the roots of his blazing hair as he faced her.

Glancing at Dominic, Reena continued, "With the captain's permission of course, I was wondering if you might not find a yard or two of fabric in the hold that could be lent to me. The captain has been most helpful, but since the decision to join you on this voyage was made in such haste, I fear all my bags were left behind. After seven days I find myself in dire need of still another dress.''

Mr. Graves turned to Dominic. "Captain?"

Dominic nodded and spoke to Graves, his warm gaze never leaving Reena's face. "Of course, Mr. Graves. Take whatever you think the lady might need. I myself find her present state to be quite lovely, but if she wishes, she may make as many dresses as she pleases."

Reena was taken aback by Dominic's gentle attitude. For a moment her eyes widened with surprise, and then they narrowed with suspicion. What was he thinking about? Except for his insistence on sharing the cabin with her, he had bestowed upon her every courtesy imaginable. Once able to leave the cabin unassisted, she was asked to join the officers each night for the evening meal and was treated by all with the utmost respect.

It was most confusing. First he kidnapped her, hoping to destroy a man she was supposed to be engaged to, and then he seemed to go out of his way to be pleasant. Why?

Had he had a change of heart? Could it be he was sorry for what he had done? Reena almost laughed at the nonsensical thought. More likely the beast sought to strip her of her guard and trick her into . . . of course! How could she not have realized it before? Did his hungry gaze not devour her at their every encounter? Did his eyes not speak volumes of the lust that lurked within, forever promising a repeat of the passion that had once raged between them?

He had said he did not desire her, did not long for her body, but his eyes belied his words.

Reena grinned smugly at the transparent ploy. Did he think her such a simpleton not to see through his plan? Indeed, more was needed here than a gentle word or tender smile. What she felt for the arrogant beast could not easily be explained. Although he might be attractive to some, she admitted begrudgingly, he was everything she despised in men—arrogant, overbearing, presumptuous. Still, she had to admit his act a good one. Had she not known the depth of his baser instincts, she would surely have believed him to be kind and considerate of her wants.

Reena pushed aside the depressing thoughts of his false gallantry. For now all that was important was that he had not attempted to bed her since that rainy afternoon in the delapidated cabin.

She could not think why he did not press for a repeat of the passion shared until a wild thought flashed. Did he expect her to come to him willingly and eagerly? Did he truly hold himself in such high regard? She almost laughed out loud at the outrageous idea and had to bite her lip to prevent the merriment that threatened. Glancing at him again, she promised a silent vow. Whatever your plan, Captain, you'd do well to keep in mind the woman you think to toy with.

Dominic turned from speaking a word to Mr. Wingate, his first mate, feeling Reena's gaze upon him, and answered her determinedly icy expression with an easy smile that caused an odd and unexplainable twisting in her chest. After a long, breathless moment, Reena managed to pull her gaze away and answered Mr. Graves's question about the type of material that was usable among their inventory.

The meal was soon at an end, and the officers made to leave the delightful company of their female guest with obvious reluctance.

Reena was offered a fourth at a game of cards, if she'd a mind. Realizing from his expression that Dominic was eager to see her stay, and wishing to keep as much distance between them as possible, she gently refused the invitation, while promising another time, and accepted Mr. Graves's stammered offer to join him for a turn on deck.

The night air was as warm as a gentle caress, and Reena breathed deeply of its clean, salty fragrance. She was content for the moment to walk in silence, as Mr. Graves proved to be most lacking in the art of conversation, and

Reena finally gave up her attempt to put him at ease when her questions produced no more than monosyllables for answers.

Reena groaned when after a few minutes a deep voice interrupted her stroll. "Mr. Graves, perhaps you might take a man and see to the lady's wants. You may bring the bolts of cloth to my cabin and see to it she has everything she needs to work with."

Mr. Graves responded with a smart salute and an "Aye, sir," before he bowed to Reena and wished her a pleasant evening.

Reena turned flashing eyes on Dominic and gave a silent curse. What was it about the man that caused her this irritation? Why could she not ignore the spark of fire that gleamed in his dark eyes? It didn't matter how often she might encounter him. He made her long to strike his face, while at the same time melt against his long lean body. Reena almost gasped aloud at the horrible thought. Nay, she didn't want that! She couldn't allow it. Had she not been punished enough for her sin? What further horrors might befall her if she acceded to these wanton urgings?

Angrily she turned from him and looked out over the calm sea. " 'Twas not necessary, I'm sure, to have your man search the hold at this moment. Tomorrow would have been soon enough."

Dominic shrugged, "Tomorrow other duties will occupy his time."

A moment of silence ensued as Reena fought to quell the trembling his nearness caused. Finally she remarked, in a voice louder and sharper than she had intended, "Captain, I fear you'd do better to stand here alone than to bear my disagreeable company, for I cannot think of a kind word to speak to you." She made to walk away, but was brought up short by a restraining hand on her arm.

"You could start by thanking me for the clothes you now wear," he snapped, his annoyance obvious.

"Could I indeed!?" she countered fearlessly, as she

wrenched her arm free. "Have you forgotten so soon that it was your actions that caused me to be lacking in my own possessions?"

Dominic chuckled at her anger. "Touché, Mary." And then stepping closer he leaned down and whispered near her ear, "Would you admit to our being even then?"

Reena stepped quickly away and glared at his smirk. She certainly would not! Did he believe the generosity of a few bolts of cloth canceled out his villainous act?

A smile threatened at the corners of his mouth, and his eyes danced with merriment as he continued, "All things being even, perhaps you might reconsider your attitude and show this poor soul a touch of kindness."

Reena faced him squarely. "Poor soul indeed," she snapped. "I've no doubt what a touch of kindness means to you. Understand me on this, Captain, I do not like you and I cannot foresee a time when I shall. I do not want your attentions, no matter that you have deemed it more seemly to act in a gentlemanly fashion. Remember, I know you for what you truly are."

Dominic chuckled softly. "And what, pray tell, is that?"

With a long, weary sigh, Reena continued, "Captain, it furthers not my cause to issue you insults. Would I not be most foolish to chance the loss of the few comforts I can now claim in order to vent my fury?"

Dominic smiled, his eyes gleaming with admiration. "You do me an injustice, mistress. I give you these things because of my own desire to do so. Whether I have your approval or not is of no importance."

"Indeed, you have made that abundantly clear on more than one occasion," she returned, and then sighed again. "The hour grows late, Captain. I think it best if I retire."

"Surely a few moments spent in idle conversation can bring no harm."

Reena ignored his request and took one step. Immediately she was brought to a stop as his hand took her arm. "I think not."

"I insist," he returned.

"Nay, I insist!" she snapped breathlessly, as she pulled her arm free. Reena shivered at the long look that passed between them. She hated him, and yet she could not deny the desire he stirred. What was the matter with her that she should feel such emotion?

Dominic recognized the answering desire he read in her eyes and laughed at her stubbornness. "What is it that so terrifies, Mary? Can you not trust yourself in my presence? Fear not, I promise I will be strong for both of us."

His white teeth flashed in the glow of a swinging lantern, and Reena had to force away the groan that threatened. A sudden emotion twisted in her chest, and her face flushed at the measure of truth in his teasing words. "Captain, I will not let you goad me into accepting your company. I am afraid of nothing but your lechery, and I will give you no cause to press for a further sampling."

"I've already told you that you need not fear me on that account. I do not desire to bed you," he lied easily.

"You speak more clearly and, I believe, more truthfully, with your eyes, Captain."

"Do you deem yourself safer in my cabin?" he taunted, not bothering to deny her charge.

Reena refused to answer him.

Dominic shrugged and took her arm. "It matters not in the end, for regardless of your wants you will join me for a stroll."

Dominic smiled as he felt her silent acquiescence to his superior strength as she allowed him to guide her around the deck.

All during dinner tonight he had watched her. His chest had constricted with an unnamed emotion at the sound of her throaty laughter. His stomach had churned with something resembling pain every time she chose to bestow her lovely smile on one of his officers, or engage one of them in conversation.

She was a stubborn wench, to be sure. She might swear her dislike, but she could not honestly deny the flame of longing that passed between them each time their eyes met.

Suddenly his arm snaked around her waist, and he breathed against her hair as he pulled her to his side. "Talk to me, Mary."

"Please, Captain!" Reena groaned, as she pried his fingers loose, only to have him close his free arm around her. She stiffened and continued breathlessly, "Very well. I will talk to you if you promise to refrain from touching me."

Dominic smiled as he pulled her stiff form closer still.

Reena choked out a breathless, "Will you?" as she desperately tried to blot out the tremor his contact caused in the pit of her stomach.

Dominic's hands fell to his sides as he breathed a ragged sigh. "If you insist, Mary, I will not touch you."

Together they walked side by side while Reena spoke and Dominic, as nonchalantly as possible, led her deeper into the shadows of the ship.

Suddenly she stopped, very much aware of where he led her. "Surely, Captain, 'tis not necessary for our walk to take us into these shadows."

Dominic chuckled softly as his hand reached around her waist. "What is it you fear, Mary? My advances, or your lack of retreat from them."

Reena trembled as she pulled herself free of his hold, but faced him fearlessly. "Captain, I'd be less than honest to deny what exists between us. Still, it matters not. I will not give in to these emotions. Surely there is more between a man and woman than a simple, carnal act?"

"Think what you will, mistress," he smiled tenderly. "The fact remains, you'll not deny your desire overlong."

Reena spun on her heel and walked away, fearful of her reaction, so filled was she with overwhelming hatred.

He smiled as the dim lantern light fell upon the gentle sway of her skirt as she moved toward the hatch. "'Tis not finished between us, Mary," he promised aloud. "I begin to believe it may never be."

Chapter Thirteen

REENA LEFT THE STIFLING HEAT OF THE CABIN AND GAINED
the deck with a great sigh of relief as the gentle, cooling
tropical breezes bathed her damp body in their delicate
caress. If she were lucky she might find Dr. Barrett in one
of his idle moments, or perhaps she might persuade the
kindly old gentleman to forego his duties till later and talk
with her instead. Indeed, she could sit for hours listening to
his endless tales. And although she suspected his affinity to
the English was somewhat exaggerated for her benefit, she
was beginning to believe he held no malice toward her
countrymen, but merely disagreed with her government's
policies.

She found no hatred harbored in the man's soul, no
matter that he had lived through one war with England and
now found himself in the midst of yet another.

He treated her most kindly, and she found she enjoyed his company above all others aboard.

It was later than she had thought. After the evening meal, she had returned to the cabin to finish the work on another dress. Apparently she had forgotten the time, for twilight had given way to night and the darkened deck loomed black and empty before her.

Realizing it was too late for her chat, she reasoned the night would not be a total loss if she could spend but a moment or two lingering at the ship's rail. Indeed, she had no desire to return to the airless cabin.

During the day, the sun beat relentlessly upon the deck until its heat slowly suffused the thick wood of the vessel, penetrating to the deepest hold. 'Twas at night alone she found some measure of relief, for after the sun cast the last of its golden light and blackness crept across the sky the cooling breezes would ease away the day's suffering.

Making her way carefully across the shadowy deck, she found herself, with no little surprise, smack up against one of the crewmen.

"Oh, I beg your pardon," she exclaimed automatically, as strong, muscled hands reached out to steady her startled form. Reena made to step back, but to her amazement, found herself firmly held in the man's strong arms, while a gasp of surprise caught itself in her throat.

"No need to hurry off, missy," came a deep, ominous sound, and the arms tightened, pressing her against a steel wall of male chest.

It took no longer than an expulsion of breath to realize her struggles were useless against the man's superior strength. In an instant her arms were pinned to her sides and she was being dragged toward a huge crate that might hide them from inquiring eyes.

Reena found she was more surprised and annoyed than frightened. What did he expect to get away with? Did he believe she'd offer no objection to his misuse? One scream and the entire crew would be alerted, with Dominic at the lead. Did this foolish man believe his captain would allow him the rights he himself was denied?

"Unhand me this instant," Reena ordered, in her most haughty and refined fashion, and felt a surge of astonishment that her words brought forth no more than an evil chuckle as a response. Reena was effortlessly dragged behind the crate and then shoved from the man to fall helplessly into the burly arms of another.

"Let me go!" she cried, while renewing her struggles, and opened wide eyes in surprise as at least four men answered her outrage with softly uttered laughter.

The man that was holding her spoke close to her ear. "No need to flaunt your high and mighty ways, missy. The lot of us know you've been pleasurin' the cap'n. We've been wantin' to know when we get our share of the piece. I ain't never had me a high-class whore."

Reena gasped in horror at the grotesque words. Her back stiffened while her heart began to pound with the terror at what was sure to come. "You are mistaken, sir." Valiantly, she controlled the urge to scream and claw at the man who held her, and her voice barely shook as she continued, "In truth, your captain offers no more than his protection, and deservedly so, if this is your usual treatment of a lady. Indeed, he will not look kindly upon this mauling."

The men chuckled, the sound so evil that Reena couldn't control the shiver that ran up her back and caused goose flesh to appear on her arms.

"The cap'n's a fair man, missy. Once he's finished with you, we are sure to have our share of fun. What we want to know is when?"

Reena opened her mouth, prepared to allow the scream of terror that had been slowly building, when a thickly fingered hand clamped itself over her lips. Another reached for her, and still another, as she was held immobile to the man behind her.

Her intended ear-splitting scream was no more than a weakly muffled sound that blended easily with the gentle wind that whistled through the ship's riggings, and Reena felt a tormented groan sound at the back of her throat as one of the groping hands caught at her breast and squeezed with agonizing fatality. They were going to rape her, and she had not a prayer in hell of escaping. Her mind swam dizzily, and behind the hand she screamed again and again, while praying to escape into unconsciousness before she knew the worst of this nightmare.

A man chuckled close to her face. "They say the cool ones burn the brightest. Be it truth?" he inquired, just before the seam at her shoulders split and his heavy hand ripped the thin fabric to her waist.

The men laughed at her renewed struggles, so engrossed in the game they forgot to keep their voices to a whisper. Still, it was appallingly easy for them to pin her to the deck. A hand pressed firmly to her mouth while her arms were brought above her head. Rough hands pulled at her legs, forcing them to part.

Reena gave a mighty kick, born of pure terror, and barely noticed the grunt and low curse as one of them was flung back and knocked his head against the crate. "Keep the bitch still," another grated, as he fought to restrain her flying feet.

So engrossed with extricating herself from these vicious beasts, Reena never heard the deep voice that cut the silent, warm night with icy rage. "Might one in this beggarly lot care to explain what is going on?"

Instantly the four men jumped to their feet, each stuttering a feeble reply.

Reena, aware only of being released at last, also came to her feet. Her mind was a fog of outrage. She knew not why the men had stopped, but felt only a rage that knew no bounds. Without a thought her fist clenched into a tight ball. Her hand swung with no little force into the face of the unsuspecting man unlucky enough to be closest to her. The man gasped with surprise as his head snapped back at the force of her blow and Reena gave a satisfied grunt to see him stagger, as his hand automatically came to nurse his injury.

Had Dominic not been so enraged, he might have laughed at the tiny bundle of pure fury. Her hair was wildly disheveled, her dress torn to her waist, she had come as close as he cared to think to being raped, yet she did not cower in fear or cry with maidenly distress. Nay, she was a power unto herself, magnificent in her rage, vehement in her need to extract a measure of justice.

Unmindful of her nakedness, she lunged at the next man and delivered a well-aimed fist to his groin. Barely noticing his cry of pain, nor the buckling of his knees, she turned to Dominic. Never realizing he had come to her aid, she dealt him a clean blow that stunned.

Instantly, he pushed her behind him and swung a huge fist in a neat arc of pure power and instantly relieved the last two men of any thoughts they might have been harboring as to what type of justice their captain might bestow upon them.

"Easy, love," Dominic crooned, as he caught her to him and turned her so her nakedness was no longer exposed. "Should I allow you to continue, I'll have nary a hand to see to the running of this ship," he continued, as he fought to restrain her struggles.

"Mary, can you hear me? Can you understand me? 'Tis over," he soothed, as he held her closer to him, her hands pinned to her sides as he ran his hand in comforting strokes along the trim line of her slender back.

Again he repeated the calming words, and yet again until he felt her body soften against him and heard a low muffled sob slip from between her lips as she pressed her face into the comforting warmth of his chest and lifted trembling arms to the strong column of his neck.

"Mr. Wingate!" Dominic suddenly called out, his voice ringing deep and clear with authority in the silent night.

It seemed but an instant later and Mr. Wingate was

115

standing with mouth agape, staring at the four men, each obviously in some degree of discomfort, while the young lady clung to his captain in a hold that closely resembled strangulation.

"Yes, sir?"

"Mr. Wingate, it seems these four worthy souls have decided not to continue on with this voyage after all. You might have a few men see to their packing while we make for the first available port. For now, you need not exhibit undue gentleness in seeing to their comfort."

"Aye, sir," the young first mate remarked, while a grin split across his surprised expression.

"Also, I'd have a parson brought aboard at the first opportunity. It appears I've waited overlong for my lady to regain her strength, and it seems some among us have jumped to erroneous conclusions."

Reena barely heard his words as she silently shivered in his arms, quietly absorbing a measure of strength.

Leaving the running of his ship in the capable hands of his first mate, Dominic guided Reena to the hatch of the ship and whispered tenderly against the golden silk of her hair, "There are men below, Mary. Perhaps you might wish to wear my coat until I can get you past them."

Reena only half heard his words and stood docile before him as he slid his jacket around her shoulders. Dominic preceded her down the steps, but the task of lowering herself while holding his jacket together was more than she was capable of, and a moment later she tumbled into his waiting arms.

Dominic's voice was filled with concern as he turned her from the inquiring eyes of his crew and whispered, "Are you all right?"

"Yes," she managed in a shaky and low voice. Glancing up into his compassionate gaze was her final undoing, and she felt the protective wall of strength she was struggling to erect begin to crumble. Her eyes filled with tears as she asked in a choked voice, "Are all men such monsters,

Captain? Might a lady not walk in their midst without fear of assault?'' Her words seemed to destroy the last of her composure, and she couldn't stop the tears that ran freely down her cheeks. Hastily, she wiped them away with the back of her hand as she tried to gain control of her emotions. "Forgive me. I detest tears, but I can't seem to . . .''

His arms were around her, lifting her trembling form against him in a comforting embrace as he gently crooned softly spoken words into her hair, "Truly, I'm sorry, Mary.''

And to the startled men who were wandering about their quarters, he explained, "Mistress Braxton has had an accident.'' Quickly they made a path for their captain as he took her to his cabin.

Reena's voice was muffled and choked with tears as she tried to speak against his chest. Dominic's heart swelled with pity, and he refused to question the wave of tight emotion that filled his being at seeing her thus. Her slender arms released their hold on his coat and circled his neck. A few quick strides brought them inside the cabin and the door was slammed shut with a backward kick of his boot.

He sat her on the bed and quickly poured two fingers of brandy into a glass. A moment later he was at her side lifting her to his lap, his coat falling unheeded to the floor as she cried out her terror into the warmth of his neck.

After a few minutes her trembling calmed and her tears lessened. His arms were around her holding her close to his chest as he coaxed her to drink the fiery brew he held to her lips. The buttons of his shirt pressing into her breast barely registered, and she was momentarily unaware of her disheveled state as she did as she was told.

'Twas not so with the man who held her. Very little about this lady escaped Dominic's attention, and the baring of her breasts least of all. Still, knowing the fright she had just gone through, he carefully kept his eyes on her face and his passions under the strictest control.

117

Tipping her head back, he gently brushed away the last of her tears and asked, "Did they hurt you, Mary?"

His whole body tensed as he waited for her answer.

She shook her head, giving a negative reply.

Dominic smiled with relief. "Better?"

The warmth of the brandy seeped into the core of her being and released a soothing warmth that slowly reached out to her trembling arms, and she found herself nodding and meaning it. Suddenly shy and embarrassed that she should have lost all control before his eyes, she brought her gaze to his chest and kept it there. An occasional hiccup was the only concession to the extreme emotional upheaval she had suffered, as she struggled to regain her dignity.

"I hesitate to leave you in this state," he remarked, his voice growing husky as the knowledge of her nakedness began to override all thoughts of bringing comfort. "But I've tasks I must see to." Still, he kept his eyes averted, not sure he'd be able to control his response should he give in to this temptation. It would be easy enough to take advantage of her in her shaken state, but he wanted her aware of her wants and desires when the time came for them to come together again.

"Shall I ask Dr. Barrett to look in on you?"

"Nay," she breathed softly. "You need not fear for me, Captain. I am made of sterner stuff than you suppose." The trembling fear was easing and her confidence began to return.

"I've no doubt 'tis the truth you speak," he smiled tenderly, as he traced her soft cheek with his fingers.

Releasing her hold on his neck, she leaned away from him; becoming conscious at last of her half-naked state, she gasped, "Oh!" as her hands went to clutch the tatters of her dress.

The temptation was too great to resist, and he instantly covered her hands and held them to her lap. "Nay," he gently insisted, "do not."

Slowly he allowed his gaze to lower from her wary

expression to the long line of her throat, to rounded, gleaming shoulders, reaching at last the gentle swell of full, thrusting breasts.

Reena watched the warmth of his eyes move ever so slowly over her and shuddered with instantly rekindled longing. His gaze darkened and lifted to her own. If she ever doubted that he wanted her, his reaction to her half-clothed state instantly put the thought to rest.

Reena couldn't seem to summon the will to do more than sit placidly beneath the burning desire that once again flared to life between them. His large callused hand came from around her back over her tiny waist to ride up and engulf her full, firm flesh, as a softly uttered cry slipped from her parted lips.

"Dominic," she moaned breathlessly, desperate he should not continue this gentle assault to her senses.

"I know," he returned. "I'm leaving," he promised, even as his mouth descended to the object his hands so gently cradled.

Reena's head snapped back, and a long hiss of breath was sucked through her teeth as the heat of his mouth contacted and enveloped, while nearly burning her cool flesh. Her body again began to tremble, although this time from a different cause, and her hands unconsciously sought the delight of returning his caress. Sliding over broad shoulders, her fingers moved to his head and entangled in his thick black hair as she held him to her.

His mouth slid a burning path up her shoulder to nuzzle the throbbing vein in her neck before capturing her lips with a husky growl of desire.

Reena's mind was spinning, and she couldn't stop the soft whimpering sounds her throat emitted. His tongue delved past her softly parted lips, deep into the warmth of her mouth, hungry for more of her sweet tastings.

A few short moments later and, with an audible groan, he tore his lips from her gasping mouth and lifted her from his lap to lie full-length upon the bed. With a few quick movements he had her torn dress and chemise thrown to the floor and was covering her nakedness with a linen coverlet, lest he find himself unable to leave her side.

Gently he whispered close to her ear just before he delivered one last mesmerizing kiss, "Upon the morn we will marry and put an end to this game we play. Thereafter not another will dare approach you."

Reena, her mind so immersed in the sheer bliss of his tender caresses and earth-shattering kisses, merely smiled blankly at his softly spoken words. It mattered not what he said, it mattered only that he continue this ecstasy and bring her once again to the fulfillment she had for so long denied herself.

An instant later he was gone, leaving a confused Reena to stare in bewilderment at the closing door, her body crying out in silent agony for still more of his touch. She blinked in confusion. What had he said?

And when, after a long moment, her mind and emotions regained some sense of normalcy, his words came back startlingly clear. She opened her mouth in astonishment and sat straight up in bed. Her voice breaking and husky with surprise and confusion she choked out a startled, "What?!"

Chapter Fourteen

"ARE YOU INSANE?" REENA GASPED WITH ASTONISH-
ment, her mind whirling as she heard yet again the
hauntingly familiar words that had left her numb with shock
and awake throughout the long night. With the light of
dawn, she had finally convinced herself 'twas only her
imagination. Of course he had not mentioned marriage. He
had not, after all, returned to her side. Surely a man did not
say such words and walk away as if it were naught but the
weather discussed.

Indeed, she now realized he had not actually offered for
her, for the words she heard held not a tender question, but
simply stated a fact, and Reena fumed that this arrogant
beast would believe her so gullible as to be brow-beaten into
an arrangement simply so he might vent his lust.

"I think not, mistress," Dominic remarked, as he slid his

arms into his blue captain's jacket and absentmindedly brushed off his shoulders and adjusted his cuffs. "In truth, you could do worse than marrying me."

"Could I?" She laughed almost wildly, while her fingers jerked nervously as she creased the sheet that was clutched to her. Her mind raced as she tried to keep at bay the hysteria that threatened to crash down upon her. "Indeed, sir, I cannot think of a less likely happening, or a more ridiculous notion. 'Tis beyond my understanding why you should suggest such nonsense."

Dominic turned with a grim look of determination. His eyes grew hard while his lips thinned in anger as he studied her obvious reluctance to his suggestion. Ignoring the pain that threatened to come to full life within his chest at her rejection, he raged silently, English bitch! Haughty domineering twit! Instead of being thankful for my offer of protection, I find I have to face still another of her blasted icy glares.

Anger flooded to the core of his being, and he had to fight to control the urge to shake her till her teeth rattled. His voice sounded a hiss, so low Reena found she had to lean forward to hear, "I suggested it, mistress, not because of any tenderness that might live between us, but in order that you might find yourself able to walk these decks without fear of further maulings."

"Damn it!" she raged helplessly, "had you not taken me in the first place I would never have known such fear."

Dominic grinned. "In truth, my conscience pricks. I mean only to make amends."

Reena forced aside the rage she felt. Surely she could talk this dolt out of this ridiculous scheme. "Captain, 'tis apparent I've done you a grave injustice, for you are most gallant indeed. More so than I would have dreamed. Still, there is no need for so drastic a step. I am sure there will never again be a repeat of last night's horror. I will, in the future, take proper precautions."

"The first one being to marry me," he insisted with an

easy smile, while his brow lifted at the pleasurable sound of her softly spoken words, even if they both knew she didn't mean them.

A vague thought came to life somewhere in the back of his mind. What would it be like if she always spoke to him thus? Quickly he dismissed the notion as not important. After all, he cared nothing for her and her words, sweet or otherwise, were insignificant. No matter what he allowed her to believe, his only reason for this marriage was to have her, to finally have her. His intention upon her abduction had been much the same, but he found, much to his disgust, he was not the villain he had supposed.

Reena returned again to her cool, disapproving attitude and tilted her beautiful nose with annoyance. "Sir, I know not the game you play, but I grow weary of anticipating your moves. I will not marry you or anyone else on this day or in the near future."

Dominic suddenly raged, realizing at last the reason for her reluctance. "Are you so smitten by your betrothed? Do you love the bastard so desperately?"

Reena's eyes clouded with confusion, for try as she would she kept forgetting she was supposed to be Mary Braxton. "Who?!"

"Coujon, damn it! Can you not remember the man you were to marry?"

Unable to control the rage that came instantly to life as his words filled her with disgust, she blurted out, "Damn your rotting soul to hell! I've promised to marry no one."

Dominic's black brows raised in surprise while a light of sardonic amusement glittered in his coal black eyes. "So it seems you are not Mary, after all. Who then might you be?"

With a dejected slump of her shoulders, Reena sighed wearily, "That, sir, is none of your business. You are my abductor and therefore deserve no explanations. Go away and leave me alone."

Deceiving little wench! Why should he care what happened to her? Like all women she was naught but a liar and a fraud.

Suddenly Dominic laughed out loud. Her name did not matter to him. She was like a sickness in his soul. All he knew was that she had to be his. He could take the torture no longer.

At the sound of his laughter, Reena thought she had convinced him to see things her way, but was quickly dissuaded of that erroneous notion at his next words.

Dominic leaned against the post at the bottom of the bed and grinned down at her. "Get out of that bed and ready yourself for a wedding, woman, lest you desire me to join you there instead. No doubt the parson will marry us regardless of your position or state of dress," his grin widened as he continued on with a glint in his eyes, "or undress, as the case may be. Still, I would have thought you to prefer the ceremony on deck." Dominic shrugged and began to slip out of his coat.

"Wait!" Reena cried, as she scrambled to the edge of the bed while pulling the sheet with her, wrapping it securely around her nakedness. "I'm up. Are you satisfied? I'm up, you beast!"

Dominic made as if to think over her question while his eyes grew dark and admiring, imagining clearly what lay beneath the togalike garment. With the temptation to reach out and touch her uppermost in his mind, he forced himself to nod. "For the moment. You have twenty minutes to meet me on deck. Twenty-one minutes from now I will return and we will be married, no matter your disheveled state."

Reena held no hopes that Dominic would change his mind or that she could somehow find a way out of this mess. There was no hope of escape. She would be his to do with as he pleased. Good God, how could she marry him? How was she to bear it? This couldn't be happening to her. What had she ever done to deserve this horror? But Reena knew what she had done, and no matter her darkest melancholy, she could not find it in her heart to curse the fates, for she alone was at fault.

Fifteen minutes later Reena gained the deck with a slow, stilted gait. Her mind numb with the enormity of what was about to happen, she hardly noticed Dominic's tender smile as he watched her walk toward him.

She wore a high-waisted gown of pale blue silk that dipped low in the front and offered tantalizing glimpses of smooth, rounded flesh. Beneath the bodice and at the hem of each puffed sleeve, she had woven green satin ribbon. A matching ribbon held the length of her hair at her nape, while curling golden tendrils fluttered in the gentle breeze to caress her temples and cheeks.

Dominic felt his heart swell with something akin to pride knowing the lovely lady would soon be his. Although her expression was reminiscent of that of the condemned journeying to the gallows, he knew she possessed the ability to accept the inevitable and, more likely than not, turn it to her advantage.

He smiled, knowing her present docile state to be of temporary duration, for her fiery spirit would soon make itself known and, although he couldn't deny his uppermost need was to bed her, he found himself longing too to witness and enjoy the vivaciousness he had so far only glimpsed.

One of the crew, when gone ashore to fetch the parson, had picked a small bouquet of daisies, while more were woven into a crown for her hair. The man, stuttering and shy, offered her his gift of flowers with a red face and a deep bow, bringing a gentle smile to Reena's pale lips.

"For you, my lady."

"Thank you, sir," she replied, as she took the offered flowers.

Gaining courage from her obvious happiness at his thoughtfulness, he dared to continue, "I only wish I could have done more."

So do I, she cried silently. I wish you could get me out of here!

Dominic was at her side, his arm possessively around her slender waist as he guided her toward the parson and Mr. Wingate, who would witness the ceremony. In a daze she found herself surrounded by the crew as the words that would join them together for all eternity were spoken.

Reena refused to look at him, positive of his grin, as she choked out her true name and promised to love, honor, and obey this man whom she barely knew and liked even less.

Suddenly it was over. A heavy gold ring had been slipped upon her finger, and she was the wife of one Captain Dominic Riveria.

The crewmen offered to the captain their heartiest congratulations and turned to shyly mumble their best wishes to the captain's lady. Only the officers dared to take the opportunity to kiss the bride, an action Reena barely noticed, although Dominic could not claim the same.

A keg of ale was broken into and toast after toast was offered throughout the afternoon to the newlyweds' happiness.

As the day wore on, Reena, with a smile frozen on her lips, had to bite her lip to hold back the tears of self-pity that longed to rush from her glittering eyes. She was sure had she cried, the men would have attributed her tears to happiness or perhaps to a touch of apprehension about the coming night.

In truth, Reena felt no fear of the night to come. If little else, she knew this much about the man she married. He would not take her against her will, and she had no intentions of succumbing to him. Once they were alone, she'd make sure he understood just that.

It was nearly dusk by the time Dominic suggested his crew might continue their celebration ashore, since his ship would not leave port until the following evening.

With gentle pressure to her back, Dominic guided Reena toward the hatch and below deck. Inside his cabin, his desk had been cleared of papers, a white cloth laid over the top. Candles glowed from pewter sticks at each side, while two plates of roast beef and potatoes awaited them.

Dominic sat Reena at the desk and filled two glasses with dark, rich burgundy before he settled himself across from her.

They ate in near silence, he not wishing to say anything that might bring to an end what promised to be a thoroughly enjoyable evening, and she trying to gather her thoughts into the least insulting terms so he might become aware there would be no evening for them to share.

After the evening meal, Dominic suggested, "If you prefer, I could step outside for a smoke so you might ready yourself."

All Reena's thoughts of delicacy fled as she snapped, "For what?"

Dominic chuckled, assuming her sharp tone to be nervousness. "'Tis usual, I believe, for the bride to wish to look her best on her wedding night."

"Are you telling me, sir, there is something amiss in my appearance?"

"Nay, madam, indeed you are quite lovely tonight. I simply thought you'd prefer a few moments alone."

"In truth, I'd prefer more than a few moments."

"Indeed?"

Reena sighed, knowing now was the time to tell him. She only prayed she'd be able to convince him to see the sense of her argument. "Dominic, I see no other way but to tell you my decision straight out."

"And what decision might that be?"

"You must know I did not want this marriage."

He nodded and gave a slight shrug. "I understand that quite well, but since the deed is done I see no recourse."

"But there is!" she smiled brightly. "We need not be held to vows neither of us want. The remedy is appallingly simple. We will divorce."

Dominic filled his glass with the red liquid and downed it

in almost one gulp. Leaning back, his elbows on the arms of his chair, his fingers pressed together beneath his chin, he eyed her from beneath heavy lids. His expression seemed relaxed, almost lazy, belying the pounding of his blood as he ached to reach across the table and shake her until her teeth rattled. His voice was low and smooth as he asked, "Will we indeed?"

"Of course!" Reena jumped to her feet and began to pace the tiny compartment. "There is no reason why we should not. You, sir, would be the first to admit to a lack of tenderness in your feelings. Surely you've no need for a wife at this point in time, and I assure you I feel much the same way."

I wonder, Dominic mused silently, as he came to his feet and blew out the candles, knowing full well he felt more than he'd care to admit, certainly more than he wanted to feel for the haughty little snip.

"Do you not think we could find contentment in our present situation? Surely others have married with less between them than we and have gone on to live together quite amicably."

Reena shook her head. "Dominic, I mean no insult when I say I have no wish to be your wife. I wish to be wife to no one. It disgusts me to realize I have now, by law, no will of my own, no properties, and no rights. In truth, once married a woman belongs to her husband as if she had suddenly become less than human. 'Tis a state I cannot tolerate."

Dominic grinned as he watched the gentle sway of her skirt as she paced before him, her slender, petite form belying the womanly curves that moved so lusciously tempting beneath the flowing fabric. He knew she spoke from the heart, for no one could make up such outrageous nonsense. He began to understand, and his temper slowly came back to normal. 'Twas not he but marriage itself that so revolted this gently bred lady. To say the least, she possessed an unusual opinion, for he'd known no other

128

woman who did not desire for herself the blissful state of matrimony.

In truth he himself had not relished the thought of marriage. Last night he had heard himself speak the words with no little surprise. Later, he could hardly back out once the orders were sent to find a parson. Dominic shrugged. What was done was done.

Walking around the desk, he leaned his hip on the corner and crossed his arms over his chest. Realizing she was bursting to complete her thoughts, he nodded, "Go on."

Her spirits lifted at his apparent interest, and she stopped pacing and stood before his relaxed form. "In truth, 'tis a simple plan of which I speak. When we reach Barbados, I will board a merchant ship and sail home. Once there I will contact my solicitor and he in turn will contact yours. There need not be a scandal. No one shall ever know." And after a moment's hesitation, she dared to ask, "Does that not meet with your approval?"

Dominic's smile did not reach his eyes. "Indeed, your plan is admirable, but for one point."

"And that is?"

"I do not wish it."

Reena's back stiffened with shock. Her eyes grew wide with astonishment, and she almost shrieked, "What?!"

"You heard me, madam, I do not wish it."

"Why? What reason can you give?"

And Dominic, unable to find the answer to her question in his own mind, found he could not respond with any logic and simply stated, "I need not give you any reason. I simply will not allow a divorce."

"You cannot be serious!"

"Indeed, madam, I am most serious."

"Very well," she snapped, her anger getting the best of her, "if you will not divorce me, I shall divorce you."

Dominic smiled heartlessly, "You and I both know that is not possible."

Desperate, she cried, "I will shame you then."

His eyes narrowed to dangerous slits. "And how do you propose to do that?"

"I will take a lover," she snarled, her own fury making her heedless of his growing anger.

Dominic grabbed her hand just as she raised it with the obvious intent to strike and twisted it behind her back as he pulled her between his legs and held her tight to him.

Reena ignored the pain in her wrist and faced him fearlessly. "I will take a dozen right under your nose. You will be a laughingstock."

"Not likely, madam. The only lover you will ever know will be myself," he warned so softly as to instill chills of fear down her back. "For at the first hint of another, the man will instantly meet his maker. Soon enough not a soul who fears for his life will come near you. And it will be your reputation in tatters, not mine."

"I care not. I will leave you in any case. I will go home and take my lovers there. You shall never know."

"Nay, madam, you will not. The width of an ocean is not enough to protect you from my wrath once incurred. What is mine is mine forever or until *I* choose to discard it."

"Including a wife? Do you intend to discard me?"

"Perhaps," he lied, and then shrugged as nonchalantly as his anger permitted, for he knew in his heart he'd never let her go. The mere thought of it left him empty and aching with loneliness. Somehow, some way she would grow to care for him. One day she would come to him. Suddenly he knew she must.

"Perhaps! Goddamn your evil soul. My life is controlled by a shrug of your shoulder? By a whim? I will know your intentions."

"My intentions should be obvious, madam, I have married you, have I not?"

Reena was nearly blinded with fury. "You insufferable wretch. How could you force me into this caring not of my wants?"

Dominic chuckled, clearly enjoying her rage. "You fare better than most, madam."

"Indeed, I see not how."

"For one thing, I have no need of your properties. Upon docking, I shall sign them back to you." He nodded at her surprised expression. "I believe you will find naught to complain of in this union, for I will not treat you as a possession, but as my honored wife."

"Why?" Reena blinked, her confusion apparent.

"Let's say, another whim?"

"And what will you ask of me in return?" she asked, while shooting him a look filled with suspicion. "I confess I cannot give you my undying love."

Dominic laughed. "Nor would I believe it should you tell me so. Indeed, I ask no more than any husband has a right to expect."

"And that being?"

Dominic grinned. "Madam, I realize you were gently reared, but I also believe you know the pleasure a man and wife can share."

"You mean a repeat of the afternoon we spent in the cabin?"

"Madam, that afternoon was naught but a sampling of the long night to come."

"And if I do not wish it?" she taunted bravely. Even trapped as she was, she dared to deny her precarious position.

He relaxed his hand and brought her wrist to his mouth and touched his warm lips to the slight injury his fingers had brought. "I'm afraid you have no choice."

"Would you be open to a bargain, Captain?" she gasped, as his mouth moved to her palm and his tongue flicked out against her sensitive flesh.

"And what might you bargain away, madam?" he asked, distractedly. For the moment his attention was focused on the taste and feel of her hand. "What do you have that I might want?"

131

Reena's eyes lowered with shame, yet she never hesitated as her cheeks suffused with heat. "This night. Anything you might want during this night."

"And for that?"

"My freedom."

Dominic's head snapped up. His dark eyes searched hers with astonishment as a thought made itself known. The little twit was willing to do much to secure her freedom. Well, he was willing to do even more to keep her. Still, it might be wise, for the time being at least, to appear to go along with her. Indeed it would save much time trying to convince her to see things his way.

He gave a long deliberate sigh and remarked as if against his will, "Very well, you may have your freedom. In six months' time."

"Six months?!" she gasped, not at all sure the cause came from his words or from the touch of his finger as it ran along the delicate line of her jaw and down her neck.

"You seem to be most anxious."

"I am."

"Indeed, it is not so very long. By that time my plans for Coujon will be realized and my revenge complete."

"Your word, Captain. Will you give it?" She was trembling as his finger continued its downward path, barely touching yet bringing her nerve endings achingly alive.

Dominic sighed with annoyance, the words almost choking him as he forced out, "If at the end of six months you wish to leave, you may go with my blessing. Does that satisfy?"

"It does," her voice quivered, and she gave a violent shudder as his finger reached her breast and slid over the sensitive tip. Her eyes closed with mounting desire.

Dominic didn't miss the softening of her eyes as desire sprang to life. Her lips parted with unconscious invitation. Purposely he continued his downward path. "And after tonight?"

She couldn't think. All she could think of now was his

touch. "What?" she asked softly, while trying to clear her mind.

His finger moved with aching torture across her flat stomach. "After tonight, what then?"

"'Tis finished between us."

"And should you change your mind, what then?"

"I shall not," she choked out in a voice that closely resembled pain, as his finger dipped lower still.

A happy grin suddenly split Dominic's handsome face. Promise or not, she was his. She couldn't deny her reaction to his touch. She wanted this as much as he. Let the wench believe what she would. If it somehow appeased her conscience to believe her actions secured her freedom, so be it. Right now, he'd promise the devil his soul to have her willing in his bed.

"Be you so sure, madam?" he asked, while continuing his deliberate taunting with only one finger. He was driving her crazy and he knew it. He could feel her trembling and heard her breathing grow shallow and gasping as he hesitated at the junction of her thighs.

"Aye," Reena breathed, as his finger moved down her leg and began to retrace its path, only to linger at the warmth of her passion. She swayed into him, her body growing soft and warm as she pressed herself against him.

His mouth came to nuzzle the throbbing hollow at the base of her throat and she unconsciously sighed softly yet again, "Aye."

Her mind was in a fog of delight as his mouth lingered at her throat and then began the scintillating movement that would end against the sweet softness of her mouth.

Hovering but a hairsbreadth from her lips, his warm breath caused Reena to tremble in anxious anticipation. She only half heard his deep whisper. "So be it, the bargain is struck." And then he pulled back and rested his hands upon the desk and dared, "Make love to me."

Chapter Fifteen

REENA'S MIND WAS AWHIRL, FILLED WITH GLORIOUS
sensation. The warmth of his lips seemed to overcome any
obstacle of reason as they moved with erotic mastery,
leaving a burning moist path up the smooth column of her
throat. Her lips trembled with yearning as they parted to
await the lusciousness of his mouth on hers. So it was a long
moment before she finally realized he was no longer
touching her. Her eyes cleared of the fog of desire to find
him leaning more firmly on the desk using his hands as if
for balance, while a confident, taunting smile played
deliciously over his lips.

"What?"

"You struck the bargain, madam," he responded lightly,
his manner and smile belying the tension that knotted his
chest and cramped his stomach. "Make good your word."

And when no sound or reaction was forthcoming, he

continued, "Did you not promise anything I might wish tonight, for your freedom?"

Reena simply stared at him, her mouth agape in astonishment.

"Very well," he continued, as if she had answered, "I wish you to make love to me."

Reena blanched at his cool, callous attitude. She couldn't become the aggressor in this act. She didn't have the slightest notion as to how to go about it. Well, perhaps she did, she shrugged mentally, but she'd never, never find the courage to be so bold.

Her eyes lowered shyly as she murmured, "I thought."

Reena felt her cheeks flush with heat as Dominic's smile grew into a soft chuckle. "Aye, you thought to offer your body up for sacrifice." Purposely he allowed his gaze to lower over the length of her before he continued with a shrug, "In truth the idea does pose a certain enticement, but at the moment it will not suffice. Nay, I want you to make the effort."

Reena's eyes blazed with a mixture of confusion and rising anger. "But how?"

Dominic's low chuckle was masterfully absorbed into a cough. And it was only when he was sure of his control that he dared to reply. "Surely you've not forgotten?"

Reena's face reddened with mortification. When she was able to raise her gaze to his she realized he was enjoying her suffering as never before. Her embarrassment fled, to be replaced by a rage that was quickly growing dangerously out of control. How dare he ridicule her thus? What had she ever done to deserve such ungentlemanly and thoroughly wretched treatment?

"Captain Riveria, you are a scoundrel of the worst sort. You sir, may take the bargain and . . . and . . ." she stammered, suddenly so filled with fury she was unable to finish the thought. She heard a low chuckle escape his throat and raged, "Damn it, I'll give you no further cause to laugh at me."

"Oh, no you don't," Dominic insisted, as she turned from him and lunged for the door. "You are not going anywhere."

"In truth? And will you keep me a prisoner if I deem otherwise?"

"'Tis no surprise to find a female going back on her word," he remarked, while catching her just before her hand reached the doorknob. He spun her back to him and held her struggling form in a steely grip.

"I said naught of being made a fool of, you beast! Release me this instant!"

"'Tis as I thought. Words come easy, too easy indeed, to the gentler gender." He shrugged. "I suppose one cannot expect a lady to honor her promises."

Reena stopped her struggles and glared up at his knowing smirk. "Indeed? Do you believe men alone may claim honor as a virtue?"

Dominic shrugged almost imperceptibly, "I've yet to meet a lady who does not put the weight of a man's purse above all else."

Reena glared, her lip curled with disgust. "Have you not?"

Dominic's hold relaxed and his hands slid provocatively up her spine, while the other molded their lower bodies together. "Show me the folly of my thoughts, Reena," he whispered close to her ear. "Prove to me my error."

"I hate you," Reena groaned, while cursing the traitorous body that a simple whispered caress could so arouse.

"Aye, but a bargain's been struck, my love. A bargain true and fair," he breathed, as his mouth lowered to her neck. Reena, despite her effort to cling to her anger, couldn't prevent the shudder of longing that shook her body. It wasn't fair what this man was capable of doing to her. She didn't want to feel longing such as this. She didn't want another to hold her in such helpless power.

Still, no matter her conscious wants, when he held her thus, it was impossible to deny the thudding of her heart, nor the dizziness that caused her to sway toward him and the longing that was beginning as an ache in the very center of her being.

His lips slid to her ear and she felt herself softening as his tongue flicked out to taste the small hollow beneath. Nibbling on her lobe brought a soft sigh from her throat.

The satin ribbon beneath Reena's breasts came undone, and her gown was easily slipped from her shoulders to fall in a swirl of pale blue silk at her feet. Her petticoat instantly followed. With a flick of his finger, Dominic disposed of the beribboned straps of her chemise and lowered the delicate fabric with titillating slowness, uncovering her body only inches at a time. The unveiling of this exquisite creature required an absorption of mind he was most willing to give.

Aye, he'd feasted his eyes on this delectable sight before, but as each day passed, his hunger to see her again, to touch her again, to love her again grew to torturous heights. His suffering knew no equal. He couldn't remember wanting such as this.

His blood pounded, creating a rushing sound nearly deafening him to all else as the fabric came away from her breasts. His dark eyes raked her body with desperate intensity as if storing her beauty forever in his mind. She wore nothing but her stockings beneath her chemise. And when the fabric fell to her feet at last and left her loveliness fully exposed, Dominic was helpless to hold back the groan of pain that wrenched his body. He lifted her free of the discarded material. On his knees, he slowly rolled the stockings to her ankles and followed the silk material with the warmth of his lips to her feet.

Reena found herself holding to his shoulders as wave after wave of pure delight left her shaking and weak. The stockings gone, he came again to stand before her. His hands at her hips slid with delicious sensuousness, spanning her tiny waist and up the sides of her ribs. His thumbs brushed enticingly against the sides of her breasts, but

137

pushed past their provocative call intent on saving that succulence for a future palatable delectation. His fingers never stopped until they reached her shoulders and finally her neck. Her pulse throbbed wildly at the hollow of her throat against the pressure of his hand, and Dominic doubted a pleasure existed to surpass this ecstasy. His fingers threaded through the clean, golden silk of her hair and brought a heavy lock to his face so he might breathe in her own special scent. His body tightened as each sense became more vividly alive. He longed to crush her to him and yet he needed to touch her gently to see the results of his tenderness. To watch as her eyelids grew heavy, her eyes unfocused with desire, her lips parting slightly so she might more easily breathe, while a rosy flush slowly suffused her flesh to grow with his every caress into pure liquid fire.

"Reena," he whispered, his voice husky and raw as he lowered his mouth to savor the sweetness of her cheek, her brow, her eyes, the delicate line of her jaw. "Reena," he groaned softly into her neck, his voice echoing his body's need for this woman he called wife.

Reena was helpless to do more than offer her lips to his, yet he avoided the contact that would bring the delight she craved.

Pulling away from her, he allowed his hands to run the length of her again. Reena gasped as his sensuously rough fingers spread over her shoulders and down her sides to linger at her waist. Her back arched with seductive enticement, offering the soft mounds of tender flesh for his exploration, yet Dominic resisted her unconscious, silent call. He needed more than her submission, he needed a conscious, equal giving.

"Show me, Reena, show me how much you want this," he managed, between desperately gasping breaths. "Show me," he choked, as his mouth slashed across hers in a kiss that threatened to draw her very life into his.

Dominic's brow furrowed as if in pain and, indeed, for the moment he could not differentiate this delight from

138

torture. Reena moaned at the unleashed power behind his kiss as he suddenly clutched her to him with all the desperation and longing he had held in check these long weeks past.

And when his lips gentled and lingered in erotic savoring, Reena could do naught but whimper her equal desire into the warmth of his mouth.

His tongue slid between her parted lips to caress the sensitive flesh inside, to graze the smoothness of her teeth and, finally to twist with her own as he pushed to discover again the sweetness he had long sought to regain.

Reena was awash in sensation, luxuriating in the exquisite feel of his hands on her body. Each indrawn breath brought his manly scent into her being, and she eagerly reveled in the taste of his clean mouth as it claimed hers for his own.

Her fingers trembled with the need to touch him as they crept up his chest and pushed aside the annoying obstacle that prevented access to the solid warmth of his flesh.

With a muffled groan, Dominic allowed her mouth to part from his as she slid eager tastings over the slight roughness of his cheek, along the column of his throat, to the mass of sinew, muscle, and heated flesh his shirt had covered.

With a sigh of delight, Reena further explored with hands and lips, inching lower, ever lower, leaving a trail of fire in her wake. Her mouth moved over the tickling hairs of his chest and followed the thin black line below his stomach until it disappeared into the waist of his trousers.

Dominic gasped for air when a moment later his pants opened to her seeking exploration. Slowly she allowed her nakedness to slide against his as she eased them down the long length of muscled thigh. Dominic's hiss of indrawn breath came sharp and loud to the silent room as Reena dared to descend lower still, gaining courage from his deep groans of pleasure as she sought out his maleness with a greediness she'd not known herself capable of.

It was fantasy come alive. It was dreams fulfilled. It was all he could have imagined and more.

His hands stroked her head and delved deep into the heavy mass of hair as he pressed her to him. With a torturous groan he forced her from him at last, fearful to let this delight continue lest it bring to an immediate close the pleasure he so longed to savor.

With his hands in her hair still, he coaxed her to retrace her path up his body until she was again standing before him. His hands held the sides of her face, while his thumbs ran roughly but deliciously over her lips and cheeks and his eyes grew as dark as pitch with a yearning unequaled.

A smile teased the corners of her mouth as she recognized a helplessness in his eyes that surely matched her own. Neither of them could have prevented what was sure to come. A force more powerful than either had known drew them on ever closer to the flame. Caught up in consuming fire, they came together with a fierceness that would know no release until the final moment of ecstasy.

With a soft cry Reena clung to his shoulders as he crushed her body to his, their mouths parting only to gasp for air, rejoining again and yet again with earth-shattering force. Beneath his shirt, her nails bit deep into his shoulders and back as she urged him closer still.

His hands were everywhere, touching her, desperate to bring her to his desire, but it wasn't enough. She wanted more, much more.

"Dominic, Dominic, please," she whispered against his neck between hot biting kisses. "Please," she begged softly.

He released her to discard his opened shirt and pants. His boots were flung away with effortless motion as his hands reached hungrily again for the warmth of her. His mouth covered her own, never parting from her as he lifted her into his arms and pressed her to the bed.

With a cry of excitement, she opened her legs, anticipat-

140

ing his next move, and groaned again as he laid his weight full-length upon her.

But Dominic was in no hurry to see to the culmination of this act. Indeed, he wished to prolong the rapture until it was beyond his power to go on.

Reena, conscious of the fact that he was holding himself away from her, lifted her hips, leaving him without a doubt as to her eagerness. Her hands clung to his hair, pulling his mouth to hers with nothing less than desperation. "Please," she cried brokenly as her tongue slid into his mouth.

Dominic groaned as he took her hands from his hair and held them, fingers entwined, at her sides. "Anything I want tonight, remember?" he asked. And when she sought to deny it he insisted, "Remember?"

"Oh God," she moaned softly knowing he would delay this longed-for ecstasy until she was mindless with need. She couldn't bear it. She couldn't!

He leaned further away so his gaze might take in the entire length of her. Her hair lay across the pillow, haloing her beautiful face with riotous curls. Her body was magnificent from her shoulders, white and gleaming, to her long, perfectly molded legs. "I cannot imagine a sight more lovely," he murmured, as his gaze took in the full rose-tipped breasts that lifted and fell in rapid succession with every breath she took and lay so softly upon a chest that appeared too delicate and slender to support them. Her waist was the tiniest imaginable above smoothly rounded hips, and he knew, had he searched the world over, he'd not find one to compare.

"Dominic, I've not the strength," she warned softly.

"Only a little longer. I promise, love, I promise," he whispered, and then groaned deeply as his mouth suddenly dipped and sought out the core of her passion, bringing a sharp gasp to her lips and a splendor unequalled to her body.

She lay helplessly pinned beneath his weight, his fingers entwined with hers while her head twisted wildly over the pillow in anxious anticipation. The drumming in her ears deafened her, and she never heard her own moans of excitement, nor his as the pressure within built to blinding force.

It was coming again, this, a repeat of the time in the cabin, a time she had pushed far from her mind, a time she had sought to deny. But it had happened and was happening yet again.

Her lower body lifted, despite his weight, drawn taut as the pressure within grew to terrifying proportions, and as his mouth moved over her warm, moist excitement, tighter still. She was moaning incoherently, as incapable of stopping the words as she was the pleasure, a steady stream of muttered, broken sounds she'd later have no recollection of.

"Dominic, please," she gasped, unable to bear it as the rapture began to close around her enveloping both body and mind, drawing her away from reality to a world she had once visited and now eagerly welcomed again. Her mind slipped from arousal to madness as her body suffered the sweet, wrenching waves of unbelievable ecstasy.

She groaned one last time as each convulsive spasm of delicious anguish flowed hot, wet, and giving into his hungry kiss, to leave her shaken and weak, silent, but for the soft gasping sound of her torturous breathing, lost for a moment in her own world of sweet enchantment.

Dominic raised up and slid his body into her warm, moist flesh with one fluid motion. His eyes closed, his features contorted into a grimace at the sensation of his swollen passion being immersed in the undeniable throbbing that still wracked her sweet body. He covered her slackened lips with his warm mouth and coaxed tenderly. "Come back to me, love," and when his words brought forth no response, he whispered near her ear, "Reena, can you hear me?"

"Mmmm," she murmured, as she nuzzled her cheek to his. "My nose itches."

"Does it?" he asked with a softly uttered chuckle. And then raising himself slightly so he might look down on her, he continued with a wicked grin. "Well, since I've seen to one itch, I imagine another no great hardship."

Reena smiled when, instead of releasing her hands, his mouth came closer and his teeth grazed along her nose. "Better?"

"Much," she grinned. "Although I seem to have gotten yet another." Her eyes glowed with satisfaction as a gleam of teasing laughter lurked in their depths.

Dominic's eyes narrowed with some suspicion. "Where?"

"I'll show you if you release my hands," she offered.

"Tell me where," he insisted as his lips moved along the line of her jaw. "Here?" he asked, as his mouth dipped to her throat.

"Nay."

"Here?" he inquired, as he followed the shadow of a blue vein along her breast with his tongue.

"Nay," she gasped, as he took her into the warmth of his mouth. "But you're getting closer."

"Tell me where," he laughed against her flesh.

"Here," she grinned, as she lifted her hips so he might enter her further.

"Oh there!" He smiled in return, as his voice grew deeper and less steady. "Are you sure?"

"Very sure," she whispered, her eyes growing large with professed innocence.

"Does it itch very badly?" he choked out, as she swiveled her hips in a decidedly wanton motion.

"Terribly," she smiled, realizing full well the effect of her movements.

"Shall I scratch it for you?" he groaned, as if in some pain as she continued the movement.

"Oh please do."

"Is that not better?" he asked, as he pressed himself closer, feeling a wave of delight, knowing he was growing immense, throbbing with heat and blood, filling her to her limit.

"Almost."

"Almost?" he asked, his brows lifting with no little surprise, and then he laughed out loud at her daring look of teasing. "My lovely English lady, I'm afraid you are witness to the entirety of my ability to please."

Reena purred softly as her lips strayed to his neck and shoulders, "I'd not deny your ability to please, sir, but it's been my experience that an itch can only be appeased when scratching is applied to the afflicted area."

"Oh," he grinned wickedly. "I see your meaning. Does this not suffice?" he asked, as he slowly withdrew and then pushed his hips toward her again and then again.

"It begins to," she managed, as sensation began to bath her body with a warming glow.

"Only begins?" he taunted with breathless yearning.

"Oh sir," she gasped, as his thrusts increased in power and frequency, suffusing her body with liquid fire, "I believe the itch grows in strength."

"And will for a time, I imagine," he growled, as his lips sought out her answering kiss.

Chapter Sixteen

A TRACE OF SUNLIGHT LIT UPON THE CALM, BLUE WATER IN the early dawn and filtered a thin path through the curtain and across the bed, caressing the entwined lovers in its dim glow.

Dominic cuddled her soft, sweet form in a sleepy embrace. His body was content for the moment merely to hold her while his mind, growing ever alert, cursed the bargain he had struck. The idea of divorce was out of the question, although he'd allow her to believe it for a time. The problem most pressing was how was he to find the strength to allow her to leave his bed? After tasting of her passion the previous night, he doubted the possibility of fulfilling his promise.

A soft chuckle sounded from the back of his throat as he realized he had indeed promised no more than to release her in six months' time. It was she who had offered the night, and should she be unable to keep her distance during the intervening period, surely he'd not be held to account.

He had born witness to her awakening and growing passion. Surely it would not be possible to deny these needs overlong. He smiled as he snuggled his face into the fresh scent of her hair. Perhaps a gentle coaxing would suffice. If not, he had no doubt a more deliberate taunting of her senses would produce its desired effect.

His eyes closed in delight as he pressed her nakedness close to his own. He did not regret his hastily spoken words. In truth, this marriage business was not the worst of happenings. Given time, this lofty English lady might grow accustomed to it.

Reena stirred as she drifted closer to the edge of consciousness. A small smile tugged at the corners of her mouth as his hands spread in delicious familiarity over her hip and down her thigh. Sleepily, she nuzzled her cheek to his shoulder and gave a long, contented sigh before the memories of the night's pleasure came to flood her being.

Her husband, she frowned as the strange word came stiffly to her mind, seemed to take this new arrangement easily in his stride. It would never be that simple for her. He might possess the power to bring her body unearthly delight, but in truth, she barely knew the man and the little she did know wasn't all she'd have liked. Certainly his abduction was appalling, and the high-handed way he had forced her into this marriage, abhorrent, but add to this the fact that he was an American! Not that she considered herself to be prejudiced, for she did not. It was simply a mismatch of the worst kind. What could she, a gently bred Englishwoman, find in common with a man so lacking in the basic knowledge of propriety?

Reena breathed in a soft gasp of building excitement when his hands began to reverse their course and slid gently between their bodies to cup her suddenly yearning breast. She whispered low and throaty, "Our bargain is fulfilled, Captain. The night is over."

146

"Nay, my love," Dominic returned, as his mouth lowered to bid good day in the most luscious fashion to the softness his hands so lovingly caressed. "'Tis not over until we rise, no matter the sun's position."

Reena smiled and closed her eyes in complete acceptance as the heat of his mouth spread a warming glow to the pit of her stomach, unable at the moment to find a flaw in his considerable logic. Her body, of its own accord, leaned closer to the object that had brought such remembered bliss. "It could be hours yet before I find the strength to rise, Captain, as this night has proven to be particularly long and arduous," she teased.

"It matters not, my love," Dominic grinned, as he released the flesh his lips and tongue had so enjoyably sampled and moved to taste the haunting softness of her lips. Pressing her to her back, he covered her body with his. "If it takes days before you find the strength to rise, I promise I shall not complain."

"No doubt," Reena chuckled, while arching her back in wicked abandonment and offering again the sweetness his hungry mouth sought.

Reena forgot, for the next few hours, her misgivings, her determination to live out her life in peaceful solitude, and her mistrust of the man who could show her the beauty of her body and the satisfaction that could be gained from a time spent in his bed.

Hours later, Reena awoke alone to the muffled sounds of male laughter and hurried footsteps as the crew came aboard. The cabin was stiflingly hot and her body moist with perspiration. Slowly she came to her feet and staggered naked to the washstand. She was exhausted. Her body felt bruised and battered. She couldn't remember the amount of times they had come together. God, he was insatiable. Then she suddenly found herself giving a throaty chuckle, for he alone could not bear the brunt of the blame. Indeed, she had been a willing accomplice in this past night of pleasure.

Reena hurried in her toilet, for it would not do for Dominic to come in and find her thus. No matter her enjoyment of the night they had shared, it could not be allowed to happen again. Should she be so foolish and find herself with child she'd never be able to shake herself free of this unwanted entanglement. She could only pray his lustiness had left no lasting evidence, for no matter the delight she found in his arms, this was an unwanted entanglement indeed.

"Can I trust you, Captain?" Reena teased, her eyes twinkling boldly, her smile one of pure mischief.

"Undoubtedly," he returned, in a similar playful tone, and then shrugged. "Of course, the truth of those words depends largely upon their interpretation."

"Shall we make ourselves clearer then? Can I trust you to act a gentleman should I put myself in your care and walk these darkened decks at your side?"

"In truth, Reena, you ask much of a man. The thought grows daily to take you from your pallet and bring you to my bed, no matter your objections." At her smile, he added arrogantly, "I've no doubt your incompliance will not last overlong."

Reena didn't answer his deliberate taunt, but chuckled at his obvious frustration and pressed on. "What say you, Captain?"

Dominic's hand tightened on her arm. "I fear I've become a beggar of late, content to accept an occasional crumb you might offer. In truth, I do not relish the torture of not being able to touch you."

Reena laughed again, her voice growing somewhat strained as she fought against the desire his words brought to life. "Fear not, Captain, to deny oneself is a true test of strength. 'Twill do no more than build character."

"Indeed," he grumbled, "before long I shall have the strongest character known to mankind."

Reena's soft laughter floated gently upon the flowing,

warm breeze to further assault his senses, and Dominic gave a silent groan at the pain it brought to his stomach as he led her away from prying eyes and into the darkening shadows of his ship.

The night was warm, a soft, refreshing breeze brought relief from the day's heat. Not one to find overly pleasing the damp chills her beloved homeland could sometimes bring, she was still less accustomed to this harsh heat of the lengthening days that left her limp and exhausted.

Reena felt completely at ease as she walked in silence at Dominic's side, her hand resting lightly upon his offered arm, and it was with no little amazement that she suddenly realized how much she was coming to enjoy this man's company.

She gazed up at his strong profile silhouetted against the glow of a lone lantern and silently cursed the sudden thudding of her heart. Get a hold of yourself, damn it! she scowled into the black night. Let not a handsome face and a few softly spoken words and remembered caresses sway you in your determination. It matters not what you think you feel. You are not right for each other and you are leaving in less than six months. 'Twould be folly indeed to imagine a growing tenderness for this man. He has promised nothing but to let you go. His words might be pretty, but he means nothing by them. His only wish is to exact revenge upon Coujon.

Still, she reasoned, he had saved her life. He had attended to her in her illness with a gentleness that had known no bounds. He could have easily taken advantage of her emotional disability, yet he had been gentle and soothing when those monsters had attempted to attack her. And although more than a week had passed since their wedding night, he had not, regardless of his legal rights, insisted she share his bed.

Reena's mind swirled in conflicting thoughts, for she could not deny her wish to be gone from his side, nor the passion that so easily drew her to him. She moved a slim

149

shoulder with a small shrug as she silently admitted, with some reluctance, it was growing harder each day to find her previous hatred, for he was, despite her determination that it not be so, becoming more agreeable to her eyes.

Try as she might, she couldn't put her thoughts in order, for they only grew more disturbing as the silence continued. Giving up her attempt, she hesitated at the railing and turned to look out over the endless stretch of black ocean, lit to a shimmering beauty by the moon's silver light.

"Have you always favored the sea, Captain?" she asked, as she allowed the motion of gently flowing waves to penetrate her being and soothe her ragged emotions.

"Nay, but it's as good a life as any," he remarked easily, as he leaned his hip against the railing and turned to enjoy the serenity of her beauty. "In truth, I prefer my home in Barbados to this constant wandering." He shrugged before he continued, "As a lad I turned to the sea when my mother died. Perhaps it was a way of forgetting." He shrugged again. "In any case it was something to do."

"And your father?"

Dominic's features grew hard and cold. "I am a bastard, madam. Riveria is my mother's name."

"Oh, I'm sorry."

"Save your pity for Coujon," he growled harshly.

With some surprise she glanced up at him. "Why Coujon? What is he to . . . ? Oh!" she sighed softly as comprehension dawned. Now she realized why he had, from the first, seemed so familiar. He was Coujon's son! It was his own father he hated.

"I'm sorry."

"There is no need."

She hesitated only a moment before she returned, "I believe there is, Captain, for no one should have to suffer the hatred you hold so close to your heart. Surely it will grow like a canker until it possesses you. Why do you allow it? What's done is done."

"What makes you think I hold such malice within?"

"Did you not abduct me simply because you believed me his betrothed?"

He shrugged aside her words, "Madam, you know not what you speak. There is a debt I owe the man. I can do naught until it is satisfied."

"And then? Will the sorrow heal then?"

"There is no sorrow, damn it! What nonsense do you speak?"

"Captain, one cannot harbor a hatred such as yours and not suffer in its holding. In the end it will color everything in your life."

Dominic laughed with no semblance of humor, "Shall I make amends then? Shall I offer him my undying gratitude for mistreating my mother and congratulate him for his hatred and abuse since my birth?"

"You need do no more than forget the past, Captain. Life is too precious to waste by hating."

"The words you speak come easily to your lips, madam. Be they truth, in fact?"

Reena looked at him with some interest, while waiting for him to continue, "Go on."

"Do you deny your hatred for all things American? Myself included?"

"I do not hate you, sir. 'Tis merely a fact that we are of different worlds, and I doubt the ability of finding common grounds."

"And if I were English? Would you then find fault?"

Reena shrugged and lifted her hands in a gesture that bespoke her uncertainty. "How can I know?"

They stood for some moments in silence, each considering the other's words until she finally asked, "Will you soon retire from trading?"

"Aye, I believe this might be my last voyage. 'Tis past the time for me to enjoy my plantation."

Reena laughed softly and teased, "You, a gentleman farmer?"

Dominic grinned while acknowledging, and perhaps agreeing with her gentle rebuke. "Well, a farmer at least."

His gaze moved with slow deliberation and obvious delight over her small form, his eyes blacker than the night as a small smile touched the corners of his mouth.

Reena couldn't control the sudden leap of her heart and the rapid increase in her breathing as his long, wicked look glittered with a promise of a repeat of the passion she so desperately tried to forget. She felt trapped, unable to breathe in or out, as she waited for him to speak again.

"The lady that was taken with you, is she Mary Braxton?"

Reena nodded and gave a silent sigh of relief that his thoughts had taken a different turn.

"Who is she to you?"

"My cousin."

"Why did you tell me you were she?"

Reena gave a silent groan. She had known once he found out her name the question would not be long in the asking. "After we . . . in the cabin . . . I couldn't think. I was embarrassed and terrified that you . . ."

"That I might make a nuisance of myself?"

She shrugged silently, acknowledging the truth of his words.

"So you gave me another's name to throw me off your trail. Why hers?"

"It was said before I thought. I know not why."

"Still, when my men stopped your carriage, you again professed to be Mary."

Reena sighed as she lifted her gaze to his. "You must understand. I knew not who was stopping the coach. She is young and gently raised. I thought she was in danger, or at the very least, by her expression, about to die of fright."

"So you sought to protect her by sacrificing yourself."

Reena shrugged. "'Twas but an impulse, Captain. Done without thought."

"Are you always so protective of the girl?"

"I was but a babe when my parents died and I came to live with my aunt and uncle. Mary was born some six years later. We were raised as sisters. I love her dearly."

"One wonders what lengths you might go to ensure her safety."

Reena's eyes rounded with fear. "Is there a need? I assumed she was being treated kindly. Was I in error?"

"Nay, you are not wrong," he responded quickly and smiled, relieving the knot of fear that had suddenly made itself known in the pit of her stomach. "Still, one never knows when circumstances might alter."

Dominic did no more than grin at Reena's puzzled expression as she asked, "What is it you are hinting?"

Still, he said nothing as his lips curved into a sensuously taunting smile, his eyes telling her clearly what his words had not.

It took but a moment for Reena to understand the hunger and amusement that lurked in the depths of his dark eyes and she laughed softly. "You really are an obnoxious beast! Is there no limit to the depths you will sink? In any case, my cousin is not with us. I doubt even your magnetism can draw her over the waters and into your arms." She laughed again. "Did you think to bring me to heel with veiled threats?"

Dominic chuckled softly, his black eyes flashing with enjoyment as he casually shrugged. "In truth, the thought has crossed my mind."

Reena gave a low, throaty laugh, causing Dominic a twisting pain in his chest, and he had to forcibly restrain the groan that threatened as her laughter brought blatant pictures of her naked and writhing with pleasure in erotic sequence through his mind.

"Have you so little confidence in your worth, Captain, that you must resort to blackmail?"

Dominic forced aside the urge to press her soft curves against him. He laughed, flashing gleaming white teeth in the dark night. He obviously enjoyed these verbal skirmishes almost as much as he would a physical encounter, particularly since he most always found her in this light-hearted mood.

"I've no doubt, my love, bargain or not, since you've tasted of my worth I'll find you soon in my bed. The day will come when I'll have to fight you off."

Reena laughed out loud. "Is there no limit to your arrogance?"

"'Tis not arrogance you hear, Reena, merely the truth. Do you deny the ecstasy we've shared?"

Reena felt her chest constrict with an emotion she stubbornly refused to name. That she had been lifted to heights of ecstasy was a fact she could not deny, but she would never admit these errant emotions to this rogue. "You stray from the subject at hand, Captain. I contend it is arrogance, not truth you speak."

Dominic grinned, realizing full well she had not answered his taunting question, but being a man of some experience he knew better than to press a lady on a point she did not wish to admit. He moved a half step closer to her and leaned down so his mouth might more easily reach hers. "Do you? What do you think might happen if I kissed you?"

Reena stepped back and grinned wickedly. "Should that circumstance come about, I doubt you'd have to fight me off."

"Shall we put it to the test then?"

The light tickling sound of her laughter was very nearly his undoing, and he groaned softly as she stepped further away. "Nay, Captain, for that would not be a test true and fair. In point of fact, I have already shared your bed and have not as yet noticed your efforts to fight me off. Indeed, the opposite might be closer to the truth."

Turning from him, she continued their stroll and wisely steered the subject to a more happy and carefree time.

"And you did it?"

"Sir, I not only climbed that tree, but when I brought my

poor kitten down, I boxed Tommy's ears until the brute cried for mercy." Reena chuckled softly. "My right fist was a power few dared reckon with."

Dominic looked down at the woman at his side, his eyes filled with amusement and ever-growing admiration. "As I and at least two of my crew can well attest," he commented as he rubbed his chin, remembering the blow she had given.

Reena glanced up and sideways beneath thick, dark lashes and gave a low, sultry laugh. The sound of her laughter caused an ache in his chest while his arms longed to reach for her.

Forcing his passions under control, he continued to lead her to an even darker corner.

"Aye, but it does not frighten you as it did Tommy."

"Oh, it frightens me well enough," he admitted, "but there are times, no matter the severity, the punishment does not deter the crime. If the prize to be attained is worthy, one might willingly endure much suffering. At any rate, Tommy was a fool."

"Why?"

"If I had you alone in the woods, I can't think of a less likely happening than torturing a cat. If you were to box my ears, I'd wager I'd give you more interesting cause for it."

"No doubt," she conceded, with a barely hidden smile, "but you have forgotten we were little more than children."

"Your age mattered little," he returned smoothly. "Even children have been known to experiment."

"Good God, I shudder to think of your childhood. I'd venture not a maiden within miles was left intact."

Dominic shrugged away her response. "I heard not a complaint."

"Your mother should have taken a stick to you."

Dominic laughed. "Reena, I forced no one. The experimenting that was done required two willing partners."

"And how old were you when you began this lechery?"

"Old enough."

"Oh," Reena exclaimed, as she twisted her ankle on a piece of rattling and fell to her knee.

Instantly Dominic was crouched down beside her. "What is it?"

"It's all right," she answered, as she came again to her feet. While leaning on his shoulder, she ventured to test her weight on the ankle and breathed a sigh of relief at doing so. "I only twisted my foot. The turn was very slight. It brings no discomfort."

Dominic stood beside her again. "Are you sure? Shall I carry you?"

Reena didn't miss the teasing note in his voice and smiled at his thinly disguised excuse to hold her close. "I'm sure you could, but there is no need."

He was standing less than a half step away, effortlessly blocking her path. Reena, had she a mind, could have reached out and touched him. The aroma of soap and tobacco mingled with his clean male scent to form an overpowering aphrodisiac, and she cursed the unnatural trembling that began in her limbs. Beside her were the twisted lines of rattling that cluttered the deck. Behind her stood a huge crate that cast the two of them into its black shadow.

Reena flattened herself to the crate, trying to create ample space between them. Her breathing grew quick and labored as she realized her precarious position. She had no wish to sample again another display of the passion his touch could produce and cursed herself soundly for allowing him to lead her into the ship's darkest corner.

Anxious to leave the privacy the shadow offered and the obvious dangers that lurked at his close proximity, she asked, "Shall we continue, Captain?" She was dismayed at the trembling she heard in her voice.

The past half-hour might have been spent in idle conversation, but Dominic, from the onset, had only one thought in mind. Being a man of no little experience, he was fully attuned to Reena's reaction to him. The breathless tremble of her voice was enough to stir the desire he only half sought to control into a raging passion. In an instant he had reached around her and pulled her slender form into his hungry embrace. Brokenly he groaned into her hair, "Reena, my God."

Reena felt rather than heard the low moan of despair that escaped her throat and gasped at the blinding force of passion that suddenly flooded her being. She never thought to break his hold, but felt herself softening against him, a willing prisoner in his arms. It was happening again. How had he gained this power over her? She didn't want this. Oh God, she didn't. It meant next to nothing to him and was growing all too important to her. She'd never find the strength to leave should this grow more important. His hands moved over her back and down her full hips, pressing her deliciously close to his obvious desire. With some effort she managed to gain some control over her seething emotions and finally choked, "Captain, please." She pushed against his shoulders and cried out, "You promised!"

Unmindful of her protests, Dominic's hand came to cradle her head and held it to await his descending mouth. Reena's heart pounded so hard she thought it might burst. Almost as if she stood at a distance, she watched in helpless fascination as his mouth grazed her cheek, her eyes, her chin with whisper-soft tastings. Again and again his lips caressed her sensitive flesh, causing an unconscious moan to form at the back of her throat. He drove her to the edge of desperation as he left her lips helplessly yearning for his touch. All at once she was offering her mouth, and still he chose to avoid the silken sweetness that silently begged to be claimed.

His hands slid smoothly around her hips and over the flatness of her belly, past the tiny waist his hands could easily span, to the swell of sweet, beckoning flesh. Cupping

157

her softness in his palms, his thumbs grazed the tips to hard buds of desire and still his lips teased the aching need only the touch of his mouth would ease.

"Dominic," she breathed softly. "Dominic, please," she begged brokenly. "Please."

"Oh God," he growled, realizing her pleading had taken on a totally different meaning, one he could do naught but yield to. His lips found hers at last in a burning kiss that threatened to char her to the depths of her soul. Reena swayed dizzily against him and groaned with tortured pleasure as her eager lips parted. His tongue plunged to discover again the sweet passion she had sought to deny. Wildly, she clung to him with a strength she never knew she possessed. And when his mouth tore itself from hers, she heard herself groan a desperate plea for more of this sweet anguish.

"Reena," he breathed huskily against her ear, "you cannot deny this longing we share."

Reena's head swam with the deliciousness of his assault. His touch and scent left her helpless to fight the desire he inflamed. "Oh God," she whimpered weakly against his throat, "I should have known I could not trust you."

"You can trust me, Reena," he breathed into her throat, sending chills down her back, "in all matters but this. I want you. It is beyond my power to say nay. I've never wanted like this before. Let me love you tonight."

His mouth closed over hers again, powerful, insistent, driving away her hard-fought resistance, leaving her without a thought but to have more.

"Tonight and every night," he urged, as he lifted his mouth from hers. "Come with me now."

It was impossible. This was not a marriage true. They were to divorce. She couldn't meet with him for a few hours of casual carnal delight. Were they not more than animals? Did they not need more than lust? "I cannot. Please don't ask me."

"Do you even now deny what's between us, what we both long for?"

Taking a deep breath, she managed to control her churning emotions. "It matters not what either of us wants. It is enough that it's wrong." She tried to push herself away. "We will soon divorce. This marriage is not a union true. If I should become with child, what then? Would you still let me go?"

"Would you want to?"

"I . . . I don't know. Please, Captain, I cannot think when you touch me thus. This is not a decision to be made in the heat of passion."

Dominic smiled as he gathered her close in his arms and forced his desire into some semblance of control. She was not ready, but he knew she soon would be. No one alive could deny the degree of passion that raged between them for long. His lips brushed the top of her head as he promised silently. But passion will play a role in your decision, my love, no matter your wants.

Chapter Seventeen

DOMINIC RESTED HIS LONG, LEAN BODY AGAINST THE heavy wooden railing. His legs were stuck out in a deliberate pose of nonchalance as his dark gaze feasted on the loveliness before him. With intense interest he followed the object of his every thought with a greediness he would not have believed possible, as she conversed, happily unaware of his presence, with the ship's doctor.

Suddenly he grinned as erotic pictures of her lying naked and pleading beneath him flooded through his mind. Aye, she could be cool and distant, but not when he had her thus positioned. His eyes closed with remembered satisfaction as he once again saw her writhing wildly, pleading for him to take her.

Jesus, what did he see in her that so enthralled? He shook himself, forcing away the luscious thoughts.

Perhaps it was her insistence not to lay with him that so perked his interest. In truth, his interest was becoming all-consuming. Even the hatred he had long harbored for Coujon dimmed in comparison to this growing obsession.

Reena's soft laughter floated gently upon the warm, tropical breezes to assault his senses and bring a further tightening across his belly, leaving him suddenly empty and aching for her notice.

He was torn between the desire to feast his eyes on her and pull her from beneath the doctor's nose and into his arms, to run his hands over her softly rounded flesh. Why in God's name didn't he simply demand her acquiescence? He knew, once in his arms, she'd respond to his caresses as no other before. Still, it wasn't enough, this carnal act. He wanted more than a leisurely taking of her body. He wanted her . . . all of her.

Across the deck Reena sipped the cooling lemonade and smiled at Dr. Barrett, who had settled himself on an opposite crate. Since the *America* had weighed anchor and again set to sea, Reena had spent many delightful hours enjoying the warm southern breezes beneath the shade of white canvas in the company of the good doctor. Together they had companionably talked away most of each afternoon, more often than not with a chess board set between them, as now.

Reena only half listened to the man's lively chatter as her eyes often strayed to the tall man who leaned so insolently against the railing, watching her every movement.

"One wonders why a newly married couple should seem to take such pains to keep apart. In truth 'tis a useless endeavor, for barely a moment passes that one of you does not seek out the other with lingering glances."

Reena felt a warming blush spread over her cheeks and cursed herself soundly that the truth behind the doctor's words should show so obviously. It was a rare occurrence indeed if she should gain the deck and her traitorous gaze

161

not seek out the ship's handsome captain. No matter her efforts to resist, she couldn't seem to stop it. But she would not, no matter the evidence, admit to it.

"Whatever do you mean?" she asked, her innocent act worthy of the stage, but not good enough to fool this charming old gentleman.

"These eyes may be old, but they see clearly enough," Dr. Barrett returned companionably.

"And what is it they see, doctor?"

Dr. Barrett chuckled. "They see two young, stubborn children. As skittish as young colts, they circle warily. Advancing, retreating, all the while striving to deny even to themselves the one thing that will, in the end, bind them together more firmly than shackles."

Reena shook her head, a smile threatening as she moved a piece on the board. "You speak nonsense, doctor, and see only what a romantic heart allows. 'Tis but a marriage of convenience and once ended neither of us will long remember the other's name."

"And yet you cannot keep your eyes from him, nor his from you."

Reena shrugged. "I cannot deny he is most handsome. Check!"

Reena's smile of victory soon turned into one of surprise as Dr. Barrett quickly took advantage of her heretofore unnoticed and unguarded queen. "Checkmate."

He leaned back against another crate and grinned. "Be wary of attacking your foe, Reena, lest they find an unforeseen weakness and turn the attack to you."

"And do I have a weakness, doctor?" Reena asked, knowing full well the man spoke not of chess.

"We all have weaknesses, Reena. If we acknowledge them we have a greater chance to withstand the siege and emerge the victor."

Reena sat in silence for some time, her mind reflecting the old man's words of advice. Again and again she tried to attribute them to her present circumstance and failed. What did he hint at? Should she not fight against the powerful pull she felt toward his captain? Would she fare better to share the man's bed? To what end? Surely a few nights of pleasure could not compensate for the torture their parting would bring. Should she allow herself to soften toward this man, she had no doubt she'd suffer indeed.

Her confusion was apparent as she finally raised her eyes to him. "I know not . . ."

"It will come, Reena," he assured her wisely. "Worry of it no more."

Reena finished the last of her stitching and broke the thread with her teeth. She turned the fabric in her hands. It was beautiful. She had sewn a trim of black lace at the neckline and at the cuffs of the long, loose sleeves and couldn't wait for Dominic to see her in it. She gasped at the wayward thought. What could she have been thinking? She cared not if he liked it. 'Twas no concern of hers what he thought.

She studied the dress with an impersonal eye, while a frown marred her smooth forehead. Now that it was finished, it was possible she had been too daring in cutting the neckline so low. The low V in front and back was indeed in fashion, but she wondered if she were not flirting with fire to display so much temptation to Dominic's ever-consuming gaze.

Again, as often of late, she found her thoughts drifting back to moments shared with the captain. Every night, after dinner, he would find her on deck. He never offered to accompany her, but allowed her to accept other invitations. And every time, bar none, he would conveniently find something for the man to do.

After the dozenth time, Reena had to laugh as the young officer was ordered to oversee the cleaning of the crew's quarters. Upon being questioned as to the reason for her sudden happy state, she had remarked, "Captain, the time draws near when not a soul on board will dare seek me out, lest he be ordered to extra duty. Why have you not offered to accompany me from the first, if that is your intention?''

Dominic had laughed at his easily seen-through ploy. ''And would you have allowed me to escort you?''

Reena had grinned slyly, ''We'll never know since you have not asked.''

Reena gave a full, throaty laugh as she discarded her gown and slipped the rose silk over her head. They had started at the end and were now, it seemed, working their way toward a beginning. At least she didn't hate him any longer. Indeed, it was difficult to say honestly what it was she felt. He had brought about her present circumstance, and unaccountably she found herself actually liking him more each day.

After dinner Reena noticed the hem of her new dress had lost its thread and excusing herself returned to the cabin to make the necessary repairs before heading for the deck and her usual nightly stroll.

Reena held to the walls of the narrow walkway as the ship gave a sudden, unsettling lurch. Trying to brace herself against another surprising movement, she made to spread her feet, but her fallen hem tripped her while her petticoats tangled themselves around her legs and left her precariously off balance.

The ship gave another sharp dip and sent her flying to land with a thud against Dominic's door. She had no time to steady herself before the door was flung open and she fell into Dominic's unsuspecting arms.

She heard his startled ''What in hell—'' just before the two of them toppled to the floor in a tangle of arms, legs, and flying skirts.

Dominic was beneath her, and she could feel his laughter before she heard it. Gently he tipped her chin so her gaze rested on his smiling mouth rather than his chest.

''I'm sorry,'' she explained with a sheepish grin. ''I should have my sea legs by now, but my skirts tangled around my legs and tripped me.''

164

"Lucky skirt," he murmured with a trace of envious laughter in his voice.

"What?"

"To be allowed to tangle around those luscious legs."

Reena's smile at his teasing was short-lived as she suddenly realized the humor in his eyes had disappeared and raw hunger had taken its place.

His arms thwarted her attempt to rise. His mouth was barely inches from her own. She needed only to lower her head a fraction and their lips would touch. Her heart pounded, her lips grew suddenly dry.

His dark eyes held her own for a long, breathless moment. God, she couldn't fight him when he looked at her like this. Drawn to him despite her constant desire to keep some semblance of control, she suddenly knew she wanted above all else to feel his mouth covering hers.

Dominic read the longing reflected in her smoky blue eyes and gave not a moment's hesitation to ending the suffering he had endured these past weeks. God, how he had dreamed of this! Each night he had lain awake, his whole body awash with pain, aching with the need to hold her near him, to breathe in her sweet, delicate scent, to touch this silken flesh, to kiss these delectable lips.

His low, hungry growl was sucked into Reena's sharp gasp as he turned her to her back and crushed her lips to his with a kiss that sent Reena's blood pounding. She didn't hesitate to part her lips, and his tongue delved deep into the warm recess, desperate to taste again the sweetness he had too briefly known and so long sought to sample again.

Reena forgot she was on the floor, lying in front of an open doorway. She forgot everything but the taste and feel of the man who pressed her willing, nay eager, form to his hard length. All her denials meant nothing. She was possessed with a fiery need to touch him, to kiss him, to feel his body press heavily to hers.

From the first there had been passion, but she had never known an intensity such as this could exist. At each coming

165

together it grew in strength, gaining such power as to threaten its participants with incineration.

Tearing his mouth from hers, Dominic gave a low curse that spoke clearly his frustration and pulled away at the sound of approaching footsteps. A moment later she was lifted to her feet and the door closed behind them.

Weak-kneed and flushed from the rush of extreme emotion, Reena leaned heavily against the door as Dominic closed the small distance between them. She lifted wary eyes to his dark gaze. She wanted to cry. She felt torn to pieces. Every argument and reason she could name to keep her distance meant nothing once his mouth closed over hers.

More than anything she wanted him to kiss her, to touch her, to love her, while at the same moment, she prayed he would not. She had never known such confusion.

Her eyes bespoke clearly of her mingled fear and longing and as much as Dominic wanted her, he knew it wasn't enough to satisfy these physical yearnings. Nay, this time he wanted more, he wanted all she had to give.

His eyes grew tender as his fingertip grazed the soft flesh of her cheek and slid over the delicate line of her jaw to the wildly pulsating throbbing in her throat. He smiled as he felt her tremble beneath his touch and murmured intoxicatingly low and husky. "There'll be no takings here, my love. What we both want is too important not to be given freely. And only you can give it."

Chapter Eighteen

REENA CLOSED HER EYES AND PRESSED HER BACK AGAINST the hardwood of the door as tears of confusion threatened to overflow. Her mind whirled with the easy admittance of his longing. He wanted her, to be sure, but he wanted more. He wanted her to admit to her desires, to come to him willingly, and God, how badly she yearned to do just that, but she couldn't, she simply couldn't!

Her whole being was atremble with a longing so overpowering as to cause her to gasp for each aching breath her starved lungs demanded. She was weak and quivering beneath his darkly searing gaze. Her blue eyes read the hungry insistence in his and she suddenly knew were he to touch her, she'd fall into his arms without another thought to the consequence.

"Dominic," she whimpered, her despair a painful ache. What was happening to her? Had she been foolish enough to fall in love with her husband? Had Dr. Barrett been right? If not, why did his every movement draw her eye? Why did his softly spoken words pierce her resistance until naught remained? Why did his smile bring joy to her soul and his kiss nearly melt her heart?

Her extreme emotions colored her blue eyes to a near violet hue as she pleaded for she knew not what. She couldn't think clearly, not with the taste of his kiss still on her lips, not with the longing so clearly seen in his eyes.

"You must say it, Reena," he coaxed shakily, his dark eyes drawing her will from her, leaving her mindless but for the need that throbbed to the very core of her being. "We both know what you want," he crooned tenderly. "You must admit to it. 'Tis past the time for us to begin again . . . this time on equal and honest footing."

"Dominic," she choked, as she mindlessly pushed away from the door and closed the small distance between them. Her hands of their own accord spread slowly over the crisp white shirt that covered his broad chest to circle his neck and gently pull his very willing mouth toward her aching lips. "Dominic, please," she begged softly, her voice breaking with mindless urgency. She knew no more than the need to touch this man, to feel his mouth on hers again, to revel in his masterful caresses. It seemed an eternity since he had held her last, an eternity and more.

Dominic gave a low, hungry growl as her trembling body leaned weakly into his and soft, eager lips lifted to his descending mouth. No matter his gentle insistence, he could no longer control his need for her. Large hands reached around her slim form. His arms brought her to him in a breathless hold. His need for her to voice her desire forgotten, his mind whirled with the scent and feel of her. He couldn't touch her enough, taste her enough, breathe her enough. His ravaging tongue sought every dark, honeyed crevice of her sweet offering, urging a repeat of an abandonment he had once sampled and ached to possess again.

Tenderly spoken words of adoration further clouded her swirling mind. A groan tore itself from her throat as he reluctantly pulled his mouth from hers to run a burning path of pleasure over her cheek, to her ear, only to return again bent on yet another tasting.

He felt her trembling and heard the softly uttered moans of pleasure his touch instilled and knew she was beyond thought or denial. She wanted him, and the knowledge that she was an eager participant in this delight nearly pushed him to madness. A firm tug of her gown freed the soft mound of burning flesh that ached for his touch.

Reena choked back a breathless gasp of esctasy, her head falling back, leaving easy access for his warm mouth to coat her throat and shoulders with burning fire, while his large, callused hands closed lovingly over the precious firmness. The tantalizing moan of pure rapture that escaped her parted lips nearly drove him past all endurance.

She leaned weakly into his strength. Her ability to stand faded rapidly as she, on the verge of madness, groaned out his name again and again, unconsciously relating her need with every softly uttered sigh.

He pressed her back to the door, lifting her slightly to allow his mouth easier access to her captive flesh.

His need to possess her burned like fire in his brain. It never occurred to him to take her in his arms and walk the few steps to the bed. So great was his urgency that it blotted out all but this moment, this one delicious moment. His hands found their way beneath her full skirt, his fingers spreading greedily to discover again the tempting, beckoning flesh that awaited his masterful exploration.

Her skirts were pushed aside with an impatient growl, and his hands contacted at last with her quivering warmth. Reena was lost to reason, her body flaming to life, burning at his touch. His questing fingers, intent on only one purpose, found the moist seduction of her at last, and, delving deep into the lushness of her eagerly responding body, brought a moan of near anguish from her lips. Faster his fingers thrust within her, leaving her helpless as the urgency began to build to a crashing force, one she vaguely wondered could she survive.

Her body tightened to a painful ache, her breathing grew shallow and labored. There was pure magic in his hands and she groaned again, urging him on, silently begging for more of this exquisite agony.

Reena's arms clung to his neck and the faint sounds of a man calling, "Sails ho!" barely registered on her fevered brain. The more clearly heard footsteps of running along deck were forced from her mind as her body arched to accept yet another full thrust of his fingers.

Reena's whole body cried out for release as Dominic's fingers slid from her, while he spat out a long round of frustrated curses. "Christ! I can't believe it," and her skirt fell in place.

His hands cupped her face. His still moist fingers teased the fullness of her lips. He licked the sweet moisture he had brought to her mouth into his with a desperately hungry growl. "God, you taste delicious."

Suddenly she was swung into his arms. The few steps to the bed were covered in a flash. He sat her down with a definite threat, "Don't move from this spot. I'll be back."

A shimmering mist blurred her vision as she stared blindly into his tender expression and wondered with no little confusion why he had pulled away. What had happened? She didn't want this to end. Not now!

Dominic had left the door ajar as he ran down the long corridor toward the ladder that would bring him topside.

Reena watched in a daze as his shirt billowed as he ran, and wondered how it had become undone, for she had no recollection of doing it. The sounds of activity on deck soon filtered through the fog of desire that had continued its hold on her, and finally released her of her temporary insanity.

Quickly she adjusted her disheveled clothing and reached shaking fingers to smooth the disorder his ardent lovemaking had lent her hair as she slid out of his cabin and followed his hurrying form. She had no intention of meekly submitting to his demands. Nay, she smiled, this lusty beast would gain little by ordering her about.

Moments later Reena gained topside amid a flurry of hurried activity. Dominic barked out crisp orders and men ran to their stations. Primed cannonades were aimed and readied for the order to fire. There was excitement brewing. Reena could taste its sharp bite in the air and her heart beat double time as she found herself caught up in it, longing to witness, firsthand, the thrill of battle these men took so easily in their stride.

Reena was suddenly stunned into shocked stillness. Three ships approached, the Union Jack flying proudly above all. Good God, 'twas her countrymen they were bent on attacking!

Dominic patiently paced the deck as the sails came ominously closer. She wondered how this arrogant beast expected to achieve his end, while the merchant was accompanied by a convoy of armed frigates.

Fear clutched its cold hand into her chest as Dominic raised the spyglass to his eye and gave a menacing grin. From the flashing look in his eyes as he once again returned the glass to his side, she knew he was not going to be dissuaded by the fact that the merchant rode protected. Nay, all that fact seemed to do was to bring a daring glitter to his eyes and a further determination to his lips.

For an instant Reena could well imagine the man a pirate, for indeed at the moment he looked more like one than a simple trader. With lips drawn tight over gleaming white teeth, his smile caused a trembling of fear to shiver down her back and gooseflesh to form on her arms.

A gusting of breeze caused her skirt to flutter and brought Dominic's attention to her. In a few quick strides he was standing before her, his expression a scowl of annoyance. "I thought I told you to stay in my cabin."

Reena lifted her chin in marked defiance. Her eyes moved past his form toward the oncoming ships.

"Go below. There's bound to be trouble here."

"Dominic, you can't mean to attack?"

"And why not?"

"They are my countrymen."

"Indeed?" His brow lifted with sardonic amusement. "In truth, madam, they were your countrymen. You are my wife now, and as such an American."

"Dominic, please. You cannot do this. I cannot let you."

"Madam," he sighed, his patience growing thin, "you have no option. You are to go below immediately or I will have one of my men take you there."

Reena raised defiant eyes and glared at him.

"Tate," Dominic called out to one of his burliest seamen, while half turning from her.

"All right, all right, I'll go," she interrupted, before he finished.

Dominic nodded curtly, his look determined as he watched her move toward the hatch. A moment later a man called out and Dominic's attention was once again brought back to the problem at hand.

Reena hesitated at the stairs and looked back to see Dominic saying a quick word to Mr. Wingate. Taking the opportunity offered, she quickly moved toward a large crate and slid behind it. This position offered her nary a view of the approaching ships, but at least she was not confined below deck. Once Dominic's attention was directed again to more serious matters, she'd be able to peer out from her hiding place.

She'd be damned if she'd obey this colonial lout. The papers at home were filled with the outrageous exploits of the privateers and how they managed to capture the English merchants, thereby claiming all aboard as contraband. Out and out thievery was all it was. She couldn't sit idly by and watch the ship taken. She had to do something to help them. She had to!

The evening sun was warm on her back as she crouched behind the large wooden crate. The gusting trade winds snapped the ivory canvas overhead and pushed the ship forward with a whooshing sound. The bow of the ship cut sharply through the blue water, leaving a trail of white foam in its wake.

Reena's heartbeat accelerated as further orders were sounded and a man continuously called off the closing distance between *America* and the coming vessel. The three-masted schooner was sleek and smooth and, Reena knew, would soon put its far-flung reputation for swiftness to the test.

Several seamen ran past her and scrambled barefoot up the mast. As they secured tangled flying lines, the canvas billowed with a loud snap and the ship lunged forward at an even greater speed.

"You'd best be gettin' below, miss," another remarked, as he rushed past her and jumped aboard the platform that held the swivel gun in midship.

A moment later the order to fire was issued and the sudden and powerful vibration of a cannon blast nearly knocked Reena off her feet. Her shriek of terror was lost in the echoing thunder of rapid gunfire. Her ears were ringing, and her heart pounded so hard she feared it would burst through her chest. The acrid smell of gunpowder closed chokingly around her for an endless moment before a breeze took the noxious odor out over the ship.

No more than five seconds passed, and an answering shot split the air overhead and landed a mere ten yards behind her. Reena gasped as the shell splashed a torrent of water and soaked her to the skin. It was then she felt her fear turn to terror. Good God, what was she doing exposing herself to this madness? Was she insane? Why had she not listened to Dominic and saved herself this torment?

Still, she reasoned, would she have fared better in her cabin? What if the ship took a direct hit? Would she be able to get out in time?

Reena glanced around the crate and was not surprised to see one frigate in hot pursuit. They were in for it now. She only prayed the warship could outrun the *America* and call an end to this horror.

Another shot blasted from the frigate and whistled through the air to land uselessly some yards behind the ship. She heard Dominic's laugh when for the third time the cannon missed its mark. "We're out of range, mates. Don't pull too far ahead. Let them think they have a chance to catch us. Mark the chart and direction, Mr. Wingate. When we return we'll have naught but the stars to guide us."

Reena's mind screamed, nooo! He was to lead the frigate astray and circle back under the cover of night to take the merchant. How many English lives would be lost in the coming battle? Nay, she could not permit it. She could not!

Her eyes darted toward the huge wooden box that held the ship's small arms. In an instant, she was on her feet and running. With a strength she had not before known, she wrenched the top of the crate free. A flicker of disgust marred her anxious features when she suddenly realized the rifles, so neatly stacked, were not loaded, and she had no idea how to accomplish that feat.

The evening sun glinted off the shining blade of a sabre, and she unhesitantly reached for the weapon.

With a guilty expression she looked around her, but all eyes were intent on the ever-widening space between the *America* and the frigate. Unnoticed by either the crew or Dominic, she made her way toward the stern of the ship and came up behind Dominic's unsuspecting figure. His hands were clasped at his back, his feet spread wide for balance, his body erect with arrogant mastery of his plan.

Reena pulled the heavy, concealed weapon from the fold of her full skirt and pressed its razor sharp tip to the hollow of his back.

Dominic gave not a clue as to the dangerous positioning of the weapon, but spoke with deliberate authority and arrogance. "Put it down, Reena. I've no time for this foolishness and less a need to see you come to harm."

"Reduce your speed, Captain," she returned, pushing

aside her choking fear, while ignoring his easy order. She applied a bit more pressure to his back. Her hands shook with the terror of her actions. Until now she had not thought, but reacted solely on impulse. Still, she reasoned, it was the right thing to do. She could not stand idly by and allow this piracy to be perpetrated upon her own countrymen.

"Would you run me through, madam?"

"Without a doubt," she returned, her voice quivering as she continued, "I'll not repeat my words again, Captain. Reduce your speed."

For a long moment Reena thought he was going to ignore her orders. Suddenly his voice rang out loud and sharp. "Mr. Wingate, reduce speed."

Reena kept the grin of victory from her face as she carefully watched the crew come to the realization of what was happening.

Incredible looks were exchanged among the men, that the captain's lady, English though she might be, should dare to hold a weapon on her husband.

Mr. Wingate called out in disbelief, "Captain?"

"You heard me, sir, I said reduce speed."

Orders were called out to that effect, and Reena felt a joy such as she had never known fill her being as the ship's speed noticeably lessened. She had only to hold her position for a short time and the frigate would overtake them. She felt a power surely unmatched by any woman before.

Suddenly a cannon burst flew overhead and sliced the top canvas most neatly from its number two mast. Reena gave a startled shriek and her hands relaxed their pressure. Still another shriek came to her lips as Dominic, taking the opportunity offered, turned and flung the offending sabre from her to clatter helplessly to the deck.

An instant later, he held her bound to his side, in a hold that threatened to crush her ribs.

Reena's struggles were brought up short as his hold tightened to the point where she had to strain just to breathe, and he growled, "Stop fighting me before I give you a true taste of the anger I feel."

"Mr. Wingate," he continued in a voice of icy calm, almost as if nothing were amiss, "disregard that last order and get us the hell out of here."

The men laughed with relief as the sails were once again stretched taut and the wind swept the graceful ship with resounding force out of reach of the cannon blast.

A moment later Reena's startled cry filled the air as she was flung, with effortless ease, over his shoulder as if she were no more than a sack of soiled clothes. Her face burned with shame as Dominic walked amid a roar of male laughter and shouts of approval as he brought her below.

In his cabin, he flung her carelessly upon the bed. Reena fairly shook with rage at his audacity. The beast! The vile, low-life, wretched beast! How dare he manhandle a lady? And to do it before the laughing eyes of his crew was the final degradation. She'd never forgive him.

With a growl of loathing, she was up and flying at him. All the unleashed fury and hatred she had held in check since their first meeting came instantly to full bloom. A small-fisted hand made sharp contact with his jaw before her arms were pulled behind her and held securely by one of his large hands.

He shook her so hard Reena felt her teeth rattle as her jaw snapped again and again. For a moment she thought he might break her neck.

"Little fool," he growled with disgust. "Did you think to surrender us to your countrymen so we might face the end of our days in English shackles, forever in bondage aboard one of his majesty's vermin-ridden ships?

"Nay, my fine English lady. I'd die first and see you in hell with me before I'd allow it."

"It was you who first attacked! You cannot blame them for returning fire," she cried righteously.

"Can I not? How many ships have they stopped and boarded upon these high seas? What right have they to take

176

American seamen against their will and press them to serve in your bloody wars?

"If I can but put a thorn to the arrogant English bastards, I will consider my time on earth well spent."

"Indeed, sir," she sneered as she tried, but failed, to wrench herself from his steely hold, "I can well attest you've done that and more to this Englishwoman."

"You, madam," he warned with blood-curdling certainty, "have yet to feel the sting of my thorn."

He flung her from him with such force that she fell back and lay trembling on the bed. The look in his eyes was so murderous, she dared not even move to adjust her skirts, somehow knowing for certain any movement would cause him to pounce on her.

His dark eyes grew blacker than pitch and flashed undisguised desire as they moved over her prone figure. "See to it you stay where you are," he hissed a warning so low Reena found herself straining to hear. "When I've finished with this business I expect to find you waiting for me. The game we play has reached its end."

Chapter Nineteen

"SAILS HO!"

Dominic stiffened, his heart accelerated with excitement as he called out in an equally low voice, "Directions, man."

The lookout atop the main mast replied, "Three hundred yards off starboard, sir."

Suddenly the deck was crowded with men running to and fro, each knowing his post and hurrying to it. From the wooden storage bins, grappling hooks and lines were unraveled and readied. Rifles appeared and were primed, while sabres gleamed eerily in the moonlight.

"Mr. Wingate, man the wheel," Dominic ordered, and immediately his first mate was standing at his side. "Bring her along side," he added in half a whisper.

A moment later the ship gave a powerful shudder as it

contacted sharply against the port side of the English merchant.

Reena was jolted from a light doze and flung unceremoniously to the floor. Her heart pounded in terror as she unconsciously rubbed her aching hip and came unsteadily to her feet. Clutching the bed's thick wooden post, she wondered if the ship had taken a hit. She could hear the muffled sounds of running feet and low screams. Were they taking on water? Were they about to sink? Had they forgotten about her in all their excitement?

She couldn't stay below and meekly await her end. She had to get out! If she were to die, it wouldn't be sealed as if in a coffin, finding her end in a watery grave.

No sooner had the thought occurred did she lunge for the door and, with no little relief at finding it unlocked, she sped down the ship's corridor to the steps that led above.

Reena was amazed upon gaining the deck to see that the *America* was in no danger, but securely held to the merchant with grappling hooks. A line of men stood facing the English ship with guns primed and aimed, should any of the crew dare not to see the wisdom of compliance.

Most of the *America*'s crew were aboard the merchant, seeing to the relieving of that ship's officers and convincing its crew of the good sense to accept the *America*'s captain as their own. The alternative was to suffer the long swim to the ever-prowling frigate.

Dominic ordered a warning shot fired as the man-of-war, under the cover of darkness, attempted to protect its sister ship and close its distance. He laughed at the frustration its captain was sure to be feeling as he beat a hasty retreat and dared not return the shot lest his countrymen's ship take a direct hit.

The English captain and his officers were coming aboard. Reena, forgetting Dominic's orders to remain below, crept closer so she might witness firsthand the meeting of the antagonists.

The captain stopped before Dominic. Even in the moon-light Reena could see the thinness of his mouth as rage contorted his features.

"Allow me to extend you every courtesy, Captain," Dominic remarked, as he saluted the man and then offered his hand. "We will be in port in less than three days. You and your crew will, of course, be released upon our docking."

"Blasted hell! You cannot expect me to submit meekly to this abominable act of piracy. This is not the first ship I've lost to your sort and I won't have it!"

"What choice have you, sir?"

"I have this."

"Nooo!" Reena shrieked. His hand reached into the deep pocket of his coat and pulled out a small gun. The metal glittered dangerously in the silvery light before the gun fired. The force of Reena's body knocked his hand aside, while from the side of her eye she saw Dominic flinch and stagger as the bullet found its mark.

At first Dominic thought the bullet had passed through her as he watched in stunned, wild-eyed panic as she slid to the deck. As his men quickly restrained the captain, Dominic hovered over her prone figure. His hands shook with terror as he turned her on her back.

Once he got his senses about him again, he realized she had no wound. With a deep sigh of relief he called for one of his men to carry his wife below. Before following, Dominic asked the doctor to join him, since Reena had not been mistaken: the bullet had indeed hit him, but, thanks to her quick movement, it had merely grazed the side of his scalp, rather than doing the destruction intended.

In his cabin, Dominic settled himself in a chair so the doctor might clean and bind his wound.

A few moments later Reena came awake to the sound of his soft groan of pain and jumped from the bed. She wobbled noticeably and nearly staggered toward the two men. Her eyes grew wide with fear at the enormous amount of blood that had covered his face. His shirt was soaked with it, and Reena felt a terror she had never before known grip at her chest as she watched its constant flow.

"Are you all right?" she choked out as she came to his side.

"I am, madam, thanks to you," he returned, his eyes glassy but aglow with admiration.

"But there's so much blood!"

"'Tis no more than a graze," he promised. "Were it not for your quick thinking," he shrugged, not bothering to finish the obvious thought.

"Doctor, should he not be in bed?"

Dr. Barrett nodded. "After I've finished."

Dominic gave another groan as the agonizing pounding in his head nearly blotted out all else. He swayed weakly as he fought away the blackness that threatened. "Would you get me a brandy?" And then noticing her look of terror, he added, "You need not look at me so. I am fine."

"Oh, my God," she groaned as he suddenly slumped toward her, nearly knocking her to the floor as she caught his full weight, before she had a chance to question him further.

Barely conscious, Dominic had no strength to argue against their combined help as they managed, amid much straining and grunting, to get him undressed and into bed.

Reena was shaking from the exertion and fright as she helped the doctor finish the bandaging.

A short time later Dominic rested comfortably, as the doctor promised a distraught Reena that her husband had suffered only a minor concussion and would soon, with proper bed rest, find himself well again.

"Reena," Dominic whispered, and she spun away from the doctor to return to his side.

"I'm here."

"Sit with me," he asked, as he reached for her hand.

Reena and Dr. Barrett exchanged a look, and at his nod she sat. His work finished for the moment, the doctor left them alone.

"You should sleep," she whispered gently, as she took his hand.

"I will," he sighed, as he pulled her down to lie at his side.

"Dominic, you must rest."

He closed his eyes, and after a long moment asked, "Why did you do it? Your problem could have been over on this night. You would have been free."

She shrugged, not knowing how to answer, for she knew not why herself. "If anyone's going to shoot you, Captain, it's going to be me."

His soft chuckle ended in a groan of pain. Again a few minutes passed before he asked, "Another impulse?"

"Perhaps," she shrugged again. "There certainly was no time to think on it."

"'Tis my good fortune, I think, that you seldom obey my orders. You should not have been out of the cabin."

"You would be dead."

He smiled as he acknowledged the truth of her words.

Reena started to move away.

"Stay with me," he breathed, already slipping into the relief only sleep could bring as his arm slid around her and brought her closer to his side.

Chapter Twenty

"GOOD GOD, MAN, YOU MAKE THE MOST ABOMINABLE patient!" Reena raged, her blue eyes glittered with anger as her hands planted themselves on her hips and she faced him with a fearless scowl. "Is it not in you to utter one kind word? I care not your head aches. The pain gives you no cause to abuse those who would see to the running of your ship.

"You, sir, are no more than a bully and deserving of a bully's reward. The next time you show this obnoxious side of your nature, you can damn well feed and take care of yourself, for I shall leave you to rot."

"Lower your voice, damn it! My head is killing me."

"What a shame," she muttered, as she flung aside the half-eaten bowl of soup that had been sitting on the bedside stand. She gave a low grunt of satisfaction as the contents splashed on his face and the bowl clattered noisily against the door.

Dominic glared as the sound brought a knifelike pain throughout his brain.

"Do not bother with your evil looks, Captain. You do not scare me," she snapped, as she threw a towel at him so he could wipe his face. "You're mistaken if you think your rage will work on me as it did on him," she pointed over her shoulder at the door, reminding him of the man who had just left.

"If I were well I'd take you over my knee for that."

"If you were well, I doubt the sound would have bothered you. Therefore, I would not have done it."

"What the hell do you want of me?" he groaned, as he clutched his throbbing head.

"Merely that you act like a reasonable human being, rather than the monster you've suddenly become. There's not a soul on board, besides myself, who does not quake with fear in your presence."

Despite his discomfort, Dominic could not control the grin that split his handsome face. "And you do not find cause to fear me?"

Reena returned his grin with her own knowing smile. "You told me once, Captain, that you would treat me as your honored wife." She shrugged. "What do I have to fear?"

"So you dare to throw my words back at me."

She shook her head and smiled as she wiped the soup from his face with clean, wet toweling, "Nay, Captain, I wish only to remind you lest you've forgotten."

"Very well," he sighed. "If I try to control my temper, would you continue to help me in my time of need?"

"I will, Captain," she smiled tenderly. "Would a cool, wet cloth bring you some comfort?"

"Aye, madam, that and you at my side would surely ease this pain."

Reena smiled and answered softly, "Perhaps some gentle massaging?"

"Aye," he breathed as her fingers gently rubbed against his forehead and temple, soothing the throbbing within. "The pain eases," he sighed with relief and a moment later added, "Kiss me, gentle, honored wife, for that more than anything will soothe the pain."

Reena smiled, "Go to sleep, Captain. We will see to your other pains at a later date."

Reena sipped from the hot mug of tea that had been generously laced with rum. Her feet braced apart for balance, she allowed the rolling movement of the ship to carry her along with its flight. The wind was warm, but as brisk as she had ever known, and it pressed her dress tantalizingly against her, leaving little to the imagination. She had never moved this fast, and she felt excitement and laughter threaten to bubble free from her chest. She felt like a bird must when it swoops through the air, light, graceful, and nearly weightless.

Her hair flew out behind her, in long and golden glory, the moonlight adding to it its own aura of silver. The hour grew late, but Reena was loathe to leave the peace and contentment of the deck for the airless cabin.

"Enjoying yourself?" a deep voice rumbled close to her ear.

Reena had no need to glance up into Dominic's darkly handsome face to know it was he who spoke. She nodded her head and smiled as she took another sip of the tea. "You should not be out of bed."

"My headache is gone."

Reena shot him a disbelieving look.

"Well, nearly," he corrected with a smile.

Together they stood at the rail as the ship sped them ever closer to his home.

"Is it always this much fun?"

Dominic's deeply melodic laughter filled the warm night air. "Might you be a lady pirate in disguise, madam? The way you fearlessly wield a sword and flout danger at nearly every turn cast doubt upon the fact that you were gently reared."

Reena smiled at his teasing. "Why are we going so fast?"

"The night holds a brisk wind. There is no need to waste it. If it keeps up we will make port in less than an hour. Would you care to join me at the wheel?"

"In truth?" she asked, with no little surprise.

"Why not?" he shrugged casually. "I've a need to stretch the stiffness from these muscles," he remarked, as he rubbed his arms. "I've lain in bed too long."

Reena had to bite her lip to prevent the laughter that threatened.

Dominic grinned, "No doubt you never thought to hear that."

Reena couldn't stop the laughter that bubbled forth.

"What I meant was, I've lain in bed too long, *alone*. Had you been there with me, I know my muscles would not be stiff from lack of use. More likely from overwork."

"No doubt," Reena grinned, as she placed her hand on his gentlemanly offered arm. Glancing up at him, she studied his strong, dark profile for a long moment. The corner of his lips lifted in a gentle smile, and she realized how easily laughter came to both of them of late.

A frown marred the smoothness of her brow as she realized the depth of her confusion. She had wanted to hate him and indeed, for a time, she had done just that. She had wanted nothing more than to be gone from him and yet now, after only a few weeks, she found herself seeking him out; her time spent alone became dull and tiresome, for only his company seemed to bring out a lightness that filled her heart.

Why? she groaned silently. What was happening to her?

Since the moment she had thrown herself against that gun things had begun to change.

She gave a small sigh and pushed her thoughts from her mind. She'd think on it no more tonight. For now she was content to stand at his side and feel the breeze rush against her. To know he was near, to feel the warmth of his arm as it circled her waist was enough. Tomorrow she would delve into the workings of her mind and settle her thoughts, if indeed that could ever be accomplished.

Dominic relieved the man at the wheel for a half-hour break and stood in a relaxed stance, his feet spread for balance before the giant wooden object. Reena, at his side, watched how his large hands nearly swallowed the wooden spokes and effortlessly kept the ship on course. His hands—she groaned silently as she closed her eyes and remembered their rough texture against her skin.

What had come over her tonight? She found herself in such a strange mood. No matter how she might try, she could think of nothing but him. How his nearness brought a rapidness to her pulse and a shallowness to her breathing. Just standing at his side caused a warmth to spread over her. Why? How was tonight different from any other? Why should she suddenly feel this closeness, this contentment, this happiness?

Dominic glanced down at her upturned face and grinned. "Have I a wart growing on my nose?"

Reena's eyes opened wide with surprise and she gave a low, husky laugh as she turned away. She hadn't realized she was staring. What must he think of her?

"You needn't stop, you know. There's only one thing I enjoy more."

Again she laughed as she returned her gaze to his, her heart beating fast, her face flushed warm as she read the silent meaning behind his words.

"Would you like to steer the ship?"

"Oh yes," Reena cried anxiously.

Dominic moved back. "Put the mug down. Step before me. Put your hands where mine are."

Reena did as she was told, all the while extremely conscious that she stood within inches of him. Her back nearly touched his chest as he removed first one and then the other hand from the wheel.

Reena laughed with excitement as she felt the power of the ship vibrate beneath her hands and strained to hold the wheel in place. "You make it look so easy," she grunted.

"Is it too much for you?"

Reena chuckled softly. "Captain, contrary to popular belief, all women are not weak and helpless. I can surely—" she gasped, forgetting what she was about to say as the wheel lifted her from the deck and threatened to spin her off to the side.

In an instant his hands covered hers, and the wheel was once again pulled back to its correct position.

"All right?" he asked, his chest now firmly pressed to her back, his hands covering her own.

She nodded and, although she could have moved a step closer to the wheel, unaccountably the thought never occurred to her. Instead, she found herself resting against him with a comfortable sigh. His jaw rested lightly on the top of her head as he asked, "Better?"

She sighed softly and nodded again, loving the feeling of his hands on hers. "I don't seem to be doing any good standing here." She smiled sheepishly as she turned her head and lifted her gaze to his.

Dominic chuckled knowingly. "You're doing more good than you know. Don't move. You fit perfectly against me."

Reena squirmed, unhappy to leave the serenity and comfort of her present position, but trying to just the same. "Dominic, 'tis most unseemly. Suppose one of your men should see us?"

"Worry of it no more, Reena," he insisted, as he held her hands to the wheel. "The night is dark and only a few

188

keep watch. And their eyes had best be on the lookout for land, or I'd be knowin' why.''

They stood together for some time, both lost in their own thoughts, each enjoying to the fullest the touch and feel of the other.

Suddenly Reena blurted out, "Where did you get that bed?" and could have bitten off her tongue once the words were uttered, for surely he'd believe her mind to be wandering along the path of beds and what could be accomplished thereon.

Dominic laughed out loud, more than a little surprised by the question. "Why?"

"I don't know." She shrugged, while silently cursing her impulsive tongue and the flame it caused her cheeks. "The thought just occurred to me."

"I once did a favor for a Turkish merchant. It was his form of a thank-you. Do you like it?"

Reena's face grew warm as she remembered the obscene miniature disporting figures that were carved into the headboard, and warmer still as vivid memories flooded her mind of the two of them upon it.

"No, I think it's disgraceful."

"But informative," he teased, low and silkily as he lifted one hand from the wheel and slid it around her slender waist, pulling her closer to his hard length.

Her free hand covered his and their fingers entwined.

His head lowered and he whispered near her ear, "Should one run out of ideas, he need only . . ."

"Please," she groaned. "Indeed I am sorry I mentioned it."

"Perhaps you should see it again. No doubt your memories need refreshing. 'Tis not nearly so disgraceful as you imagine."

"No doubt," she agreed with a soft laugh, delighted to be able to join his teasing.

Her eyes danced with merriment in the silvery moonlight as she lifted her gaze to his again.

Dominic groaned at the loveliness his eyes took in, his arm tightened, pulling her more firmly to him. "Would you box my ears until I cried for mercy if I kissed you?"

"Aye," she breathed with a hint of a smile, for this was the first time he had asked her permission, and her heart raced madly at his softly spoken request. She watched his lips, her mind silently crying out for the touch of his warm mouth on hers.

"I'm holding your hands," he gently reminded. "How will you do it then?"

"Surely you will not always hold me thus?" she sighed, as she lifted her willing lips toward his descending mouth.

"Perhaps I shall," he murmured, an instant before his lips touched hers.

For a long moment his mouth pressed gently against her own in a kiss as chaste and pure as if it were their first. Warm breaths mingled as firm flesh pressed close. His control was pushed to its limit, but he rejected the passion that could so easily flame.

Each held back, reveling in the pure ecstasy of this magical moment until Reena pulled her hand from beneath his and turned in his loosely held embrace. With a devilish glint in her eyes, she leaned against him, her head tipped back so she might more easily see his face as she ran her fingertip along the firm line of his jaw. "If I'm going to box your ears, Captain, you'll have to give me more reason than one gentle kiss."

Dominic grinned at her saucy taunt, "Could it be you've relented at last? Would you cancel the bargain?"

Reena laughed softly and pressed closer still. Her arms circled his neck in easy familiarity as she responded to his teasing. "Nay, Captain, you misunderstand my words. 'Tis a kiss I speak of, no more or less."

"Oh?" he responded, feigning surprise. "Is it a kiss you be wanting?"

Reena grinned. "Only a wretched beast would force a lady to ask for a kiss."

190

His eyes grew suddenly serious as he studied her lovely face. "It would please me, Reena, if I knew you wanted it enough to ask."

Reena returned his long searching look with one of her own. Suddenly she realized he was as wary of her as she was of him. Was he too feeling something growing between them . . . something more than lust? She smiled, feeling suddenly wild and free as she flung back her head and stood on tiptoe, brazenly responding to his tenderly spoken appeal. "Would you kiss me, Dominic?"

He almost groaned out loud, the temptation to crush her to him almost beyond bearing. He could tell from the flicker of fear that had shown itself briefly in her eyes how foreign this request was for her, and still she had asked. His heart beat wildly with joy, but he forced himself to go slow. It would be enough for now. She would soon realize there was no going back. This kiss would seal a new beginning and she would soon admit to it.

"Now?" he teased softly. "In front of anyone who might care to look?"

He watched with no little satisfaction as her lips lifted in a teasing smile and he felt the pressure of her arms pulling his face down to hers. "They'd best be watching for land, or I'd be knowin' why."

Dominic intended to only brush his lips against hers in a sweet, searching kiss, but the moment their lips touched his arm closed her in an explosive hold of brute strength, and his heart leaped with blinding joy. A strangled groan sounded in the back of his throat as his mouth opened and slashed across hers with devouring hunger.

Reena felt her knees buckle with the force of his unleashed power and the answering desire that came instantly to life. Her lips parted eagerly to his ravenous exploration, and her head spun as his tongue sought out the sweetness he knew awaited him.

Dominic's hand left her waist to slide up her back beneath the silken veil of gold to caress her neck and bring her mouth closer still. His tongue moved past the softness of her lips to run along the smoothness of her teeth to the roof of her mouth and then entwined exquisitely with her own in dazzling, delicious tastings.

His hips pressed into hers, his passion becoming more obvious with each second that passed until he pulled abruptly away. Breathlessly he watched her for a long moment before his raging desire caused him to groan out her name and again take her mouth in a joining of feverish urgency.

Reena gave a gasp as he tore his lips from her own at last. Weakly she leaned into him and groaned, "Now *that* was worthy of an ear-boxing if I know anything about it."

Dominic chuckled softly in agreement, his lips brushing lightly against her hair, one arm holding her close as he struggled for control. "Aye, but which of us will box the other? You asked me to do it, did you not?"

She didn't answer him, but kept her face pressed to his chest.

"Remember?"

"Vaguely," she murmured in contented bliss, as she nuzzled the small V where the opened shirt exposed his warm, hard chest. "I will not do it again, however," she vowed, "for you are most unchivalrous to remind me."

"Will you not?" he asked, his disappointment obvious.

"Nay," she grinned. "Do you not know if you want something done right, you must do it yourself?"

Dominic blinked in surprise. "Are you telling me I don't know how to kiss?"

Reena laughed and glanced up at him. "Is it always so easy to deflate the male ego? Indeed, sir, you have no cause to worry, and much to boast of. I meant only that should I feel the inclination, I will simply oblige myself, rather than ask."

"Mmmm," he murmured, as her lips slid up his neck to his jaw. "Might you be feeling so inclined at the moment?" he asked hopefully.

"It appears I might," she whispered, as her mouth reached his chin and slid ever closer to joining with his.

It was a long moment before Reena could breathe again and she gasped heavily into his neck. Her warm breath sent a delicious chill of longing down his back, and his body gave a violent shudder.

"Cold?" she teased impishly, knowing full well the reason for his trembling, since she was caught in much the same throes.

Dominic grinned at her teasing. "You'd best turn around. I know not how much longer I can stand this before I leave the wheel unattended and take you to my cabin."

"To that awful bed?"

"I'll throw the damn thing overboard," he growled, as she opened one button and then another and proceeded boldly to dip her mouth lower, leaving a burning path wherever she wandered.

"Reena, please, my God," he groaned helplessly. "If you mean to kill me be done with it, for I cannot bear this torture."

"Am I torturing you, Captain?" she asked so innocently that for a moment he almost believed she didn't realize what she was about until he saw her grin.

"God's truth, were I upon the rack, I'd not feel this pain."

"Perhaps I should go below," she suggested, with a low, husky laugh that bordered on being outright evil as she tried to move out of his embrace.

"Nay," he cried out, the desperation clear in his voice. "Turn around and lean against me and for God's sake be still for a moment."

Reena did as he asked, and after a few minutes inquired softly and with much mock concern, "Has the pain passed, Captain?"

Dominic only grunted for an answer and pressed her pliant form closer to his as he attempted to keep a menacing tone but failed miserably, "Woman, should you ever do that to me again, I promise dire punishment."

Reena couldn't contain the laughter that bubbled forth when she glanced at his pained expression, and Dominic was powerless but to join her.

A moment later the couple's soft laughter was interrupted by a loud cry from high above. "Land ho!"

Chapter Twenty-one

"SHALL I HAVE DIAH BRING THE WATER IN HERE FOR YOUR bath?" he asked casually, his voice and stance belying the tension that wracked his body as he anxiously waited for her response.

Dominic was experienced enough to realize her actions aboard ship had been no more than an unguarded moment. Should he pressure her now, they could easily lose the tenderness that was slowly growing between them. His body ached for her with desperate need, but he would wait until she was ready. He had to. He only prayed the time was now.

Reena didn't answer. Her eyes lowered to the red carpet as she worried her bottom lip with her teeth and cursed her foolishness. What in God's name had gotten into her tonight? She had never before behaved in so wanton a fashion. It was almost as if she had been caught up in some magical spell that could only be broken when land had been sighted. She despised women who teased and yet she, in a wild, uninhibited moment, had done just that. Surely Dominic had every right to believe she would willingly share this room and his bed. How could she get out of this without causing their growing friendship irreparable damage?

Dominic shrugged out of his jacket and flung it to the small settee before the unlit fireplace. A quick glance at her white face left him without a doubt as to her decision and he prayed to God he had the stamina to withstand the torture he would surely come to know.

"On second thought," he sighed, feigning exhaustion as he moved to stand before her and allowed his arms to enfold her in a gentle embrace, "it might be wiser if you took your bath in your own room. I fear I am weaker than I supposed and long only for a good night's rest."

Reena brushed gentle fingers against the small bandage that covered his wound while her eyes grew wide with concern. "Are you all right?"

"I will be after you kiss me good night and allow me to get into bed."

"Do you need anything?" she asked unthinkingly, and then closed her eyes with a silent groan at her stupidity. Was she never to gain control of her tongue? Would she never learn to think before she spoke?

Dominic's lips twitched as he tried to suppress a grin. "Do you have anything in particular in mind?"

Reena lowered her gaze to his chest, trying to think of something light and airy . . . something that would relieve the sudden tension between them.

Dominic smiled at her flustered look and placed a tender kiss on her forehead. "Forgive my teasing, Reena, but you are so open and honest and blush so prettily, I am hard put to resist."

Over his wife's head Dominic noticed his housekeeper move past his open door and called out, "Diah." And when the beautiful coffee-colored woman returned to face him, he continued, "Would you have one of the girls bring water for a bath to my wife's room? I feel the need to retire early. I trust she'll want for nothing if I leave her in your care."

"Yes sir," the young woman replied, while keeping her eyes demurely to the floor as she backed out of the room.

"Shall I show you to your room?" he asked, as his embrace loosened and one hand held to her waist.

Reena smiled as she gazed up at her husband and realized the depth of his consideration. He knew she wasn't ready. He knew she might never be, and yet he treated her as if she were his precious wife, as if nothing stood between them, her every desire his, while asking nothing of her. Her gaze filled with appreciation and undisguised esteem, for he was growing more admirable as each moment passed.

She smiled softly and nodded as she allowed him to lead her to the adjoining room.

Reena inhaled a soft gasp as her gaze took in the beauty of the room. All the furniture was white. The only color to soften the almost sterile appearance was the blue of the lush carpet beneath their feet and a matching satin spread upon the four-poster bed. A double door stood open to a vine-covered, bordered terrace.

Dominic's whisper was filled with tender humor as he breathed close to her ear, "I trust this bed meets with your approval, madam."

Reena smiled at his teasing. "You have a lovely home, Dominic. Everything is so beautiful. I can hardly wait to see it in daylight."

He turned her to face him, his arms pulling her close as he murmured into her hair, "This is your home, Reena, for as long as you want it." He knew his words a lie, for he grew more certain daily he'd never let her go. "In the morning I will take you to Mary."

"Where is she?" Reena asked with growing excitement.

"Not far."

"One hopes she has fared as well as I."

"I'm sure she has. I've no doubt Mr. Steele has treated her with the utmost care and respect."

A knock sounded at the door, and upon Dominic's call to enter two young maids struggled to bring in huge pails of water.

"Enjoy your bath, love," he whispered, his mouth close to her own. "I will see you in the morning."

"Thank you, Dominic," she returned, as her mouth lifted and joined with warm regard to his, and they both knew it was more than a bath she thanked him for.

The girls hustled around the room in a flurry of activity, preparing the bed, securing toweling, while still another brought hot chocolate to her bedside stand, all under the watchful gaze of the housekeeper.

Reena smiled and closed her eyes as she eased her tired body into the warmth of the copper tub. Her head rested along the tub's rim and she felt the tensions of the day dissolve as she breathed in the gentle scent of tropical flowers. It was a pleasure beyond compare, and she sighed softly in enjoyment until a knowing grin teased the corners of her mouth. Well perhaps not beyond compare, but the only one she could allow herself.

A prickling sensation ran up her spine, and Reena's eyes opened to the intense glare in the hostile, dark eyes of the beautiful woman who ruled Dominic's home.

"Is something amiss?"

"Nothing at all, madam," Diah answered quickly, and lowered her head in a subservient manner.

Was it her imagination, or had the lights played tricks with her tired eyes? Surely she was mistaken. Diah could not harbor hatred for Dominic's wife. After all, they barely knew each other.

Reena pushed aside her thoughts as wild imagination. Obviously she was more tired than she had thought. After weeks spent sleeping on the hard pallet on Dominic's cabin floor, her body longed to recline upon the inviting softness of the beckoning bed.

A moment later she dismissed the girls, dried herself, and eased her body beneath the cool sheet and into the soft comfort of the down pillow and mattress.

A soft smile touched the corners of Reena's full lips as consciousness slowly returned. Her eyes remained closed against the bright glow of the early morning sun as he leaned over and whispered near her ear. "The hour grows late. Do you intend to remain abed all day?"

"Perhaps," she said and sighed softly, her voice low and husky from sleep. "This bed is sinfully comfortable."

Dominic smiled and watched as she curled tighter into a ball. Leaning close again, he teased, "Were you to sin, Reena, one hopes the bed could be put to better use than sleeping."

"Go away," she grinned, while smothering a low laugh into the pillow.

"Breakfast is ready. Would you care to join me downstairs, or shall I have one of the girls bring it up?"

Reena turned her head and opened one eye with a suspicious glare. "One wonders why a man would employ so many women and not an ugly face among them."

Dominic laughed, his heart growing light at her obvious jealousy. "Shall I dismiss them simply because they are pretty?"

"So you admit to it," she returned, lifting herself to her elbow.

Dominic shrugged, his silence all the answer needed. "Should I have surrounded myself with ugly servants?"

"Are they . . . are they your . . . ?"

"Harem?" he finished for her with a decidedly lecherous grin.

Reena lowered her eyes, her cheeks colored with embarrassment. "I'm sorry. I have no right to ask. How you live is of course none of my business."

Dominic brushed a golden lock of hair from her eyes, the temptation to nuzzle his face into the luxurious shining curls almost more than he could bare. "If it brings you distress, Reena, I shall replace them, and you may choose the ugliest women on the island to serve us, for they are naught but servants."

Reena couldn't control the smile that softened her lips. She had not a doubt that he spoke the truth, but she couldn't resist the temptation to ask, "Not even Diah?"

"Diah's mother has served me since I built this house. She was old even then. When Lena died, her daughter asked for the position. Since her mother trained her, I saw no reason to deny the request. She does an excellent job. The house runs smoothly."

Reena remembered the odd look the girl had given her last night and knew, in the light of day, she had not imagined it. It was easy enough to believe Diah in love with her master. Had Dominic given her just cause? Was she, Reena, the interloper?

"She is very beautiful."

"Not half so as you," he breathed, as his head bent and his lips brushed tenderly against her own. "Now get up," he finished, as he pulled quickly away while slapping her rounded rump and grinning at the look of aggravation that clouded her eyes.

The coverlet dipped as he moved and brought to his delighted view the nakedness the sheet had previously hidden. Dominic gave a strangled groan as his eyes feasted on her loveliness and Reena, noticing where his gaze had strayed, quickly snapped the sheet into place.

He came instantly to his feet, knowing full well should he linger his control would soon dissolve and it might be hours before he'd find the strength to leave her side.

"In truth, I find myself hard put to object to what you're currently wearing, but for now I think it wise to forego that delight and see to the addition of your wardrobe. This afternoon would not be too soon to visit the seamstress."

It was bad enough knowing she was so close while he was unable to have her, he couldn't bear it knowing she was lying in bed naked, warm, and luscious, and he on the other side of her door. God, he'd never get a moment's sleep.

Dominic walked away from the bed and turned his back to her as he forced aside the hunger that had nothing to do with his need for the morning meal.

Two girls came shyly into the room only moments after the door closed behind Dominic. One of them Reena remembered from the night before. That one, Halie, curtsied before she spoke. "The captain has asked that we assist you, madam."

Reena threw off the cover and slid into her one and only chemise as the other girl poured fresh water into the pitcher on the small white table in the corner and gathered fresh toweling from the top shelf of the armoire.

"Thank you, Halie," Reena returned with a cheerful smile. "I want to hurry this morning. Captain Riveria is waiting breakfast for me."

After Reena completed a quick toilet, Halie helped her into her petticoat and rose silk gown. Her hair was brushed to long lengths of rippling golden waves and a green ribbon used to tie it neatly at her nape.

She fairly flew down the stairs, for the moment unsure if she hurried to find Dominic's company or the promise of seeing Mary after all these weeks.

Less than an hour later Dominic helped Reena into the open carriage that stood waiting at the door of his huge white house. Harnessed to the carriage were two perfectly matched white horses, held in check by a giant black man dressed in white livery. A driveway of crushed shells and bordered with a lush array of the most exquisite flowers she had ever seen curved to the door and back to the road again in a half circle. As the carriage pulled away, Reena couldn't control the urge to turn in her seat and stare with open-mouthed astonishment at the breathtaking sight she was leaving behind. The house stood three stories high and sported six huge columns which evidently supported the terrace that ran the full length of the second floor. Enormous trees surrounded the structure, and against the dark green background the house appeared startling white in the early morning sun.

"Would you prefer to sit opposite me? You could then see without twisting your neck."

Reena smiled at his teasing. "You cannot fault my curiosity, Captain. When we arrived last night, all was masked in darkness."

Dominic, with a sudden thudding of his heart, impulsively gathered her into his arms and lifted her to his lap. His eyes glowed with delight as he tilted her chin so she might face him. "I find no fault in your curiosity, Reena, nor anything else about you."

Reena lowered her gaze to stare nervously at her fidgeting fingers, every inch of her body keenly aware of the warmth and strength of this man. "'Tis most unseemly, sir, our sitting thus."

"We are man and wife, are we not?"

She lifted her eyes to his amused gaze. "But should someone see us."

Dominic smiled as he allowed a lone finger to trace her silken cheek and jaw. "Should someone see us they'd no doubt remark, 'Look at that lovely lady. What a fortunate man to have her positioned thus.'"

Reena couldn't prevent the soft smile that came to her lips. "I often think of our first meeting, Captain. Truly you were an abominable wretch. Sometimes I compare that man to the one I now see and wonder how you could have changed so."

"I have not changed, Reena. Perhaps you have simply grown accustomed to my barbarian ways."

Reena allowed a shy smile to curve her full lips and replied softly, "I think not, for of late I see nothing in you that does not appeal."

Dominic gave a silent groan, suddenly wanting no more in life but to crush this lady to his chest and somehow bring her sweetness into his own soul. His head dipped, his eyes aglow with yearning, his mouth brushed tenderly against hers.

"I'm afraid you are a temptation beyond my control to resist," he murmured, as his lips reluctantly broke from hers. "Should you continue to speak to me thus, I fear these folks here about will have a sight to see that will light their days for some time to come."

Reena gave a soft husky laugh. "Perhaps I should refrain from doing so. I'd not willingly set tongues to wagging."

"Willing or not, I've no doubt your presence alone will achieve that end."

Moments later the carriage pulled into a long drive bordered on both sides by flowering trees. At the end of the avenue, against the background of a cloudless blue sky, stood a majestic mansion of mammoth proportions.

Once the carriage pulled to a stop at the double front doors, Dominic lifted Reena from it with effortless ease and, keeping his arm at her waist, held her close to his side.

Before another step was taken, one of the doors flew open and a tiny blond blur raced from the house, down the steps, and with a shriek of laughter lunged into Reena's arms.

Reena pulled Mary into a tight embrace as tears misted each woman's eyes. It had been but a few weeks since they had parted, still the circumstances of that parting had left each of them with fear for the other's safety.

"Oh, I'm so happy you've come at last. I expected you days ago. Richard was forever telling me not to fret, but I could not help but worry of your safety."

Reena smiled as she hugged her again, realizing how badly she had missed her sisterlike cousin. "You have worried for naught, Mary. As you can see I am well and quite safe."

"Come in, come in," Mary laughed happily, while nearly jumping like a child with delight as she pulled her cousin and Dominic. "I have so much to tell you." Turning to Dominic, she asked, "You are Captain Riveria, are you not?" After his short nod she turned to Reena with a knowing grin and led the way into the house.

Once the three of them mounted the few steps to the front door, Mary called out, "Richard, come quickly, they are here."

Her excitement was barely controlled and she fairly danced down the long hall and pulled them into a large day room. Mary whirled around with bubbling energy and faced Reena and Dominic with a huge grin. "I thought he was in here. Don't move, either of you. I'll be right back."

And as the tiny whirlwind flew from the room Dominic couldn't suppress the grin that had been threatening. "Is she always so melancholy and lethargic?"

Reena laughed at his teasing and allowed him to seat her upon the small settee, while following with his long form at her side. His legs stretched out and crossed at the ankles as he leaned back comfortably.

Mary's voice could be heard down the hall as she called out, "Matie, bring refreshments right away." And again she called, "Richard!"

A smile teased Reena's lips as she faced the man at her side. "Can she come back with us? Would you welcome her in your home?"

Dominic grinned as he listened to the bubbly voice of her cousin, while his eyes caressed the beauty of his wife's face with a long, tender look. "I've told you before, it is your home. If you wish your cousin to live with us, I have no objection."

Mary reentered the room with a rush of flying skirts and nearly fell into a chair opposite them as Richard came into the room. The two men exchanged friendly greetings with handshakes and hearty slaps to their backs.

"I'm so excited, I can't think what to say first," Mary breathed enthusiastically. "First of all, you must stay with us. Richard wouldn't mind, would you, dear? Heaven knows this house is big enough."

Reena's mouth dropped open with surprise. Dear? Mary had called this tall blond stranger *dear!*

"I don't understand. You intend to stay here? I thought you might want to live with me."

Mary's light, tinkling laughter filled the room before she replied, "Reena, this is my home. Richard and I were married the day after the ship docked."

Dominic interrupted Reena before she had a chance to do more than gasp. "It appears you are not alone in your blissful state."

For an instant confusion flickered in Mary's blue eyes as she watched the possessive look that passed from Dominic to her cousin. Suddenly a brilliant smile curved her tiny mouth. "You too?" And at Reena's nod, Mary jumped to her feet with a cry of pure rapture and hugged Dominic. "Oh, I'm so happy. Who would have thought such wonder could come from being kidnapped?"

"Indeed," Reena remarked dryly.

"When? When did you marry?"

"We put the ship in on the coast of Florida and were married there."

"Oh, you must be ecstatic," Mary sighed, as she hugged her cousin again. "It sounds like a fairy tale."

"I'm afraid . . . ." Reena began.

Dominic interrupted yet again, this time with a note of strained laughter in his voice. "Afraid this has been quite a shock. We had no idea the two of you might have also fallen in love. Is that not so?"

Reena took her cue from his long, searching look. It was apparent he wanted no one to know their relationship was less than ideal. A moment later she gave the tiniest of nods as his arm came around her.

Dominic breathed a silent sigh of relief as Reena finally murmured a low, "Aye."

"You must stay to lunch. Perhaps Richard might show you our newest addition, Captain. We had a mare foal last night. It was an experience I'll not soon forget."

"You were there?" Reena asked, with no little amazement. Could this be the same Mary who fainted at the sight of blood? Who blushed at the merest hint of reproduction, whether it be among animals or humans.

"She wasn't only there," Richard commented proudly, his eyes resting with obvious admiration upon his wife, "she worked harder than all of us."

Reena was quiet during the short ride home. Her amazement could not have been greater had she seen her cousin sport a full-grown beard. The change in her was phenomenal. She fairly shouted happiness. Had love for her husband brought all that about? She had grown from a girl into a woman in a few short weeks, and Reena couldn't deny the new Mary was even more appealing.

An unexplained emotion tugged uncomfortably, and Reena wondered if she were jealous of Mary's new-found happiness. Nay, she reasoned after some thought. She wished the best for her cousin and always would, for the girl was most dear and deserving.

If it wasn't jealousy she felt, what then? Envy! Aye, she mused silently, for she had never realized just how lovely the state of matrimony could be. Of course, there were young girls at school who were wild with joy at finding a man, but Reena had always supposed that to be a reaction others expected, rather than truly felt. Till today, she could not bring herself to believe another could so influence one's life.

Now, for the first time, she had witnessed this phenomenon and wondered how these emotions could have passed her by. Perhaps she was never to know, firsthand, the happiness Mary felt.

Reena gave Dominic a sidelong glance. The only thing between them was lust. A lust she could not in good conscience give in to. For soon she would be gone, and her indulgence in this basest of instincts would have accomplished naught. Reena couldn't help but wonder, if circumstances were different, whether she could grow to love him. He was watching the scenery as the carriage drove over the bumpy dirt road. The strong sunlight glistened off his uncovered head and caused his skin to glow darker than ever. She gave a slight shrug as her thoughts continued in some confusion, for she could not of late look upon the man without a fluttering in her chest. Still, it mattered not. What was done was done. She would soon leave, never to see him again.

Somehow her dream of opening her own school for young girls felt strangely flat. Why did the notion now feel such a chore?

Dominic turned to look at her. With a smile he took her hand in his and brought it to his mouth and then pressed it familiarly to his thigh, his own hand holding hers in place. "You are unusually quiet, Reena. Are you somehow distressed?"

"I was thinking of Mary."

Dominic smiled. "From the few times you mentioned her, I confess I had a completely different picture."

"You didn't know her before, so you can't begin to imagine the change in her."

"'Tis doubtful she changed so drastically. More than likely she never had the opportunity to show you this side of her character."

As Dominic's carriage entered the half circle drive before his home, Reena noticed a carriage standing near the front door and lifted inquiring eyes to Dominic.

"Ah, it appears Madame Simmons has already arrived." And when he swung his gaze back to Reena, he continued, "The seamstress, remember?"

"Captain, you can't mean to stay and watch my fittings," Reena whispered, as she bent low to the chair he was sitting in, while unknowingly giving him a splendid display of her charms when the neckline of her chemise gapped wide.

"And why not?" Dominic almost groaned at the lovely sight before him and felt an uncomfortable throbbing in his loins. He shifted in his seat and crossed his legs lest his desire grow more noticeable, while the chatter of female voices at the other end of the room went on.

"'Tis most unseemly. I shall feel on display."

"I ask little enough of you, Reena. Surely this will pose no inconvenience."

"Captain, 'tis not done," she pleaded.

"It is now. I wish to see what I'm paying for," he insisted.

"I will not do it!"

"You will, madam," he responded easily, his presence and tone leaving her little choice, lest she tell Madame Simmons her reasons, and more than likely look the fool. He was her husband, after all. She could not expect these women to understand her plight.

Reena mumbled a disparaging remark and turned from his grin. She'd show this beast his presence meant less than nothing to her. If he wanted to watch, she'd give him something to see, and she hoped the beggar suffered untold agony, for she knew not another more deserving.

Her jaw was set in a tight, angry line as she rejoined the women. "You may begin."

With a mouth full of pins and measuring tapes strung over her arms, Madame Simmons proceeded to lift off Reena's chemise and cast the offending article to the floor.

Reena gasped with surprise. She had not expected to stand before the mirror unclothed. Her cheeks flamed with mortification, for she knew without a doubt should she raise her eyes, she'd find Dominic's dark gaze studying her reflection.

The tape rested a moment across the peaks of her breasts and, as Madame Simmons routinely went about the business of calling off the measurements to her assistant, it slid to her midriff and then her waist.

A short, muffled cough caused Reena to raise her gaze to

the mirror, and she watched as Dominic's dark eyes drank in the sight of her lush figure with an expression that could only be described as torture.

A corset was placed above her waist and pulled to close at the back, causing her breasts to lift enticingly toward the mirror and Dominic nearly to cry out with the painful yearning that suffused his body. He cursed himself soundly. What a fool he had been to subject himself to this torment, for he could imagine no suffering to compare.

Beyond his control, his gaze was drawn to her, and no matter his silent beratings he could not stop. He dared not move, for should he stand, everyone in the room would know of his condition.

Reena squared her shoulders and shifted slightly. The action caused her breasts to sway provocatively, and Dominic closed his eyes against the pain that shot through him.

The voices dimmed behind a cloud of growing passion and he heard nothing but the throbbing of blood in his ears and the laboring of his breath. There was not a part of her he could not see. Her back was exposed to him, while the front of her reflected in the mirror. One after another, materials of every color and texture were draped across her nakedness, only to be pulled away and replaced by still another.

"I have a few pieces at the shop, Captain. Do you want them delivered today?" Madame Simmons was asking, and from her expression, Dominic wondered if she hadn't repeated it more than once.

"Today would be fine." He cleared the huskiness from his voice and after several tries continued, "When will the rest be done?"

"Most of them by the end of next week. I have left the few things I brought," she nodded to the stack of folded garments on the bed. "'Tis a shame her luggage fell overboard."

Dominic nodded and watched as Reena slipped a satin robe over her nakedness as the women prepared to leave.

He breathed a sigh of relief as they finally left the two of them alone.

Reena was sitting at the dressing table seething with rage. Angrily she brushed her hair, while fervently wishing with every stroke that she was using the brush on him. "You may leave now. The performance is at an end," she sneered arrogantly.

Dominic waited a full minute for his desire to recede to a bearable point before he came to his feet and moved to stand behind her. His dark hands showed in sharp contrast against the white robe as they rested on her shoulders, and he pressed her stiff form back to rest against him.

"Be there a sight more lovely than you, madam, these eyes have yet to know it."

"Thank you, Captain," she returned, her anger only barely under control, "but your compliments will not suffice. I know not when I've felt such anger nor suffered more humiliation."

Dominic turned her to face him and lifted her to stand. His knuckles ran along the smooth line of her jaw as he confessed, "I, too, in my own way, have suffered, Reena, for I never expected to see you naked, and when I did it was too late. I could not have left you even if I had wanted to lest I display for all to see the effect you have on me."

His voice was so filled with pain that Reena had not a doubt he spoke the truth. A smile touched the corners of her lips and her blue eyes twinkled with mischief. "Good! Perhaps the next time you will listen."

"Perhaps," he grinned in return. "Still, despite the torment, it was pleasure beyond belief."

Chapter Twenty-two

"I CAN'T BELIEVE IT," DOMINIC LAUGHED SOFTLY. "I thought I was wild, but you were a terror."

Reena answered his laughter with her own. "My poor aunt, I'm sure she was never quite the same once the constable showed her the note."

"Can you remember what it said?"

"I'll never forget," Reena grinned. "It read, 'If you wish to save the parsonage, kindly leave a small pony for Reena Braxton at Mr. Braxton's stables. Thank you, sincerely, The highwayman."

Dominic laughed again. "At least you were polite. I can't see why everyone should have gotten so upset."

Reena flashed him a devilish grin. "That's exactly what I thought at the time."

"Where did you get the idea?"

Reena shrugged. "At the time there was a highwayman

about. He didn't hurt anyone, but managed to leave a trail of terror wherever he went. I heard some of the adults talking and figured if it worked for him, it would work for me. Unfortunately, I didn't wait long enough, for they soon caught him and left the poor man to decorate a tree."

"But the church? Good God, what gall."

Reena shook her head. "It didn't take gall. I'd say it was closer to stupidity."

Dominic's smile grew tender as his dark eyes surveyed the beauty of his reluctant wife as she sat across from him. With a determined effort, he tried to imagine this lovely woman as a hoyden and failed miserably. For although she possessed a certain vivaciousness, and at times a twinkle of mischief might add a devilish glint to her eyes, no sign could be seen of the girl she described.

There was no hope for it, he grinned, in silent amusement, if he wished to behold a younger, slightly uncivilized facsimile of the lady, it would be necessary to provide a duplicate model, a chore he found he had no aversion to.

The evening was warm, and they had had their dinner on the terrace outside the dining room. Glass-enclosed candles cast her lovely face in their golden glow, and Dominic longed to reach across the table and stroke the satiny texture of her skin.

"Was that the extent of your mischief?"

"Hardly," she returned. "I'm sure I should not be telling you of my misdeeds, lest you come to believe the unconventional attribute lingers still."

"You need not fear influencing my beliefs, for I know you for what you are."

Reena gave him a long, inquisitive look, but couldn't muster the courage to ask what knowledge he presumed. A moment later she shrugged, belying the notion that his opinion held any importance.

"In any case, I'm sure the escapades of my youth gave both my aunt and uncle more than one gray hair."

Dominic refilled her glass with the rich, dark, fruity wine they were sharing and coaxed her to continue, "Go on."

Reena shrugged again. It mattered not the impression he might come to know of her childhood. She snickered evilly as a waywood childhood action was remembered. "The Harrington estates were situated across the park. The owners were the most outrageous snobs. Thinking back, I believe their thoughts and feelings and particularly their speech originated not from the heart or brain, but from the nose. Upon being introduced at some social gathering Mrs. Harrington might inquire, 'How do you do?' " Reena gave a comic nasal imitation of the lady's greeting and Dominic chuckled. "I was present at one of these gatherings, and when I heard her I asked in a voice that was never too soft and ladylike to begin with, 'Is there something wrong with her?'—only to receive a steely look from the horse-faced lady and a pinch from my aunt. Needless to say, my family was never again invited to the manor house, a circumstance I knew to be my fault. Still, I could not find it in my heart to forgive the snobbish fools for snubbing a lady as sweet as my aunt and went out of my way to answer their cruelty in kind."

"I'm afraid to ask the means of your retaliation."

"Oh it wasn't as bad as all that. Just the usual childish pranks, I imagine. Usual for me, in any case. I pushed their sweet son in mud puddles. Dared him once to climb a tree and when he couldn't get down, I left him there. One time I hid in the underbrush and threw rotten tomatoes at him and his nurse. Tomatoes stolen from his own garden, by the way. They caught me that time. His nurse was faster than I had expected. She dragged me back to Mr. Harrington.

"What a to-do," Reena sighed with disgust. "Mr. Harrington brought me to the constable himself. My uncle hugged me afterward and from the look in his eyes, I knew he was secretly amused. Of course my aunt was totally mortified and came as close to tears as I can remember."

"And you felt no remorse?"

"Of course not. I'd not have done it if that were the case."

Dominic laughed. "Remind me never to make an enemy of you."

Reena grinned. "You need not fear, Captain, for I can abide most anything but a slight to those I love and snobbery least of all."

"And yet you possess a degree of the trait yourself."

"What does that mean?"

"It means upon our first meeting you portrayed an aristocrat in every sense of the word. I doubt there was another present that held herself in higher regard."

Reena laughed. "That was merely to keep those like yourself at a distance." She shot him a knowing look. "Obviously, it did little good."

"I see," he grinned. "So you believed me to be beneath you."

"Captain, I did not know you or anyone else at the inn. No matter the station in life, one does not speak with strangers."

"And yet you did just that. Deny if you can your haughty disdain because I was an American."

"That's not true!" Reena snapped all too quickly, as she came to her feet and walked to the terrace railing. For a long moment she looked over the darkening gardens trying to examine her motives. At his prolonged silence, she finally turned to see him standing behind her, a look of disbelief clearly in his eyes. Reluctantly she admitted, "All right, so I once mistakenly considered all Americans barbarians. Certainly you will agree I had ample cause. Your actions were abominable. Still, I never held myself in such high regard as to consider you unworthy of me."

"In truth? Why then did you find the idea of marriage so repugnant?"

214

"You never asked me, damn it! You gave yet another order."

"Didn't I?" Dominic asked with some amazement, and then gave a sheepish grin as he remembered back and knew the truth of her words. "It must have slipped my mind." He grinned again. "Shall I ask you then?"

"It's a bit after the fact, don't you think?"

"Perhaps, but I've a need to know your answer." He took her hand and led her from the terrace into the beautiful gardens that stretched almost endlessly beyond the house. Beneath a flowering tree, he finally pulled her into his gentle embrace. "Will you marry me, Reena?" And at the touch of her body against his, he couldn't prevent the low groan that escaped his throat. "Will you?"

"You're teasing me, Captain, and I think it very unkind."

"And if I weren't teasing? What would you say?"

"I would say we should get to know each other first."

"What if we married first and then grew to know each other?"

"Suppose we find no mutual accord? Shall we spend our remaining years in agony?"

"Do you like me now, love?" he asked, his voice low and husky as his mouth brushed against her hair.

"I do," she breathed shakily, the touch and scent of him causing her heart to beat erratically. "But I hardly know you. Suppose, after a time, I find much to detest?"

Dominic chuckled softly, while gathering her closer still, "I think you worry overmuch. I harbor no hidden faults, love. I am what you see."

"Are you, Captain?" she sighed softly, as his mouth came to nuzzle the side of her face, his warm breath sending chills down the length of her back. "And what might that be?"

"A man who right now wants nothing more than to kiss you."

"Nothing more, Captain?" she asked, while restraining the impulse to press herself close to him and run her hands over his powerful form.

"Nay, Reena, the touch of your lips will suffice for a time."

With a ghost of a smile she lifted her lips to his and wondered, as his mouth brushed against her, how she would manage to leave him when the time came.

Chapter Twenty-three

REENA SPLASHED HAPPILY IN THE SMALL, SECLUDED pond. For the second time this week she had answered to its silent beckoning call, unable to resist a quick, cool soaking during her early morning ride. Yesterday Dominic had questioned the dampness of her hair upon her return, and even though he had obviously suspected her answer, Reena had let the excuse lie in the day's intense heat, rather than disclosing the truth. This was her private spot, hers alone to enjoy, and she intended to keep it that way.

Her horse snickered contentedly as he drank from the water's edge, and Reena smiled while treading water as she allowed her gaze to roam over the peacefulness of the setting. The pond was deep within the island and fed by a small trickle of cool water that ran off a huge black rock, and totally surrounded by thick, sweetly scented foliage. In truth this was an island paradise and, try as she would, she could not imagine greater beauty.

The day after her fittings, Dominic had given her a beautiful mount, and she had often accompanied him as he had seen to the workings of the plantation. His property seemed to stretch on endlessly, and it was one day when she had gone off on her own that she had come across this pond.

Reena was just making her way to the water's edge, moving slowly over the precariously slippery rock, when a voice from the foliage startled her and caused her to slip and fall back with a giant splash. Terror pounded in her chest as she surfaced again only to find Dominic leaning casually against one of the many trees that grew to the water's edge. His arms were folded across a loose white shirt that was opened nearly to his waist, his legs encased in tight white pants that left no doubt about his delight in finding her thus, while a grin threatened the severity of his mouth.

"I see you've found the means to alleviate the heat, my love."

Coming to her feet, the water reached only to her knees.

Reena stood unconsciously naked; her hands, curled into fists, rested belligerently on her hips. Her whole body shook from the fright she had just suffered, while anger suffused her being.

"Was it necessary to sneak up on me? How long have you been standing there?"

"Long enough." And at her obvious reluctance to close the distance between them, he added, "You needn't hesitate on my account."

Reena felt a slow blush creep up her neck as she realized her naked state and Dominic's obvious enjoyment. She tipped her head stubbornly. "Perhaps I've not yet finished."

Dominic shrugged, finding it harder with each passing moment to profess nonchalance, as his eyes wandered freely over her damp, naked loveliness. "In that case, perhaps I will join you," he returned easily, as his hands reached unerringly to his belt buckle. "Indeed, the thought of a cooling swim grows more appealing by the moment."

Reena muttered a low curse as she stormed past his grinning form, bent on reaching her clothes lest he should make a move toward her. She had not a doubt, no matter her anger, should he touch her, she'd be helpless to prevent the inevitable conclusion.

Her thin chemise was pulled quickly over her soaking wet body, but rather than protecting her nakedness from his dark gaze, she succeeded only in intensifying the desire he kept so strictly under control. Her chemise reached only to midthigh and molded to the dampness of her skin so provocatively that Dominic found he had to look away and take deep, calming breaths lest he take her now, willing or not, upon the earth's soft bed.

"Why did you follow me?" she asked, her voice muffled against the material of the dress that was being pulled over her head.

Dominic smiled as she quickly buttoned the bodice and smoothed her skirt in place. "Shall we say I was curious as to why my wife should return home in such a dampened state?"

Reena stiffened at his words. She wished he would stop referring to her as his wife. Somehow his light, teasing use of the word seemed to cause an ache of despair within her breast, and for the life of her, she couldn't understand why.

"Now that you know, I expect I'll have to go elsewhere to be alone."

"Reena, if you wish to return here you need only to say so and I will be most willing to accompany you."

"I will not bathe if attended, Captain," she returned, as she pocketed her tights and slid her naked feet into soft leather boots.

"In that case you may do so in the privacy of your room."

"Or?" She turned just as she was about to mount her horse and glared at him.

"Pardon me, have I left you a choice? If so you may dissuade yourself of the notion."

"You beast!" she snapped, as she pulled herself atop the horse. "How dare you invade my privacy and then have the gall to issue yet another order? I care not for your demands. I shall do as I please."

Dominic moved to her side, his expression closed and unreadable as he took the reins in his large hand and held the prancing animal still. His free hand moved over her booted foot to the bare skin of her leg, and Reena couldn't stop the shiver that shook her body.

"Reena, I have no wish to bring you to heel. I fear only for your safety."

Slowly his hand slid beneath her full skirt and up her leg. They were both fully conscious of the fact that she sat naked beneath her petticoat, and Dominic felt a rush of anger that he should be allowed what he desired most.

Reena held her breath as his warm, rough fingers traveled the length of her calf to her knee. She tried to pull away, but his hand held firmly to the animal and kept her in place. Her body tensed as his fingers passed her knee and pressed into the soft flesh of her thigh.

"This will not change anything," she breathed shakily as she stared straight ahead, desperately trying to ignore the effects of his caress. "I will continue to do as I please."

"You may, of course, do just that, Reena," he soothed, his voice growing husky and thick as his fingers reached the junction of her thighs. Unconsciously Reena shifted to allow his access and breathed a sigh of delight as his fingers slid between the soft fold of her warmth. "As long as your actions bring no danger."

Reena had not the strength to object to his words, for they barely registered on her dazed mind. She almost cried out her disappointment as he released her warm flesh and swept her from the horse. Dominic ignored her soft whimper of protest as he held her firmly to him and buried his face in the softness of her loosely flowing hair.

220

"What are you doing?" she choked, as she strained to clear her mind, while her whole body shook with a fire only he could extinguish.

"What I should have done from the first," he returned determinedly. His head dipped, his intent obvious.

"Nay!" she sobbed softly, while holding her hands to his chest, trying to create space between their bodies. "Let me go."

A look of annoyance flickered in his eyes and disgust was clear in his words. "Jesus, but I'm sick to death of chasing you, fighting you and cajoling you. Try if you can, just this once, to act the woman and meet me halfway."

"Dominic, listen to me."

"Nay, my English miss. 'Tis past the time for you to put aside your virginal role and be my wife in truth."

"You promised. What of the bargain?" she cried helplessly, for she knew the limit of her strength lay in his word. If he chose to take her to his bed, she could not hope to fight both of them.

"I promised to let you go in six months' time. Ask no more of me."

"Dominic, please," she begged to deaf ears, as his heart pounded so hard he thought it might burst, and his arms circled her body and pulled her to him again. With a deep hungry growl, his mouth found hers at last.

He felt her soften against him and heard her weakly whispered sighs of protest turn to moans of longing as his mouth moved from hers to taste the clean flesh of her throat and knew she was as caught up as he in the throes of a fiery passion that was beyond their control.

His heart swelled to bursting as she wrapped her slender arms around his neck and held him to her. Why couldn't it always be thus? he wondered, as he lowered her to the ground. After tonight, he vowed, he'd allow no less.

There was no sense in denying her need. She might not want to feel this longing, but the fact was she was dying to touch him. Her fingers threaded through his thick, dark hair and crushed his mouth to hers. Her lips parted beneath the probing of his tongue, and Dominic inhaled her soft sigh deep into his being with a hungry growl.

He was absorbing her into him, so starved for the taste of her his mouth left not a portion of exposed flesh untouched. And when that was no longer enough, his fingers disposed of the buttons of her bodice and his mouth dipped to seek out the sweet, swelling mounds that had so long haunted his dreams.

Reena felt his hand reach beneath her skirt and slide up the naked length of her thigh again, just as his mouth left her breasts. He watched her face as his fingers teased her body, running accurately up her thigh to touch lightly upon her moist warmth and then down again. A slight smile curved the corners of his mouth. "Tell me, love," he coaxed gently, "tell me what you want."

"You," she cried desperately. "I want you."

"Do you want me to do this?" he asked, his voice straining for control as his fingers slid into the folds of her warm flesh.

"Yes," she gasped. "Yes!"

"And more?"

"Oh yes, more," she moaned, almost delirious with need as her hips lifted, her body crying out for his touch.

His strong fingers entered the warmth of her with a powerful thrust, just as his mouth, hot, almost burning, fastened to the tip of her breast and bit down with less than gentle pressure.

She couldn't prevent the soft cry of ecstasy that slipped from her lips. Her blood pounded in her ears as she gasped again and yet again at the mind-exploding pleasure that suffused her body.

"Dominic, my God," she moaned with a deeply guttural sound. Desperately her hands pushed aside his shirt to seek out the hard, warm strength of his muscled chest.

Never stopping the movement of his hands, he lifted

himself so his mouth might taste again the sweetness of hers.

Her hands, too, dipped lower. Unable to open his belt in her anxiousness to touch him, Reena slid her hands over the straining material of his trousers and rubbed her fingers in delicious torment against the undeniable power that ached for release.

"Sweet Jesus," Dominic groaned, his voice echoing the torture that wracked his body as he quickly lowered her dress. He sat up, and as his fingers did justice, for their size, to the tiny buttons of her bodice, he choked, "Should I be forced to stop yet again, I've no doubt serious damage will ensue."

Reena watched with no little amazement until the high-pitched squeals of laughing children and the deeper murmurs of adults began to seep through the thick foliage. Sitting up beside him, she ran her fingers through her hair and adjusted the folds of her long, blue skirt.

He didn't look at her again, but stared toward the sounds of the family some yards away. "Tonight, Reena. I'll wait no longer than that."

Giving her no option but to accept his decision, he stood and mounted his horse. A moment later Reena sat alone in her confusion amid a cloud of flying grass and soil.

Chapter Twenty-four

REENA FORCED HER MIND FROM HER BLACK THOUGHTS and listened to Mary's happy chatter.

"To say I was surprised is a grave understatement. Richard is, after all, but a first mate. I had no idea he lived in such luxury."

"But Mary, do you not realize he has attained his riches through many acts of piracy perpetrated against your own countrymen?"

"I know well enough what he has done, Reena. In truth, I do not condone such action. Indeed I deplore it most vehemently. But the two countries are at war, and I am but a woman who loves a man. Surely you do not believe one small voice will put an end to these happenings?"

"Mary, never believe a voice raised in objection to be of no consequence. Should we all speak out, our governments would have no option but to listen."

"To a woman?" Mary laughed softly at the absurdity of the idea. "I hardly think so."

Reena sighed in disgust. What her cousin said was true. A woman held no voice in anything of importance. She was considered by most to be on a child's level of intelligence. 'Twas more than likely Reena would be scorned and probably sorely abused should she be so daring as to voice her objections.

As a man's wife, the fragment of rights she had possessed had faded to nothing. To all the world she was simply her husband's possession, to do with as he wished. Reena wondered if she'd ever grow accustomed to the ways of the world. Why did she feel so out of place? Why could she not accept the subservient role others felt as right? She cursed this wayward longing, for she knew she'd never find peace as long as she fought against the dictates of society.

For a time the two women walked through the lovely gardens at the rear of the house in silence. Reena watched as Mary cut yet another flower and added it to the assortment the basket already held.

"This will make a beautiful bouquet, don't you think?"

"Indeed."

"I want the table to look especially lovely tonight."

"Are you expecting guests?"

"Not tonight," Mary giggled.

Reena shot her cousin a curious glance. "Is tonight a special occasion?"

"It will be." She laughed again.

Reena smiled at the obvious delight that filled her cousin's bright blue eyes. "I can see you are nearly bursting to tell me. What is it?"

Mary spun away from her with a happy laugh. "Do you see anything different?"

Reena's eyes narrowed with some puzzlement as she studied her cousin's petite form, while Mary swirled in a small circle.

"Do you?"

"What would you have me see?" Reena asked, as her full lips curved into a tender smile. "I can see you are disgustingly happy, but naught else."

"Oh Reena," Mary laughed, "why do you try so hard to act the grump? Before long you will have to try less and then not at all, for you will achieve your ends."

Reena laughed, knowing full well the truth of Mary's words, for she often restrained the deviltry and laughter that threatened in an effort to act the demure lady.

"I believe we were speaking not about myself, but of you."

Mary pressed her high-waisted, light cotton dress to her flat stomach and asked hopefully, "Do you see a difference now?"

Reena gasped as she realized the message behind Mary's actions and asked, "You're not already with child?"

"I am," she laughed happily, as she hugged her cousin. "Is it not wonderful? Richard doesn't know yet. I can't wait to tell him. Do you see it?" she asked again as she moved away, and with bubbling excitement rested her hand against her flat stomach.

"Mary, I hardly think the child could make itself known quite so soon. How can you be sure? You've been married no more than five weeks."

Mary giggled. "Oh I'm sure. Three weeks have past since my last time. I can feel the difference."

At Reena's look of disbelief she laughed and insisted, "I can!"

"Do you feel well? Have you seen a doctor?"

"I feel wonderful."

"And the doctor?"

"I will see him this week." And at Reena's obvious concern she continued. "You need not fear for me, Reena. I want this above all else. Will you not say you are happy for me?"

Reena laughed at her cousin's gentle look of inquiry and hugged her close. "Of course I am happy for you, darling.

How could I be otherwise? It is a wondrous thing to be able to bring a child into the world.''

Reena sighed as she later walked alone amid the lush growth of flowers. Her plan to avoid her husband and his promise of the coming night would not come to be. She could not ask Mary to keep her here tonight. In truth she knew Dominic would not have allowed it in the first place. The man was determined to have her, she could not hide from him for long.

She had no choice but to return home. Her thoughts alternated between despair and growing excitement, for she could not deny the power that lay in his hands to sway her to his will. In a few seconds' time, she could become a lusty wanton pleading for more of the touch of him. She didn't want this, damn it! God help her she didn't want to love him. A wave of despair washed over her, for she knew it was too late. She loved a man who felt only lust in return.

Reena jumped and gave a small sound of surprise at the deep voice that suddenly shook her from her reverie. ''The hour grows close to dinner, Reena. I think it is time to bid our hosts farewell.''

''How long have you been here?''

Dominic gave a slight shrug of a muscled shoulder, and Reena cursed the sudden tightening that clutched at her chest as the trembling ache to touch the hard flesh that was barely hidden by his opened shirt filled her being.

''Richard and I had business to discuss. I was here for much of the afternoon.''

Reena lowered her gaze from his as vivid pictures of this morning's happening flashed through her mind in erotic sequence. Had they not been interrupted, she would have surely allowed him his way with her. Oh God, she groaned silently, at least speak the truth to yourself! You would have demanded it.

A soft flush spread up her neck to brighten her cheeks as she acknowledged the need that throbbed to her very core. Again she lifted her gaze to his and a weight seemed to fall from her shoulders as she made up her mind. She might be leaving here in five months, but she loved him, and for the time being she was his wife. It mattered not that he did not love her in return. It mattered not that this marriage was not a union true. She would use the time she had left. She'd need its memories to fill the empty lifetime that stretched ahead.

"Are you ready, my love?"

Reena's lips lifted into a tender smile as she laid a gentle hand on his offered arm, and Dominic felt his heart thud heavily at the provocative glance she flashed as her smile turned tantalizingly secretive.

"I am, Captain." And then she lowered her voice to a husky whisper that gave clear promise to all she was to give. "More than ready."

Chapter Twenty-five

REENA CHATTERED NERVOUSLY AS SHE DOWNED HER
third glass of wine. Her face was flushed, her eyes sparkled
with a new, fiery glow, while Dominic studied his usually
serene bride from across the small table. His fingers toyed
with his own scarcely tasted wine as his eyes feasted on the
deliciousness of her barely concealed form.

They had taken the evening meal in the private seclusion
of his chambers. Candles, glowing from the mantle and
bedside table, cast them in soft, flattering light. Open
French doors that led to the terrace and gardens allowed a
gentle, warm breeze to stir the flickering flames, while a
few moths circled endlessly about the light, drawn, yet
afraid of the tantalizing warmth that summoned.

Reena watched as one by one they came, mesmerized by
the light, impervious to the danger, only to end their

existence, drawn by a need they were powerless to control. And try as she might, she could not deny the comparison, for Dominic was the flame. Dressed as he was in a loosely tied robe of black silk with most of his dark chest exposed, she could no longer resist the silent call that beckoned.

The silence hung heavy between them when she finally ran out of things to say. No matter the effort, she could not keep up this one-sided conversation.

"May I have another glass?" she asked as she held up her now empty vessel.

Dominic was aware of the turmoil of emotions that raged within his gentle wife, for her face gave clear evidence to her agitation. He longed to ease her fears with a comforting word, but could find naught. That she was willing to lie with him was obvious by her choice of garments. Still, he was more than certain she was nervous about the night to come.

Upon entering the house, he had ordered dinner served in his room, and they had both made their ways to their respective chambers to prepare themselves for the coming night. After a bath and shave, Dominic had sat comfortably relaxed, paging idly through a book on planting, while his mind strayed to the woman who dallied beyond the closed door that separated their rooms.

At Reena's timid knock, he had dropped the book to the floor and made his way across the room. His heart had nearly stopped at the beauty that greeted his dark eyes. An opened robe of gold silk hung in gentle folds from her shoulders, while a gown of gossamer golden tissue displayed her curves and left little to the imagination, but for the strategically placed cambric lace that taunted him to envision what lay beyond. His heart had swelled with joy at finding her thus, and he knew no matter her intention, he could never let her go.

Her hair hung down her back in soft waves of heavy gold, while a thick tendril slid over her shoulder and lay tantalizingly over her breast. He longed to take her instantly to his bed, and would have, but for the knock that announced the serving of their dinner. His fingers had trembled slightly as he pulled the fabric of the robe around her and tied it securely at her waist as he called for his servants to enter.

Once the girls had departed for the night, leaving them alone at last, Dominic had turned again to face her, and his hands had unerringly untied her robe and taken it from her shoulders.

Reena shivered at the dark look of longing that flickered behind his coal black eyes.

"Are you chilled?" he asked, as he ran the tips of his fingers up her bare arm to her shoulders and across the straps of her gown. He raised her chin so he might clearly see the answering desire grow to life in her eyes.

"Nay," Reena whispered, almost unable to speak as his touch sent her nerve endings to tremble violently and her voice to grow husky and raw to her ears.

"I think we should dine before the food cools overmuch."

Reena nodded and moved past him, and Dominic had to force back the groan of pain that twisted at his stomach at the sight of her. The gown dipped down her back, leaving her naked to the rise of her hips, while the transparency of the fabric showed the roundness of her smooth curves and the length of her long, shapely legs.

Dominic smiled as he rose from the table. "You may, of course, have another glass, my love. We will share it later," he promised, as he filled her glass again and took it from her to the bedside stand.

Instantly he was again at her side, his dark fingers covering her small white hand as he silently urged her to her feet and led her toward the bed.

He could feel her tremble as he ran his hand up her arm, his dark gaze moving with tender admiration over her small upturned face as she gave a tiny smile.

"I do not exaggerate, madam, when I say you are easily the most beautiful woman I have ever known," he whispered, as his fingertips played against the fullness of her bottom lip and caused her to tremble yet again.

Reena's eyes clung to his as the tip of her tongue grazed his finger and upon seeing his reaction to the impetuous movement, she closed her lips and drew it more firmly into her mouth.

Dominic closed his eyes as the erotic sensation filled his mind and body with a need he had never before known, and he pulled his hand away, lest the pleasure of this small, shared gesture cause him to hurry this act he longed to prolong.

His fingers, as light as thistle down, moved over the smoothness of her jaw and down the silken length of her throat to her shoulders, and Reena was barely aware that the thin straps of her gown were slid from her shoulders. She saw his eyes widen with pleasure as the garment fell silently to the floor and heard the quick intake of breath he was powerless to prevent.

His eyes feasted greedily over the luscious curves and hollows of her flawless body and Reena knew her vows to leave were empty promises at best, for she suddenly wanted nothing more than to remain at his side.

She watched with eyes heavy with passion as his gaze moved over her. Her shoulders lifted in an unconscious beckoning gesture and it was beyond Dominic's control to resist her silent call. His hands slid to her hips and drew her closer to him and, with a tortured groan, his mouth dipped and caught the tip of her breast between his teeth.

Reena felt her breath catch in the back of her throat at the unexpected touch of his mouth and she swayed dizzily, her knees weak and shaking with a need that seemed to grow in strength at his every look and touch until she was finally no more than a mindless being aching with but one need, one torturous, aching need.

"Dominic," she sighed softly, as her arms locked around his shoulders, holding to him for the only solidness in a swirling world of pleasure. "I can stand no longer."

Dominic's mouth lingered but a moment before he tore his lips from her softness with a strangled moan. His breathing was heavy and ragged as he pulled her close to him. His mouth moved slowly over her golden hair as he fought for control. His hands slid up the slenderness of her back and down again over the fullness of her hips, lifting her slightly as he moved against her. "This is not what I planned. I've a need to prolong this time between us and yet the sight of you leaves me powerless to stop."

Reena's hands slid over the warmth of his chest and circled his neck, her mouth moving with lingering tastings over his throat as she murmured softly, "What is it you had planned, Captain?"

"Would you have me show you?"

"I would." Surprised at her own straightforwardness, she chuckled low and throatily at the obviously brazen invitation, and threw her head back to gaze up at him with total abandon.

Dominic steeled himself against the joy that suffused his being, fearful, should he relax, his control would vanish and bring to an instant conclusion the pleasure he planned. He realized she, too, wished to linger in this act. Of course, it could mean no more than that he was capable of stirring her passionate nature. Still, he suspected there was more to it than that. She was a gently bred lady and would need a deeper involvement, whether she'd admit to it or not, to find true enjoyment in their coupling.

Dominic kicked away her gown and reached behind him for the vial of lightly scented oil he had earlier placed on the night stand. Pouring a dollop into his palm, he rubbed his hands together for a moment before he reached for her shoulders.

"Mmm, gardenia," she sighed as she inhaled the light fragrance. "My favorite scent."

"I know," he returned, his tender gaze locking with the smoky blue of her eyes as he began to massage the liquid into her smooth skin. "When you first spoke to me, actually snarled at me is a more accurate description," he grinned to her low laughter, "I very nearly took you in my arms, and this scent was half the cause."

Reena's eyes opened wide with surprise. "And the other half?"

"You, a tiny bundle of pure outrage. All I could think of was making love to you."

Reena smiled, her eyes half closed with the pleasure his hands brought. "Is it a common occurrence? Do all men think such thoughts upon first meeting?"

"I've no doubt upon meeting you the idea grows rampant."

Unwilling to part from her, he pressed her to him as his hands moved over her back with slow, masterful touchings. His hands slid lower, and he felt the warmth of her softly uttered sigh against his neck as his fingers reached the firm flesh of her rounded hips and kneaded gently. Continuing his downward path, he dropped to his knees, his head pressed firmly to her stomach, his mouth tasting of her clean flesh, until he rounded her ankles and began an upward motion.

Reena gasped as the soothing sensation became more determinedly erotic. His fingers grazed along her inner thigh until she thought she'd go mad if he didn't touch her. Her hands clung to his shoulders for support, and she marveled at her ability to stand at all, as her body trembled with wave after wave of longing growing to terrifying dimensions.

"Dominic," she choked, as his long fingers reached the junction of her thighs at last and delved into the moist, heated flesh he found there.

"Aye, love," he murmured, his voice muffled against the softness of her as he lowered his mouth to nuzzle his lips to the sweetness his fingers had rediscovered.

"Do you think we could lie down," she gasped, and sighed a long, purring sound as his tongue slid between the folds of her sweet, warm body.

Dominic came to his feet again, a sheepish grin lifting the corners of his mouth. "I didn't mean to do that, but I seem to have some difficulty keeping my mind on my original plan."

"Do you?" she sighed, only half realizing she was speaking out loud, as she leaned into him, her fingers running up his neck to the firmness of his jaw and over the sharp contours of his cheeks to the lustrous, curling hair held neatly at his nape with a string of cowhide.

Dominic hesitated, his eyes closed as he allowed her a moment, reveling in the pleasure of her answering caress.

"I love to touch you," she sighed into his chest, as she pushed his opened robe from his shoulders. "Did you know that?"

Dominic's chuckle as he pulled her tighter against him turned into a deep groan as his naked flesh contacted hers. His breathing was shallow and shaken as he gasped into her hair, "Madam, you've done an excellent job of hiding the fact, thus far."

Reena's laugh was low and husky. "I have, haven't I?"

"In the future, should you feel the need to indulge in that particular pastime, you have my permission to do so."

"Have I?" she asked dreamily, her eyes half closed, while her soft lips curved into a lusciously inviting smile that Dominic gave not a moment's hesitation to answering. His mouth covered her parted lips as she ran her hands between their bodies over his chest and stomach to the core of his burning passion. At hearing the strangled moan that escaped from the back of his throat at her delicate touch, she brazenly dared to examine more fully the object that had twice brought her such mindless pleasure.

"In that case, I might do just that," she gasped, as his lips left hers to trail a path of fire to her ear.

"Oh please do," he grinned as he moved away from her, "but not just now."

Reena laughed as she watched him reach again for the

bottle. "If you use any more I shall probably slip out of your arms."

"Not these arms, madam," he returned, as he again rubbed the oil between his palms and proceeded to spread a thin, hot film over her neck and shoulders, down to the soft, heavy flesh that so enticed.

Reena threw her head back, her long, golden hair swirling at her waist with the movement, her eyes closed with sheer delight as she concentrated on the tantalizing strokings that brought such wonder. His hands slithered past her breast and over the rounded flesh of her stomach. Reena swayed noticeably. A low moan was heard at the back of her throat as his fingers slid deep into the moistness of her heated body.

"I grow to believe you begin to enjoy my touching in return," he teased, his eyes studying the blissful expression on her hauntingly beautiful face.

"In truth," she gasped, "should I grow to enjoy it further, I doubt my mind could bear it."

Dominic gathered her into his arms and lifted her to lie across his crisp white sheets.

Reena felt the mattress dip as he knelt beside her, and she looked up to his dark eyes with a puzzled expression as he purposely held himself from her. "I've waited so long for this night. I've a need to see it linger."

"Do you?" she teased softly, a smile curving the lushness of her mouth into an agonizing temptation as she trailed a lone finger down his chest. "What do you suppose we might do to see to its lengthening?"

"Not that," he groaned, as he removed her ever-lowering hand from him.

"Why not?" she taunted brazenly, her mouth forming a beautiful pout. "Do I not allow you the same?"

Dominic's low laugh sounded strained and uncertain as she returned her hands to his chest. "If you continue along this path, madam, you will bring to an instant close the pleasure I've in mind for you. I've waited so long, my control is strung to its limit."

Reena pulled her hands away in a startlingly quick motion. Her eyes rounded with feigned innocence and a smile lifted the corner of her mouth. "Far be it from me to dissuade you from your proposed task, sir. You may proceed."

Dominic laughed. "May I?" he asked, as his head lowered to her breast and took the rosy tip into his mouth.

"Oh, indeed, you may," she whispered softly, as her hands reached for his face, her fingers threaded into his dark, crisp hair. "Is it permissible to touch you here?"

He nodded, and, as his mouth was already occupied, his affirmative answer was somewhat muffled.

"Here?" she asked as her hands moved to his neck and shoulders.

He grunted for an answer.

"Here?" She laughed as she slid her fingers down his sides.

Dominic sat back on his heels. "It appears you've grown a bit cocky, madam. I think you should be shown who is the master here."

"Do you?" she grinned, "and how do you propose to do that?"

In an instant he settled himself between her legs and penetrated her body with a powerful and most welcomed thrust as he grunted, "Like this!"

"Ohhh," Reena groaned, as blinding stars chased each other through her mind. Her eyes were glassy when they opened again.

"Will you concede me the master?" he asked, his voice faltering as she answered his movement with her own.

With willful determination, she forced the pleasure he inflicted from her mind and grinned. "Nay."

Dominic increased the force of his thrusts and brought a sharp gasp from her throat. "Will you?" he demanded.

"Nay," she cried, as she lifted herself. Her arms held to his neck as she rubbed herself purposely across his chest. Her mouth lifted to his and he closed his eyes against the pain of taking it.

"Will you?" he groaned into her opened mouth.

"Dominic, please," she cried out with urgent need against his lips, her body tightening around him.

"Not yet, my love," he breathed as he lowered both of them to lie upon the bed again. "Be still for a moment."

"Dominic," she murmured impatiently.

"Please?" he coaxed as he took her face between his large hands. "For me?"

A smile curved her lips, and she didn't know it, but pure unadulterated love shown within the depths of her blue eyes.

Dominic's chest swelled with triumphant joy, and for an instant he forgot his intent as his mouth reached greedily for hers. There was no question of her leaving him. This beautiful woman was his forever. His arms tightened with desperation. God, he'd never let her go.

His lips left hers with a deep groan and he looked down upon eyes glazed with passion. Her lips, swollen and moist, begged to be taken again. Forcing aside that need, his mouth luxuriated in the texture and taste of her as he lowered his head and allowed his mouth and tongue the pleasure of running the length of her body. He hesitated for a time at her breasts and then stopped again to linger at the heat of her passion. She was as hard as he and equally ready. If he could time this right, it would be something neither would ever forget.

His tongue moved with slow, leisurely strokes over the sweet moistness of her skin until he felt the erection soften and then grow harder than ever. Her hips were lifting from the bed urging him to complete this delectable task as she groaned out her longing.

With a sudden movement, he flipped her to her stomach

and pulled her up against him. With a merciless thrust he entered her softness and heard her sharp cry of delight as he pressed wildly into her warm flesh.

His one hand reached around her hips and continued the gentle massaging where his tongue had been, while the other gently cupped her swollen breast and caressed the tip as he moved his hips with almost violent thrusts.

It happened then, almost immediately, and neither could stop the ecstasy as it crashed around them like a billion lights exploding in a black sky.

Chapter Twenty-six

REENA STIRRED IN HER SLEEP AND GAVE A SOFT, LEISURE-ly sigh as she leaned more fully into the arms of her husband. Her head nestled upon his chest, while a small smile curved the corners of her mouth as she rubbed her silken, smooth leg against his scratchy one and felt his arm tighten around her.

Reena's eyes opened, and her fingertip slid over the smooth muscles of his chest, following the thin black column of hair across his stomach to search out again the strength she knew could grow to life.

A soft blush of pleasure warmed her skin as she realized his passion was again throbbing with need for her. The endless past night and the rapture shared seemed only to instill a greed for more.

She glanced up to his grinning expression and announced in mock surprise, "Oh, you're awake."

"Did you think to have your way with me while I slept, my love?"

Reena giggled as he pulled her to lie over the length of him. "Are all men so hairy?" she asked, while finding it impossible to contain her laughter.

Dominic grinned. "In truth I've not noticed, but the next time I see a naked man, I'll be sure to take note and report back to you."

"Better yet," she returned with a taunting smile, "the next time I see a naked man, *I'll* take note and report back to you."

"It may be some time before that happens."

Reena shrugged and replied with growing preoccupation as she slid her body down the length of his and dipped her mouth to his firm flesh, lower and then lower and finally lower again. "It matters not, right now I have something else to occupy my mind."

A knock sounded at the door and Reena gasped and came instantly from beneath the covers and bounced from the bed.

Dominic took the opportunity offered to watch her slide her creamy body into the shimmering gown. Reena stopped all movement at the sound of his low laughter. A quick look at his amused expression brought a sheepish grin to curve her mouth, while her face warmed with embarrassment.

"Where are you going?"

She shrugged and tried to act as nonchalant as possible, "Oh, I thought since it's such a beautiful day we might go for an early ride."

Dominic grinned at her obvious lie and came smoothly from the bed to stand before her unashamedly naked and heartstoppingly beautiful. "Did you forget you were married?"

"Of course not!" she snapped, and then bit at her lower lip trying to stop a smile. She raised her eyes to his teasing look and couldn't prevent the soft giggle that soon bubbled into full, throaty laughter. "I think I did. I'm afraid I've not yet grown accustomed to this."

"You will in time, my love. Soon it will not seem so illicit," he assured happily, as he lifted her and brought her back to the bed. "It's a shame you went to the trouble of putting that gown on."

"Is it?" she asked feigning puzzlement. "Why do you suppose?"

"It will only have to come off again," he sighed wearily as he flung himself down beside her.

"Have I sapped your strength, Captain?" she laughed softly. "Could it be you're too weak to manage the task?" she asked and, as a teasing light twinkled in her eyes, she came to her knees and ran her index finger down his chest.

"And if I were, what then would you suggest?" he grinned wickedly, as his hand reached beneath the hem of the gown and slid up her thigh.

"See who is at the door and I will show you," Reena sighed, and closed her eyes with pleasure as his fingers found their intended destination.

"Will you?"

"Will I what? Answer the door?"

"Will you show me?"

Reena laughed. "Are you going to answer it or not?"

"No one is there. One of the girls leaves my breakfast outside every morning."

"In that case," she stated, as she slid the silky tissue with slow, deliberate provocation up her body and smiled wickedly as she flung it to a far corner.

Dominic's eyes narrowed with pure enjoyment as the sight of her naked body brought an instant rekindling of a throbbing to his loins.

"Getting pretty brazen for a bride, don't you think?" he grinned, his dark brow raised in a decidedly lecherous fashion.

Reena laughed. "Are you complaining?"

"And if I were?" he sighed, as he folded his arms

beneath his head and closed his eyes as she began to trail her fingertips down his body.

"If you were, I'd not believe you, for there is a part of you that likes me well enough."

Dominic gave a low chuckle, knowing full well of which part she spoke. While their breakfast cooled in the hall, the sound of soft, happy laughter filled the room.

"I'm not taking another step until you tell me where you are taking me."

"Don't you like surprises?"

"I don't know you well enough to know what your idea of a surprise contains. And that particular look in your eyes sends shivers down my back."

"I think it's time you started to trust your husband, madam."

"Not another step, Dominic," she warned with a happy grin, as she dug her heels into the soft earth.

"Very well," he shrugged, and Reena gave a startled cry as he swung her up over his shoulder and held her there.

Reena laughed as he then proceeded to pick up the picnic basket and continue nonchalantly on his way. "Put me down this instant, you wretch! How do you expect me to trust you if you treat me thus?"

Dominic slid his free hand beneath her skirt and up her leg as he ignored her chatter.

"Dominic, stop that!"

"Stop squirming before you fall." He laughed as she jumped when his hand slid higher still.

Reena slapped at his back and squirmed all the more. Between gasping breaths, she cried, "Stop! You're tickling me."

Dominic lowered her to stand before him. His eyes glowed with happiness as he kept his hand beneath her skirt and, holding to her hip, he pulled her closer. " 'Twas not my intention to tickle you, madam."

"I know your intent well enough, Captain," she replied

243

with eyebrows raised and lips puckered with haughty disdain and then collapsed against him in a fit of giggles.

"God," Dominic groaned as he held her to him, "for just a minute I thought you had reverted back to that prim and proper miss I married."

"Was she so awful?"

"On the contrary, she was most delightful, if a bit of a prig."

"In truth?" She grinned innocently. "I thought she was very sweet."

"Oh, indeed she was, but hardly the type to let me lift her skirts in broad daylight."

"I fear you are correct, sir. It seems I have grown accustomed to your barbarian ways."

Dominic chuckled into the softness of her hair and felt his body harden as he breathed deeply of her own special scent, knowing that to touch her only caused him to want her more. "Will everything I say come back to haunt me?"

Reena gave a soft, husky laugh as she allowed her face the pleasure of nuzzling his chest. "If so, you must carefully weigh your every word, Captain."

"In the future I will do just that," he assured, as he lowered his mouth to caress her cheek.

"What is that sound?"

"That's the surprise. Are you ready to trust me now?"

"I fear I must, Captain, for my stomach rebels at the thought of repeating my last position."

"Come along then," he coaxed gently, as he took her hand and once again led the way.

Dominic stepped from the thickly bordered path into a clearing. Holding aside a heavy branch, he guided her to stand before him. Reena's eyes grew wide with wonder as she took in the clear, white water that bounded over magnificent black boulders into a deep, frothy pool.

"Oh Dominic, it's lovely," she gasped, her eyes aglow with delight as she took in the natural beauty of the tiny, secluded cove.

Dominic's arms circled her petite form as he held her slim back pressed to his chest. His head lowered and his chin rested on her head as he spoke, "Since you seem to have a penchant for swimming, I thought you would enjoy this."

"Will I be swimming today?" She grinned and turned her head to look up at him.

"You will."

"Will you be joining me?" she teased, knowing full well his intentions.

"I will."

"Perhaps I shall forego the swim today and simply enjoy the beauty of this cove—and your delightful company, of course," she teased, as she rested comfortably against him.

"Perhaps," he agreed, with an elaborate shrug. "But then again, you might as well swim since you will be dressed for it."

"Will I?" she laughed softly, as he stepped back from her and began to undo the many buttons that secured her dress.

"Suppose someone should come across us?"

"You gave not a care to that possibility yesterday."

"Aye, but I was far inland then and protected by thick greenery. This cove offers a clear view of the sea and equal sightings to anyone who might pass by."

"As you can see, there are no boats about, madam. The cove is not noticeable at any distance. We will be safe from inquisitive eyes here."

Reena smiled with delight and offered not a word of protest as Dominic eased her dress and chemise over her arms, leaving her shoulders delectably bare and inviting. Dominic, not being a man to resist this sweet beckoning, could not help but kiss the softness of her luscious flesh. And as the dress and undergarments fell away, his mouth continued to follow its delicious path down the length of her.

"I think perhaps I should use you for my maid, sir, for you have an obvious talent for helping a lady undress."

Dominic chuckled at her comment. As he pushed her stockings and pantalettes down her legs, his teeth grazed over the fullness of her derrière.

"Surely, you've had much experience along these lines."

Wisely he did not respond to that dangerous question.

But Reena, feeling an unaccustomed twinge of jealousy at his silence, was not of a mind to let the matter drop. "Well, have you?" she insisted, as she looked over her shoulder.

"Not as much as you'd like to believe, I'm sure."

"I'd like to believe you've had none," she snapped before she thought, and then gave a silent curse, knowing that her impulsive words implied a jealousy she wanted to deny.

Dominic laughed as he stood and pulled her into his arms. His breath was warm against her neck as he spoke, "Reena, surely you'd not expect a man of a score and thirteen to have remained celibate?"

"Indeed? And why not?" she returned, as she lowered her face so he'd not see her smile, while wondering how he would try to soothe her supposed anger.

"Reena, be reasonable. A man, well, a man . . ."

"A man is to be accepted, no matter the extent of his whoring, while a woman is to remain pure. Is that it?" she snapped, and silently applauded herself at her acting ability, for she knew he believed her to be upset.

"The ways of the world are not always fair, my love. Reena, please, I'd not see this beautiful day spoiled with angry words," he coaxed, as he ran his hand down her back.

Reena grinned at his chest and murmured, "I hope you *mean* that," just before she grabbed his shirt, swung him off balance, and finished with a mighty shove.

Reena knew the look of pure astonishment that crossed

his face would forever live in her mind's eye. She was doubled over with laughter as he went over the ledge and into the water fully clothed.

Slowly he pulled himself back to dry land, but Reena felt not the slightest trepidation. No matter his reaction, the look on his face was worth any retaliation.

Water ran from his hair in smooth rivulets down his face. His shirt and pants were plastered to his muscled form, and Reena couldn't control the leap of her heart as she studied his manly physique.

"I hope you realize that was a serious mistake," he taunted, as he discarded his soaked shirt and reached for the buckle of his belt.

"Oh, I don't know," she giggled softly, trying to rein in the merriment she felt, "I rather enjoyed it myself." Reena laughed at the humor she found in his eyes as she backed away from his obvious stalking. "I'd say 'twas gentle enough retribution for a life of debauchery."

Dominic removed his pants and boots, never taking his eyes from her. "You should thank the ladies in question, madam, for without their expertise, I would not have gained the knowledge I now possess, and you would have lost out in the end."

Reena grinned as he backed her into the trunk of a tree. She ran a fingertip down his wide, hard chest and over his flat belly with taunting deliberation. "Oh indeed, sir, I do thank them, but I do not thank you." She shrugged almost imperceptibly, "One would think a man of such intelligence and capabilities could have found other means to come across this knowledge."

"Being?"

Reena shrugged again, while having a hard time controlling the grin that threatened, "Conversation, literature, perhaps a visit to a farm."

Dominic laughed at the devilish gleam in her eyes. "Madam, as a child I was often told the best way to learn my lessons was to do them myself."

Dominic watched in rapt fascination as droplets of water fell from his hair and trickled into a smooth stream to the tip of her breast. Without hesitation, he cupped the heavy mound in his palm and lifted it to run his tongue with aching sensuality along its rosy tip, catching the cool water in his mouth.

Reena gasped as his lips lingered and drew her cool flesh deep into the heat of his mouth. "I begin to see your reasonings, sir," she managed weakly. "Perhaps another lesson is in order, for I suddenly feel an uncontrollable thirst for knowledge."

"Do you?" Dominic asked, as he straightened again, a grin teasing the corners of his mouth.

"Oh aye," she sighed, as she lifted her hands and slid them over the sinewy muscles of his shoulders to entwine around the strong column of his neck.

"Do you realize now my need to have learned so much?"

"Mmmm," she moaned, as her lips seared a path against his throat.

"Are you sorry, then, for your mistreatment of this poor student?"

Reena giggled as she relaxed her hold. "Not likely."

"Somehow I didn't think you would be."

With a suddenness that left her dizzy, he swooped her into his arms and jumped into the pool. Before she had a chance to squeal out her surprise, she was under the water.

The pool was frothy only at its surface, and when Reena opened her eyes, she could clearly see her husband smiling broadly before her. She lifted a small fist and made to hit him in the jaw. Dominic never bothered to deflect the blow, for she moved against the weight of the water as if in slow motion.

His hands reached instead for her waist and pulled her against him, enjoying fully the feel of her wet, slippery nakedness against his as he guided her to the surface.

Barely had she a chance to gasp for air before she punched his shoulder and ranted, "You wretch! That's the second time today you have flung me around. Is this a taste of what I should expect?''

Dominic chuckled as he pulled her to him yet again, while keeping them afloat as he effortlessly treaded water. ''If I remember correctly, madam, you pushed me in first.''

''Aye, but you flipped me over your shoulder and *then* you threw me into the water.''

''Does that mean you owe me yet another form of retaliation?''

''Doesn't it?'' she teased evilly, while grinning a secret smile.

''Oh, no you don't,'' he groaned as he released her. ''I'll not be able to sleep thinking you might sneak up on me at any moment. Whatever you're going to do, do it now.''

Reena laughed, suddenly filled with delight that she could instill trepidation in this huge man. Her eyes grew huge with mock disbelief. ''It couldn't be that you're afraid, Captain, not of one so small as me?''

Dominic groaned as he pulled her back into his arms. ''Woman, I'd be a fool not to fear you no matter your tiny stature.''

Reena chuckled low and huskily as she gladly succumbed to the intoxicating warmth of his body. Her arms circled his neck and she tugged so she might again feel those wonderful lips against her own. ''You need not fear me, Captain,'' she murmured, as his lips left hers to taste the sweetness of her tiny ear. ''Right now I have but one thought in mind.''

Slowly, they sank beneath the water's surface, so involved had they become with each other they didn't even notice.

Chapter Twenty-seven

REENA SIGHED WITH LAZY CONTENTMENT AS SHE RAISED her soapy leg and watched the water run in smooth rivulets from her skin back into the bath. A tiny smile tugged at the corners of her full, pink lips. After spending most of the afternoon in the pool, she was certainly clean enough. Still, no matter the beauty of the cove, it could not compare to the luxury of a warm, scented bath.

Resting her head back against the rim of the tub, she eyed the filmy, muted rose gown that awaited her use. Her closets overflowed with garments since the second week of her arrival and she finally had had to insist Dominic stop ordering more. Reena had not actually counted them, but she was sure she could go two months without wearing the same dress twice. Even though she knew her husband to be wealthy, this kind of extravagance embarrassed her.

Dominic had allowed Reena free choice in her daily

wear, but when it came to the nights his opinion held forth, and she owned nothing but the sheerest of garments.

"'Tis well the climate is constantly warm," she mused to the empty room. "Back in England I'd likely freeze in these gowns."

Reena came to her feet and blotted her damp skin dry with a towel. A moment later she slid the Grecian-style gown over her head and secured the catch at one shoulder. The thin material barely covered her breasts as it plunged from her shoulder to beneath her other arm, and Reena wondered why she bothered wearing anything at all, for it left nothing to the imagination.

She took the combs from her hair and brushed the golden waves into a mass of free-flowing curls that ran nearly to her waist. The slightest touch of fragrance between her breasts and she was ready.

Dominic was waiting for her and, although they had made love countless times since last night, the look in his dark eyes when they had returned to his home left her without a doubt that his hunger had yet to be appeased. She laughed softly as she reached for the door that separated their rooms, for she hoped it never would be.

Dominic waited impatiently for his bride to finish her preparations and join him. Already his arms ached to hold her. He had sworn never to let a woman close to him again, but he couldn't help it. She was an obsession, one he knew he'd never tire of, for no matter how many times he held her in his arms, he only wanted her more.

He was nearly at the point of seeing what was taking her so long when a soft knock sounded at his door. At his call to enter Diah timidly pushed open the door, "Captain, the mare is in foal and Jackson thinks she's in trouble."

Dominic nodded. "I'll be right there. Will you let Mrs. Riveria know where I've gone? And tell her I'll be back as soon as I can."

"Yes, sir," the housekeeper responded, her head held subserviently low.

Dominic never noticed the gleam of satisfaction that filled her dark eyes as he opened his closet and set out a clean change of clothes, nor did he see the tiny smile that threatened her soft lips as she left the room.

A few moments later, Diah watched from the shadows of a bedroom doorway as Dominic left his room and dashed down the wide, curving steps that led to the enormous front entrance. She moved quickly, for if her plan was to succeed, she had to be found already in his room.

The door closed soundlessly behind her and she instantly opened the buttons that secured her bodice. She hated the dress she was forced to wear as his housekeeper and longed for Dominic to see her in the comfortable, flowing garments of an island woman. The bright garb she wore by night cast her coffee-colored skin in its best light and allowed her full figure the freedom to sway with her every step.

Diah had no doubt once she rid this house of that English bitch Dominic would take notice of her at last. Perhaps he would need her comfort then. She knew he was tired from his travels. He could not stay here and continue to ignore her. She'd make sure he couldn't.

Diah rumpled the bed with one quick toss of the spread and was pulling her arm from her dress when she heard the door open behind her. She spun on her heel, her naked breasts swaying free of the gown as she reversed her action and began to pull it up around her.

"Oh, I'm sorry, madam. The captain led me to believe you were asleep. I should have hurried. He will be so angry with me. Please, madam, you will not tell. Please!" she begged, suddenly filled with real fear that should the captain hear of this, she'd not only lose her position, but any chance she might have had with him as well.

Reena's eyes widened with shock and disbelief as she watched the young woman straighten the bed and finish with the buttons of her bodice. But no matter how she wished it not to be, she could not deny what her eyes saw. The woman was obviously terrified at being caught. This was no act.

For a long moment Reena couldn't manage to breathe in or out and thought she might faint dead away from the simple lack of oxygen as she listened to the woman's terrified pleas. The room seemed to tilt at an odd angle and she clung to the door jamb for support as she finally freed her mind of its stranglehold of shock.

In her heart she had suspected from the first. Why then had she been so surprised? Many men took mistresses and saw nothing wrong in the act. Simply because he denied involvement with his staff, did not make it so. Diah was a beautiful woman. Even Dominic had admitted it to be so.

He never professed a tenderness for you, she cried silently. Simply because he enjoys your body does not ensure fidelity. You knew he did not love you!

Reena raised her head a little higher and struggled to keep at bay the pain that threatened to crush her with its force. If he wanted Diah, he could have her, but by God, he couldn't have them both.

To her amazement her voice barely shook at all when she finally interrupted the frightened woman's tirade. "You need not fear, for I will tell no one."

And after watching the terror subside in the servant's eyes, she asked in a more tender tone, "Would you come into my room, please? I'd like you to pack a bag for me."

Diah looked at her with no little amazement. Was it this easy? Why hadn't she thought of it before? Controlling her urge to laugh was probably the hardest thing she'd ever have to do.

"Yes, madam," the housekeeper whispered, as she lowered her head and preceded Reena into her room.

"Do you know where the captain is Diah?" Reena asked, as she stripped away her gown and began to dress.

"At the stables, ma'am," Diah returned, as she quickly folded a dress and two changes of underclothes into a bag.

"Will he be long?" Reena questioned, as she took several pieces of jewelry from her case and a handful of coins from her top drawer and stuffed them into the bag.

"A mare is in foal. He has gone to help."

"You may retire for the night, Diah. If the captain asks for me, remember you know nothing."

"Yes, ma'am."

Diah watched, no longer hiding her satisfaction. A broad smile spread across her lips as Reena moved quickly down the steps and out into the night.

In her wildest dreams she'd never imagined it could be so simple. Diah felt not a flicker of remorse. "Stupid girl," she murmured softly, "a woman who won't fight for her man doesn't deserve him in the first place."

Hours later Dominic came slowly up the stairs. He was tired, but elated. Jezebel had foaled a beautiful black colt, and he couldn't wait to show Reena the much-prized addition to his stables. She'd be sleeping now. He hoped she was in his bed. Right now, he wanted a few hours of sleep, but he wanted it at her side.

Silently, he opened the door to his room. Even though the room was dark, he knew it was empty. Somehow, even asleep, her presence seemed to fill it with warmth, and he felt only a cold emptiness. Dominic gave a low grunt of annoyance. Now he'd have to bring her to his bed, the bed in her room being too short to accommodate his length. He lit a candle on the bedside stand and crossed to the connecting door.

"Good God!" he gasped as his eyes took in the chaos. Clothes were flung every which way. Dress after dress had been taken from the closet and now littered the floor. Drawers were left open and undergarments hanging out. Reena's jewelry box was upside down and pieces of jewelry glittered coldly in the soft candle light.

What the hell had happened? "Reena!" he called, unmindful of the sleeping house as he dashed from the room. "Reena, where the hell are you?"

A quick, fruitless search of the lower floor only caused his heart to hammer wildly in his chest. He could hardly breathe as the fear clutched at his heart. What had happened to her? Sweet Jesus, had someone taken her? Is that why her room looked like that? "Reena!" he bellowed, as he took the stairs three at a time to the third floor.

"Diah! Diah, answer me," he yelled as he pounded on her door. "Damnation, girl, open this door!"

An instant later Diah opened the door and stood facing him in a loosely tied robe that covered little more than the dusky rose of her nipples, but Dominic never even noticed.

"Have you seen her? Have you seen Mrs. Riveria?"

And when she rounded her eyes as if surprised and shook her head, it was all he could do not to spread his fingers around her throat and squeeze the life out of her, and he hadn't a clue as to why he should feel this sudden rage.

"Dress yourself and wake up the girls. I want this house searched . . . now!"

In a flash he was gone, running so fast down the three flights of stairs that he nearly lost his balance and tumbled down the last few steps. The front door slammed against the wall. In his terror he had pulled it from its hinges. He was outside now, jumping over the vine-covered railing that bordered the front steps and running as if the devil himself gave chase.

"Jackson, get your lazy ass out of that bed," he bellowed as he entered the stables. By the time he reached the room at the back, the small man was running out to meet him.

"My wife is missing. Get every man you can find and search the grounds. Don't come back till you've found her."

As he spoke he was leading his horse from its stall. Too hurried and panicked to saddle the stallion, he gripped its mane and pulled himself on top.

"I'm going to the Steeles' place to get more men. Take a rifle with you. If you find her fire it three times."

Dominic rode through the black night, pushing his horse

to its limit, unmindful of the dangers of the unpaved country road, as a stream of unconscious curses mingled with prayer and echoed in the night.

He had to find her . . . he had to! Nothing could happen to her. Not now! Please God, not now. But despite his insistence, an icy cold certainty filled his heart and held him almost paralyzed with terror. She wouldn't just leave, not after the things they shared last night and today. She wouldn't!

As Dominic pushed his horse at breakneck speed, Reena squirmed around the lump in the mattress and punched the flat pillow into some semblance of comfort. Lying down again, she forced away the heaviness that nearly crushed her chest and made it almost impossible to breathe.

You suspected it from the first, Reena. You have no one to blame but yourself. The man is a rotter and you're better off without him. My God, he promised you nothing! He merely wanted your body for a time. Can't you get that through your head?

She stared up at the dark ceiling over her bunk, her eyes burning with the need to cry as she felt the ship begin to sway as it put out to sea. Every moment took her further away from the beast, and yet she felt no relief, but instead the discomfort in her chest intensified to pain.

You can't allow his lechery to affect you so. You were a fool to love him, she raged, but surely you can just as easily stop. Of course, she sighed, and gave a weak imitation of a smile. In a few weeks you will have forgotten this ugly mess and everything will be as it was.

He is not worth a single tear, damn it, and I'll not give him the satisfaction. "I'll not, oh God, I'll not," she cried out loud, as her throat closed with choking emotion and her face turned with wracking sobs into the pillow.

Chapter Twenty-eight

REENA SPLASHED COOL WATER OVER HER PUFFY EYES AND cursed her own weakness. It had been two weeks since leaving Dominic's home—weeks of pure torture and near starvation, and she had done it all to herself! What is the matter with you, Reena? she questioned silently. How could you allow that beast to hold you in such power?

Can you not understand his kindness was no more than an act? A devious plan to break down your defenses. How could you let him hurt you so?

"'Tis over, Reena," she sighed softly, as she straightened her shoulders. You're made of sterner stuff than this. You will not spend the rest of your life whining because of the heartlessness of one man. You do not need him. You never have. 'Tis past time for you to put this nightmare behind you and begin again.

Quickly she pushed her brush through the heavy mass of

golden curls and tied its length at the nape with a soft, pink ribbon. She was going up on deck. After spending days on end in this airless cabin, she'd had enough of self-pity. It was time to begin anew. She'd go home and open that school and she'd be damned if she'd ever think of the brute again.

Dominic paced the deck of his ship endlessly. His fingers ached with the need to spread around the deliciousness of her throat and squeeze the life from her. How had he fallen so fully under her spell not to have known her for what she was? You fool! You goddamned, stupid fool! he ranted in silent frustration while his fisted hand swung constantly into his opened palm.

Not a man on board dared address him, for the look of murder was clear in his eyes and had not diminished since he realized the means of her escape.

In his mind he relived the night of terror upon finding her gone. Only one ship had left port that day two weeks ago, and he knew she had to be on it. Without a moment's hesitation he had set out to follow. An evil smile crossed his lips. He would find the bitch, he vowed, and when he did, she'd curse the day she was born.

They were all the same. Why was he fool enough to have believed this one different? Why did the erotic pictures of her writhing beneath him, begging for his touch never leave his mind? He felt bewitched and knew, no matter his hatred, he'd never be free of wanting her.

His hands clasped together behind him. His feet spread for balance as he stood in the bow of the ship and silently urged the wind to hurry them toward Charleston and Reena. He had to get there in time. He had to find her.

Reena forced a smile to her pale lips as the crew and passengers hustled about in varying degrees of excitement. Charleston was in sight, and the captain had informed her they would be docking in no more than three hours.

"I'm happy to see you have gotten your sea legs of late, madam. I've known many a stout lad to succumb on their first voyage."

Reena smiled and allowed him to believe she had stayed in her cabin due to illness. In truth it had been an illness of sorts. An illness of the spirit. An illness she'd never suffer again. "Thank you for your concern, captain, but I am quite well now."

"Do you have someone waiting for you in Charleston?"

"Nay, Captain," she smiled gently. "I know no one in that city. My intent is to book passage home as soon as possible."

Captain Cummings shook his head and gave a kindly smile to the lovely woman at his side. "Not an easy task, Madame Riveria, what with the war and all."

"I am aware of the difficulties, sir," she returned. "Still, I've no doubt I'll find a way."

"Would you be in need of a place to stay while you work out your plans? I know of a number of boarding houses I could put you in touch with."

"Thank you again, Captain, but I'm sure that will pose no problem."

With some puzzlement, Captain Cummings realized an instant anger. What the hell was the matter with this lady's husband to allow her to travel unescorted and in such dangerous times?

He shrugged aside his thoughts. 'Twas no concern of his how a man treated his wife. Still, he couldn't resist one last offer, "My ship will be in Charleston for close to two weeks while we unload and take on a new shipment. If you find yourself in need, please do not hesitate to call on me."

Reena thanked the captain, but remained adamant. She'd depend on no man, for no matter their degree of civility, she knew not one among them that she could trust.

Reena bid goodbye to the solicitous captain and left the ship almost as soon as the wooden planks were set in place. First things first. She had to find a man of business in order to sell her jewelry. Then she would secure a place to stay and begin inquiries about a ship home.

The docks teemed with bustling humanity. Reena looked about with wide-eyed amazement as ships were unloaded by huge, half-naked black men, singing out a rhythmic foreign chant, while white men, in stiff-necked white shirts and jackets, stood about with sweaty faces, arguing for the best price on a particular shipment.

In a few cases, cartons and crates were opened right on the dock and the wares loaded into open carts. The new owners of this merchandise added their own voices to the chaotic atmosphere as they began calling out their spectacular bargains, no more than a few feet away.

Ragged children ran in and out of the busy crowd, laughing as one of them snatched a lady's purse. Suddenly a group of angry men gave noisy chase, one of them almost knocking Reena over in his haste.

A few men gave her leering, knowing looks, but Reena breathed a sigh and felt more at ease once she noticed the number of lone women that seemed to wander aimlessly about. Apparently, no one thought it unusual for a lady to travel unescorted in this country. Her relief was short lived however, once she came close enough to notice the indecent cut of the lady's clothes and the brightly painted lips that curved into a hungry smile every time a man crossed her path.

Reena couldn't control the heat of embarrassment that flooded her cheeks when she clearly overheard one of the women offer a seaman a time he wouldn't soon forget, for a tidy sum of cash.

Unconsciously, she hurried her step, anxious to be gone from this place. Quickly, she moved away from the endless line of huge ships toward what she hoped was relative safety, only to find herself more firmly surrounded by an even seedier populace. She had noticed no carriages for hire and dared not ask one of these leering louts who wandered lazily through the hot streets for help.

Perspiration began a slow trickle down her sides and back, and she could feel the small hairs on the back of her neck grow rigid, while a shiver of gooseflesh spread over her. Two men were definitely and quite obviously following her.

What a fool she had been to have rejected Captain Cummings' offer of help. The thought occurred to return to the ship, but she dismissed it as impossible, for she'd have to turn and face the men and somehow get past them.

Again she increased her pace, but ignoring their jeering and suggestive remarks only seemed to entice them into bolder action.

Reena stopped short and gasped as the contents of a full slop pot flew from the open doors of a dark doorway. Its vile contents came horribly close, and Reena almost gagged and momentarily forgot her tormentors at the obnoxious odor.

The bawdy laughter at her back instantly reminded her of the danger of dallying overlong and she again hurried on.

Her light bag grew heavy as she struggled to keep up the pace, and she silently prayed for help. The men were on each side of her now, casually stroking her arms and hair at will and there was not a soul about to lend her aid.

From the swinging doors of yet another building stepped a tall dark man to the uneven wooden sidewalk. The cut and fit of his coat and the cleanliness of his shirt and breeches professed him to be a gentleman of some consequence and Reena lunged toward him without a moment's hesitation.

"Sir, please, excuse me for being so bold, but I've a desperate need to impose upon your kindness. Would you hail me a cab?"

Jack Reed looked down at the beautiful young woman whose wide blue eyes clearly begged for help. A soft smile curved his thin mouth beneath a neatly trimmed mustache as his gaze slid down the length of her in frank appreciation.

Christ, his luck was good today. His pocket bulged with the rewards of a night spent at the gaming tables. No sooner did he call it quits when a lovely fresh piece dared to stop him in broad daylight to offer a good toss. Jack Reed was accustomed to the women of the street and in his time had heard every excuse imaginable to start a conversation, with the purpose of ending under the sheets. He gave her a beautiful smile as he realized hers was the most original yet.

A closer look proved most agreeable, and he felt the beginnings of a stirring in his loins as he studied the fullness of her lips. In truth, this one looked less a whore than a lady, which only seemed to further entice. Still, it was obvious what she was, and he absentmindedly patted the bulge in his pocket, wondering how much she would cost him.

Were these her pimps? he wondered, as his gaze shifted to the two men who were now edging back. If so, she definitely needed to raise her sights, for they could only bring her the lowest in trade.

"Do you know these men?" he asked, waiting for either of them to name her price.

"Nay, sir," she breathed with a wave of relief, as she realized he was about to help her. Still, a quick look at the viciousness of their expressions caused her to hold back the worst of her condemnations. "My ship docked some two hours past and it seems I've become hopelessly lost while trying to find lodgings." Her voice shook as she continued, "I believe these two gentlemen were trying to help."

Jack was momentarily taken back by the refinement of her speech, but a moment later reasoned her to be English, and in all likelihood they all spoke like that. He allowed another smile in the hopes of coaxing her to name her price. A quick glance at the two behind her reaffirmed his first thought. These two bastards wouldn't help their own mothers out of a burning pit. They were her pimps all right, if not she would have surely complained of their presence.

"How much?" he asked, wanting done with the game.

"Excuse me?" Reena asked, more than a bit confused at his question.

"How much do you want?"

"Oh," Reena returned, still puzzled at the oddness of his phrasing. These Americans certainly had a most peculiar way of speaking. "Well, I have no idea the usual cost of a room. Do you know?"

Jack smiled and decided to play along with her game, knowing, of course, she was discussing her price. "Well, I imagine cleanliness and age play a factor."

Reena frowned. "Aye? I thought the prices rose according to their elegance. The most expensive are usually in the better parts of town. Is that not so?"

"It is," he returned quite honestly, for he himself had once had a mistress set up in her own house in one of the better neighborhoods, until his luck had forced him to find her another protector.

His dark eyes again studied the softness of her lips and he wondered if it wasn't time to begin again. The last one cost him a pretty penny, but it was a pleasant experience knowing she was only his and waiting for him to come as he pleased.

Still, he'd need more cash than he could now lay his hands on for that circumstance to come about. For the time being, a room would suffice. Perhaps, if his luck held and she were available in the near future, he might take advantage of her obvious offering on a more permanent basis.

"I live around the corner and down the block."

Reena started, her eyes opening wide with dawning fear. "Excuse me?"

So she wanted to go to her place did she? Well, Jack wasn't a lad, still wet behind the ears. No doubt the minute he got his pants off, her two friends would come barging in and take him for all he was worth.

He gave a flippant shrug. She could take it or leave it. He

wasn't going anywhere but home. "Like I said, I live around the corner and down the block." And then to keep up the game she seemed intent on playing, he added, "I think there might be rooms to let, if you've a mind."

"Oh indeed, sir," Reena smiled brightly, her fears washed away in a rush of relief. He was going to help her. Thank God! she groaned silently.

Reena wobbled noticeably; the torment of the past weeks had taken its toll. She had missed most of her meals aboard ship, too embarrassed by her weepy appearance to leave the cabin, too miserable to care.

Jack noticed her sudden trembling. "When was the last time you ate?"

"I think I had something yesterday," Reena answered weakly, and felt herself lean helplessly into him as a gray mist closed over her eyes and turned the sunny world into night.

Jack muttered a low curse as he lifted her limp form into his arms. What the hell was the world coming to, when a beautiful whore couldn't make the price of a meal? Jesus, he groaned silently as he gazed down into her exquisite face. Her skin was creamy white, her lashes unusually dark for one so fair. He laughed softly and wondered if she was truly fair. Her mouth was full, and he knew it would be deliciously soft beneath his. This one deserved diamonds and furs and the best home in the city. How the hell had she gotten herself involved with these two bastards? They must be taking every cent she made.

Jack kicked aside the bag that had fallen from her hands and watched the two blokes lunge for it. With a shrug he turned to reenter the gaming hall. "Molly!" he called from the open door. "For Christ's sake, Molly, get your fat arse up and lend me a hand."

A moment later a woman, a bit more than pleasantly plump and just past her prime, stepped from behind a red, threadbare curtain that led to a hall off the large room.

"Jack!? What are you doing back here?" And then

noticing the girl in his arms, she snapped, "Oh, no you don't. Get her out of here!"

Jack ignored her as he passed her rigid form and headed for one of the rooms at the back.

"I told you to get rid of her," she complained, as she followed him down the hall. "This is a respectable place, damn it. I ain't motherin' any street whores back to health."

And as he continued to ignore her, she ran up behind him and raged, "Damn it, Jack, did you hear me?"

"Open the door, Molly, and shut that wailing. She's not sick. She hasn't eaten since God knows when. As a matter of fact, neither have I. Ask Jess to rustle up something, will you?"

"It's goin' to cost you for the room and the food. I don't give nothin' away anymore."

"All right, all right, just get going and close the door behind you."

Chapter Twenty-nine

REENA OPENED HER EYES A FEW MINUTES LATER TO A darkened room that smelled nauseatingly of stale whiskey and unwashed bodies. She was lying on a bare, dirty mattress; three buttons of her high-necked dress were opened to allow unrestricted breathing, while a strange man sat rubbing her wrists in an apparent attempt to revive her.

But he wasn't a stranger. She remembered him from somewhere. Who was he? Where was she? She started suddenly. Where was her bag? "Oh my God!" she gasped as she tried to sit, only to be forced back.

"Take it easy. You fainted. There's no need to fret. Molly is bringing something to eat, and when you're feeling stronger we can go." Damn if she didn't act the prim and proper miss. This one missed her calling, all right. She should have been on the stage.

Tears misted her blue eyes, causing them to glow almost

iridescently. She dreaded asking, but she had to know. "Where is my bag?"

Jack shrugged. "The two you were with took it when you fell."

"Oh no! Oh God, what am I going to do? Everything I owned was in there. I can't even pay for the food you ordered."

"Don't worry about that now," Jack grinned. God, she was good. "I'm sure we can think of something that will put you to rights."

He turned from Reena's suspicious look at the sound of a knock.

Reena's eyes narrowed. What kind of a place was this? Where had he taken her? And how did he mean to help her? For the moment Reena pushed her doubts and fears aside as the aroma of hot beef came to tease her senses. God, she was starved. She'd worry later of her precarious position. Right now, she had to eat.

At that very moment, Dominic was walking away from Captain Cummings' ship. His face was set in a grim mask of cold rage. She was gone. She lost no time leaving the ship. It would be nearly impossible to find her in this city, but by God, he would do it. He would do it if it took forever, and when he did, he was going to kill her.

"Mr. Wingate," he called, when once again aboard his own ship.

His first mate came immediately to his side, "Aye, sir."

"Mr. Wingate," he began, his barely controlled rage making it difficult to talk as a rational human being. "I want you to take every available hand and search this city from top to bottom. She is here and I intend to get her back. I want you to find her. Find her tonight!"

Dominic paced the nearly empty deck throughout the day. At dusk he gave a vile curse born of frustration and moved down the gangplank at last. He was doing no good here, and this waiting was tearing him to pieces. He would find her himself. He'd find her if it meant taking this town apart plank by plank until it was nothing more than a huge pile of rubble.

Elijah Boone was disgusted. This wild goose chase his captain had sent him on was a waste of time. The town practically overflowed with whores, and here he was searching for the captain's missus and losing out on all the fun.

If she didn't want to stay, why didn't he just let her go? Christ, he grunted, thinking of his own harpy. We should all be so lucky.

There wasn't a port in the world where a man couldn't find a juicy piece. Why did he insist it had to be her? With his luck some poor bastard would find her, and they'd all be ordered back to the ship before he had a chance to accommodate even one of these ladies.

"Oh God," he groaned, as a luscious piece came up to him. How the hell was he going to refuse her? Shit! Where was the fairness in this godforsaken world?

Elijah closed his eyes against the pounding of his blood as the gaudily dressed whore sauntered up close. He could smell her perfume, and if it wasn't splashed on the cleanest body in the world, what matter was that to him? Her eyes widened with obvious hunger and fastened themselves to the growing bulge at his groin as she licked at her lips.

Elijah groaned a silent curse. That damn blouse she wore gaped so low she nearly lost it all as she swung her shoulders in silent invitation. Her skin was white against the red ruffled material. She looked soft and cushiony, just the way he liked them, and he could easily imagine how good she'd feel lying beneath him.

He'd have her, damn it! To hell with his captain. To hell with orders. But what if he was seen? Oh Christ, he couldn't give up a ripe piece like this.

"Suppose I make it worth your time," he asked, his voice already growing husky and thick as he forced aside his passion, "do you think you could help me find some-one?"

"Honey," she grinned, her expression showing her clear reluctance and obvious disappointment, for she had been sure this one was a likely customer, "I might be a lot of things, but I don't snitch."

The hell she didn't. There wasn't a soul that walked these streets that wouldn't rat on their own kid if the right temptation was offered. "Lady, I ain't askin' for you to turn anybody in to the law. I just want to know if you seen or heard of a lady new to these parts. She's blond, and about this tall," he held up his hand to his shoulder. "She ain't used to bein' on her own. Her husband's afraid she got herself in some trouble."

"I ain't seen nobody like that," she shrugged, and Elijah almost groaned out loud as the darkened tip of her breast showed itself before it settled down again into her blouse.

"She had some jewelry on her. A couple of pairs of earrings, a necklace, and a heavy ring. You seen any of that?"

"I ain't seen nothin'," she returned, her eyes glittering with greed. "Is her husband offerin' a reward?"

"There could be." He shrugged. "My captain's mighty anxious to find her. I reckon he'll do most anything."

"If I was to help you, what's in it for me?"

"What do you make on a good night?"

She named her figure.

Elijah pulled a roll of bills from deep in his pocket. "Twice that for everything you know," he offered, "and later, twice that again for havin' just me for the night."

The whore's eyes bulged. She had never seen that much money in one place before. She wet her lips again, her eyes growing more eager as each moment passed and never leaving the wad of bills.

"There's this bloke. Word has it he's been tryin' to sell some stuff. It could be the same you mentioned."

"Where is he?"

"He's usually at the place down the street." She nodded over her shoulder at the long block behind them and turned huge eyes laced with fear back to his. "You ain't goin' to say I was the one that told?"

"I ain't sayin' nothin'. You and me is goin' to see my captain. You can tell him what you know."

"I can't just leave! For Christ's sake, I've got me a business to run. Every minute I'm gone costs me."

Elijah took a couple of bills off the roll and stuffed them into the low-cut blouse; his fingers lingered as he stroked a nipple to hardness. "We only have to go to my ship. You won't be gone all that long. Besides, I told you I want you for the night."

"Just you? All night?"

"Just me."

The whore laughed. "You got the strength, mister?"

Elijah returned her laugh with his own, his mouth watering with the promise of the night to come as he loosened his hold on her breast and moved to the other one. "Don't you worry none. I got strength enough for both of us."

An hour later Dominic pushed the swinging door of the Hungry Dog Inn aside and moved toward the crowded bar. The place stank of sweat, smoke, and rotting garbage, and he couldn't prevent a shiver of revulsion as he imagined Reena held in a place like this.

His eyes narrowed into slits as his gaze scanned the smoke-filled room, searching out the bastard that was trying to sell Reena's jewelry.

If anything happened to her, he'd kill him. He might even kill him anyway. His fingers ached to smash into somebody's face, and he forced aside the rage that boiled just below the surface, lest he scare off the only one that could help him.

He ordered an ale, and after flashing a goodly sum of cash for the benefit of the men who stood gaping at the bar, he brought it to a table near the door. Purposely, he sat with his back to the wall, knowing full he chanced getting his head bashed in for the leather of his boots, never mind the money in his pocket.

His nerves were stretched to the limit as he forced himself to appear a picture of a sea captain, with nothing more on his mind but a bit of relaxation.

Of course the whores who serviced the clientele hadn't missed the neat roll of bills and soon sought to show the handsome bloke just how best his money could be set to use.

A voluptuous dark woman whose aged eyes belied the obvious fact of her youth approached him. "You lookin' for a good time, Captain?" Her huge breasts nearly overran the low neckline of her gown at each breath.

"I might be," Dominic returned as he eyed the woman with obvious interest. "What are you offering?"

The woman's smile revealed a gaping space in the front of her mouth, and Dominic felt a moment's pity, wondering if she had lost the teeth to one of her clients.

"Why don't we go in the back room and I'll show you."

"Why don't you show me here," he remarked. "I'd like to see how much of that is you."

"Oh honey, it's all me," she assured with another grin.

"I have only your word for that."

Without a moment's hesitation, and mindless of the tavern's occupants, she reached into her dress and lifted her milky white breast free of its confines. Expertly, she rolled the coral nipple between her thumb and forefinger. "See?"

Dominic nodded, "How much?"

The whore named her price. He nodded again and came to his feet. His arm circled her waist as she led him down the darkened corridor to the rooms at the back.

The moment they entered a small room, Dominic pulled her against him and shoved her forcefully to the closed door. In a flash his mouth was covering hers and his hands reached for her huge breasts.

271

She moaned softly as he rubbed the nipples into a tight nub. "Shit, but you feel good," he groaned into the smoothness of her neck. "I'm sorry I didn't bring that little trinket with me. It would have looked beautiful nestled right here." His mouth dipped to the swell of her breasts. "Do you have something to put on? I'd like to see you naked, wearing only a necklace."

The whore was pressing her hips against his, enjoying this job more than usual, for this bloke smelled like none of her other customers, and could he kiss!

"What?" she asked, not quite comprehending.

"I said, I'd like to see you wearing only a necklace, do you have one? Maybe one that would fall to here?" he asked, as his fingertip traced the upper curves of her breasts.

"I could borrow one."

"When?"

"Later," she sighed, as she ran her painted mouth over his jaw.

"Now!" he returned, while answering the pressure of her hips, seemingly caught up in the moment of passion.

Christ, she moaned in silent aggravation. Why was it the ones who looked the most normal turned out to be cracked? Couldn't they simply enjoy a good lay without all this perversion? The longer she was in this business, the worse it got. She couldn't seem to pick a customer who was straight anymore. But then she remembered the roll of bills and shrugged. If the bloke wanted her to wear a necklace, she'd wear a goddamned necklace. What the hell did she care?

Maybe, just maybe, if she was real good, she could get this one to give her more than her usual fee. Jake had a passel of sparkling gems he was just aching to part with for the right price. Of course, none of them were real, but she didn't care. They were dazzling, and the green glass in the necklace would look right pretty nestled between her swelling sugar loaves.

"Jake has some stuff he's tryin' to sell," she murmured between kisses. "He might let me borrow a piece."

"Is it expensive?"

"Naw," she giggled. "Where would he get anything expensive?"

"Maybe I'll buy it for you. Then you could wear it for me the next time."

A smile split her soft mouth and showed again her lacking teeth. She had been right about him after all. "Wait right here," she grinned, as she pulled away and then glanced over her shoulder just before she opened the door. "Don't move."

The minutes ticked by, and Dominic's nerves screamed out. He was almost ready to lunge after her and find the bastard himself when the doorknob turned and a rag-covered man entered the dingy room.

"You interested in buyin' somethin'?" he asked, his eyes shifting nervously around the room.

The man smelled so bad Dominic had to force himself not to flinch. "I am."

The whore entered. Dominic turned to look at her. "You want to wait outside? I'd like this to be a surprise."

She nodded and returned to the hall, closing the door behind her.

No sooner had the door closed when the man pulled a handful of Reena's gems from his filthy clothes.

"Where is she?"

"What?"

"You son of a bitch! I said where is she?" Dominic growled as he pushed the smaller man up against the wall and held him there with his arm pressed, not too gently, to his throat. Exerting a bit of pressure caused Jake's eyes to bulge and his skin to grow motley with red patches.

"I don't know what you're talking about," the man gasped, knowing from the look of death in Dominic's eyes he was about to meet his maker, and he hadn't a clue as to why.

"The lady you took these from. What did you do with her?" Dominic grunted, his rage nearly out of control.

"I didn't, I swear it. I didn't steal them. She dropped the bag when Jack grabbed her. He kicked it away. They didn't want it," he almost screamed in terror. "I swear I didn't do nothin'."

"Jack who?" Dominic inquired, so silkily as to cause gooseflesh to grow over the man's arms and back. Jake didn't even think to answer him, so lost was he in this madman's icy rage, until he felt the pressure increase on his throat. "Jack who?"

"Jack Reed," Jake squealed. "Everyone around here knows him. He's always at Molly's. I swear it was him that took her. Has her still for all I know."

"You'd better be right," Dominic grunted as he deposited a powerful fist to the man's midsection. "I'll be back if you're not."

Jake gasped as the punch sent slivers of pain through his stomach while his knees buckled beneath his weight. "I swear," he choked. "Ask down at Molly's. Jack has her."

It was with no little satisfaction that Dominic watched Jake slide down the wall and crumble into a ball at his feet.

Chapter Thirty

DOMINIC WALKED INTO THE NOISY GAMBLING HALL. HIS mouth was grim, his mind of one purpose: to kill Jack Reed and his darling, deceitful, bitch of a wife. It hadn't taken her long. Christ, she had only docked this morning and already she had found herself a protector.

Dominic's imagination had run rampant during the short walk to Molly's place. His mind's eye saw them in bed, imagining every position and pose, watching as a faceless man ran his hands over his wife's body.

Forcibly, he shook the gut-wrenching pictures away. If Jack Reed frequented this place, he was obviously a gambling man. He didn't know it, but the biggest gamble of his life was about to be played out, and Dominic doubted not who would emerge the winner. He allowed the thought of killing him outright to cross his mind with savorous pleasure, but instantly thought better of it. Should he be so fast to see to the demise of this unknown yet hated opponent, he might never find her. No, he would watch for a while and follow once he left the table.

Dominic leaned over the bar and ordered a tankard of ale. A pretty woman sauntered up and rested her elbow on the bar near him. "You new in town?"

Dominic shrugged, ignoring her question. "I've got business with Jack Reed. You know him?"

"Over there," she nodded toward a table of men. "The one that's dealing."

Dominic flipped a coin in her direction. She caught it easily and slid it into the bodice of her dress as Dominic, unable to stand the strain of worry and fear, moved to join the men.

Jack Reed glanced anxiously at his pocket watch for what seemed like the hundredth time in the last hour. God, could that woman sleep! He had wanted to take her to his rooms right after she had eaten, but she had asked so sweetly to be allowed to rest for a minute that he hadn't the heart to insist.

He too had caught a few winks, but it was hours since he had awakened and she was still asleep. What the hell had she been doing lately? Suddenly he gave a knowing grin. Fool question, he knew well enough what she'd been doing, and he felt a stirring in his loins, for he wanted his share.

"I've a proposition for you, if you're Jack Reed."

Jack looked up at the sea captain standing relaxed and confident at his side. "Yeah? What is it?"

"Could we go where there's a bit more privacy?"

Jack laughed. He didn't care how the man dressed or what he looked like. He didn't trust anybody. He was winning again, and he wouldn't put it past any one of these low lifes to put a knife between his shoulder blades. "Mister, you can say anything you want right here!"

Dominic pressed on, "Perhaps one of the rooms in the back? I'll make it worth your while."

Christ! Jack groaned beneath his breath, this was all he

needed. Don't tell me the man has a hankerin' for a sturdier piece of flesh. What the hell ever gave him the idea I'd be interested in somethin' like that?

The men around the table began to snicker.

Jack's face flushed and his collar grew unusually tight as he snapped with no little disgust, "I ain't interested."

"Not even for this?" Dominic asked, as he pulled out the wad of bank notes.

Jack's eyes widened with surprise. Jesus! How much money did he have?

"If that's not enough, I can get more," Dominic continued, knowing full well what the men thought and caring not a damn.

Jack smiled. He'd play the whore to no man, but if the bastard wanted to part with his roll, he'd be more than happy to oblige. He winked at the surly group of men as he came to his feet.

"Go get it, Jack! Give him one for me," were the remarks accompanying the two men as they made their way past the red curtain and into the narrow hall to the rear of the building. Jack led the way down the dimly lit hall and out the back door.

Dominic smiled as he followed. The man was in for a surprise. No sooner had they reached the dark alley did Dominic's hand reach around Jack's chin and pull his head backward, while a knife glittered in the moonlight and came to press with ominous deliberation against his neck.

"Christ!" Jack groaned, momentarily held helpless. "What the hell do you want?"

"My proposition, sir. The possibility of you retaining your life if you tell me where she is," a low voice whispered close to his ear.

"Who?"

The knife pressed harder, splitting the tautly held neck as easily as cutting through softened butter. Jack could feel the sting of the blade and cursed as a warm wetness began to trickle down his throat.

He was bleeding! The goddamned crazy son of a bitch cut him! Jack's voice trembled as he tried to talk some sense into this madman. "Look, mister, if you tell me what you want, I'll give it to you."

"My wife, man. Where is she?"

"Who the hell is your wife?" he cried out, his fear growing into impotent rage as he was held frustratingly immobile.

"Reena. You know Reena," the low voice purred deceptively calm. "The one you took in your arms today. Tell me, what else did you do to her?"

"Nothin', I swear to God, nothin'," he gasped, as the blade sank further into his throat and he felt the flesh of his neck split. "She fainted, that's all. I gave her somethin' to eat. She's been sleepin' ever since. Christ, mate, don't kill me on that account. I swear I didn't know she was married."

"Where is she?" Dominic's voice grated.

"I'll . . . I'll show you."

"Tell me," he coaxed, all too softly.

"Inside. The first door on your right." Shit. He'd never help anyone again. This bastard was going to kill him. He almost laughed. He had thought himself lucky to find her, now he knew he'd be lucky to see tomorrow.

"You'd better be telling me the truth, Mister Reed," Dominic commented lightly.

"I am. I am."

Dominic's knee came up high and plunged into the small of his back and sent Jack sprawling across the dirty alley. He stood over the bleeding man as he resheathed his weapon and warned, "I'll be back if you're not."

An instant later he was gone.

Dominic felt a full range of emotions assail his being as he watched his wife's sleeping, beautiful face. His relief at finding her knew no bounds, but then again neither did his rage. How could he still want her knowing what she was? Christ, he must be demented!

With an angry growl, he shoved her. "Get the hell out of that bed. We're leaving."

Reena's eyes opened slowly. A soft smile touched her lips as she saw her husband standing over her. "Dominic," she said softly, and then the memory of the past weeks returned in a rush as she scrambled to the other side of the bed and came to her feet. "What the hell do you want?"

It was definitely the wrong thing to say. In most likelihood, there wasn't a right thing to say, but her words cut into him like a knife, and he found himself lunging at her with a terrifying roar.

In an instant he was across the bed. His hands were no more than a blur, so fast did they reach for her. There wasn't anything he wanted more than to beat all hell out of her, but somehow he managed to control the impulse and instead shook her until her teeth rattled.

Suddenly he flung her from him. Her head hit the wall and her knees wobbled, but she forced herself to stay on her feet through pure willpower.

"We are leaving, Reena," he remarked as he took huge, calming breaths deep into his lungs.

Reena was shaken to the core. Besides being dizzy from his rough treatment, her emotions were in an uproar, and she didn't recognize the further threat of his icy, calm manner. All she could think was how much she despised him, how much he had made her suffer. His deceit. His lies. "We?! Captain, I beg to differ, but there is no 'we.'"

Dominic growled out a long stream of curses as his body pressed her into the wall, for he dared not touch her with his hands. "You have two choices. You can go with me, or I will take you, and I promise I'll not mind using force."

"Who the hell do you think you are? You can't come barging in here and order me about. I'm not on your damned ship. Get out!"

Dominic didn't bother to answer her, but effortlessly slung her small form over his shoulder. He ignored her shriek of surprise and gave her rear a sharp, stinging slap as she punched his back and tried to kick his stomach.

"There is little else I'd rather do right now than beat you, madam. Were I you I'd tempt me no further."

Reena's backside smarted from the one slap and she wisely refrained from using further force as he walked out of the back of the building, through the narrow alley way and whistled for a passing cab.

The next thing she knew, Reena was lifting herself off the cab's floor. A restraining hand held to her shoulder as he ordered, "Stay there."

Reena had no choice but to endure the bumpy ride back to the docks in silent discomfort. His hand stayed at her shoulder, but he never looked at her. She was at a loss as to what to say. Why had he come for her? Did he think to have her and Diah too? No! Never! She'd not allow it. She didn't care if he beat her to a pulp. She'd run away again and again.

The hired cab pulled to a stop in front of the *America* and Dominic jumped down and dragged a struggling Reena after him. He twisted her arm behind her back and almost lifted her from the ground as he boarded his ship. With a shove he pushed her away and ordered icily, "Get below."

Reena stiffened and was about to refuse, but thought better of it as she glanced at the look of rage that thinned his mouth and glowed eerily from his dark eyes. It was obvious it wouldn't take much to bring him to murder.

Dominic leaned against the closed door of his cabin and idly crossed his arms over his chest as he studied his wife. Reena could feel his eyes on her, but stared at the wall, refusing to make eye contact. She sat and forced her fidgeting hands to still as she fumed in silent frustration. How dare he drag her back? Who did he think he was? Damn it, she'd not stand for this abuse!

Reena's nerves screamed her anxiety. What was he going

to do? Why didn't he say something? She couldn't stand it any longer. She felt like a rabbit cornered by a fox, waiting, waiting for him to open his jaws and finish her off.

Suddenly she jumped to her feet and faced him. "Now that you've brought me here, what do you plan to do?"

Dominic's dark gaze wandered freely over her tiny form. His expression was purposely filled with disgust, but in truth he was drinking in the sight of her with a greediness he had never known. He had wanted to kill her, but all he could do was thank God he had found her at last. His body throbbed with an aching need. God, how he had missed her. He longed to hold her in his arms and make love to her until she was too weak and exhausted ever to leave his side again.

"One question."

She lifted her head and waited.

"Why?"

Reena knew well enough of what he spoke, but she couldn't bring herself to admit to the reason. She shrugged. "I left you. Is it so impossible to believe I simply did not want to stay?"

"After that day at the cove?" he bellowed, instantly enraged. "Without a goddamned word? What the hell kind of a woman are you?"

"What the hell do you care?" she managed to yell back, while almost jumping at the fierceness in his voice. "I don't owe you any explanations. You got what you wanted."

Her anger inflamed him so that he didn't know if he wanted to knock her on the floor or carry her to the bed.

"Not quite," he returned, his voice growing low and husky with his need for her as he walked the few steps that separated them. God, he couldn't think if he loved or hated her more. Suddenly he gasped at the thought and stared at her with nothing less than shock. His eyes closed with a wave of helplessness. Sweet Jesus, he loved her. He loved her and she was no better than Amanda. God, he couldn't live through this torture again. He couldn't bear the rage . . . the pain.

His long fingers bit deep into the soft flesh of her shoulders. "I could kill you," he growled between clenched teeth.

"I don't care. I hate you," she sobbed, as he pulled her struggling body roughly against him. "I hate you!"

"Maybe," he groaned thickly, "but you like this well enough."

Chapter Thirty-one

"No!" SHE GASPED AS HIS WORDS REGISTERED. "DOMINIC, please," she begged. But he never heard her pleas as he reached for the high neckline of her dress. As if made of paper, the thin material ripped to her waist. Buttons popped and rolled ominously, the sound of their spinning along the oak floor holding her oddly immobile as her eyes watched in stupefied fascination.

Suddenly her mind came sharply back to the moment. She couldn't let him do this! Her hands came up to push his from her. "Dominic, listen to me!" she cried as she struggled to free herself of his steely hold. "You cannot do this!"

His eyes glazed over, lost as he was in an overpowering need that could no longer be controlled.

Reena's fisted hand contacted smartly to the side of his face. "Let go, damn it. Let go of me!"

Dominic barely noticed the blow as he gave yet another yank and the dress split to the hem of her skirt. An instant later her chemise and drawers followed the dress's fate and fell in a ragged heap to the floor.

Dominic drew in a sharp breath as his gaze lowered from her face. She stood in nothing but black cotton stockings and soft kid boots and he felt a wave of yearning so intense as to blot out every rational thought. She was beauty beyond his ability to imagine and the knowledge seemed to come anew each time he saw her thus.

Reena shoved against him, her arms swinging at will, yet posing no threat to his strength. She was filled with a wide range of emotions, anger not being the least of them. She felt a twinge of fear, but knew, even in his rage, he would not hurt her. No, the fear she felt was directed more at herself than at him, for Reena could not deny the thrill standing naked before him brought. And even though she didn't want this it was an intoxication to know she could bring him to the brink of madness.

"Oh God," Dominic groaned on a ragged sigh. His voice echoed the torment that ravaged his features. "Why do I have to want you like this?"

His hands at her waist lifted her as if she were weightless, until her breasts were level to his mouth.

Her small hands pummeled his broad shoulders as she continued her useless struggles. "Dominic, damn it. Can you hear me? Stop!" she cried, but when he drew the tip of her breast into his burning mouth, all thoughts but of wanting more fled.

Reena's back arched and a choking gasp hissed through her clenched teeth. "No! Oh God, no. I don't want this," she whimpered on a broken sob, for all hope was lost. No matter her denials, she had never known this rush of longing to exist.

Of their own volition, her fists opened, her fingers spread over his shoulders, trying to gather the warmth of him into her grasp. Her fingers slid to his neck and then moved to thread through the thickness of his hair and she groaned a soft sound as she held him to her.

She wanted him. She needed him, and for this one last time she would love him. Aye, she would love him until she was free of this insane yearning.

"Reena," he choked in mindless desperation, as he pulled his mouth from her and nuzzled his face to her luscious softness. Slowly he slid her body down the length of his until his lips could reach her mouth. His tongue flicked out, stroking the softness of her lips with hot wet fire. "It terrifies me, the things we do to each other."

"I know," she moaned, as she guided his mouth to hers and kissed him with all the pent-up hunger and despair that had haunted her for these past weeks.

Her arms clung to his shoulders and her lips parted beneath the hunger of his answering kiss. Reena pressed herself into the hardness of his body. She swiveled her hips and felt a thrill ripple through her as the obvious sign of his need made itself known.

"Dominic," she gasped breathlessly, as he released her mouth at last. "I need you. Please, I'll die if you don't take me now."

She felt on fire. She couldn't remember ever being this hot.

"Open my pants," he growled, as he covered her shoulder and breasts with hot sucking kisses.

It took a moment before his words penetrated the thick fog of desire that encompassed her mind, but when it did, she murmured, "I can't reach you. Dominic, lower me."

He did as she asked and a moment later his pants fell unheeded around his legs.

Reena cried out a low sound of pure ecstasy as he instantly impaled her upon his throbbing manhood. Her legs circled his hips and her arms clung to his shoulders with wild desperation. She couldn't believe this pleasure. It couldn't happen this fast. It couldn't feel this good.

"I can't stand," he groaned against her mouth, as his body shook violently. A moment later he sat upon the bed and placed her legs on each side of his hips as he fell back.

Reena reached beneath his shirt and spread her hands over his chest and stomach.

"Sweet Jesus, this feels too good," he groaned as she rocked her hips over his. His body lifted, pressing deep into the warm wetness of her. "I can't hold back," he gasped, his voice breaking as she increased her pace. His features contorted as if in pain. "I cannot!"

Reena fell forward, unable to resist the magic lure of his mouth. Her tongue dipped deep and tasted of his delicious maleness as she breathed his haunting scent. The last of his control vanished as she gave a low, seductive growl and the achingly sweet heat came flooding into her. Hot, so deliciously hot. Her body quivered and with a strength she'd never known, she thrust hard to him. "Oh God," she cried out in wild frenzy as sparks of light ricocheted throughout her body, each one bringing her closer to the ecstasy she knew awaited her, until she was totally encompassed, swirling, glowing amid the dazzling specks, light as air, content to stay forever among the stars.

For a long moment the only sound in the room was the labored breathing of the two young people sprawled across the bed. Each held to the other, positive should they release their grasp, they'd find themselves falling off the edge of the earth.

"It's not enough," he growled only moments later and, still in her, he rolled her beneath him. Reena's eyes opened wide with amazement as he began to move again.

A smile touched the corners of her mouth as she began to open the buttons of his shirt. "We were in a bit of a rush, weren't we?"

Dominic smiled down at her. "Aye, but not this time." And then his eyes closed as he allowed the sweet beauty of being held within her warmth to bask his soul with enchanted bliss.

It was close to an hour later that Reena murmured dreamily against his warm, damp chest. "This doesn't solve anything, Dominic."

"The hell it doesn't!" he growled in return.

She stiffened noticeably beneath him, her determined gaze locking with his. "I don't care how many times you drag me back. I'll run again."

Dominic's brow furrowed with confusion. "Goddamnit, why? Are you so unhappy?"

"Yes," she choked, refusing to meet his dark gaze, as huge tears spilled from her eyes and ran into her golden hair. She'd never let him know how much she needed him, how much she loved him, how much he had hurt her.

"Were you happy when you left?"

"Yes," she sobbed, no longer able to contain her misery. "I was very, very happy," she murmured into his chest.

"'Tis as I thought, Reena," he whispered arrogantly. "You love me."

Reena gasped, her eyes lifting to his. "I . . ."

He waved away her attempts of denial with a quick shake of his head. "Do not bother to deny it. I suspected as much before you left, and I know it for fact now."

He kissed away her tears, his breath hot against her damp skin, while murmuring, "The only thing I don't know is why? Tell me, my love."

Holding to the last of her pride, Reena snapped, "Don't call me that. I am not your love. I hate you. I hate everything about you. And stop kissing me, damn it!"

Dominic gave a low, tender laugh. "You're going to tell me. It doesn't matter how long it takes. I have all day, I have tonight, I have tomorrow and . . ."

"Ask Diah then, if you insist on knowing."

"Diah? What the hell has she to do with this? . . . With us?"

Reena shoved his relaxed body from her and rolled from the bed. Her chest heaved as the remembered pain came yet again to assault her being and penetrate every living cell. Unmindful of her nakedness, she forced aside her tormenting thoughts, her hands on her hips, and snarled, "You need not try to deny it! I saw her and she admitted everything. I won't live with a man who shows so little respect for his wife that he takes his mistress in the same house. *In the same bed!*"

Dominic's eyes feasted on the loveliness of his wife's body. His heart swelled with adoration and joy, for he was confident as never before of her love, and the time was at hand when she would explain her actions.

"Reena, I know you think you are making sense, but I have not a clue as to what you are talking about."

"Dominic, it pleases me not to see you act the innocent. I know Diah is your mistress. I will not live with a man who takes his vows so lightly." She shrugged as she slid her arms into his discarded shirt. "I realize our promises meant less than nothing to you. But for a time, I thought . . ." She shook her head and forced away the tears that threatened and breathed a long, calming sigh. "In the end it matters not. I will not go back."

"Damn," she muttered as she eyed her ruined dress. "Now I have nothing to wear."

Dominic reclined upon the bed, a contented grin spread across his mouth. His hands folded behind his back. "Do not worry of it. You will need nothing."

Reena shot him a contemptuous look, and he grinned again. "What was it you thought?"

Startled at his question, Reena's gaze lifted to his, and his dark eyes seemed to draw the words as if she had no will.

"I thought you cared."

"And if I told you I do, what would you say?"

"I'd say you speak not the truth, for a man does not make use of a mistress if he cares for his wife."

Dominic chuckled softly. "In truth, Reena, there are many men who do just that and were you to ask, they'd swear their undying love and respect for their spouse."

Reena blinked, her expression confused. "Then why?"

Dominic shrugged, "For many reasons. Some need more than a dutiful response. Others fear an unwanted child. Still others insist that a man should know the favors of many women. Somehow it makes them feel more the man. Undoubtedly there are still more reasons I've not yet touched upon."

"And which of these do you claim?"

"None," he returned, his eyes never wavering from her blue gaze. "I have not touched another since our first meeting. And I will not."

Reena gave a deep, shuddering breath. She longed to believe him, but the evidence was so damning. Diah couldn't have made up the fear she displayed. Still, a nagging doubt came to her mind. Maybe Diah felt the fear for an entirely different reason than she had supposed. Maybe she had allowed Reena to believe what she would and had counted on Reena's reaction to the supposed misdeed and then felt real fear at the possibility of being exposed.

His eyes did not falter as she returned his gaze. Could he so easily profess the truth if it were not so? 'Twas unlikely, she reasoned, for no matter the faults of this man, she knew him not as a liar.

"Why?" she asked, suddenly timid, almost fearful of his response.

"Why what?"

"Why have you not touched another?"

Dominic grinned. "Woman, 'tis not so hard to understand the workings of my mind. In the first place, I love you. In the second, you are the most beautiful woman I've ever known. In the third, your responses to our lovemaking leave all others lacking. Indeed the question should be, why would I need to touch another?"

Reena's eyes misted with tears of joy, and she asked with delighted anticipation, "Do you?"

Dominic grinned. "Do I what?"

"Do you love me?"

Dominic laughed. "Do you know, standing as you are, you remind me of a lady I know. She, too, stood in a shirt of mine, looking just as small and so endearing as to take your breath away. If I'm not mistaken it was in a cabin, deep in the woods, that I saw her thus. I found myself irresistibly drawn to her that day. I knew not why at the time."

Reena smiled through happy tears. "Do you know now?"

"Oh aye. It took a while for the truth to dawn, but I realized I loved her."

Reena shot him a disbelieving look.

He shrugged and then grinned wickedly. "Well, perhaps it was not love at first, but something just as basic. Soon enough I was lost forever in her beauty."

Reena gave him a taunting grin. "So you love her because she is a comely wench? What will happen then in years to come when her beauty fades?"

"Her beauty will never fade, Reena, for it comes from within. Her skin may crease with age, but not her spirit, nor her gentleness, nor her zest for laughter. I believe the sparkle in her eyes will be there when she holds her tenth grandchild snug in her arms."

Reena threw her head back and laughed. "Her tenth? Indeed you have great plans for this woman you love, but don't you think you should begin with just one child at a time, and they in turn can worry of the grandchildren?"

Dominic's dark gaze and accompanying grin made Reena's skin tingle in anticipation. "Agreed. Now, if I could persuade her to join me in the bed, I could set about that laborious task."

Reena's eyes hungrily took in every detail of her husband's masculine form, and her voice lowered to a husky drawl as she knelt at his side and leaned over him. "If the truth be known, Captain, it will take little persuasion, for I have a feeling this lady you love would like nothing better than to see to the fruition of your plans."

"Why?" he taunted, as he pulled her on top of him, his hands running beneath his shirt to caress the length of her slender back and rounded hips.

And just before she surrendered to the pressure of his hand to bring their mouths together, Reena sighed, "Because she loves you."

Chapter Thirty-two

REENA GRINNED IN ANXIOUS ANTICIPATION AS SHE WAITED in the garden. From the house came the clear sounds of lively music and much gaiety as light spilled from the open windows to the lawn. Her first party as his wife was a success. All night she had basked in the glow of his love as they danced and joined their guests' merrymaking.

Indeed, tonight was a night to celebrate, she mused in silent joy, for she knew at last the ecstasy Mary had felt since the beginning of her pregnancy and she couldn't wait to tell Dominic.

Purposely, they had planned this party for tonight, for it was six months from the day they had wed, and they both knew the miracle of their love had changed their lives forever. She gave a soft smile as she examined the leaves of an orchid. Tonight could have been the last night she spent in his home. Stretching out before her could have been years of loneliness, and she thanked God for this perfect gift of love.

The muffled sounds of approaching footsteps took her from her thoughts, and she turned to face her husband with outstretched hands and a tender smile. "Darling," she whispered, and then choked on a startled gasp as a huge, roughly dressed man stepped out of the shadows and grinned lecherously as his eyes moved insolently over her tiny form.

"Yes dear," he chuckled, while another moved behind her and clamped his hand over her gaping mouth.

Reena's eyes opened with shock as the man at her back easily subdued her struggles with bone-crushing strength. Almost before she could blink, her hands and feet were bound, a gag was shoved between her lips and secured with another tied around her mouth.

Her screams were no more than muffled moans carried on the soft island breeze to mingle with the gentle strains of music that caressed the darkened garden.

What was happening? Good God, not again! She wasn't being kidnapped again! It wasn't possible that this could happen twice in a person's lifetime.

"Dominic!" she screamed, although her moans gave little semblance to her intended words. The wind was knocked from her as she landed with a hard bounce on one of the men's sturdy shoulders.

Through a haze of terror, she watched as a piece of paper was put to the same tree she had waited under and held in place by a dagger. "Dominic," she cried again. Dear God, she wasn't sure she had the strength to go through this again.

The ground moved dizzily above her head as she strained and struggled against her bonds, only to hear the satisfied chuckle of the man who held her so firmly in place.

After what seemed an endless walk through thick foliage, Reena was finally flung from his shoulders and knocked almost senseless as she landed in a small boat.

She moaned softly as one of the men tried to step over her, but in the dark stepped on her shoulder. Her cry of pain brought about further chuckles, and Reena vowed not to give them future cause for merriment.

The soft tropical moon shown brightly upon the dark water as the small boat holding three shadowy forms made its way across a short stretch of iridescent water to a large schooner anchored some hundred yards from shore.

When they reached the ship, she was again tossed upon a shoulder. "If you squirm and fall, I don't know if I'll find you in these waters, or even if I'll try," a gruff voice warned.

A chill of fear penetrated the terror that had numbed her into docility. With hands and feet bound, she had no doubt as to her fate should she fall.

"Did everything go all right?"

"Just fine, Captain," the man who held her replied.

"And you left the note?"

"Just like you ordered."

"Bring her to my cabin," the voice from the dark continued, "and lock the door."

Reena was positive she was in the midst of a nightmare. The voice sounded like Dominic, and when she raised her head, through the curtain of her hair, her eyes swore they saw him. Could she be asleep? Could this simply be a dream? She tried to call out his name, but he turned away and signaled his men to put out to sea.

Reena landed with a hard bounce upon the bed. A low, evil chuckle sounded above her, but she closed her eyes and remained perfectly still, too terrified to imagine what might happen next. To her immense relief, the door to the cabin closed, and she was left alone.

The cabin was in shadows. The only light came from the moon's rays shining through the small windows. The bindings on her hands were tight, and the pain excruciating when she tried to twist free, but regardless of the pain, she continued her struggles until she was positive she had worn away most of the skin on her wrist.

The usual sounds of men singing, or murmured conversations, were nonexistent. The ship ran as quiet as a graveyard, and Reena shivered in the dark, her fear bringing its own sense of cold to the warm room.

Were they going to leave her alone until a ransom was paid? Oh God, she hoped so. For no matter her terror of the unknown, it was better than the certainty of what they would do if given the chance.

Reena assumed it was money they wanted, otherwise why the note? If Dominic worked quickly, she might be back before anything more happened. Oh please, God, let him hurry, she prayed, the chant repeating itself again and again, until the monotony soothed her into an exhausted sleep.

The sun shone a warm stream of dust-laden light through the porthole when Reena next opened her eyes. Her body ached, her head pounded. She must be ill, she thought, until she tried to move her hands and remembered. A soft sound of pain came from her throat and a voice behind her caused her to start.

"So you're finally awake."

Reena tried to turn, but bound as she was managed only to twist her head to its limit and still could not see the owner of the voice.

"Curious are we? Well I have to admit, I would be too. Will you promise to remain calm if I release you?"

Reena nodded her head and groaned again as pain shot through it. She had been so terrified, she had barely noticed the knock to her head last night . . . till now.

The bindings were severed with one stroke of a blade and Reena nearly screamed as the blood rushed into her hands and feet causing her the most agonizing pain imaginable.

It was a long moment before she could bring her arms around her body. Slowly she rubbed at her swollen hands and fingers until the color began to return. Her gag was roughly torn away and Reena tried to wet her teeth, but her mouth was parched.

"Water," she whispered in a raspy voice, and then added a soft, "Please."

Her fingers were stiff, and the water spilled over the front of her dress as she gulped it down, but she couldn't have cared less. She couldn't remember being so thirsty. A sigh of relief escaped her as she emptied the tankard and turned to face her abductor.

A soft gasp of air caught in her throat. Dominic! How could he do this to her? Why?

It wasn't until the dark man stepped from the shadows and grinned that Reena realized it wasn't Dominic at all. This man was older, and the closer he came the more vicious he appeared. There was a cruelty in his eyes that was absent in his son's.

Coujon! Reena closed her eyes with sudden disgust. First the son kidnaps the father's intended bride and now the father kidnaps the son's wife. They were madmen playing with her life, and at this moment she hated them both.

"I see you have not forgotten me, Mistress Braxton. How do you do?"

Reena almost giggled at the absurdity of it all. Was she now expected to pass the time of day with this monster? Was he insane?

Coujon shrugged at Reena's lack of good humor. "I'm afraid I must apologize for my men. It appears they have made an error. It wasn't you but Riveria's wife I sent for."

Reena almost snapped that she was Dominic's wife, but suddenly thought better of the notion. Apparently she had been mistaken for Mary. Perhaps it was wiser and safer not to disclose that information at the moment.

"Indeed, sir, you have a most unusual way of sending for someone. And, at the very least, your treatment upon arrival leaves much to be desired."

Coujon grinned an evil sneer. "Perhaps, and for that I

have already apologized. In the end, the mix-up is of no matter. The note was left. I know Riveria to be a man of conscience. He will come for you, regardless of who's wife you might be."

"Suppose he sends another with the money?"

Coujon laughed. "It's not money I want, mistress. I want Riveria. I mean to see him dead and be done with it."

"No! You cannot!" Reena gasped, as she came to her feet.

Coujon laughed again, and Reena felt like crying, for her impulsive words had disclosed clear enough her feelings.

"Could it be you have a tender spot for Riveria, my dear?"

Reena didn't answer, but sat again on the bed silently cursing her all too quick tongue.

"Perhaps he returns those feelings. Ah yes, I believe he just might. In that case he will most definitely come."

Reena spent the rest of the day alone in the cabin, endlessly pacing the small wooden floor. She prayed Dominic would come and then prayed again he would not. For it would mean his death.

Her mind raced on as she walked, discarding one plan of escape after another until at last she flung herself to the bed with the sure knowledge of her doom.

She had been lying on the bed for hours, her tortured mind leaving her incapable of sleep, when the sound of a man calling "Sails ho," filtered into the cabin.

Dominic! He had come. She knew it was he and, although her heart leaped with joy, the accompanying terror that closed over her left her nearly breathless. Had he come for her only to meet his end? Oh please, God, no!

It seemed only moments before a small boat rocked against the wooden hull of the ship and she could only pray he had not come alone.

Soon footsteps sounded outside the door and a key turned in the lock.

Reena was in his arms, smothering his face with desperate kisses before the door closed. "Oh Dominic, you shouldn't have come. It's you he wants. You should have sent another."

Dominic smiled. "Reena," he soothed, "you mustn't fear so. All will be well."

"How very touching," came the deep voice from behind him. "But you see, I have plans of my own concerning the girl. Now sit!" Waving a gun at Dominic, he motioned for him to take a seat, while pushing Reena toward the bed.

"Tie him well, mates," Coujon ordered the two burly seamen who were standing at the opened doorway. "It would not do for our guest of honor to gain his freedom on this night."

The men did as they were ordered and soon left.

Dominic's eyes glittered with murderous rage from across the small cabin and Coujon laughed. "We have been waiting for you, haven't we, dear?" Coujon asked, as he pulled a stiff Reena into his arms.

Dominic's glance lowered to his wife's terrified face, and he groaned and cursed his helplessness. He had had no thoughts but to come as ordered. He couldn't chance her life by attacking the ship. Nay, no matter the outcome, he knew he'd do it again.

Dominic watched in horror as Coujon ran his hands over Reena's breasts. "No!" he cried, trying to come to his feet. "Coujon, you have no need to do this. You promised her freedom if I came. Kill me and be done with it, but let her go."

"It's true I did want you, Riveria, but upon seeing this lovely piece again, I believe I'll have her, too."

Dominic heaped a stream of curses upon Coujon's head, only to hear his father's exultant roar of laughter in return.

"Oh Christ, it does the heart good to see this. Do you realize how many years have passed since we've last met . . . How many years I've waited to destroy you?"

"Why?" Reena gasped as she watched the hatred pass between father and son. "Why is this happening?"

Coujon chuckled. "You don't know do you? You don't know that this bastard took away from me the only woman I've ever loved."

Reena's mind raced, trying to make sense of this madman's wild words. "Who?"

"His mother!"

"His mother? You loved his mother?"

"Aye, but she turned out to be an ungrateful bitch in the end. I had the pleasure of watching her suffer for her betrayal."

"Oh aye, he loved her all right. He loved to beat and abuse her. He loved to treat her like an animal."

"What do you know of the ways of men? You never were more than a sniveling brat!"

"I know a woman should be treated with tenderness and care. Something that has never occurred to you."

"Enough of this bickering. That's not why I brought you here."

Coujon turned from Dominic and reached for Reena's dress. With one mighty pull, he ripped the material to the hem. Reena screamed and tried to pull away, but Coujon had the greater strength, and a moment later she stood naked, shaking with exhaustion before the man.

"Ah, a prize, Riveria. She's even better than Amanda. Oh, Amanda," Coujon taunted with a gleeful chuckle. "There was a beauty indeed. She came to me to plead for you, you see, but decided to stay awhile."

"I doubt not, after being favored with your abuse, she thought she could never go back to Dominic again." Reena glared. Unable to cover herself, she stood proud and disdainful before the gloating beast.

Dominic's eyes softened with love for his wife, her voice, a healing salve, seemed to penetrate to the depths of his soul, and he had never loved her more. He had not imagined Amanda too ashamed to come back to him. He had thought she preferred Coujon to himself, and he felt a wave of sorrow that he had accused his first love so harshly.

Coujon laughed again. "She enjoyed it enough, after a time."

"At least she stopped fighting, eh, Coujon?" Reena sneered.

"Whatever," he returned with a careless and dismissing shrug. "She was unimportant, merely a means to an end."

"Something like myself. A means to hurt your son."

"Exactly," Coujon grinned. "And now that you know your place, you can get on the bed."

"You might take me, Coujon, but I'll not give you an easy time of it."

"You will only suffer in the end," he warned with a careless shrug.

"So be it!"

Coujon gave a low, wild laugh that sent gooseflesh down Reena's back as he placed the gun on the bedside stand and began to discard his clothes. "I've always enjoyed women with spirit, Mistress Braxton. That damned Amanda wouldn't fight me, no matter what I did. All she could do was cry. I tired of that soon enough."

Reena felt a wave of pity for the woman. "Perhaps I shall not fight you then. I'd do much to see your pleasure thwarted."

"It matters not your reaction," he shrugged, and then motioned toward Dominic. "'Tis enough for him to watch."

The man was clearly insane, and no amount of talking was going to dissuade him. Reena looked wildly about the room for an object with which to protect herself. Suddenly Coujon's hand reached out and grasped her hair. An instant later she was on the bed.

Dominic almost screamed out his pain. He thought he'd go insane as he strained against the bonds that held him to the chair. He couldn't bear it. He could feel his blood pound in his head and a wave of dizziness overtook him. His body shuddered as Coujon ran his hands over his wife's breasts. He'd kill him, my God, it was too much for any man to take.

The pressure was building in his brain, and he felt ready to burst. He longed to scream out his agony, but he would not, for Coujon would only take more pleasure in his suffering.

Reena lay across the bed docile and calm as she endured the fondling of a man she despised. He was whispering something, but she could not hear him, for she was no longer there. Nay, she was with Dominic at the small cove and they were resting upon the warm sun-drenched sand after taking a cool swim. A soft smile touched her lips as she felt the warmth of the sun caress her naked body. She was telling Dominic of the child they were having and his face glowed with radiant joy at the happy news.

A hard slap to her face brought Reena sharply back to the present, and Dominic growled, the ropes cutting deeper into his skin as he continued his endless struggles.

"Stay here," Coujon warned as Reena's eyes cleared of the lovely dream. "I want you to know everything that's happening."

Tears filled Reena's eyes as her cheek smarted from the vicious blow. "That's better," Coujon grunted with satisfaction, and watched her jump as he pinched her nipple between his fingers. He laughed. "That's good. Can you do that again?"

He pinched her again and then lowered his head so his mouth might reach her. His teeth bit down so hard she couldn't prevent the moan of agony that came from her throat. "That's it! That's what I like to hear," he murmured against her skin, caught up in blinding passion that knew nothing of tenderness or love.

Reena couldn't bear the pain. She'd go mad at his pawing and biting. She had to do something to stop it. Her head twisted across the pillow as she blindly reached out for help.

Her fingers grazed along the glass chimney of a lamp. Instinctively she reached for it and brought it down with a strength she'd not known she possessed to the back of Coujon's head.

Barely conscious, he slumped against her as kerosene and broken glass covered them both.

Reena wasted no time in shoving him aside. An instant later she was working at the knots that secured Dominic's arms. "Hurry, hurry," he panted anxiously.

Once free Dominic slid his jacket over her nakedness and pushed her toward the door.

"Stop," came the desperate cry from the bed. "She's mine. You'll not take her, too!"

Dominic ignored the order. The door opened beneath his hand just as a shot rang out, and Reena screamed as the wood splintered an inch above Dominic's head. But her scream was nothing compared to the roar of anguish that came from the bed as a spark from the fired gun set the kerosene ablaze.

Coujon's body was instantly aflame, and he jumped from the bed in a frenzy of agony while his hands beat the flames in wild desperation.

Dominic shoved Reena out of the door and slammed it shut.

Aghast, Reena stared into the grim face of her husband. She watched as the cries from the room lessened and then disappeared altogether. He shuddered with revulsion. "There is nothing we can do but get out of here. In a few minutes the whole ship will be ablaze."

The corridor was empty. The ship's deck dark and quiet. It was almost as if it were already a ghost ship. Dominic pulled a stumbling Reena to the rail and just as someone cried, "They're getting away!" he jumped.

Chapter Thirty-three

"YOU FOOL," REENA RANTED, HER WHOLE BODY SHAKING with almost uncontrollable rage. "You're going to let him win. In death he has had the last laugh."

From the moment Dominic had flung her from Coujon's burning ship, he had barely spoken ten words. Two weeks had passed, and she couldn't take this silence any longer.

At first she couldn't imagine the cause, but more and more she came to realize his change of attitude had been brought about by his own feelings of inadequacy, and then the unforgivable, *She had saved his life!*

"Can't you understand you cannot be expected to control every imaginable situation! For God's sake, you are but a man."

Dominic's voice filled with self-loathing. "At the very least, I should be able to protect my wife. Do you realize the humiliation to see you the protector?"

"Do you honestly believe it would have been better to let him take me and then watch as he killed you?"

Dominic shrugged, unable to believe that end could have been worse than the guilt and utter revulsion that had assailed him these past weeks.

"Damn your pride, Dominic. Damn you to hell!"

Dominic said nothing as he continued to gaze out to the blackness of the night, a blackness that rivaled the blackness of his spirit and soul. No matter the arguments, he could not find himself worthy of her. He knew it illogical, but he could not control the emotion. What good was he as a man if he could not protect his love? How could she continue to love him knowing him so lacking? He knew she couldn't!

Perhaps it was best to end this now while he had some pride intact. His voice was devoid of emotion as he spoke. "There was a time when you wanted only to be gone from my side. I believe your first instinct was correct."

"You want me to leave?"

"I think it's for the best."

"My God, Dominic, I can't believe you intend to throw away all that we mean to each other over a damaged ego!"

"It's useless to pretend otherwise, Reena. I know you could never respect me as a man. Not after this failure."

"Good God, am I talking to a man or a child? Perhaps it is one and the same in your case. It matters not what you believe," she insisted in her most stubborn tone, "I will not leave you."

"And I cannot keep you. To watch your love diminish daily until there is nothing between us."

"Dominic, if that circumstance should come about, 'twould be your present behavior the cause, not a single happening you were incapable of controlling."

Dominic's face might have been cast in stone for all the emotion he allowed. "I will arrange for your departure."

"I'll not go!"

"In that case, I will begin to trade again, for we cannot go on like this. Soon enough you will come to despise me and in return, I you."

Reena gazed up at him with astonishment. She couldn't believe it! How could pride play such a role in a relationship? She had half a mind to fling herself in his arms and beg him to stop, but knew from the look in his eyes the uselessness of the action. He would simply and coldly disengage her arms from him.

Reena gave a long weary sigh. "Very well, Dominic, I will do as you ask."

"You will, of course, be well taken care of. I will contact solicitors in London and see to an income for you."

"Keep your money," she raged, as tears of helplessness glistened in her eyes. "I want nothing from you." Her hand touched the slight roundness of her belly. She had all she'd ever want. She'd not tell him of his child. He had to want her first. He had to put aside his pride. A child could not breach the gulf he had put between them.

Reena dragged herself through the next two days in a listless cloud of despair. There was nothing she could do. Nothing that would make this stubborn man understand what he was throwing away. Maybe someday, she tried to believe, someday he would come for her.

She was leaving in the morning. Her trunks were packed and already loaded on the ship that would take her to England. Her eyes misted with tears. She couldn't say take her home, because this was now her home, and it was surely going to break her heart being forced to leave it.

Reena's gaze moved to the door that separated their rooms. Dominic had kept himself from her since the rescue. And all day today he had sat in his room drinking. Damn, she raged in silent frustration, she hoped the bloody fool suffered on the morn.

As she brushed her hair an idea began to make itself

known. What would he do if she went to him and made it impossible for him to resist? Would he have a change of heart? Would he realize he could not live without her?

Reena gave a sad smile as she slid out of her gown and into her white satin robe. It mattered not if she failed. She knew he loved her beyond all else, save his damn pride. She would show him pride had no place between them. If, in the end, she lost, so be it, at least she had tried her best.

Silently she opened the door to his room. He was lying on the bed; an empty bottle of brandy stood on the bedside stand, another on the floor. His arm was flung over his eyes as if he would blot out the sight of the world and all its glaring misery.

"Dominic," came her softly uttered sigh from the darkened shadows. "Are you awake?"

"Aye," came the deep voice from the bed.

"Dominic," she started hesitantly. "Can I speak with you for a moment?"

"What is it?"

Reena bit at her lip, suddenly at a loss as to how to go on. Her raging had no effect, her pleading fell on deaf ears. What the hell was she to say? "Well I . . ."

"Should you not be in bed? The ship leaves early on the morn."

"Well, actually, that's exactly what I was thinking. I should be in bed. Yours."

Dominic lowered his arm from his face. His body tensed, knowing what she was about to do.

Slowly she untied her robe and allowed the satin to slide from her shoulders and slither to the floor as she walked toward the bed.

"Reena," he choked, unable to resist this offered treasure. Was he insane? How could he think of letting her go? My God, he loved her more than his own life.

"I'll leave, Dominic. I promise," she assured. "I ask no more of you than your comfort for this one night."

"Oh my God, Reena," he groaned, as she leaned over him and touched her soft lips to his eyes, his cheeks, his jaw and, as his arms came to lift her to the bed, his mouth.

Dominic snored softly. His head rested comfortably on her breast, his arm flung across her middle as he held her to his side. Reena watched the first, hesitant rays of the dawning sun come to light the indigo sky and breathed a shaky sigh of sorrow. How was she to find the strength to see herself through this day, and the next, and the next? He loved her, of this she had no doubt, for all through the long night, he had murmured the words and shown her with the most delicious actions.

Still, he had not spoken of his need to see her stay. Nothing was changed. Upon awakening he would expect to find her gone. Reena almost gave in to the temptation to stay, despite his wants, but knew in her heart the uselessness of it all. She knew his pride could not take her presence as a constant reminder of his supposed failure. Soon enough, he'd come to hate her.

Valiantly, she fought back the tears that threatened and turned to look upon him for the last time. A sob closed her throat as she watched the sunlight fall across his features, softened with sleep. He was so beautiful. Even when she had hated him most, she couldn't deny his handsomeness. Perhaps her child would be a boy. Maybe he would have his father's coloring. Maybe once she held him in her arms she wouldn't feel this utter desolation.

Gently Reena disengaged herself from his loosely held embrace. If she didn't hurry, the servants would be knocking on the door and Dominic would awaken. Right now she didn't think she could go through with it if she had to face him again.

Two hours later Reena stood alone at the ship's stern gazing out over the endless expanse of clear, green water.

Tears of remorse, for all they could have had and lost, glistened in her blue eyes as she waited for the ship to put to sea.

All the passengers were forward, each saying their farewells to family and friends. She could not bear to watch. Should she stand among them, she knew her eyes would endlessly search the shore, and she doubted she could bear the disappointment, for she knew in her heart he would not come.

"And where might you be going, madam?" a deep voice whispered close to her ear.

As once before, Reena had no need to turn to know who had spoken so gently at her side. Her eyes closed with the sheer ecstasy of the moment, and she breathed a long sigh of thanks. He had come for her. And the joy that filled her heart knew no bounds.

"I awakened this morning to find you gone." His hands circled her waist and drew her back to rest against him. "I thought I was too late," he breathed into her hair. "Tell this fool he's not too late."

Dominic sighed with relief as he turned her to face him; his heart beat erratically at the sight of Reena's smile, for surely, like the early morning sun, its power could light the world. His chest twisted with pain, knowing he had almost lost her, and he was helpless to resist pulling her into the warmth of his arms and covering her mouth with his.

He breathed a ragged sigh against her lips, "Oh Reena, how could you pick this time to listen to me. You never have before."

Reena laughed. "Are you giving me permission to ignore your orders in the future?"

"You need not my permission, my love, for I doubt not you will, as always, do as you wish."

Reena smiled, her heart bursting with joy. "I love you, Dominic."

"And I you, my love."

They held to each other in quiet desperation for a long

308

moment before he ventured. "It's best, I think, if we continue this at home, lest you wish to visit your beloved England, for the ship sails momentarily."

Reena gave a devilish grin as she shrugged her shoulder. "In truth I think we should wait until the babe comes, don't you? They say a long ocean voyage is hard on a woman with child."

Dominic's eyes were aglow with happiness and, he thought, a joy to match this could not exist, as he laughed. "Who says?"

"Me," Reena giggled, as he reached behind her knees and lifted her into his arms. "You little wretch. What kind of a way is that to tell your husband of an impending heir?"

Reena laughed, her mouth tasting with relish the clean maleness of his jaw while ignoring the staring crowd as they left the ship. "What would you have done?"

"I would have given you flowers, moonlight, candles," he shrugged, "you know."

"Mmm, that sounds nice enough, but I had something a bit different in mind."

"Being?" he looked down at her, one brow raised with suspicion.

"If you could get me home, I could show you."

Dominic laughed at her teasing as he sat her in his carriage, "Madam, we're almost there."

Epilogue

IN THE PREDAWN STILLNESS OF A GRAY DAY, THE BED-room's antechamber was cast in dark, eerie shadows. He shivered from the cold. His bare feet were nearly numb as he stood upon the uncarpeted floor. It wasn't the first time he had stood in the darkness and listened to her whispered murmurs. For as long as he could remember, her soft voice in the dark of night had left him somehow comforted. The sound was welcome, especially when he had a nightmare.

A heavy hand touched his shoulder as he reached for the doorknob and he spun around in surprise to find his sister behind him. His pounding heart nearly obliterated all other sounds as he gasped with fright.

"Why are you not in bed?" she whispered softly.

"I had a dream," he returned, his babyish voice tight with fear. "I want to sleep with Mama."

"If you promise not to keep moving, you can sleep with

me," she offered, as she slid her arm around his small shoulders and led him to her room.

"Why do you think she laughs at night?" he asked, his young mind unable to comprehend any happening capable of bringing merriment in the scary darkness. He climbed into the high bed and snuggled deep into the warmth of the soft mattress.

With a sleepy sigh she lifted a dark brow, pinning him with a look only a sister is capable of giving to a younger brother. She tucked the covers under his chin and pressed her back to his thin form and, just before she drifted off to sleep once more, she murmured, "What a silly question. Why does anyone laugh?"

About the Author

Patricia Pellicane lives in Long Island, New York, with her husband and their six children. She loves to read, particularly about America's Revolutionary War. *Sweet Revenge* is her fourth novel. Readers can write to her at Post Office Box 2250, North Babylon, NY 11703.

Tapestry

HISTORICAL ROMANCES

POCKET BOOKS